Summer at the Garden Café

Summer at the Garden Café

A Novel

Felicity Hayes-McCoy

HARPER LUXE

An Imprint of HarperCollins*Publishers*

Originally published in Ireland in 2017 by Hachette Ireland.

SUMMER AT THE GARDEN CAFE. Copyright © 2018 by Felicity Hayes-McCoy. All rights reserved. Printed in the United States of America. No part of this book may be used or reproduced in any manner whatsoever without written permission except in the case of brief quotations embodied in critical articles and reviews. For information address HarperCollins Publishers, 195 Broadway, New York, NY 10007.

HarperCollins books may be purchased for educational, business, or sales promotional use. For information please e-mail the Special Markets Department at SPsales@harpercollins.com.

FIRST HARPERLUXE EDITION

ISBN: 978-0-06-286095-8

HarperLuxe™ is a trademark of HarperCollins Publishers.

Library of Congress Cataloging-in-Publication Data is available upon request.

18 19 20 21 22 ID/LSC 10 9 8 7 6 5 4 3 2 1

For Roberta, with love

People who live in Finfarran say you can see four seasons of the year there in a single day. Then, in case you'd think they were being poetic, they point out that you'll never know what you ought to wear, so you'd better be prepared for anything.

The county town of Carrick to the east is the gateway to the Finfarran Peninsula, which stretches into the Atlantic from Ireland's rugged west coast. It's a place of fishing ports and villages, the little town of Lissbeg with its shops and school and businesses, high cliffs, a deep forest, isolated farms, and long, golden beaches. As the clouds whirl in from the ocean, they bring rain on the wind followed by rainbows. Cool, dew-spangled mornings can change to long days of burning turquoise skies and end in red-gold sunsets with a chill in the air that sends you home to hot whiskey and crackling fires. With fuel from the forest and turf from the bogs, Finfarran's homes have never lacked comfort. Yet scattered along the peninsula are emigrants' houses where the souls of the buildings have flickered out along with the fire on the hearth.

The house that people still call Maggie's place stands on a cliff in a rutted field with its back to a narrow lane. For years it stood empty, its blind windows facing the ocean and its slates shattered by storms. Self-seeded willow trees and yellow furze smothered the sloping field that ran down to the clifftop and the boundary walls were lost in curling briars. Inside the house, dead ashes lay on the hearthstone and crows' feathers drifted from the chimney onto the stone floor. Outside, by the gable end, were the fallen walls of a stone shed that had once held a turf stack. At some time or another half the rubbish of the parish seemed to have ended up in Maggie's field. Among the rusting washing machines and fridge freezers were broken bits of furniture, old bikes, and knackered lawnmowers. Each summer they disappeared among waving flowers and grasses and each winter they stood out starkly like the bones of starving beasts.

So every year the house and the field looked more

decrepit. Yet each autumn when seeds fell from the flowers and the grasses, the promise of renewed life entered the earth. And under the fallen stones at the gable end were hidden the seeds of a story, waiting in silence and darkness to emerge into the light.

1

Although Hanna had lived here for over a year, she still opened her eyes each morning to a rush of astonished delight. Now, stretching luxuriously in a shaft of sunlight, she looked around. Her room was just big enough to take her double bed, a chair, and a chest of drawers. She had painted the walls herself, using a soft shade of yellow to contrast with the rich gray color she'd chosen for the window frames. A ceiling-high, built-in cupboard, which was a paler shade of gray, served as a wardrobe, and the rails of the old brass bed had been painted in deep cream enamel.

The front door of the house opened onto a narrow field that sloped down to a low stone wall, beyond which was a grassy ledge and a sheer drop to the churning Atlantic. The building stood alone surrounded by fields, so, eager to allow as much light as possible into the small rooms, Hanna had hung no curtains on the windows that faced the ocean.

Beneath the duvet on this unhurried Sunday morning, her toes curled with pleasure as she watched dust motes in sunlight drift round the battered brass balls on the bedposts, which she'd polished to a golden sheen.

It was late spring, when the weather on Ireland's Atlantic coast veered between balmy days that brought green shoots, and days of howling, bitter gales that brought floods and freezing sleet.

Yesterday Hanna had puttered between the fireside and the slate worktop by the cooker where she'd measured out buttermilk, flour, and soda in a green glass tumbler and kneaded and cut a batch of scones before sliding them into the oven. Then, with a scone piled with butter and jam in her hand and a book on her knee, she'd sat by the fire while the wind hurled rain against the window. But now sunshine beckoned her outdoors. Pushing back her duvet, which was patterned in yellows, greens, and grays like her spring garden, she reached for her kimono and made for the bathroom.

Later, still wrapped in her kimono and with her feet pushed into Wellingtons, she carried a coffee and an apple down the field, climbed the stile, and settled herself on the wooden bench on the clifftop ledge beyond her boundary wall. The sun on her face was warm and the view stretched for miles from the edge of the cliff to the shimmering silver line where the sky met the ocean.

Lazy mornings like this one belonged to Hanna's weekends. The rest of her week began with the bleep of her alarm, a snatched breakfast, and a quick shower before the three-mile drive to work, and, though she loved her job in Lissbeg's public library, she took huge delight in the hours she spent at home. What she cherished most was her sense of independence. After a painful divorce she'd spent several years living with her teenage daughter, Jazz, in her widowed mother's retirement bungalow. It hadn't been easy. By any standards Mary Casey was a difficult woman and, now that Jazz had flown the nest, Hanna's pleasure in moving to her own home was augmented by the relief of averting what had seemed like an inevitable future cooped up with her bossy mother. Physical distance had made their relationship easier, but Mary could still be infuriating. Today she had summoned her daughter and granddaughter to a family lunch which Hanna would have been glad to get out of. Still, it would be great to see Jazz. And, opinionated and volatile though Mary might be, her Sunday roasts were delicious.

Tipping out the dregs of her coffee, Hanna reminded herself that she had several hours to enjoy in her own garden before driving to her mother's bungalow. As she wandered back up the field toward the house, she wondered if she ought to clean its windows. The wind from the ocean had crusted them with salt, making them as opaque as the windows of greased paper she'd read about in a book about the American frontier.

The simplicity of her house delighted her and she'd wanted to retain its integrity when restoring it but, having been born and raised in the locality, she'd opted without hesitation for triple glazing. This was no holiday home to be enjoyed in high summer and locked up and left empty when winter roared in from the north and the east. Like every other house of its kind on the Finfarran Peninsula, it had been built for a family who farmed the fields, burned turf on the open hearth, and, in many cases, ended their days by the fireside crippled with rheumatism. Hanna knew that if her father's Aunt Maggie, from whom she'd inherited the house, had had the chance of installing triple glazing, she'd have grabbed it with both knotted hands. So, even though integrity had mattered and money had been a major consideration, Hanna had cut no corners herself when it came to practicality—a tiny extension at the back of the house contained a well-heated bathroom and utility room; her oven was electric and her stove-top was gas, in case of power cuts; and her glazing came with a proper guarantee.

She smiled as she remembered the frontier log cabins she'd read about. The window lights had often been made from marriage certificates: the precious documents, frequently the only suitable piece of material that a frontier couple owned, were carefully greased or waxed and installed by the man of the house when building a home for his family. There was no man in Hanna's story now, and, approaching the house through the rutted field, she could honestly say that she felt no lack of one. She was Hanna Casey again, not Mrs. Malcolm Turner. Her marriage was behind her and her future was ahead and, whatever the future might bring her, right now she was reveling in solitude.

Her great-aunt Maggie had left her the house and the clifftop field more than forty years ago and, when she'd first heard of the bequest as a twelve-year-old, she'd been baffled. "But why?" she'd asked. "What would I want it for?" Her father had shrugged and smiled at her. "Life is long, pet. You'd never know what might happen."

Time had proved him right and, having forgotten about her tumbledown inheritance for most of her adult life, Hanna had come to thank her stars for it. It was all she possessed that was unencumbered by the grief and anger of her divorce and, in the process of restoration, it had become both a sanctuary and a solace.

Maggie Casey, who had lived well into her eighties, was a termagant. Like most of her generation she had spent time in England, but Hanna remembered her here in the house as a pinched, bad-tempered old woman always shooing hens out the door and bewailing the price of paraffin. By the end of her life, having alienated most of her neighbors, she depended heavily on her nephew—Hanna's dad, Tom—for help and company. But the claim on Tom's time and attention had infuriated Hanna's mother, Mary. To begin with, having no option, she'd put up with it. Then, as soon as Hanna was old enough, she took to sending her round to Maggie's to give her a hand: Wasn't it good for a young one to make herself useful, she said, and wasn't there plenty of work at home for Tom to be getting on with? Torn between two demanding women, Tom had acquiesced, presumably deciding that that would be best for everyone. As a child Hanna was unaware of those interwoven threads of adult resentment, dependence, pity, and acceptance. But what she did know was that her own relationship with her gentle, loving father stirred up deep wells of jealousy in her mother, who adored him. And, as a result, she had been glad of any escape from the cramped rooms where she had grown up, over the family's post office.

For the last few years of Maggie's life it was Hanna who did her chores and kept her company. The old woman's conversation consisted largely of curt commands to wash the teacups and bitter complaints about the nosiness of her neighbors, the incursions of her hens, and the cost of lamp oil. All the same, she and Hanna got on well together. Maggie accepted no diktats but her own, which were always arbitrary. She had a love of the little new potatoes she called *poreens* so, although grown-ups usually disapproved of lifting spuds while they still had some growth in them, Hanna was sent out each year to tease the smallest potatoes from the sides of the ridges, leaving the rest to mature for a few weeks longer. She'd wash them in running water before Maggie shook them into the black pot that hung from the iron crane over the turf fire. Later they'd eat them straight off the kitchen table, dipping each mouthful first in salt and then in a bowl of buttermilk.

Part of the pleasure of those meals lay in the shared knowledge that Mary would disapprove of them. According to Maggie, God made spuds to be eaten in the hand. According to Mary, He knew all about germs and bacteria, which was why He also made cutlery. The same opposing rules applied to laundry, which Mary washed with the latest biological detergent and Maggie scrubbed with yellow soap. And to leftovers, which

Mary sealed up in plastic bags and Maggie shared with the cat. Enchanted by the pleasures of food dug straight from the earth and sun-warmed sheets dried in the salty wind, Hanna had learned to keep house according to Maggie's rules in Maggie's place, and to keep quiet about it at home. And now, over forty years later, more than twenty of which she had spent living in London, the house and the field were once again Hanna's fortress against her mother. Though she still couldn't think why her great-aunt Maggie had left them to her.

Reaching the top of the rutted field she decided to forget about windows and think instead about gardening. She had plans to use the land near the edge of the cliff for vegetables, and to make an herb-and-flower garden close to the house. Last year she'd cleared the garden plot, rooting out furze and briars, pruning the willow trees at the south gable end, and marking out beds. At the edge of the plot, close to the house, was a pile of fallen field stones, once part of an old shed wall. Rather than remove them, she had decided to turn them into a rock garden into which she would sink tubs for herbs like marjoram and wild garlic that grow wildly if unconfined. It was going to be a hard slog, but Hanna reckoned the result would be worth it. Throwing on a pair of jeans and a paint-stained fleece, she fetched her thick gardening gloves and set about shifting stones.

An hour or so later, having paused for another coffee, she stood back and considered her work. In piling the stones into heaps of different sizes, she had exposed a couple of slabs set at right angles to each other, presumably the foundations of a corner of the vanished shed. Thinking that their flat surfaces might be useful elsewhere, she went to see if they were too heavy to lift. Then, as she squatted down to look at them, she realized that a gray object which she'd thought was a stone was actually an old tin box. It was set in the angle between the slabs, half buried in earth and dented by falling stones. Fascinated, Hanna fetched a spade and managed to lever it out.

As the spade released it from the earth, something solid moved inside it. Picking up the box in her gloved hands, she looked at it. It was an oblong biscuit tin with traces of a colored design still clinging to its tarnished surface. The rim where the lid met the base was thickly caked in earth. Carrying it to the doorstep, Hanna went and found a kitchen knife. Ten minutes later, sitting on the step with earth and chips of paint scattered round her, she eased the lid from the tin with her hands. Inside, wrapped in an old waxed sliced-bread wrapper, was a penny copybook bound in a thick cardboard cover. Handwritten on it in ink was Maggie Casey's name.

2

High under the eaves in The Old Forge Guesthouse, Jazz scowled at herself in her bedroom mirror. She dabbed blush on her cheekbones and scrubbed it off again angrily. Then, shaking her hair out of its ponytail, she decided to trust to luck. Whatever she did, Mum and Nan were sure to say she was looking peaky, and there was no time to sit here trying to assume camouflage. Lunch in Nan's bungalow, always called "dinner," was served promptly at one, and God help you if you weren't there ready for it. Twenty minutes in the oven to the pound, plus twenty more, was Mary's rule; then twenty minutes while the meat rested on the worktop and the greens were strained and the spuds set on the table. She organized her Sunday mornings precisely and expected her guests to do the same. That was one of the many things about Nan that drove Mum crazy, though Jazz herself didn't mind it. There was something very dependable about Mary Casey's rules and expectations, even if she did peer and poke at you, and despite her massive sulks. Grabbing a sweater from the bed, Jazz ran down the stairs and went round to the kitchen.

The old forge and its adjoining house belonged to Gunther Winterhalder, a young German, and his Irish wife. There were four en suite guest rooms in the house, where the Winterhalders also had their living accommodations, and the forge had become an open-plan space where meals were served on long wooden tables and guests could relax by a fire. Gunther was the cook, Susan did the housekeeping, and together they grew vegetables, kept goats, and made cheese that they sold to local shops. It had been a struggle to begin with but now business was improving, which was why Jazz had been taken on to help with this season's guests.

It was less of a choice on her part and more the fallout from a stupid car crash she'd had last year. Before the accident she'd been a cabin crew member with a budget airline. It was her first job and had brought her the freedom to travel the world and a buzzy, exciting life in a flat-share in France. But, after her accident and surgery to remove a ruptured spleen, she'd found herself grounded; constant travel would require constant vaccinations to support her impaired immune system, so, although she'd made what the doctor called "a great recovery," she'd also been told that she'd have to change her job.

From her dad's point of view, serving drinks on cheap flights to Malaga hadn't been suitable work for her anyway, so, for him, Jazz thought darkly, the crash had produced the perfect result. As soon as she'd got well, he'd started making noises about her returning to London, where she'd spent most of her childhood, and going up to Oxford to take a degree. She's always had an entrepreneurial flair for marketing, he'd said, obviously seeing her as a future mega-tycoon. But without consulting anyone, she'd gone off by herself and taken a job in the guesthouse. She liked Susan and Gunther, who treated her more like family than an employee. The work was easy and she loved the old forge, which was beautifully positioned between an oak forest and the cliffs. And her decision had really annoyed Dad, which provided a savage satisfaction.

As she stuck her head round the kitchen door, Gunther looked up from the sink. He was due in Lissbeg at a quarter to one and had offered to drop her at Nan's. Mum would give her a lift home later, so there was no point in taking her own car. It was Jazz who'd suggested the lift, but Gunther was fine about it. He was like that—easygoing, blond, and good-hearted, nothing like Dad with his smooth weasel ways.

Gunther smiled as she looked into the kitchen and, taking his jacket, gave Susan a hug on his way to the door. Jazz waited as he backed his car out of the shed and leaned to open the door for her. Then he swung the car onto the road with the same easy competence with which he did everything else.

Sitting back against the scuffed leather passenger seat, Jazz told herself that today was the day that she'd have the whole thing out with Mum. Not in Nan's hearing, of course, because this was between the two of them. They'd go somewhere quiet, like the beach, if she could contrive a walk after dinner. Because, one way or the other, the time had come to make her position clear.

She turned to Gunther as they approached the turn-off for Lissbeg. "You might as well leave me here, it's only a bit of a walk."

"You're sure?"

"Of course. Drop me at the turn and you won't have to double back on yourself."

As she walked along the main road, she wished she could have stayed with him. Or stayed back in her room in the forge with the duvet over her head.

꩜

Carrying a bunch of late narcissi from her garden, Hanna arrived at the bungalow where the smell of roast lamb was delicious. Jazz was leaning on the worktop, tugging shreds of meat from the joint and dodging vengeful flicks from Mary's tea towel.

"Would you stop pecking and poking like some class of a savage!" Mary removed the joint to a platter. "Take that yoke, put an edge on the knife and sit up there to the table."

The "yoke" was a piece of sandstone picked up on a beach fifty years ago and used ever since as a whetstone. A succession of carving knives had succumbed to time and Mary Casey's violent handling, but the unchanging sound of steel on stone was as much a part of Hanna's earliest memories as the Good Coat worn by her mother to morning Mass and the sixpenny bar of chocolate bought with the Sunday papers.

With the narcissi in a vase on the dresser, they sat round the table while Mary piled food onto plates.

Jazz shook her head at the potatoes. "Honestly, Nan, I've got loads already!"

"Ah, Name of God, child, you're skin and bone, there's no pick of flesh on you."

Hanna watched from under lowered eyelashes as

Jazz shook her dark hair forward as if to hide her face. Mary was right. Jazz's residual childish roundness had disappeared months ago when she was convalescent after her accident. Now, at twenty-one, she was slimmer than she'd ever been, and the newly revealed angles of her face were strikingly like her father's. And last year's car crash hadn't just left her looking peaky. There was a nervous tension about her that hadn't been there before. Hanna wondered if the child was enjoying her work. It was lovely that she'd decided to stay in Ireland but, seeing her strained face and tense shoulders, it was hard to believe she was happy.

When the meal was over Jazz and Hanna went for a walk on the beach. Mary had refused to come, waving them off briskly with her tea towel and announcing that she'd no intention of getting sand in her shoes. Hanna and Jazz, who were both inveterate beachcombers, left their shoes on a flat rock as soon as they crossed the sand dunes, and wandered the tideline in bare feet picking up shells and stones. Later, with their pockets full of their finds, they sat on a balk of driftwood, gazing out at the ocean.

There was silence for a moment. Then Jazz spoke, still looking at the horizon. "I always thought Nan disliked Dad because he was English. Well, a foreigner. Not One Of Us. But that's not it, is it? There's more."

Hanna stiffened, wondering what was coming next. According to Mary Casey, Malcolm was nothing more than a wily egoist, an appraisal Hanna herself now considered pretty apt. After years of marriage and a huge emotional investment in his career, she had found him in bed with one of his colleagues, a woman she knew as a friend. Furious and grief-stricken, she had swept Jazz, then still a teenager, over to Ireland where Mary's admittedly generous welcome had been accompanied by a commentary on Malcolm's iniquity that had nearly driven her mad. For the next few years she had poured all her energy into raising her daughter and not murdering her mother. Above all, she had protected Jazz from the knowledge of what Malcolm was really like. It hadn't been easy and she wasn't even sure that it was wise. But Malcolm, a high-powered London barrister and an expert in manipulation, had assured Jazz that the divorce was entirely amicable, saying nothing about his long-standing affair. And, unable to deny it for fear of upsetting their daughter, Hanna had found herself having to collude in his lie.

Now Jazz, who had continued to stare at the horizon, turned round and looked at her. "He sat me down a few weeks ago when I was over in London. I'm not sure why he decided to tell me the truth." She drove her heel into the sand. "All that stuff about no one being to blame. I don't know why I bought it. Well, I do. Dad had the story lined up and you said practically nothing. And Daddy's Little Princess believed everything she was told."

Hanna chose her words carefully. "Look, when there's holy war going on in the background, people want to protect their kids."

"No. *You* wanted to protect me. Dad wanted to protect his squeaky-clean image."

Hanna looked down at her feet, which were stippled with grains of sand. Jazz's were more slender than hers and the nails were painted. But you could tell they were mother and daughter by the shape of their toes.

"But he's told you now."

"He's told me he was having an affair with Tessa. And that you found out and left him, which was why we came over here to live with Nan. Nice to find that your dad was shagging a friend of your mum's since before you were even born."

Hanna flinched, remembering Malcolm's voice pontificating over dinner tables to his colleagues. He'd always told his clients that there was never any point in making half a confession. "Admit nothing unless you have to, and when you do, don't hold back." If you did, it would only be dragged out of you, he'd said, and you'd look much worse in the end.

Jazz glanced at her. "You made him tell me, didn't you?"

"I said that now you're a grown woman, I wouldn't lie if you asked."

Jazz looked out at the ocean. "And you never did lie, did you? You just prevaricated for years and went round panicking in case Nan let the cat out of the bag."

"She thought you should know. And maybe she was right."

"Yeah, and maybe she wasn't." There was a pause while Jazz continued to gaze at the ocean. "Look, Mum, it doesn't matter, you did what you thought best. I'm the fool for believing him."

Hanna swung round and grasped her by the shoulder. "You're not a fool and you're never to think so!"

Jazz shrugged and smiled wryly. "'The one sure way to be a winner is to make your opponent feel like a fool.'"

It was another line that Malcolm frequently used at dinner tables, though Hanna hadn't realized that Jazz had noticed.

"And that's what he's really good at, isn't he? Malcolm Turner, Queen's Counsel. Gets you where he wants you and keeps you there under his thumb." Jazz scuffed the sand with her heel again. "I bet he never even made you a decent settlement."

Hanna grinned. "No. But that may have had something to do with the fact that I told him where to stick his money."

"So that's why you've ended up living in Maggie's place. I thought you were just being eccentric. But it's all you can afford."

"And hasn't it turned out to be exactly what I want? I love it. Okay, it's all been a bit touch and go, but I knew he'd never leave you unprovided for."

Telling Malcolm where to stick his money had given her great satisfaction, though in hindsight she'd often asked herself if it hadn't been pretty stupid. Since then, time had taught her to choose her words more carefully and now she took a deep breath before she spoke.

"Look, love, don't go making a monster out of your dad. I whipped you over here without asking him, and he must have been frightened of losing you."

"So he wove a net of lies to keep me safe? Sorry, Mum, I don't buy it. And I don't think he's a monster. I think he's a pathetic cheat."

There was another pause while Hanna struggled for a reply. Malcolm was certainly a cheat and his behavior had been pathetic. But life in general, and their life together in particular, seemed far too complex and nuanced to sum up in a single soundbite.

Then Jazz bumped her gently with her shoulder.

"Honestly, Mum. It doesn't matter. It's water under the bridge."

Her reassuring smile hadn't reached her eyes, though. And though she'd spoken with absolute conviction, Hanna hadn't been convinced.

3

As Ameena walked down Broad Street she caught a glimpse of her reflection in the window of the deli. Squinting at her dark upswept hair, neat jacket, and plain white shirt, she decided she looked okay. She had had her nose pierced a while back, not just to please her mum but because she liked the look of it. A nose ring might look dodgy to some people, though, so today she was wearing a discreet gold stud.

It was Miss O'Rourke, her high school teacher, who had spotted the piece in the *Finfarran Inquirer* about the new gift shop in Lissbeg Library needing summer staff and called Ameena into the staff room to tell her about it.

"I know you'd prefer to find summer work here in Lissbeg, so you might try for this. If you turn up looking interested and respectable, they'll probably give you some hours. I don't think you want something full-time, do you?"

Ameena didn't. She'd be lucky if her mum could be reconciled to her taking even a part-time job this summer, and she guessed that Miss O'Rourke was aware of it. But to talk to a teacher about stuff like that would sound as if she was criticizing her family, so she'd just smiled and said thank you. After that she'd considered her options. As soon as her Leaving Cert exams were over, most of her friends would be off finding jobs in Cork or Dublin. Some were even planning to fly over to London and look for work when they arrived. If they got the right points in the exams and a place on their preferred courses, lots of them would be home again in September and off to college or uni. Ameena wasn't looking that far ahead. All she wanted, to begin with, was a chance to show her mum that a life of your own didn't automatically mean you'd reject all the things you'd grown up with.

As she peered at her reflection in the window, she realized that, beyond the piles of cheese and bowls of olives, the girl at the counter was looking at her. Embarrassed, Ameena ducked her head but the girl just smiled: she was small and pretty, with red hair tied up in a bright-colored scarf. The deli, which was called

HabberDashery, was across the road from the library, beside a shop where an old clock with SEED MERCHANTS written on it hung permanently stopped with its hands at a quarter to three. Broad Street, Lissbeg's main thoroughfare, got wider here in the middle of town. At its broadest point, which had once been a marketplace, there was a stone horse trough planted with flowers, and the far side of the street was taken up by The Old Convent Centre, which had once housed a big convent and the town's girls' school. In what used to be the nuns' private garden, there was now a café that served cakes and sandwiches made at the delicatessen. Half of Lissbeg seemed to have taken to gathering there and the place had a great buzz.

Ameena crossed the street and approached the library. You got to it through an arched gateway that led to a little courtyard. On the wall by the gate was a plaque giving the opening hours, and a big laminated poster. There was a diagonal strip across it saying EXHIBITION AND GIFT SHOP OPENING JUNE. She stopped to inspect the poster which showed the open pages of an old book with Latin writing and little jewel-like illustrations. Taking the *Inquirer* cutting from her pocket, she wondered if it was really okay to turn up uninvited asking for work. But Miss O'Rourke had said it would be, so Ameena raised her chin and walked into the courtyard.

Immediately opposite the arched gateway was a door that had once been the main entrance to the school. It was approached by shallow steps and there was a sign over it saying RECEPTION. Ameena was about to climb the steps when she realized that the entrance to the library from the courtyard was through a glass door on her left. Though she'd lived in Lissbeg since she was small, she'd never been in there. People sometimes studied in the library after school, especially with exams coming up, but, as far as her mum and dad were concerned, she had a perfectly good bedroom to study in, and hanging round town after school hours wasn't allowed. When she complained, her dad laughed and made a face at her. How much work actually got done, he said, and how much time was spent checking phones and texting? Ameena didn't know because she never got a chance to find out. Though, according to her mates, Miss Casey, the librarian, was actually very strict about turning off your mobile.

She checked hers now to make sure it was off, though she already knew that it was. Then she went through the door and found herself in a vestibule. A second glass door, straight ahead of her, had a sign on it saying EXHIBITION. OPENING JUNE. Another, at right angles to it, said LISSBEG PUBLIC LIBRARY.

Conor McCarthy, the guy at the desk, looked up as

she opened the door. He was sitting with his back to the floor-to-ceiling glass wall that divided the library from the exhibition space which would soon be ready to open. Ameena could see that the work beyond the glass was still ongoing; there was a ladder propped against a wall and tools scattered on a dust sheet. The contrast between the library, which was paneled in dark wood, and the bright, modern space beyond it was kind of attractive. She knew Conor, who was about six years older than she was, by sight, but she'd never spoken to him. Glancing round, she could see no sign of Miss Casey.

"I was looking for the librarian."

Conor grinned. "That's me. Well, it's not me because I'm the assistant. But Miss Casey's out in the mobile library, so maybe I can help?"

"I came about a job in the gift shop."

"Well, the gift shop won't open till the exhibition does."

This was news to her but she kept her cool. "Right so. Could I leave my name or something?"

"You could, of course." Conor scrabbled round on the desk for a piece of paper. "I don't know if it's going to be Miss Casey giving the jobs out, but I'll pass it on anyway."

Ameena tried to look intelligent. It obviously didn't work because Conor held out a leaflet.

"It'd probably help to read up about it if you're here looking for a job."

Determined not to look too glad to get it, Ameena glanced at the leaflet. "It's the Carrick Psalter, isn't it?" She'd seen the name written up outside. Conor nodded, so she kept going, taking a stab at what a psalter might be. "I'm not really well up on medieval manuscripts."

"Well, I'm no expert, I'd know more about cows." She looked at him blankly and he grinned again. "I'm a part-timer. Half the time here in the library and the rest on my dad's farm. I'd be here all the time if I had the chance, mind, but I'm wanted at home."

"Oh I know!" Ameena nodded emphatically. "I don't mean about farms but about being wanted at home."

She wasn't sure why she'd said that, except that he seemed so nice. But she didn't want him to feel she was wasting his time. Fortunately, there was a man approaching the desk with a pile of books. As Conor turned to him, she tucked the leaflet into her bag, smiled her thanks, and left the library.

Later, sitting in the Garden Café, she spread the leaflet on the table. The Carrick Psalter, it turned out, was indeed a medieval manuscript. It was a book of psalms, handwritten and illustrated by eighth-century monks in a monastery here on the peninsula. Ameena wondered why it was going on display in Lissbeg Library, which was far smaller than the County Library in Carrick; but since it was a gift from some rich guy whose family had owned it for ages, she supposed he could choose where it went. According to the leaflet, he'd given money for the exhibition space, too. There was a plan that showed how it would be laid out. Each guided tour would begin in the room she had seen from the library, where the psalter would be displayed in a glass case, and interactive digital displays round the walls would give access to digitized images of the different pages. The guide would talk and answer questions. In the next room, the group would watch a film. Then they'd leave through doors that led into the gift shop and out again onto the street. It didn't look like you'd need to know much about the psalter if you were selling stuff in the gift shop, but Ameena could see how it might be a good thing to talk about at an interview for the job. If she'd had sense, she realized, she'd have guessed that a public library in a town as small as Lissbeg wouldn't have its own gift shop, while an exhibition like this one would be sure to attract tons of visitors, all wanting to take home souvenirs.

Miss O'Rourke had banged on so much about the importance of work experience on your résumé that had really been all Ameena was thinking about. But now she realized this job looked pretty stylish and exciting.

4

As always, Hanna was happy to be driving. Her route in the library van extended from the county town of Carrick at the eastern end of the peninsula, to the thriving tourist center at its western end, which had once been a little fishing port. She covered it in two days each week, one trip serving the communities on the north side of the peninsula and the other those to the south. There was a particular pleasure in these solitary hours spent driving through stunning scenery, as well as in the regular contact with people from outlying farms and villages whose busy lives kept them from making the journey to the library in Lissbeg.

Swinging the wheel to avoid a pothole, she was looking forward not just to the day ahead but also to the evening after work, when she'd investigate Maggie's book.

What with Mary Casey's roast lamb and the talk with Jazz on the beach afterward, she simply hadn't had time to get back to it yesterday.

The crossroads by The Old Forge Guesthouse was one of her regular stops on the northern side of the peninsula and, as she pulled into the parking lot, the usual line was waiting. Most people were sitting on the wall outside the forge, just as their parents and grandparents would have sat while they waited for the smith to do his work.

Having dealt with returned books and issued new loans, Hanna paused for a chat with Susan Winterhalder, who'd emerged from the guesthouse to bring her a mug of tea. There was no sign of Jazz, who was presumably at the reception desk. Susan was full of praise for her, though. It was easy enough to get help with the housework or the washing up, she said, but Jazz was really exceptional. "Honestly, Miss Casey, she's gold dust. Not just computer literate and happy to handle bookings, but experienced in working with the public. *And* she can talk intelligently about marketing—she's got a real sense of what our business is about."

It had taken ten years for Susan and Gunther to develop the old forge from B&B accommodations for passing hikers to an up-and-coming guesthouse with fabulous food and luxury en suite bedrooms. They'd done most of the restoration work themselves and, in

the same period, they'd set up an artisan cheese business and established an organic vegetable plot. It was
exhausting work. But now, finally, they'd reached the
point where they could afford to employ full-time help.

And they could hardly believe their luck. Gunther
wasn't one to show his emotions, Susan told Hanna,
but she'd known he'd been really stressed. Neither of
them had taken a break for ages and, with a six-year-old
daughter as well as the business, at times it all felt a bit
too much. Tall, fair-haired Gunther with his broad
shoulders and steady temperament had twice the stam-
ina of most men. Even so, Susan said, she had worried
about him. But now the pressure had lifted. With Jazz
on board they could factor some downtime into their
schedule and be an ordinary family again for the first
time in years.

As Hanna drove away from the guesthouse, she remembered the troubled months and years she'd lived
through on returning to Finfarran. Back then, she
herself had always seemed to be worrying. How would
the sudden change of schools affect Jazz's education?
Would the loss of the home in London be too much for
her to take? And, tossing and turning in Mary Casey's
back bedroom, she'd spent sleepless nights tortured by
her own collusion with Malcolm's lying. By suppress-

ing the truth of their divorce, she'd hoped to lessen its trauma for her daughter. But what would happen to the lot of them when Jazz grew up and found out?

Now, driving between the forest and the clifftop, where gulls wheeled over the ocean, she smiled and told herself ruefully that one's daughter never grew up. No matter how tall or competent she became, or how far away she traveled, in your mind she was still the little girl that you'd move mountains to protect. And no matter how much you worried and tried to do the right thing for her, you could never conquer the feeling that you hadn't done enough. But that was ridiculous. Sooner or later you had to stand back and stop feeding your own neurosis. According to Susan, Jazz was doing brilliantly at the guesthouse. And she knew the truth about Malcolm now. So maybe the best thing her mother could do was let her get on with her life.

❦

Jazz watched from a guestroom window as the van turned a bend and was lost behind towering oak trees. Last Saturday she herself had driven off, in a new skirt and top, with a free half day ahead of her, planning to have a great time. Emerging onto the peninsula's main road, she'd crossed the stream of westbound traffic and driven to Carrick. It wasn't exactly the metropolis, but in summer it always had a buzz. Lots of people she'd been to school with in Lissbeg now worked in Carrick's shops and businesses or drove there at the weekends. The shopping wasn't bad and you could usually find someone to grab a coffee with or just hang out for a chat. It didn't take long after parking the car to come upon some people she knew. A group of girls waved to her from the window of a coffee shop and, going in to join them, she found friends she hadn't seen for months. After the crash she'd gone over and spent some time in London and, since starting work at the forge, she hadn't been out much at all.

At first it had been a really great afternoon. They'd giggled and caught up on news and taken selfies and sent them to friends. A few others had joined them, including Conor, her mum's assistant. Conor was a year or two younger than Jazz, though she remembered him from school. His girlfriend, Aideen, was younger still and quiet compared to the rest of them, but everyone was laughing and relaxed and having fun. And that was brilliant.

After yet another round of coffees two of the guys had ordered pancakes. The coffee shop was nothing like the cafés Jazz and her flatmates had frequented in France, and the pancakes came with chemical-colored syrup out of a bottle. But that was fine. And in the end, as they'd prepared to leave, someone suggested they come back later and rendezvous at a nightclub. Jazz wasn't working again till the morning, so she knocked back the last of her coffee and agreed.

On the road back to the forge she'd been planning her evening's outfit. The tourist traffic was heavy, streaming off into the west. Up ahead was the turnoff that would take her back through the forest. She didn't even need to cross the road to make her turn to the left. But suddenly she panicked. Every muscle in her body tightened and her hands seemed stuck to the steering wheel. She could feel cold sweat on her forehead and her feet were blocks of ice.

Looking back now, she still couldn't tell how she'd managed to make the turn, but as soon as she'd got off the main road she must have pulled in to the verge. She'd sat there shivering violently with the birds singing in the oak trees. It wasn't fair. When she'd taken the job at the forge, she'd been looking forward to a great summer. She'd planned to hang out at the new Garden Café in Lissbeg and to drive to the beach after work, in the long summer evenings. She had left the hospital certain that she'd put her car crash behind her. But she'd been wrong. None of it was fair, she'd told herself, and she couldn't bear it. It had taken twenty terrified minutes before she'd managed to start the car again. Then she'd gone back to her room in the forge and cried herself to sleep.

5

Hanna's mobile days invariably ended with a drive back to Carrick, where the library van was based. On the way she passed both Mary Casey's bungalow and the narrow turnoff that meandered away through farmland to her own house on the cliff. Five miles farther on was the signpost to Lissbeg, and fifteen minutes later she reached the outskirts of Carrick. Slowing down, she made her way through the busy streets to the County Library. Then, having left the van in the parking lot and the key at the desk, she edged her car back into the traffic and returned the way she had come.

There was nothing left to do today but to enjoy her evening—Conor would have locked up the library in Lissbeg and shot off home on his Vespa to spend his own evening at work on his family's farm. People his age on the peninsula tended to be divided into two groups: those determined to build their lives here in Finfarran and those who were desperate to raise enough money to get themselves onto a plane. Having fallen into the latter category herself as a teenager, she hadn't relished the idea of returning home as a divorcée. But she'd had no choice. Yet now, she thought with a wry grin, there was nowhere she'd rather be.

As soon as she turned off the main road she relaxed. It was an exceptionally warm evening and swarms of midges were rising from the streams. Driving between ditches smothered in primroses, she pulled in at a passing place while a herd of cows plodded slowly toward the milking. The farmer raised his stick to her and Hanna idled slowly after them till they turned in at a gate and she could drive on.

Before leaving for work she had taken a tub of homemade soup from the freezer. Now, pouring it into a saucepan, she left it on a low heat while she grabbed a quick shower. Then, using a few sticks and a sod of turf, she lit a fire on the open hearth; later, if it got chilly, she would build it up with more turf and driftwood but for now it brought a bright focus to the room, which was enough. The vegetable soup was as thick as a stew and, with a scatter of cheese and some whole wheat toast, it was all she needed. She carried her meal to the table under the window and ate looking out at the dusk.

Then, with the meal eaten and a half-finished glass of wine in her hand, she crossed the room to the fireside and took the tin box off the mantelpiece. There was earth still clinging to the rim of the lid. Carefully setting the box on the hearthstone, she lifted out the book and removed its waxed paper wrapping: it had once contained a loaf from the Ballyfin Bakery, which was still a local business, though its wrapper design had changed. Maggie had died in 1975, so the tin must have been placed in the corner of the vanished shed before then. And it had remained there ever since: while Hanna herself was growing into a teenager; in the years that she'd lived in London, believing her marriage was happy; and in the stressful years she'd spent with her mother before moving here to live in Maggie's house.

She looked at the book in her hand. Whoever had bound the pages to the cover had used an ordinary sewing machine. When she herself had first cleared the garden, she'd stumbled on the base of a treadle sewing machine she remembered from her childhood. Tom, her father, had given it to Maggie as a gift when Mary Casey had abandoned the treadle machine for an electric one. Now, painted and fitted with a timber top, the cast-iron base served as a garden table. It was strange to think of Maggie's feet on the treadle, which was now wedged immobile with a rock.

Opening the book, Hanna turned the pages carefully. It seemed to be a series of diary entries, interspersed with lists and other material stitched into the copybook. The first page, which was closely written in blue ink, was headed with a date: "July 20th, 1920." The handwriting was careful and upright, like a schoolgirl's. Hitching her chair closer to the fire, Hanna began to read.

I never thought that I'd have to leave Finfarran. But I suppose I won't be the first or the last who's had to go this way. I'm worried about Mam even though I know the neighbors will mind her. Mrs. Donovan will anyway, she's always been good to us, though these days you wouldn't be sure of anyone. When there's a price on a neighbor's head people do be sorely tempted, and every family on the peninsula with a son or a father out in the hills fighting does be frightened of informers. All we can do is pray that Liam will be safe.

I don't want to go away but now there's no help for it. Still, it's not like it isn't a well-worn road to the boat. Paud Donovan sold the cows for us anyway. Mam couldn't cope with them on her own. He's taken the grazing too at a fair rent. I have a share of the money put away for the journey and enough to keep me in England while I look for a job. I don't know why I'm writing this really, there's so much I can't and I won't say. I don't know what's ahead of me either and I've no way of letting Liam know that I'm going. Maybe Lizzie Keogh will manage it for me. She has a brother too is in the same brigade.

I got up this morning early and was looking away toward the forest. You can't see it from here but I know the trees were there in the morning sun and the fallen leaves still deep underneath them. There'd be birds singing on the bog too where we left the turf drying. I never thought I wouldn't draw it home myself for Mam.

The entry ended there and, turning the page, Hanna saw that the next one was a memorandum, dated the following day.

TO BUY
Stockings.
Soap.
Notepaper. Envelopes.
Bootlaces.
Bull's-eyes for Mam.

TO DO
Lizzie's for suitcase.
Pay account at Cathcarts.
Ask Mrs. D. to send in the Inquirer *to Mam.*

How many versions of that pathetic list were made in emigrants' houses up and down the peninsula in the past? Hanna traced the items gently with her finger. It was hard to imagine Maggie as a young girl setting off on a journey so different to the one that she herself had made when she'd gone to England as a student.

What had sent Maggie away? There was no mention of her father, so perhaps, if her mother was widowed, she had simply needed a job. Glancing back at the date, Hanna reminded herself that Ireland's War of Independence had still been raging in 1920. Liam, Maggie's brother, must have been away from home in the fight. Holding the book on her lap, she wondered why she'd never heard of him. But, of course, her own mother had been so incensed by Maggie's demands on her father that any talk of his side of the family always provoked a row. And, as a child, it had never occurred to her to question Maggie herself. Now, all these years later, she wished that things had been different. It was sad to think of Maggie as someone so lonely that she'd poured her heart out on paper and buried it in the earth.

6

The old horse trough in the middle of Broad Street was once the center of Lissbeg's marketplace. Then when a new cattle mart was built outside the town, the council put parking spaces in the middle of Broad Street. As a result the horse trough and its surroundings became so unattractive that, despite the gallant geraniums planted in it by officialdom, no one ever sat on the benches that flanked it. Things had languished that way for years until the council bought the former school and its adjacent convent and removed the parking spaces to a new parking lot on the site of the old school yard. And the town didn't just gain The Old Convent Centre, it regained its previous sense of spacious charm.

Every time Conor McCarthy whizzed down Broad Street on his Vespa, he told himself triumphantly that none of these improvements would have happened if it weren't for Miss Casey.

Finfarran's policy makers had been dead set on implementing a plan for new all-singing, all-dancing council offices in Carrick, a massive marina in Ballyfin where all the tourists went, and practically no investment in the rest of the peninsula. But when it turned out that the plan involved centralizing all the county's services, Miss Casey had started a big campaign to stop her library being closed. In the end the council had been forced to develop the nuns' old buildings in Lissbeg instead of putting up a new one in Carrick, and to spread the investment more evenly so everyone got a fair whack. Admittedly, there were a few fat cats in Ballyfin who were fed up about it, and a rake of council guys in Carrick bemoaning the loss of their grand, fancy offices, but, with the whole peninsula behind Miss Casey, the decision had been made. The Old Convent Centre development was happening in stages, so some bits hadn't been finished yet. But already there were all classes of new rooms and studios for rent, a herb garden minded by volunteers, and a café. And the library, which was housed in the old school hall, had been given a facelift and was about to get an exhibition space that was seriously state of the art.

Swerving the Vespa over to the curb outside Habber-

Dashery, Conor popped in for a word before going to work. Aideen, who was behind the counter making coleslaw, smiled when he stuck his head round the door. Looking at her, Conor was reminded of a poem that he'd had to learn at school: *Veiled in that light amazing | Lady, your hair so wavy | Has cast into dispraising | Absalom son of Davy.* Something like that. He'd never got the measure of the Absalom bit, but he'd liked the next verse: *Your golden locks close-clinging | Like bird-flocks of strange seeming | Silent with no sweet singing | Draw all men into dreaming.* Mind you, Aideen's hair was red, not gold, but it looked great with the sun shining on it and little curls at the front coming out from under her scarf. But she'd think he was daft if he went quoting poetry at her at this hour of the morning. So instead he asked what time she'd be taking her lunch. He was on an early break himself because Miss Casey had to look in at some meeting at one o'clock.

Aideen grinned at him. "Are you hoping I'll feed you?"

Actually he'd been thinking of buying her lunch across the road at the Garden Café. There was a statue of St. Francis there, with water falling from carved flowers round his feet, and Conor reckoned that if you got a table next to it you could almost be on vacation. He and Aideen had just come back from a trip to Italy, and he kept trying to recreate the magic. The only thing was that half the women in the parish seemed to use the café as a place to hatch plans and share secrets these days, so it got awful crowded. And the other thing was that he and Aideen had sort of agreed that, now they were back, they'd start saving their money for the future. Still, he told himself cheerfully, the café's sandwiches were supplied by Bríd and Aideen, so you could almost say that buying her lunch there was investing money in the deli.

She agreed to meet him at twelve, so he wove his way happily through the morning traffic on Broad Street, parked the Vespa in the new parking lot, and bounded into the library. Miss Casey had arrived before him and was going through the mail.

Leaving his helmet in the kitchen at the end of the room, Conor set about changing the books on the Recommended Reading stand for the new ones chosen by Miss Casey the day before. Then, he put the old ones in their proper places on the shelves, making sure the plastic covers were clean and removing the little diagonal stickers that said things like RECENTLY PUBLISHED, POWERFUL STORY, and SUMMER READING. The library's biweekly book club had come up with the idea of the stickers and Miss Casey hadn't been crazy about it at first. But she hadn't been crazy about the idea of the book club either, when it was first suggested, and now it was she who led it and helped them choose the books. In fact, all sorts of things happened now in the library that used not to, and Conor thought they were great. There was even a beginners' computer class for seniors, started by Pat Fitzgerald, the butcher's wife, and now taught by Conor himself because Mrs. Fitz was up to her ears getting ready to visit her grandkids in Canada.

It was mainly women who came to the book club. What Miss Casey called the "core group" was usually about five or six. They met in a side room that had been opened up as part of the library's facelift. The room, which had chairs and a table, could be isolated by a sliding glass door etched with the words READING ROOM, giving the same effect as the glass wall that separated the library from the exhibition space. According to the local newspaper, the County Architect had used translucence to infuse what was a communal public space with both public and private resonances. According to Fury O'Shea, the builder who'd done the work, architects tended to come out with stuff like that. But apparently this guy was sound enough.

There was a new security drill to get used to before the psalter arrived. In the past you just pulled the door behind you and turned the key in the lock. Now you had to set an alarm and press a button to let down an inner security door before going out the front. Miss

Casey said it was a big responsibility. Though, as Fury O'Shea said when Conor told him about it, they didn't pay you any more money for it.

⚶

When Ameena looked up from the book she was reading, she saw Conor at a table by the fountain. He was sitting with the red-headed girl from the delicatessen across the road. Ameena waved and he called her over and introduced them. The girl's name was Aideen and she said she remembered Ameena from school.

"I'd say you were going into ninth grade when I was doing my Leaving."

This was often the way. No one forgot you if you were the only Pakistani kid in the schoolyard, but they always seemed surprised to find that you didn't remember them. Ameena had no memory of Aideen as a senior, but she smiled and said she was sorry to interrupt their lunch.

"Not at all, it's lovely to meet you. Are you going to be working in the library?"

"Well, kind of. I'll be working in the exhibition gift shop." Ameena turned and beamed at Conor. "It was fine. Miss Casey said I could have whatever hours I wanted, since I was the first to come in and ask."

"That's mighty. Didn't I say you'd be grand?"

Ameena explained to Aideen that her mum wasn't really up for her working full-time. "She tends to be at home a lot and when she goes out, she likes me with her."

When Ameena had gone back to her own table, Aideen raised her eyebrows at Conor. "Is her mum sick or something?"

"I dunno, I was only talking to her for a minute and she never said."

"I'd say she'll be a real hit in the gift shop. She looks like some class of a model, even in that awful school skirt."

Conor glanced at her sideways. "Are you fishing?"

Aideen skimmed foam off her coffee and flicked it at him. "For a compliment from the likes of you? You wish!"

She had a way of screwing up her eyes when she jeered at you that Conor loved. Picking up his cheese-and-pickle on rye, he bit into it happily. Not only was Aideen great altogether but she made the best cheese-and-pickle sandwiches on the peninsula.

7

Nell Reily was the first to arrive at the library for the book club. A quiet woman in her late sixties, she lived with her mother on the southern side of the peninsula near the village of Knockmore, where Hanna had a regular mobile library stop at St. Mary's Day Care Centre. Nell and her mother often went to St. Mary's, but, like the rest of the peninsula's seniors, they were delighted that The Old Convent Centre in Lissbeg now offered day care as well. Because, as old Mrs. Reily always told Hanna, a change was as good as a rest.

It was in The Old Convent Centre that the Reilys had met Paul Cox, a picture-framer who'd rented a space there for his business. Having chatted with him across adjoining tables in the Garden Café, Nell had come up with the idea of earning what she called pin money. She and her mother were lace-makers. Why wouldn't they do some designs based on the curly capital letters in the Carrick Psalter, make them in lace and get Paul to frame them? People always loved things with initials on them because they made great gifts. You could choose the first letters of popular names like Mary and Seán—indeed M would double up for Mother and Mammy—and stick a label on the back of the frame saying the design was inspired by the psalter. So Paul and the Reilys were now hard at work producing the framed initials ready for the height of the tourist season.

Today, as Nell put her head around the library door, Hanna marveled at the knock-on effects of the gift of the psalter. Its donor, Charles Aukin, was the widower of the last of the de Lancys, the Anglo-Irish family that had once owned all of Finfarran. Being almost a recluse, Charles was the last person Hanna had imagined would come to the rescue when her library had been threatened with closure. But that was exactly what he had done. Having stipulated that his gift must be housed in Lissbeg Library, he had not only provided the money to create the exhibition space, but matched the council's investment in the development of the Convent Centre. And as a result, now the library had been saved, the peninsula was buzzing with a new spirit of enterprise.

Nell paused by the desk and beamed brightly at Hanna. "Don't mind me at all, Miss Casey. I know I'm early but Paul's been waiting on the latest batch of initials. We've been wondering if maybe we should think of foreign names, too. I'm going to ask Susan today if she knows any common German ones."

Hanna nodded, trying not to lose her place in a column of figures on her computer screen. Nell dug in her oilcloth bag and produced a couple of library books.

"Do you know what it is, they say there's a fierce lot of Japanese tourists coming to Ireland these days? But, you see, they'd have a different alphabet and, if you started down that road, you'd be losing your USP."

Putting the books on Hanna's desk, she carefully removed the Post-it stickers bristling between their pages.

"Now, I read this and Mam whipped through the other, and they both made the same point, Miss Casey. With a start-up business the one thing you need to do is hang on to your USP. That'd be your unique selling point. And ours is the link with the psalter. So we thought we'd leave Japan for the moment and focus on a tighter demographic."

Hanna remarked that research was always helpful.

"It is, of course. Though half of it's common sense. Sure the dogs in the street could tell you to control your overheads and keep a sharp eye on your outgoings."

Clearly the plan to make pin money had morphed to a vision of an empire. But as Hanna left her desk and went to set out chairs in the Reading Room, she told herself that the framed initials really were impressive, so who knew where Nell's dreams might lead the Reilys? Up to now, they'd spent much of their time watching TV in their stuffy living room, and the exquisite lace that they made as a hobby had mostly ended in jumble sales. Now their life had a purpose and, while Mrs. Reily delivered the initials to Paul and chatted with friends in the Garden Café, Nell, who was her elderly mother's sole carer, could take time out to join a book club.

Five minutes later, Susan Winterhalder slung her waterproof jacket over the chair beside Nell's. Darina Kelly, who arrived next, was nothing like Susan in appearance. Her tousled blond hair came from a bottle, and, where Susan was smartly but simply dressed in a top and well-fitting trousers, Darina, who was a good ten years older, wore an oversized t-shirt and orange Doc Martens. She swept into the Reading Room in a whirl of scarves and patchouli.

"Hi everyone! How's it going? I'm just going to dump my bag here. It weighs a ton and God knows what's in it, but I seem to haul it everywhere!"

The bag, which was almost as large as a bin liner, was made of grubby brocade. Darina dumped it on a chair where it tipped sideways, spilling half its contents onto the floor. As Susan bent to restore them, the circle was joined by Gráinne Doran, who worked in the tourist office in Ballyfin. Hanna was always mildly surprised that someone who spent half the year dealing with questions, assertions, and non sequiturs appeared to find the book club so enjoyable—it was a cheerful group but its sessions had a habit of disintegrating into social occasions at which the book they were supposed to be discussing hardly got a mention.

This week's book choice was Darina's. She was rooting in her bag for her copy when the sliding door opened and Oliver Bannister entered and sat beside Nell. He was squat, short-sighted, and middle-aged, with pebble glasses, a combover, and a rucksack worn clasped to his chest. His input was usually limited to his opinion of a book's cover design, but he turned up dead on time and had the best attendance record of any of them.

Having dropped two hairbrushes, her purse, and a paint-stained hat, Darina emerged from her bag with a copy of Harper Lee's *Go Set a Watchman*.

As the others produced their own copies, Hanna found herself remembering the days when the library had been the school hall. As a teenager she had sat here under the cold eye of Sister Consuelo, counting the days to her freedom. And more than thirty years ago, when she'd left Ireland to study in London, she'd had no intention of returning to work in Lissbeg. Indeed, had she stuck to her guns and not been side-tracked by marriage and motherhood, she might now be an art librarian working in a famous gallery. It was strange how life took you in unexpected directions, and stranger still how you reacted to them. Once, the idea of ending up in the little town where she'd been to school had appalled her. But now Lissbeg was about to become home to a book so rare and beautiful that she fizzed with excitement when she thought of it. And each week, wearing cotton gloves, it would be her job to unlock its display case and turn yet another painted page.

"So, *Go Set a Watchman*!" Darina brandished her copy in the air and beamed at the others. "As I said before, I chose this book because I knew that we'd find it riveting. Harper Lee's themes are timeless. Childhood. Well, we've all been children. Parenting. That's something I personally relate to very deeply."

There was a pause in which everyone studiously avoided looking at each other: Darina's inability to control her noisy, acquisitive children was notorious.

Oblivious to the frisson she'd created, Darina lowered her voice dramatically. "And Gregory Peck! Such a sensitive portrayal of that deeply sensitive character. So much conveyed by those wonderful dark brooding eyes!"

Susan frowned. "Er, sorry, Darina, which book are we talking about? Wasn't Gregory Peck in the film of *To Kill a Mockingbird*?"

Darina blinked. "Well, yes. But *To Kill a Mockingbird* was the prequel or, possibly, the sequel to *Go Set a Watchman*. And the genesis of those two books demonstrates the author's lifetime obsession with the same deeply troubling themes."

Gráinne said that was all very well, but they hadn't arranged to read the two books, just the one of them.

Susan said that, in fact, she had read *To Kill a Mockingbird* but ages ago, when she was at school.

Darina, who was from Dublin, said that astonished her. "Surely the nuns here wouldn't have seen it as suitable?"

Nell Reily shook her head. "But she wasn't taught by the nuns, were you, Susan? Wasn't the convent here well closed by your day?"

Oliver mentioned that he didn't like the color of the cover of *Go Set a Watchman*.

Susan said there was no point in talking about *To Kill a Mockingbird* unless everyone had read it.

Gráinne said she hadn't but that she remembered the film. "It was on TV there a while back when I had that awful flu."

There was an extended discussion of the tenacity

of the particular flu virus. You'd think you'd got over your dose of it and then you'd be flattened again. According to Nell, old Mrs. Reily still hadn't really recovered. She got a tight place in her chest at times when the wind blew from the north. What everyone needed, they all agreed, was a good long spell of decent sunshine to knock all the bugs on the head.

Then, before Hanna could suggest that they get back to the book, Darina was off again. "What struck me most in that film was the sense of place! Those rolling fields of cotton, that wonderful mansion and the deep terror of Atlanta swept by flames!"

Realizing they were about to veer off into a discussion of *Gone with the Wind*, Hanna intervened. Maybe they should focus on their chosen title? After all, that was the book they'd all read.

Oliver announced that, in fact, he hadn't read a word of it. "If I go at a thing I stick with it, Miss Casey. Start at the beginning, go on till I come to the end and then stop. But with that method you could waste a fierce lot of time. So I take a sharp look at a cover and if I don't like the look of it, the author's had his chips. It might not be your way, but it's my way. And it saves me a lot of hassle."

Gráinne said she'd be happy to stick with *To Kill a Mockingbird*. "To tell the truth, I've had so much going on that I've only read half of the other one. And Darina's right about Gregory Peck. He was fabulous."

Darina beamed at her. "Wasn't he? So tall." Actually, she said, she hadn't quite finished *Go Set a Watchman* herself.

Susan grinned at Hanna. "And I whipped through the last six chapters far too quickly. I think it's the time of year, Miss Casey, we're all gearing up for the height of the season."

Fishing in her bag again, Darina produced her iPhone. She was pretty sure, she said, that Gregory Peck had Irish ancestors. Or maybe Spanish. Anyway, that rugged, dark thing was terribly Celtic, wasn't it? And, according to something she'd read on the internet the earliest Irish settlers came from Iberia. Or Greece. She'd have it in a minute because she'd bookmarked the piece. With a whinnying laugh, she stabbed at her phone and the others leaned in to look at it.

Hanna, who had enjoyed *Go Set a Watchman*, gave in to the inevitable and the rest of the hour was spent happily googling Gregory Peck.

8

It had been a long day and Hanna was tired as she locked up the library. With her mind on Maggie's book, she was halfway to the parking lot before she realized who was coming toward her. His mind seemed to be elsewhere, too, so, in the moment before he could raise his head and see her, she stepped hastily into the road and crossed to the far pavement. Once there, she spotted Ameena Khan coming out of the post office. Acutely aware of the tall figure visible beyond the horse trough and the moving traffic, Hanna smiled brightly at Ameena. "What are you planning to do when you leave school?"

Clearly a little startled by the unexpected interrogation, Ameena smiled back politely. "I think I'd like to study chemistry, maybe be a researcher."

"Good. That's great." Hanna's eyes flicked across the road to where Brian Morton, the County Architect, had paused and was looking straight at her. Madly, she bared her teeth again at Ameena. "Well, I hope you'll enjoy your summer job."

Ameena lowered her long, beautiful eyelashes, saying she was sure that she would. Feeling like a complete idiot, Hanna fled. From the far side of Broad Street, Brian continued to look at her. She knew perfectly well that he knew she was running away from him. The two of them had been avoiding each other for at least the last six months. Now she hung round till she knew he was gone before she went back to the parking lot. The look on his face had wrung her heart and she told herself her behavior had been foolish. Perhaps tonight she'd take up her phone and ring him. But it would have been far too hard to talk just standing there in the street.

After her dinner Hanna carried a glass of wine to the bench that looked over the ocean. It was made of a single plank painted a peculiar shade of red, the last color she herself would have chosen. But Fury O'Shea, who'd been her builder, had used it without consulting her, announcing later that it was the original color of the built-in dresser by her fire. He'd also applied it to the dresser, again without a word, and waited to see how she'd respond. At first she'd planned to repaint them both as soon as she'd seen the back of him. Later, and to her surprise, she'd come to welcome the jarring color as a token of Maggie's acerbic presence in the garden and in the house. Fury had observed her reaction without comment and she'd never told him he'd been right. But they both knew what had happened, and, as time passed, she'd realized that there was a whole lot more to Fury O'Shea than first met the eye. Though they'd fought like a bag of weasels to begin with, he was someone Hanna now knew she could rely on if ever she should need to. Though the bottom line with Fury was that he'd always do things his own way. Never yours.

Getting to her feet, Hanna left the bench and returned to the house and the fireside. Her phone was on the table and she thought again of ringing Brian Morton. But Maggie's book lay on the dresser in its box. Ignoring the phone, Hanna crossed the room and reached up to the shelf. Immediately she remembered making the same gesture to lift down a library book for Maggie. In the past the house had had no bookshelves and Maggie had never been a book buyer. But each week she had gone to the library in Carrick. Her favorite books were classic detective stories but her sight was failing so, as well as carrying water and digging poreens, Hanna had been required to read aloud. A chapter a day was Maggie's rule and no book could be opened till the day's jobs were done. Tormented by this slow progression through endless whodunits, Hanna had frequently sneaked a look at the last page of a Ngaio Marsh or an Agatha Christie. But the deception had always troubled her. It had seemed wrong to take advantage of the milky cataracts that were forming on Maggie's shrewd eyes and in breaking the rule Hanna always felt a touch of superstitious dread.

Now, as expiation for those sins of her childhood, she decided to apply the same rule to the book in the box. To consume it all in one go felt disrespectful and, indeed, to read it at all felt slightly impertinent. Yet why had Maggie preserved her story if not so that it would be read?

The next entry was dated July 30th, 1920, ten days after the previous one. But as Hanna turned the pages, she realized several had been cut out. Close to the line of stitching that held the copybook to the cover, someone had removed them with a blade so sharp and a hand so steady that their absence was almost imperceptible. It was impossible to tell when or why it had been done, and pointless to speculate, so instead she began to read.

You'd think I'd never weathered a storm before, the way I am on this boat. And you'd wonder how someone reared next to an ocean would be bothered by a little stretch of sea. I suppose the size of the boat gave me a fright when I first saw it there beside me like an iron cliff with the big cables holding it to the quay and the steep ramp leading up to it. I felt like a cow driven to market in that crowd of strangers, not knowing what I'd find at the top. The third-class cabin is awful, full of people being sick and babies crying and young fellows half drunk. There was a bit of singing at first, like there'd been on the train, but it didn't last.

One lad on the train was singing in Irish but he shut up when the soldiers got on. I put my head down and moved away from him because there'd been a poster up on the platform in Carrick with a photo of Liam on it. It said he was a known dissident who'd shot a policeman in Crossarra. That would have been the night of the raid. The photo was the one that was in the paper the time he won the prize for his poem. I don't know how the police found it because John Joe Quinn, the editor of the Inquirer, got the word last year to destroy all photos of the lads out on the hills. Mam had a copy of it that she cut out of the paper. She had it folded up between the stones above the chimneypiece but Dad made her take it down and burn it. But they got hold of a copy some way and it's up on the posters with five hundred pounds reward on Liam's head. I was afraid the police on the train would see my name and ask me questions. But the policeman who looked at my papers only glanced at them. There's plenty of Caseys in Ireland anyway, and I'd say by the look of the policeman he was dying to get home to his tea.

I'm writing this up on deck. There's a gale of wind and every bit of timber and iron is wet with the spray, but it's better than being down below there in the cabin. I've found a place between two benches. The cold and the wet would strike up if you'd sit on the deck itself but I have the suitcase here under me. It's a good leather one I borrowed from Lizzie Keogh. God knows when she'll ever see it again but I said if I met someone who'd take it with them I'd send it over. One thing's for sure anyway, I won't be bringing it back to her myself.

Lizzie said there's always someone on the boat that'll tell you where to find digs. Maybe in a while, if the sea gets calmer, I'll go back down to the cabin and ask. I have ten pounds out of the money Paud Donovan got us for the cows. I don't know if Mam understood what I was saying when I told her I was taking it. I told her I'd send money regular when I *get a job in Liverpool. Mrs. Donovan will look in on her. I don't think Liam would want me to leave Mam and I'm sure Dad wouldn't. But I was given a choice that was no choice, so what would they have me do?*

The entry ended there. Despite her determination not to rush through the story, Hanna was about to yield to temptation and read on when the phone on the table rang. It was Jazz sounding stressed. "Mum, have you heard from Dad?"

"No. Should I have? Is he okay?"

"Oh, he's fine. Not a bother on him. Which is hardly surprising, given how he shoves his problems off onto everyone else."

Hanna closed Maggie's book. "What is it this time?"

"He's coming over for your exhibition."

Hanna blinked. "Are you sure?"

"Of course I'm sure. He just phoned me. Right in the middle of my shift, as it happens, but when did anyone else's schedule ever matter to Dad?"

"So what's his ulterior motive?"

"It's Granny Lou."

This was Malcolm's widowed mother, Louisa, an elegant, dignified woman who lived alone in his family home in Kent. Hanna, who was fond of her, had occasionally wondered how Louisa was coping as she grew older. But, having an aging mother of her own to deal with, she hadn't given it too much thought. Now she felt guilty.

"Is she all right?"

"Oh, stop it, Mum. Nobody's dead or dying. Granny Lou just fancies a trip up to London. Dad's damned if he's going to take time out to entertain her. So he's told her that what she *really* fancies is quality time with me."

"And what's this got to do with the exhibition?"

"Oh, for God's sake, you know the way Dad operates. He's squiring her over to Lissbeg for your opening. And I'm telling you, Mum, he's planning to dump her on me."

The phone went dead and Hanna pulled a face at it. Then, taking the bottle and the glass with her, she went back to the garden and stared out at the ocean. So much for getting her courage up to make that call to Brian Morton. Now, just when she could do without his presence, Malcolm was coming to Finfarran. Malcolm, who had no more use for her but had always been possessive. It was as if he had read her mind and seen she was ready to move on.

9

When Ameena came home after sitting her math exam, there was a gorgeous smell in the kitchen and her mum was on Skype in the living room chatting with Auntie Fazeen. Mum was the one who kept in touch with all the family in Pakistan, probably because Dad's crowd was more footloose than hers. Ameena's grandad had moved to the city long before Dad was born, but Mum was raised in the countryside, where her family had lived for ages. Actually, both sides of the family originally came from the same village and, while Dad's had gone all urban and techno-savvy, they still tended to return to their roots when it came to finding a wife. Which was how Mum and Dad had met.

Ameena could hardly remember Karachi, where she was born, and she'd only been in Mum's village once, when she was twelve and the family had turned up en masse for her cousin's wedding. It had been a strange time, half celebration, half mourning, because Nani, Mum's mum, had had cancer and they'd known it was the last time they'd see her. Before they came back to Ireland, Nani had told Mum not to travel back for the funeral. There was no point in wasting good money, she said. She'd lived a good life and they'd all be together in Paradise. That was the way Ameena remembered Nani—devout, loving, funny, and sharp as a tack. You could see why Mum hated having to go away and leave her when the rest of the family could be there with her right till the day she died.

As Ameena went through the hall Mum called her into the living room.

"Come and say hello to Auntie Fazeen."

Ameena went in and waved and said hi before going upstairs. On her way up she could hear Auntie Fazeen exclaiming about how tall she'd got and tutting about her uniform.

"So ugly and unattractive!"

Mum laughed and said that at least it meant she was unlikely to pick up any unsuitable boyfriends; then, seeing Ameena lingering on the staircase, she told her to go and get changed quickly or the food would be spoiled. Ameena clattered cheerfully up to her room. After hours crouched over an exam paper, she was longing for dinner and Mum knew to a nanosecond when to whisk a meal out of the oven and onto the table.

As she wriggled out of her uniform, she found herself grinning at what Mum had said about boyfriends. She'd had a couple of major crushes when she'd been in tenth grade and had gone out for a few months with Eamonn Cowan when they were both in the eleventh. But Eamonn had turned out to be the jealous type, and, although she'd had plenty of offers, she'd steered clear of anything heavy after that. A couple of her friends were already talking about settling down with guys they were dating, but Ameena thought that was dumb. How could you settle down without seeing what else might be out there? Not just who you might spend your life with, but what you might do on your own. She wasn't quite sure herself of what she'd do or where she'd go, but she was determined to keep her options open. That was why she'd fixed to go celebrating after the exams with Lar Walsh, who'd recently broken up with his girlfriend and wanted an uncomplicated date.

The whole class had planned to go out together, and, when Lar had asked Ameena to go with him, he'd laid it on the line without a blush. "Are you up for it? We could have a laugh. And you're going to look drop-dead gorgeous so you'll really knock Nuala's eye out."

Ameena knew that no bones had been broken when the relationship with Nuala had ended. She also knew that she and Lar would have a great night. He was a good laugh and he wasn't the kind to act like an eejit or get drunk. So she'd said yes at once, and Mum had promised to lend her a green-and-silver sari that had once belonged to Nani. It was all fixed for July when the exams would be over, which couldn't be soon enough for her.

At the table Mum served Daal aur Chawal and Dad asked about the math exam.

Ameena shrugged. "It was fine, no problem."

Her little sister, Rimal, made a face at her. "Geek."

"I am not a geek, I just concentrate on my course work. You should try it sometime."

Rimal ignored her and swiped an extra papadum while Mum's back was turned. Then Mum joined them at the table and pointed to an envelope on the window-sill. It had come for Ameena that morning, she said, and the postmark was local. Everyone looked expectant so, licking her fingers, Ameena went over and opened it. It was a fancy-looking invitation to the official opening of the psalter exhibition with "And Guest" printed in the bottom right-hand corner. At the orientation day in the library, when the volunteer guides and the gift-shop staff had been told they'd be invited to the opening, Phil, who managed the bookings in the center, had smiled round at them. "You'll be there as members of the team, but you won't be expected to work. And, of course, you may want to bring a partner or a friend, who'll be very welcome, too."

The opening was due to take place before the end of Ameena's exams, so she'd planned to broach the subject carefully, and preferably not over dinner with Rimal flapping her ears. But, since there was no help for it, she sat down now and smiled at her mother.

"Do you fancy coming with me? It's from six to eight in the evening, so we wouldn't be out late." She'd love her mum to see the place where she was going to work, she said. It was all new and beautifully designed and the psalter was really fascinating. "The man who donated it lives in Castle Lancy—that place above the road when you drive in to Carrick. He's an American banker or something, who married the last of the de Lancy family."

Mum wasn't looking too fascinated, so Ameena turned to Dad.

"The de Lancys used to be landlords here, back when the English were in Ireland. And the psalter really is a beautiful book. The monks who made it were inspired by the peninsula. We've got postcards in the shop with illustrations from the psalter alongside photos of the same places as they are today."

Dad looked interested, but not overwhelmed.

"And they're identical . . ." Ameena was aware that she was gabbling, but she couldn't seem to stop herself ". . . well, not identical, obviously. I mean the perspective's a bit weird in the psalter and there are hares wearing hats in the margins. But it *is* remarkable."

Mum picked up the invitation and looked at it. "I thought you were going to be working in the shop, not the exhibition."

"I am. But I'm part of the team. That's why we're all invited."

Mum handed the invitation to Dad and asked him what he thought.

Dad smiled at her. "You should go with Ameena. You'd enjoy yourself. And the invitation is very courteous."

Ameena held her breath. Part of the reason Mum didn't go out much was because her English wasn't great. As a result, her social life was pretty limited and, though she covered it with an air of dignity, she was always shy around people she didn't know. And now, with school nearly over, things were coming to a head. Mum knew perfectly well that Ameena wouldn't be at home forever. But Ameena suspected that, in another part of her brain, she'd imagined a future in which the two of them would go shopping and hang out together, and drive off to Carrick at the drop of a hat without needing a lift from Dad.

So when Ameena had first told her about the gift shop, it was like it was the beginning of something that Mum had dreaded for ages.

"What are you talking about? You don't need a job."

"Well, it can't hurt to save some money if I'm going to college."

"Ameena, that's foolish. Your father makes plenty of money and we've always paid for whatever tuition you want."

Determined not to be sidetracked, Ameena had said no more. But later, when Dad had been okay about the job, she'd talked about how great it would be to plan trips to Carrick with Mum in the summer break, if she was going off to college next year. Everything she did felt manipulative, though, and she could hardly bear to see the hope and apprehension warring in her mother's face.

Now Mum looked at Dad with the same uncertainty. "You really think I should accept this invitation?"

"I think Ameena would like you to. And it won't

hurt for her to have a bit of a break toward the end of her exams. It's a Saturday and, as she says, it won't be a late night."

"I'd love you to, Mum, honestly. I'll hardly know anyone there, so I'd love your support."

Mum shot Ameena a look so shrewd that she suddenly reminded her of Nani. Then she nodded. "Perhaps I should see this place for myself."

Getting up, she went to the cooker and, with her back to the table, began fussing with the saucepans.

Leaning back so Dad couldn't see her face, Rimal winked elaborately across the table. As far as she was concerned, this was game, set, and match to Ameena. Ameena glared at her. Okay, Rimal, who was only ten, had been born in Finfarran, so it probably wasn't her fault that she didn't understand. But Ameena could remember the scent of red earth after a monsoon shower, the taste of Nani's Daal aur Chawal, and the sound of Mum trying to hide her tears on the flight back to Ireland from Karachi. She knew that this wasn't a game. It was emotional stuff and, because she loved Mum dearly, she wanted to get it right.

10

During Jazz's interview for the job at The Old Forge, Susan had taken her upstairs and showed her the room in the eaves. It wasn't en suite, she'd explained, but the bathroom across the corridor would be all hers.

"You wouldn't feel cramped?"

"Not at all. It's lovely."

It was, too, almost as big as the shared room Jazz had had in France, where the state of the bathroom, used by all four flatmates, was always leading to rows. Not that she wouldn't go back to the flat and her old job in a heartbeat. But there was no point in ignoring the doctor and asking for trouble. Besides, it wasn't just her physical health that had been affected by the accident. Somehow, she seemed to have lost her nerve as well.

Everyone, including the guards, had told her the crash hadn't been her fault and, intellectually, she knew they were right. She hadn't been drunk or speeding or texting while driving, and when she turned that corner she couldn't have known that a cow would suddenly break through a gap in the ditch. The moment the huge body had lurched onto the road in front of her, Jazz had instinctively swerved. Then, hitting the animal's shoulder with a horrible thump, the car had spun off sideways and crumpled against a stone wall. She had been incredibly lucky. A driver coming toward her had pulled up safely and immediately called the police. According to the surgeon, she had the classic injuries associated with a crash, and her routine operation had been successful. She could thank God things had not been worse, and get on with living her life.

It appeared that no one had noticed her loss of nerve except herself. No one had warned her about the nightmares either. They had started in the hospital where the heat and constant noise on the ward had made it hard to sleep. Time and again, having tossed and turned for hours, she'd be jerked back into consciousness sweating and terrified by a dream. Weirdly, she seldom dreamed about the wall. When she was awake, she could remember the gray stone spattered with mustard-colored lichen and the searing pain as the hood reared up in front of the windshield and her ribs cracked against the seatbelt. But her dreams were about the cow. The impact of metal on hair and hide and muscle. Yellow teeth and long ropes of drool. The animal's flaring nostrils and bloodshot eye seen through the window before the glass shattered. And its bellow of fear and pain that seemed far louder than the sound of the car hitting the wall or her own wail of terror. Once, she had screamed aloud in her sleep, waking the women in the beds on either side of her and bringing a night nurse scuttling down the darkened ward. Feeling foolish, she'd said that her broken ribs were unbearable and asked for pain relief. Annoyed by having to deal with several grumbling, wakeful patients on a shift that, up to then, had been uneventful, the nurse had handed her a couple of pain relievers and reminded her tersely of the bell beside her bed.

"I'll come just as quickly if you press it and you won't be disturbing other people."

Still sweating, Jazz had waited till the nurse had gone, slipped the pills into her locker, and tried to will herself back to sleep. But each time she'd closed her eyes, the cow's mud-stained hooves hung in the air above her head and torn metal slashed through its stomach, spilling bones onto the road.

11

Surrounded by shopping bags, Mary Casey sat in the bar of The Royal Victoria, Carrick's most respectable hotel. Because it was one of Hanna's mobile library days, she was assured both of a lift home from town and a chance to show off her purchases. Everyone seemed to be making a song and dance about this exhibition at Hanna's work and, having received a grand printed invitation, Mary wasn't going to be backward in coming forward at the opening. She'd been prepared for the possibility of failing to find the right outfit in Carrick and having to make a trip all the way to Cork. But there was no need to. The perfect dress with a matching jacket and exactly the right neckline for her pearls had been right there in The Carrick Couturier. It was blue, as well, and Tom had loved her in blue. Of course, Tom was so daft about her that she could have gone round in a dish rag and he still would have thought she was lovely, but she was fond of the color blue herself so she'd always indulged his preference. It was nice to think that he'd like the outfit she'd chosen today. God knew that he wouldn't have grudged her the cost of it—a more generous husband than Tom Casey you wouldn't find in a long day's walk.

PJ, the bartender, placed a clinking glass and a small silver bowl on the table. It was a bit early in the day for Mary. Normally she'd take her little martini after the evening news. But wasn't it great altogether to have someone else do the pouring for you, and to have the bowl of olives on the side? When visitors came to the bungalow, she'd always open a packet of chips and serve them in the Belleek dish with the shamrocks on it, but there was no point in doing that when you'd just be sitting there on your own. The silver bowl of olives came with a saucer under it and a little paper doily. That was The Royal Victoria there in a nutshell—proper standards. They had real flowers in the ladies' room, too. And roller towels. None of your hot-air hand driers that announced they were protecting the planet and were really just saving on the laundry.

Mary sipped her martini with approval. She missed her outings with Tom, and the times when her birthday and their anniversary were celebrated with dinner and a night in a hotel. Tom used always to be planning treats and surprises for her. In fact, whatever the begrudgers might say of him, it had been his greatest joy in life.

Thinking about Tom made her wish that poor Hanna would find herself a decent man. There was that fellow from the council who'd turned up on the dreadful night when Jazz had her accident. He'd given Hanna a lift home from the hospital and anyone with half an eye could see he'd be taking her dancing if she'd give him half a chance. Well, maybe not dancing, because people didn't do that these days, and they both were a bit long in the tooth for it. But Mary had liked the cut of him.

She'd kept her mouth shut and her ear to the ground afterward and discovered his name was Brian Morton. By all accounts he'd been some class of a pen pusher when Hanna met him, but he'd been made up to County Architect since, and that came with a proper wage. No house, mind, but a rented flat in Carrick. And not local, which she'd have preferred, but sure beggars couldn't be choosers. Yet, from that day to this, she hadn't seen sight nor light of him, and when she'd ventured to ask a question she'd been slapped down for her pains. And wasn't that typical of Hanna? Prickly as a burr since the breakup with that Malcolm Turner and full of daft notions about reclaiming her independence. Let her try a few years of it there on her own in Maggie's place, and see how she felt in the dark winter months. Anyway, she might fool herself as much as she liked, but she couldn't fool her mother. Hanna-Mariah fancied your man the architect and that was as clear as day.

Mary was mopping the condensation from her martini glass with a Kleenex when Hanna arrived. PJ appeared to take her order. "I'll have a coffee please, PJ, and a huge glass of water. It's thirsty work driving round in the van."

Mary sniffed. She'd have her head bitten off if she opened her beak, so she'd say nothing. But if the same madam had played her cards right and got a decent settlement from her pup of a husband, couldn't she have her feet up now without a care in the world? Instead of which she was inside in that library, or out in that van, five days out of seven. And living in what, with all said and done, was no more than a spruced-up shack.

Hanna smiled across the table at her. "How was the shopping trip?"

"Grand."

"Give us a look."

Mary smacked her hand aside, tucking swaths of tissue paper firmly back into place. "Are you out of your mind, or what are you? You'll have the whole of Finfarran gawping at us! You can come in when you drive me home and I'll give you a twirl." And why, she asked, wouldn't Hanna-Mariah stay for a bite of dinner? Nothing big. Just a few bits and pieces thrown together out of the fridge.

As meals at Mary Casey's never happened on that kind of ad hoc basis, this was clearly a setup. Hanna, who had planned to spend the evening reading more of Maggie's book, opened her mouth to refuse. But, recognizing that there was no fun in buying a new outfit and then having no one to display it to, she smiled and said okay. "But don't call me Hanna-Mariah, how often do I have to tell you?"

"I'll call you what your poor father called you, so you can stop wasting your breath. And I'll have you know that if I'd had my way, your name would have been Shirley."

Hanna gave up and moved on. "Did you have to go far to find what you wanted?"

Mary explained that the dress and jacket, which she'd found and bought before ten that morning, had been laid aside for her and that she'd spent the rest of the day puttering round town, having lunch and choosing accessories. "Because as your father, God be good to him, always said, 'You couldn't go out in front of the neighbors in shoes that screamed at your frock.'"

To Hanna's recollection that pronouncement had been Mary's, not Tom's, but she smiled again and listened to the list of carefully chosen tights of exactly the right denier, the slip with precisely the right shoulder straps, and the shoes with just the right heel.

"I couldn't be standing round on stilettos at my age, but you'd have to have a heel that worked with the hemline so I went for a little wedge. They're a lovely shade of midnight blue, suede with a strappy detail. Not fussy, now. But summery. And I got a little fascinator. Mind you, they had the cheek of the divil asking that kind of money for a couple of flowers and a feather. But Pam Pearse said she'd only just got them in last Monday, and you might as well be out of the world as out of the fashion."

"I'd say you'll be the belle of the ball."

"Ah, don't I know well that you're laughing at me. But, sure, I'd have to be decent. Isn't it your big night in the spotlight? I couldn't go letting you down."

"I wouldn't call it *my* big night."

"Isn't it your exhibition?"

"Well, it's in my library . . ."

"That's what I'm saying. And won't *the Inquirer* be there with the cameras?"

Hanna grinned. "Apparently there'll be press down from Dublin as well."

"Holy God Almighty, I'm glad I got the new slip!"

As her mother regarded her shopping with satisfaction, Hanna made up her mind. She'd spent the last week working up to the next thing she needed to say to Mary, knowing it wouldn't go down well and dreading the ensuing scene. But she couldn't put it off forever, and raising it now in a public place might well contain the fallout.

"Actually, Mam, you're right. It is going to be a big night. And it really will be lovely to have my family round me."

Mary's face settled into folds of massive suspicion. Seeing that beating round the bush was a bad tactic, Hanna went for the jugular.

"Malcolm and Louisa are coming over for the opening. I know you won't like it, Mam, but there it is."

Two pink spots appeared on Mary Casey's cheeks. Hanna dropped an olive stone into the saucer where it made a loud clink in an ominous silence. It was going to be a difficult evening.

12

Phil from The Old Convent Centre had asked Bríd and Aideen to come up with some menus for the opening. She'd have to ring around and get other quotes, too, she said, but it'd be great to make a big thing of Finfarran's local produce.

Aideen and Bríd spent several evenings brainstorming ideas and a week later when Phil came over for a meeting, she was delighted by what they'd come up with. They could play safe, Bríd explained, and do canapés on trays and a table with cakes or desserts. "But people always drop cutlery and put plates down in the wrong places. Anyway, you don't want to clutter up the exhibition space with caterers' tables." So she'd spoken to Trish Murphy, who'd just started a company called Luscious Lissbeg Chocolates.

"She could make little discs with a squiggly design on them, based on the ones in the psalter. We'd serve them on those wooden platters you're going to sell in the gift shop, and Trish could do boxes of samples for goodie bags. And we'd offer bite-sized honey cakes for people who didn't like chocolate. Trish and the lad that works with her would help us serve on the night. Then for the savories, we'd do a monastic theme—rye bread and oatcakes topped with local smoked salmon and cheeses."

Phil said chocolate didn't sound very monastic, but that she saw what Bríd meant.

Aideen backed Bríd up. "I did some research. Cheese, oatcakes, and fish turn up in medieval Irish stories. Hazelnuts too. But half the world has nut allergies these days, so we said that we wouldn't risk them."

"But we could do berries." Bríd showed Phil some photos of samples. "Trish suggested cherries, which will just be in season. Some plain and some half-dipped in chocolate."

As Phil swiped through the photos on Bríd's phone, Aideen chipped in again. "And we'd use herbs and flowers from the nuns' garden for garnish and decoration. Dill, rosemary, watercress—watercress turns up all the time in Irish monastic poems. There's a Seamus

Heaney poem about a mad king who eats watercress. That's based on a twelfth-century manuscript."

Phil smiled. "Well you've certainly done your home-work and it all sounds great. The price looks right, too, so I'd say you have the contract. We can finalize the details later."

Gathering up her notes, she asked if Aideen would consider writing a leaflet about the food, to go in the journalists' goodie bags. "No harm in selling other as-pects of Finfarran when we've got the press here. We can put it on the Edge of the World website while we're at it."

The website, which was both a community notice-board and a tool to showcase Finfarran to potential tour-ists, had been started as part of the campaign to save Lissbeg Library. Now, funded by the council and admin-istered by Phil, it was going from strength to strength.

Aideen had felt a bit uncertain about writing stuff for a leaflet, but Bríd had leapt in and told Phil it would be no problem. "And if you'll set up relevant links from the Edge of the World website, I'm sure more people will offer samples for the goodie bags. We're going to use Knockmore Honey, and they've got a website, and we get our bread from the Ballyfin Bakery. We could say that whatever goes in the bags has to relate to the psalter. But it's full of images of Finfarran so that'll be a no-brainer."

Ever since the meeting they'd been refining their menu for the opening, as well as dealing with their normal workload in the deli and preparing food for the café. On top of that, Aideen had been sitting up at night to do the leaflet. So this morning she was dying for an evening off.

As they worked at double speed behind the deli counter, Bríd asked about her plans.

"Nothing exotic. I just said I'd meet Conor after work and we'd go to Trawbawn for a swim."

Trawbawn Strand, the nearest beach to Lissbeg, had three miles of golden sand and high dunes scattered with star flowers. Just mentioning it made Aideen smile.

Bríd shot a quick glance at her. "Then what? Is he taking you out to dinner?"

"God, no. We're both broke. We spent a fortune in Italy. Anyway, we're supposed to be saving."

"What for?"

"How d'you mean?"

"Oh, come on, Aideen, what's the story? Are you and Conor getting together or what?"

Aideen turned pink and said nothing. But Bríd, who was more like a sister to her than a cousin, had never been one for tact.

"Seriously, what's going on? If you're about to retire into married bliss, I think I should be told."

"Like anyone these days retires when they marry!"

There was a pause while Bríd fixed her with a gimlet eye and Aideen pulled off her plastic glove and tucked a curl under her scarf. Then she shrugged.

"Truth be told, I dunno."

"You don't *know*?"

"What are you, deaf? And don't lecture me, Bríd, I'm not like you."

"Which would be?"

"Clear-minded. Organized. Able to cut to the chase."

"So you've agreed that you ought to be saving, but you haven't a clue what for?"

"That's about the height of it."

"You are definitely out of your mind."

"Oh, shut up, you weren't there! We were sitting by a fountain in Florence and it was all lovely and Conor was all romantic and . . ."

"And what? He clasped you in his manly arms and suggested you share a piggy bank?"

"Kind of."

"I suppose it beats saying, 'Would you like to be buried with my people?'"

Aideen looked harassed. "But, that's the thing, isn't it? Maybe that's what he *was* saying—that we ought to get married. But I don't know." They'd had an expensive bottle of wine, she said, so he might just have meant that they'd want to stop spending money like sailors on shore leave.

"Well, isn't it time you found out?"

"How?"

"Ask him."

"I couldn't."

"Ah, for God's sake, Aideen, what century are you living in?"

Aideen hunched her shoulders and said nothing, so Bríd gave up and went back to buttering bread.

A few minutes later, passing with a tray of sandwiches, she gave Aideen a friendly nudge with her hip. "Well, you're either engaged or you're not, girl, and I'll tell you this much—if I were you, I'd want to know where I stood."

13

Conor did a three-day week in Lissbeg Library. Two were mobile library days, when Miss Casey was out, and the third meant that he could man the desk while she did meetings and paperwork or took charge of the book club. Today was a mobile day and she'd fussed a bit about leaving him to lock up on his own. The toughened-glass display case had been put in place last week and, a couple of days later, Charles Aukin had strolled in with the psalter under his arm in a scruffy-looking attaché case. He was closely followed by Fury O'Shea, carrying a Jack Russell terrier.

As Miss Casey led Mr. Aukin through to the exhibition space, Conor had cornered Fury by the door.

"I thought the psalter was worth a fortune."

Fury grinned. "'Tis far worse than that, boy, 'tis priceless."

"And your man's just walking round with it in a bag?"

"What did you expect? An armored car and security lads in dark glasses?"

Seeing Fury's quizzical expression, Conor had felt like an eejit. "I suppose not."

"G'wan out of that, it's exactly what you expected. But that wouldn't be Charles's style at all. Sure, his people were Wall Street aristocracy."

"God, that was a great match, wasn't it? Wall Street aristocracy and the last of the de Lancys of Finfarran."

"That's how the rich make their money, boy. This fella's no different than the rest. He's a sound man all the same though and, by God, he's sly as a fox."

Fury nodded at the glass case into which Miss Casey, wearing cotton gloves, had just placed the psalter. "There it is, safe as houses and no one a penny the wiser. Come in and have a gander yourself now it's here."

As they'd entered the exhibition space, Miss Casey had looked severely at the dog under Fury's arm. "How often do I have to tell you that a library's no place for The Divil?"

"God knows, woman, because you never stop telling me. Anyway he's here in an official capacity, so I don't give a damn what you say."

Fury, who was wearing a long waxed jacket with torn pockets, had hitched the little dog more securely onto his skinny hip. The Divil pointed his nose at Miss Casey and growled deep in his throat.

Fury winked at Conor. "See? If he was off duty, he'd be wriggling round the floor making up to her. But give him the word he's on guard duty, and he'd bite lumps out of the Pope."

That evening Conor and Miss Casey had locked up the library together. Admittedly it felt a bit different with the psalter actually on the premises. But, as he'd told Miss Casey, you didn't get a tractor for peanuts and a prize bull could set you back a good hundred thousand euros. So he wasn't fazed now about being left to lock up on his own. When you worked on a farm you couldn't keep doubling back all the time to check that you'd done something right. It was like his dad taught him years ago, you just learned a procedure, applied it, and got on with the rest of your day.

Today he was looking forward to scooting off to Trawbawn with Aideen. She'd promised to come over the minute she finished work. As he trundled the Returns trolley between the shelves, he told himself that life was great now they were officially together. Well, not officially, because they hadn't actually told anyone, but they knew where they stood and that was the great thing. He'd had girlfriends before but, from the first day he'd met Aideen, he'd felt she was different. She was so shy you could easily think that she hadn't much to say for herself but, once you got to know her, you found she'd a mind of her own.

He hadn't been sure at first if she'd be up for the trip to Italy, and he wasn't sure either how to raise the question of bedrooms. But she'd been fine. She'd even made it easy for him, giving him a secret smile and clicking on the double room icon herself when they'd trawled the net for hotels. Then when they got there, she told him she'd never been to bed before with anyone, which could have amounted to a fierce load of pressure. But somehow they'd got on grand. None of that wild, vacation stuff people go sticking up online and then regret afterwards. But grand. No, actually, brilliant.

The big question now, of course, was where they were headed next. Conor's dad, Paddy, had injured his back several years ago. He could still get about, but the heavy farmwork was more than Conor's brother, Joe, could do on his own, and the place didn't yield a decent wage for the three of them. So Conor's part-time library job was a godsend. But it was also a stopgap and he knew it. He'd always told himself that, if things changed at home, he could train to be a librarian like Miss Casey. But things showed no sign of changing, except that Paddy was being treated for depression these days as well as for pain in his back.

Whatever else might happen, Conor had promised himself that he'd never be the cause of the farm having to be sold. McCarthys had worked that land for generations. Besides, where would his mam and dad live if the place went to strangers? So he and Joe staggered on, keeping the farm going with no real sense of what would happen in the long term. And now, with Aideen on the scene, the future looked even more complicated. But that would just have to be dealt with because, from the moment he'd first laid eyes on her, he'd known that she was The One.

14

Jazz's job at The Old Forge involved helping with the housekeeping as well as working in the office. At first she hadn't been sure what she thought about that, but as soon as she'd seen the rooms there'd been no problem. The four guest bedrooms and the big room with the long tables, cozy chairs, and wide fireplace were cleverly designed. One glance had told Jazz that there would be no need to unplug and replug lights to use a vacuum cleaner, and no clutter to be dusted. Susan had gone for the perfect mix of minimalism and comfort. The beds had feather pillows and down duvets, the bathrooms had walk-in power showers, and there were no welcome baskets of mini muffins to leave crumbs on the upholstery, or towels to be folded into swans.

Jazz hadn't done housekeeping before but, as she'd

assumed, it was mainly a matter of common sense. And it was surprisingly easy to get the knack of shaking out a sheet so that it fell perfectly onto a bed and didn't need tweaking when you came to miter the corners. Now, as she replenished a tea tray, she remembered a hotel she'd once stayed in herself, where the bedrooms had signs saying PLEASE FIND YOUR TEA AND COFFEMAKING FACILITIES IN THE WARDROBE. In paroxysms of giggles, she and her boyfriend Carlos had discovered sachets, crockery, and an electric kettle crammed onto a tray beneath the clothes hangers. The Old Forge was very different. There was a little fridge in each room for fresh milk, and Susan had got Gunther to build units for tins of tea, coffee, and homemade biscuits, and shelves for a kettle and china.

Jazz wondered how Carlos was now. He had been a colleague when she'd worked for the airline and their relationship had hardly begun when she'd had her accident. They'd been in the first flush of romance then, so the way things had ended was a bit crap. "The first flush of romance" was Mum's ghastly expression, but it did kind of describe how she'd actually felt. She and Carlos had tried to keep things going with texts and FaceTime but, eventually, it had just petered out. That probably would have happened anyway, so it wasn't a huge deal. But Carlos had moved in with her former flatmates, and the thought of him in the little French flat she'd loved, hanging out with the others and drinking coffee from the mugs that she and her roommate Sarah had bought in the market, was pretty crap too. None of it was his fault. Before he took the offer of the room in the flat, he'd even rung her and asked if she'd mind and, of course, she'd said she wouldn't. But he and Sarah had apparently got together and, while Jazz didn't begrudge them, she wished she hadn't heard. After getting the news, she'd been in touch with her former flatmates a lot less frequently, and now she hardly contacted them at all.

Telling herself firmly that people move on, she left the room, put the vacuum cleaner back in its cupboard and went downstairs to the office. Susan looked up as she came in.

"Well, here's good news for you."

Jazz saw that she was looking at an email. It was an apologetic message canceling two single rooms.

Susan spoke as she rattled off a reply. "One lady's fractured her hip so they can't travel. At least she let me know at once. There's many that wouldn't." Swiveling round on her chair, she beamed at Jazz. "So that frees up those dates you were looking for."

Jazz bit her lip. This was exactly what kept happening to her life. Everything would be grand and under control and then it'd all go pear-shaped. And she could never tell what disaster would happen next.

A week ago, when she'd been sitting in the office herself, she'd taken a call from Mum. "Hi, love, I'm not looking for a chat, I'm calling about a booking."

"Really? What's the story? Has the roof fallen in on you at Maggie's place?"

There was a kind of pause that sounded iffy, so immediately Jazz had heard alarm bells. Then it had all come out in a rush.

"Listen, love, I've just had your dad on the phone and Granny Lou's apparently got the notion that she'd love to stay at The Old Forge when they come over. The thing is that it *is* the nicest place to stay locally and since I've only the one room it's really the best option. It'd be two rooms for a long weekend and I'd say they'd want dinner most nights."

Jazz had hissed into the receiver like a goose. "For God's sake, Mum, can you not see what Dad's playing at? He's determined to dump Granny Lou on me so he won't have to mind her himself. Anyway, if they're looking for someplace high class couldn't they go to The Royal Victoria?"

"Don't be silly, darling, it's not about high class or low class . . ."

Jazz interrupted her furiously. "No? Well, that'll be a first where Dad's concerned."

". . . it's about being out in the beautiful countryside and spending some time with you."

"I'll be working."

"Yes, but not twenty-four seven."

"I've already said I'll do long shifts that weekend."

"Right. Fine. So I'll entertain them. But they do need somewhere to stay, love, so will you please make the booking?"

Seething, Jazz had opened the schedule and discovered to her satisfaction that all the rooms were booked out.

Thwarted, and clearly unsure whether to believe her, Mum had sighed and hung up. As soon as she'd heard the sigh, Jazz had felt guilty, though no one could possibly say it was her fault. And now Susan was beaming at her, delighted that things had changed.

"I'll put your dad and your gran in now and you can give your mum a ring. Whose name should I put the booking in?"

Jazz gave her dad's email address, since at least that meant he'd have to handle things himself and not dump them on her or on Mum. Then she went outdoors to call Mum on her cell phone. When she explained what had happened, the relief in Mum's voice startled her.

"Oh, thank you, sweetheart, that's one less thing to panic about."

"Are you panicked? Why?"

"I'm not really. It's just that your nan's as ratty as you are about your dad coming over. And, frankly, I'm not that ecstatic myself."

Stricken by the thought that she'd been selfish, Jazz made soothing noises. "It'll be nice to see Granny Lou anyway." That was true enough, since she loved Granny Lou's company when Dad wasn't forcing her into it. Then, feeling that more was required of her, she kept going. "And I bet she'll turn up to the opening looking stunning."

There was a hollow laugh at the other end of the line. "Yes, and that's part of what's worrying me. Your nan's being dressed for the night by The Carrick Couturier and I've a feeling that Granny Lou's London style is going to win hands down."

15

Aideen got to the library just as Conor was saying goodbye to the seniors in his computer class. One of them grabbed her hand and told her how great he was. Apparently the woman, who had a new laptop, had swiped the touchpad some weird way, and all the stuff on the screen had suddenly magnified. She and her daughter had spent a whole week trying to fix it; then she'd brought the laptop to the computer class and Conor had done it in a minute. He was brilliant, that's what he was—a born teacher as well as a lovely lad.

Aideen wriggled her eyebrows at Conor, who grinned and asked her to wait while he closed up. Then a tall man arrived looking at his watch. Unsure of where to put herself, Aideen went through and sat on a corner of the desk. According to Conor, this was always happening; you might have no one in for half an hour before closing time but someone would turn up just as you locked the door. Glancing through to the vestibule, she could see him talking to the man, who looked kind of awkward. A minute or two later the man left with a bit of a wave and Conor put the bottom bolt on the door and came to join her at the desk.

"Who was that?"

"His name's Brian Morton. He's the architect with the council in Carrick."

Aideen stayed sitting on the desk while he shut down the computers. "What was he coming in so late for? Was he looking for a book?"

Conor threw her a wink. "Don't go quoting me now, but I'd say he was looking for Miss Casey."

Aideen was intrigued. She followed him through to the kitchen, where he made sure things were turned off and tidied up.

"Every couple of weeks or so he's been at the same crack. Wanders in all casual, like he's hoping he'll find her here."

"How do you know? He might just want to use the library."

"Three minutes before the door closes? I don't think so. Not only that, but the one time she was here he turned tail and ran."

"Ah, no!"

"I'm serious. He spotted her through the glass door and he sort of dithered and ducked."

"You're making the whole thing up."

"I am not. Anyway, don't you know yourself what it's like when you fall for a librarian? You can't keep away."

Conor reached out and pulled her gently toward him and, knowing the door was bolted, she moved into his arms. She knew exactly what it was like to fall for a librarian—or at least for someone who was going to be one any minute now. And she still couldn't really believe it had actually happened to her.

A few minutes later he took her to check the video room and the gift shop. The shop wasn't open yet but the shelves were stocked. Aideen noticed there were packs of paper napkins with medieval-looking designs on them and told herself to remember to tell Bríd. They might use them at the opening.

When she'd told Conor that she and Bríd had got the contract his face had fallen. "But that means you'll be working. I'd wanted you there as my guest." Then he'd cheered up and said he supposed that at least she'd be well paid for it. "I mean Miss Casey says the council's throwing money at everything to do with the psalter, so I suppose they'll have offered you two a decent whack."

Aideen was a bit disconcerted. Just now, as she'd left the deli to cross the road to the library, she'd been fuming because Bríd had cracked a joke about Conor being one of those fiendish murderers who marry people for their money. It was only Bríd being daft but, all the same, it had got to her. The thing was that she'd never been much to look at and she hadn't been that good at school. So God alone knew what Conor saw in her.

Having locked the internal doors, Conor pulled down the blinds in the exhibition space and went to set the alarm system. Then he stopped and pressed a switch that turned a light on over the psalter. "Come and look at this."

Taking her hand, he drew her over to the spotlit glass case in the center of the room. The book stood open on a carved lectern. It was about the size of a novel you'd buy in an airport. There was a picture on the right-hand page and writing on the left. Aideen couldn't read the words, but they were beautifully shaped, like a design on fabric. The first letter on the page was bigger than the others. It was like a little Twitter avatar of a long-legged bird whose beak curved round to touch his knees to make a *P*. The pages were ivory colored and looked very thick.

"They're vellum. Made from the skin of a goat."

"Didn't they have paper?"

"I dunno. That's just what Miss Casey told me. You'd have to ask one of the guides."

Aideen looked at the picture on the right-hand page. It had a checkered border in red and gold and every inch of the space inside it was crowded with different things happening. In the middle was a mountain with a file of identical women in gold robes and veils going up it. Their trailing sleeves brushed the green grass, which was scattered with tiny white flowers. One side of the mountain was covered in trees with curved branches, framing nests of colored birds. On the other side, little men, much smaller than the golden women, were trudging behind a plow pulled by horses. Behind them was another man, scattering seed from a basket. Several vicious-looking crows hovered above his head, and he wore a hood that dragged like a plowshare along the furrow behind him. At the top of the mountain was a tall tower backed by a golden sun. And, at an implausible angle in the distance, a fleet of ships was being sunk by wind farted by writhing sea monsters.

There were pictures on the other page, too, in the margins and set among the writing. Aideen leaned closer to see them and her breath fogged up the display case. She wiped it away with her sleeve. According to Conor, you could bring up each page on the digital screens round the room and zoom in to the detail. But she didn't care. It was the thought of the moving brush or the quill pen that fascinated her, the drag of the ink or paint responding to the texture of the vellum and the depth of the color emerging as it dried.

"What were the paints made of?"

Conor said he didn't know.

"Honestly, Conor!" She thumped him on the arm and turned back to the psalter. "I looked up medieval food on Wikipedia, maybe there'd be stuff about paint."

"Well, there you are, google it. Or"—Conor made big eyes at her—"you could try dropping in to a library." Then he laughed and said he did know a bit about it, actually. "I asked Miss Casey. They used eggs and stuff as a base, and minerals and plants for color."

"What plants?"

"Saffron, I think—don't you use that in cooking?"

"Yes, it's yellow. And really expensive."

"Well, making something like this didn't come cheap. That's real gold leaf. And I think the blue is lapis lazuli."

"Wow, it must be worth a fortune."

Conor grinned. "According to Fury O'Shea, it's worse than that. It's priceless." He put his arms round her and kissed her. "One of a kind, no more than yourself. Now—are you and me going swimming?"

16

August 3rd, 1920

If the woman of this house knew about Liam I'd say I'd be out on my ear. She was a Miss Nelligan from Mayo and she married a man called Spencer who used to deliver coal. He got gassed in the trenches in France at the end of the war. When he came home he wasn't well enough to go back to work so now he's a night watchman. That's why Mrs. Spencer takes lodgers. You'd have to be sorry for her, the way her husband is, but she's a right besom. I'm only here because Peg, a girl I met on the boat, had the address written down on a paper. She has a sister in here already called Kate who serves in a drapery. Peg has a place got there as well, so that's why she's come over. It was terrible late when we docked and I'd no notion where to go, so she brought me here.

Mrs. Spencer looked at me like I was something the cat dragged in. Then she said she wouldn't lodge just anyone who came to her door knocking, but if I was vouched for by someone she knew, she'd make an exception. By the grace of God, Kate had come down to the door when we arrived and Peg tipped her the wink behind the Spencer one's back, so I was in.

We're splitting the rent of the room between the three of us. They're sharing one bed and I have the other and, to balance things out, I'm carrying up water from the basement and emptying the chamber pot. That's the bargain we made anyway and it's working out fine so far. You wouldn't get more than a dash of boiling water from the Spencer one in the mornings to take the chill off the jug, and the good of that's gone once the water's put into the basin. But sure what matter? At home I'd have to go down to the well with a pail. That Miss Nelligan that was is a tight bitch, though. She wouldn't give you the steam off her porridge.

Liverpool's big. The streets in the middle are grand and wide but round these parts they're woeful. Peg and Kate have clean work in the drapery.

They're up early but they'd be used to that at home with the milking. They've had to put out a lot of money for the frocks they wear at work though, and they have to have a good coat and a hat to wear over them. The boss in the shop is very strict about that. He checks the heels of their shoes too, to see that they wouldn't be shabby. I don't know why it matters to him what they look like when they're not in the shop working. And the frocks he has them rigged out in have no style at all. Kate says it'd be more than your job's worth to complain, though. The wages are good.

The first thing the Spencer one did the first morning was to ask me if I had work. I told her the parish priest at home had a place fixed here waiting for me. I knew if I told her the truth that she'd think I'd be dodging the rent. I'd no mind to tell her I have savings. That's the worst story you can tell in a strange place where anyone could knock you down and rob you. That worries me. I carry my money with me everywhere, for there's no lock on our door. I have my purse under my pillow at night always, and I'm glad enough that I don't share the bed because, if the truth be told, I know nothing of Kate and Peg either. Only Peg was awful nice to me when I got sick on the boat.

The sick feeling hasn't left me yet really. I went out the first day to a newsstand and I was nearly dizzy by the time I found a tea shop where I could sit down and read the paper. There were places advertised in the back pages, and one of them was in a biscuit factory. The woman in the tea shop told me it was on a tram route that would get me there quick from Mrs. Spencer's. She said if I walked down to the corner I'd see where the trams went by.

There were two girls in the queue when I got there and I showed them the paper and asked if I had the right tram stop. They looked at each other and giggled and then one of them said that I had but I'd have to be careful. She said the tram that I'd want would be green. There was a man standing in the queue as well and, when she said that, he turned round and looked at them. If I'd had a brain in my head I'd have asked myself why. Then a tram came along and they all got into it. I waited a good while and a lot more trams passed but none of them was green. It started raining but I was afraid to leave the stop in case I'd miss my tram if I sheltered. I thought that maybe the right one came very seldom since I'd been such a long time waiting. Lots of people came and went from the stop and I don't know why I didn't get talking to them. But I thought that people in England mightn't talk to strangers because the man who turned round to look at the girls I'd spoken to looked kind of shocked by them, and one of them had put a bold face on her like she was daring him to interfere.

I stood there like an eejit for what must have been over an hour before a young fellow who looked a bit like Liam came up and stood smoking a fag. It was getting on for dinnertime so I asked him if he knew when the green tram was due. And it turned out that the two girls were only making a fool of me. They must have known from my accent that I was Irish and thought it was great gas to leave me there waiting for a green tram. The man in front must have known it was shite but he didn't let a peep out of him. The young fellow was Welsh. He kind of laughed all right himself, but he said that all the trams from there would stop near to the factory. So I could have taken any one of them.

The factory looked like a nice clean place with a decent forewoman and I'd say you'd get your fill of sweet stuff to eat on the sly if you worked there. But by the time I got there the job was gone.

Hanna closed Maggie's book and put it in a plastic folder. For the last couple of weeks she'd been up to her eyes in preparations for the opening, so today she'd resorted to reading it at her desk on her lunch break. Now she put the folder into a drawer and went into the Reading Room to set out chairs for the book club. After the previous session she'd suggested that their book choices might relate to their personal experiences.

Oliver had looked at her owlishly. "Sorry, Miss Casey, you've lost me there. What do you mean exactly?"

"Well, books that inspired you when you first came across them. Maybe the first book that made you a reader."

"You mean *Janet and John*?"

"No . . ."

"I remember having a great love for *Noddy and Big Ears*. I wouldn't say I read the text though. With me it was more a case of looking at the pictures."

Hanna had explained that she didn't mean children's books. It would need to be something adult. "Something that really got under your skin and spoke to your own experience."

What she'd wanted was to wean them off the latest bestseller lists and on to books they'd found and enjoyed for themselves. That way, she'd told herself wryly, there was an outside chance that the club's discussions would bear some relation to its book choices.

They had trooped off fairly enthusiastically at the

end of the previous session and this morning she'd jotted down a few titles herself, scribbling the list without thinking and putting it into her pocket.

As soon as they began it appeared that Oliver was still fixated on Noddy. The loss of the Golliwogs, he announced, was a bit of a body blow.

Seeing the others' shocked reactions, Hanna intervened. "As we said last week, today's discussion will emerge from personal responses to *adult* books that speak to our experience." Reaching into her pocket, she produced her own list. These were just a few, she explained, that appealed especially to her. "So—*Tess of the d'Urbervilles* by Thomas Hardy, Jane Austen's *Pride and Prejudice*, Charlotte Brontë's *Jane Eyre* . . ."

Nell Reily cocked a critical eye at her. "God, Miss Casey, that's a lot of boy meets girl stuff."

Glancing down, Hanna saw that the next title on her list was Shakespeare's *Much Ado About Nothing*.

Actually, Nell said thoughtfully, it was more like girl meets boy, girl loses boy, and what's going to happen next? She turned to Susan. "You know the sort of thing. They meet in the first chapter and she thinks one thing and he thinks the other and it all goes horribly wrong. And then after pages and pages of fighting like cats in a flour sack, they realize they're made for each other and that's the end of that."

Suddenly Oliver raised his hand and the conversation lurched back to Noddy. "I know the logic, Miss Casey, and God knows I'm the last man to approve of racist sentiment. But didn't the Golliwogs bring a great splash of color to the pictures in them little books? I don't mean color, as in people of color. I mean with their grand stripy trousers."

Darina Kelly tossed her head like a war horse. "Due respect and all that, Oliver, but trousers are hardly the issue. I mean we're talking full-blown racial stereotyping here. Surely that's not acceptable?"

"Well, of course you couldn't have Golliwogs in this day and age, sure that'd be only farcical. Any more than any of us here would be happy with those *Punch* cartoons that made Irishmen look like apes. *Autres temps, autres moeurs*, Darina, that's the height of it. But no one can deny that those trousers looked great on the page."

Darina could and did deny it and, as the discussion grew heated, Hanna struggled to keep order. The fact was that her mind was doing somersaults. Her list of titles had been scribbled down at random. And what, she asked herself ruefully, did it reveal of her state of mind? How much was she actually reveling in her newfound independence if her subconscious mind had come up with those apparently arbitrary choices? Could she really be thinking of Brian Morton as some kind of

Mr. Darcy? Or was it all to do with the impending visit from Malcolm?

Jerked back to the present by the raised voices around her, she saw that Oliver had produced a copy of *Here Comes Noddy Again*. The Golliwogs, he declared, had nuanced roles in the canon; here they might be presented as villains, but elsewhere they were figures of authority on whom Noddy was seen to lean.

Announcing that this was a discussion that they might return to, Hanna turned briskly to Nell Reily. "How about you, Nell? Did you think of something? Something that matters to yourself?"

Nell shook her head emphatically. "Do you know what it is, Miss Casey, I don't have to think at all. There's one book cuts straight to the heart of my life since I was a teenager. God, that was a great book. It was my mam gave it to me."

Nell was lit up like a candle. "It was empowering. It was fascinating. And it opened doors. To science. To creativity. It's no word of a lie to say that book was instrumental in making me the woman I am today. I still have it, Miss Casey, and I still turn to it."

Hanna nodded encouragingly.

Slapping her knee, Nell beamed round at the others. "I'm telling you, lads, it's a great book altogether—*All in the Cooking: Part One*."

17

When Conor came in on Saturday Phil had a sign on the library door saying CLOSED IN PREPARATION FOR THE OPENING. Miss Casey was in the kitchen making a coffee. Aideen and Bríd were working away in the Reading Room already, with two big fridges plugged in, trestle tables covered in white plastic cloths, and piles of boxes waiting to be unpacked. Aideen waved as Conor passed her, but he could see that her mind was on her work. Bríd, who was signing for a delivery, didn't even notice him.

Down in the kitchen Miss Casey poured him a coffee. It was weird to stand there leaning against the counter watching other people bustle round the library like they owned it. Conor sneaked a glance at her and she laughed.

"It is strange, isn't it? But exciting. And you have to remember that if it weren't for the psalter, we wouldn't be here at all."

That was true. Not long ago half the council officials on Phil's guest list had been desperate to close Lissbeg Library, and even the County Librarian had weighed in on their side. Yet tonight they'd be swanning round raising their glasses as if they'd been there in the vanguard of those who'd fought to keep the place open.

Miss Casey winked at him. "'Live long enough and you'll see everything,' Conor."

"Is that out of a book?"

"It was a favorite saying of my great-aunt Maggie's. And the older I get, the more I can see that she was right."

Hanna had arranged to open up the library and leave the keys with Phil, who'd take things from there with Conor's help. All she herself had to do now was spend a lazy Saturday in her garden before showering, changing, and turning up for the opening. Or that would be all if it weren't for the fact that she now had to cope with her family.

Malcolm and Louisa had arrived late last night and were ensconced in the guesthouse. When Jazz had phoned first thing this morning, Hanna, who was still in her kimono, could hear the stress in her voice.

"I've a full day's work to get through here, Mum, I don't want Dad and Granny Lou hanging round my neck."

"Of course not. I've told you already. As soon as I've touched base at the library, I'll drive over to the forge and we can make plans."

"Well, they'd better not involve me." Jazz's voice had wobbled. "Honestly, Mum, we're fully booked and I've more than enough on my plate."

Suppressing a strong desire to call her daughter a drama queen, Hanna had told her not to worry. Then, having put the phone down, she'd cursed Malcolm loudly. Having finally admitted the truth about the divorce, he should have given Jazz some space. And he probably would have, Hanna told herself angrily, if it hadn't been for his mother. Back when she and Malcolm were married, she herself was the one who'd had to entertain Louisa whenever she came to London. They'd visit the shops or a gallery, take in a matinee and go for walks. In the evenings Hanna would cook dinner or book a restaurant table and Malcolm, who'd have left the house first thing in the morning, would turn up late and spend the meal on his phone. And back then it hadn't bothered her. She enjoyed Louisa's company, and supporting Malcolm's high-flying career had given her a sense of purpose. But now she could see that she'd sown the wind and that Jazz was reaping the whirlwind.

And it wasn't fair to think of Jazz as a drama queen when she truly had a right to be upset. Knowing Malcolm of old, Hanna knew exactly what had happened. Louisa's impulse to take a vacation had clashed with some high-profile court case. Anyone else would have called her and explained. But, just as he'd needed to be the perfect father in Jazz's eyes, Malcolm needed to retain his image as his mother's perfect son. So, with Hanna no longer on hand to act as his social secretary, the exhibition had offered an excuse to take Louisa to Ireland. That way, as soon as the urgent calls began to arrive from work, he could leave her entertainment to Jazz. He wasn't stupid, so he must have seen that the timing was less than perfect. But he also knew that Hanna would be there in case things should go wrong. It was a rotten way to behave, not just to Jazz and to Hanna herself but to poor Louisa. Although you could say that Louisa was the root cause of the problem, having raised such a rat-fink son.

But now, driving from the library to the guesthouse, Hanna was determined to relax. Malcolm could come

or go as he pleased, but the sun was shining, so she and
Louisa would take a picnic to the beach. She'd need to
get her back to the forge by midafternoon, and get home
to shower and change. Then she'd have to drive over to
pick up Mary Casey while Malcolm brought Louisa to
the opening in the rental car. The Winterhalders were
on the invitation list but, since someone had to hold the
fort at the guesthouse, Jazz was coming with Gunther,
and Susan was staying at home. Hanna guessed that
the decision to accept a lift from Gunther was all about
avoiding Malcolm, but Jazz had presented it as a practical solution, and there was no point in picking a row.

Given the tight schedule, Hanna laid out her dress for
the evening before leaving the house. It was black silk,
long sleeved with a V-neck and a calf-length skirt. Back
in her London days she'd had wardrobes full of designer
outfits; Malcolm's place in his chambers' pecking order
had been enhanced over the years by the dinner parties
at which she'd been the perfect hostess, networking and
establishing contacts that were vital to his career. Practically everything she'd worn in those days had been
abandoned in London when she'd left him. But this
dress and a few other timeless pieces had come with her
to Ireland and when she'd taken it from the cupboard
this morning, it had still looked as good as new. While

she might not have Mary Casey's perfect shoes or her fascinator, she could be quietly confident that she'd look okay.

When she reached the guesthouse, she found Louisa sitting in a fireside chair. Breakfast had been cleared and the windows were open to sunlight and birdsong. There was no fire on the wide hearth, but the fire basket was full of dried hydrangea blossoms and their dusky crimson petals glowed against copper and iron. There was a cup of tea at Louisa's elbow and, when she saw Hanna, she got up quickly, rattling the spoon in the saucer.

"How lovely to see you, and looking so well! My goodness, it's been an age!"

Hanna felt a pang of guilt. It had indeed been ages since they'd met and the last time was no barrel of laughs. It was at the funeral of Louisa's husband, George. Jazz, then a teenager, had sat in the front pew with Louisa and Malcolm while Hanna, the ex-wife, had lurked at the back. Louisa, who'd been devastated by George's sudden death of a heart attack, probably hadn't noticed but, all the same, the occasion had been strained. Since then she and Hanna had exchanged postcards and Christmas presents and chatted now and then on the phone. But although Jazz had continued to visit her grandmother in Kent and in London, Hanna hadn't seen her again until now. Louisa looked older.

A tall, slim, elegant woman who seemed born to wear cashmere twinsets and Jaeger skirts, her fine hair with its subtle gold rinse was drawn into a bun at the back of her head, and her hand seemed too frail for the heavy diamond eternity ring she wore with her gold wedding band. Acutely aware of the naked fourth finger of her own left hand, Hanna hugged her briefly, urging her to sit down.

"I haven't come to whisk you away or anything. It's just that I know how busy Jazz is, so I thought you and I might go to the beach in my car."

To her annoyance, Hanna had to restrain herself from glancing round for Malcolm. There was no reason why his presence or absence should make the slightest difference to her, but somehow the knowledge that he might walk in was disconcerting. They hadn't met since Jazz's car accident. It had been a weird, confusing night on which, huddled together for hours while Jazz was in surgery, all she'd been able to think about were the times they'd shared in the past. Later, as they'd waited in the chilly dawn for a taxi to take him to the airport, there'd even been a moment when it seemed that they might get back together. For a split second, as he'd held her in his arms, she'd been ready to believe that he was sorry—that he'd leave Tessa after all these years if she herself would come home.

Then, alerted by some note in his voice that she still wasn't sure she could pinpoint, she'd pulled away and, cross-questioning him, found Tessa was already gone. Even now, the memory made Hanna gasp with anger. He hadn't wanted to rekindle their marriage. He'd just wanted her to come back to him so he wouldn't be living alone. What had kindled in her at that moment was unexpected resolution. She'd sworn she was done endorsing the lies he'd told Jazz about their divorce. That night in the hospital parking lot six months ago was the real end of their marriage, the moment when she'd promised herself that he'd never hurt her again.

18

As she looked in the mirror, Ameena reckoned that her dark uniform trousers and white t-shirt looked pretty good. Printed on the back of the t-shirt was an image of a cat, taken from the psalter. The original picture was detailed and painted in bright blocks of color. On the t-shirts it was an eye-catching monochrome line drawing—blue for the guides and red for the gift shop staff. Squinting over her shoulder, Ameena admired the cat, which was reading a book. It had long whiskers and what looked like stripy rugby socks. Deciding it would be a shame to hide it, she twisted her hair onto the top of her head, found a pair of trainers with red laces, and clattered down the stairs in search of Mum.

In the kitchen, Rimal was doing boring little-sister stuff about no one ever inviting *her* to *anything*. Ameena ignored her and glanced in the mirror by the fridge to check that her hair was up properly. Actually, she thought, she kind of matched Mum, who was wearing black leggings and a white lawn kurti with red embroidery. Except that Mum never left the house with her hair uncovered. Ameena and Rimal were always sneaking into her room to borrow her scarves. The most beautiful had once belonged to Nani, who had always just thrown them over her head where they'd fall in perfect folds. Mum had the same knack, but whatever inherited scarf-draping ability she'd brought from Pakistan hadn't made it as far as Ameena.

When they walked down Broad Street there were masses of people already arriving at the library. A gaggle of photographers was descending on a car that had just pulled in to the pavement, and the man getting out was clearly someone important. He stood at the entrance to the courtyard for a moment, offering suitable angles to the cameras, before waving and going inside. Just behind him was Oliver Bannister, wearing a guide's uniform t-shirt over a fleece with a frayed collar and a pair of baggy cords.

Phil was sitting at a little table in the vestibule taking people's invitations. Looking into the exhibition space beyond her, Ameena noticed that two other members of the gift shop staff had already arrived. Both were middle-aged women and neither had come in uniform. Phil's text had been circulated fairly late in the day, so perhaps they hadn't got it. More likely they'd decided to ignore it, though. Which wasn't surprising, since the ladies concerned were a tad too large to look great in t-shirts and trousers.

As more guests arrived behind them, Ameena drew Mum into the room where people were standing about holding drinks. A girl she recognized as Trish from Luscious Lissbeg Chocolates approached with a tray of glasses. But before Mum could say anything, Bríd from the deli appeared as if from nowhere.

"Thanks, Trish, could you see to the press guys in the corner?"

As Trish bustled away, Bríd smiled at Ameena and her mum. "May I get you a drink? Orange juice? Or we have tonic water that comes with iced cucumber slices. It's lovely and summery on a sunny evening."

Mum said tonic water would be nice and Bríd brought two big goblets clinking with ice. Mum swirled the tonic round, sniffed it, and raised her eyebrows. "Juniper berries?"

Bríd smiled. "Yes! We add a couple when we serve gin and tonic. And a while back we realized that the bruised juniper tastes great in tonic served without the alcohol."

Mum nodded and sipped her drink, murmuring that it was good. Then, when Bríd moved away, she nodded again approvingly. "A polite girl. That was very nicely done."

Ameena relaxed. For a moment she'd thought she was going to be dealing with embarrassing cries of, "Oh *sorry*! Of course Muslims don't drink wine, what can I get you, a beer maybe?"

A boy who'd been one of last year's high school seniors arrived with a wooden platter. Mum had a little square of rye bread topped with dill and smoked salmon, and Ameena chose an oatcake with watercress and cheese.

As he turned away, the boy winked over his shoulder at her. "Looking good in the t-shirt."

Ameena blushed and Mum looked after him severely as he moved away. But she wasn't angry, really. Anyone could see with half an eye that the guy was just an eejit.

As the exhibition space filled up with guests, Phil left the table in the vestibule and went through to prepare for the speeches. As soon as she'd gone, Aideen hurried over and slipped a platter onto the table and Conor, who'd fixed things with her beforehand, positioned himself in the doorway where he could reach back unnoticed for the odd fistful of food. As he stood there, half in and half out of the exhibition space, the door to the courtyard opened and Fury O'Shea slid in beside him.

"Have we got to the speeches?"

Conor shook his head. "Nope. Phil's still organizing photographs."

He nodded at the far side of the room where a photographer was moving Ameena Khan into the center of a group that was posing with brochures.

"The Arts Minister from Dublin's arrived in a swanky car and Charles Aukin's below in the library kitchen. He said he was no good at mingling, so he'd lurk till he had to speak."

Fury grinned. "I'd say he would." He picked several slivers of expensive cheese off a neat arrangement of oatcakes and flicked each of them separately into his mouth. "Some night, though, wha'?"

There was a sharp bark from the doorstep. Fury stepped backward and returned a minute later with The Divil under his arm. He stood him on the table where the little dog immediately thrust his nose onto the platter. Fury scratched him fondly behind the ear. "Look at him there now, straight for the salt caramel. He's a great man for the old artisanal chocolates."

From the far side of the room Hanna could see that Ameena Khan's mother was feeling lost. Phil had hustled Ameena off to be photographed. With her dark hair and skin and flashing smile she looked stunning in the gift shop's white t-shirt, and she posed for the cameras as efficiently as if she were a trained model. But she kept glancing across at her mum, who was standing alone in a corner.

Louisa, who was chatting to one of the guides, had obviously noticed as well. Dressed in a beige shirtwaist dress with a gold chain belt, she was looking perfectly at home in her surroundings. She had a slim quilted clutch bag under her arm, a glass in her hand, and a cream cashmere cardigan round her shoulders. And in marked contrast to Mary Casey, whose fascinator was turning up in far more photos than Phil had probably bargained for, she was clearly content to keep a low profile. As Hanna watched her, Louisa moved unobtrusively over to the corner, smiled, and made a remark to Ameena's mother. Moments later they were deep in conversation. It was nice of her to have spotted a stranger's shyness, thought Hanna, and typical of her to solve the problem herself.

Over in another corner, with his sleek head at an attentive angle, Malcolm was listening to a monologue from the Arts Minister, who, Hanna suspected, was practicing his speech. She had only seen Malcolm for a moment this afternoon, when he'd pecked her on the cheek and refused an invitation to the picnic, saying he had to take an important call. Superficially he seemed as handsome and urbane as ever, but Hanna had detected a sense of strain that at first she couldn't place. Then, with a shock, she had recognized the fashionable tailoring and elaborate charm of a rich, powerful middle-aged male attempting to cling to his youth. Now, inevitably, he had gravitated toward the most important man in the room but, as Hanna watched, his head turned as if by instinct and, following his gaze, she saw Jazz appear in the doorway with Gunther. With a perfunctory word to the minister, Malcolm moved toward them. But, as he crossed the room, Jazz met his eyes and deliberately turned away. Hanna's heart lurched when she saw the desolate look appear on his face. He was a ratfink and a liar and he didn't deserve her sympathy. But nothing could change the fact that she knew how much he adored Jazz.

There was a popping noise as somebody switched on a microphone. The minister abandoned his wine glass and Phil stepped up to the podium.

"Good evening, everyone, *tá míle fáilte romhaibh go léir*, you're all very welcome! This is an extraordinary night and one we've been looking forward to with great anticipation. I can't tell you how honored we all are here in Lissbeg—in The Old Convent Centre and here in Lissbeg Library—to have been chosen to be custodians of this important, remarkable book."

As Phil worked her way fluently through her list of people to thank, a television reporter set up his camera. Hanna could see the girl from the *Finfarran Inquirer* carefully listing county councillors, Tim Slattery the County Librarian, Brian Morton the County Architect, herself, Conor, and a long roll call of volunteers and helpers, from Bríd and Aideen at HabberDashery to Jimbo the security man. The journalists from the national newspapers continued to sip their drinks. Uninterested in the local stuff, they were waiting for the big story.

Then Phil flicked from one cue card to another and they suddenly looked alert.

". . . and now I'm more than delighted to introduce the man whose extraordinary generosity has brought us here together tonight, the donor of this state-of-the-art exhibition space and, of course, of its precious exhibit—Charles Aukin!"

There was a huge round of applause followed by a moment of dead silence in which everyone looked expectant and nothing happened at all. Then Phil signaled frantically to Conor, who was standing in the doorway. The assembled crowd swung round in a body as Conor, realizing what was required of him, plunged into the library. Moments later he returned with Charles Aukin by the elbow, and propelled him through the crowd and up to the microphone. The camera swiveled back into position, Phil led a second round of applause from the audience, and Charles raised a deprecating hand.

"Thank you, thank you! Everyone. Friends! You'll have to forgive me because I really am unaccustomed to public speaking. I'm a booklover, you see. Not a politician. Though, of course, the two are not mutually exclusive."

His gaze traveled mildly to where, with one eye on the cameras, Tim, the County Librarian, had edged close to the minister. With a flicker of malicious delight, Hanna saw Tim edge hastily away again. She had expected the opposition she'd met from the council's officials six months ago, when she'd led the battle to save Lissbeg Library—after all, she'd been bent on undermining a proposal that the council had worked on for months. But Tim's refusal to support her still rankled, particularly as it was rooted in naked self-interest. The centralization of the county's library services would have given him a swanky new office and—despite the fact that Hanna was a friend and a colleague—that had been enough to decide which way he'd jump. Charles Aukin was clearly a man who kept his finger on the pulse of things. Equally clearly, he was not at all unaccustomed to public speaking, though his woolly-minded eccentric act had most of his audience fooled.

Now Charles smiled again and ducked his head toward the microphone.

"I am more than happy to make this gift, a wonderful book created in a monastery library and treasured for many generations by my late wife's family. Since it was created here, one can truly say that it belongs to this peninsula. So what could be better than to have it here in Lissbeg's public library, where the people of Finfarran will treasure it in their turn."

Phil registered proprietorial gratification followed by intense interest. It was clear that she assumed he was just about to get into his stride. Instead, Charles rose on tiptoe and pointed over her head.

"But I see that The Divil is in the doorway. Which means that my lift has arrived, so I'll wish you goodnight."

He descended from the podium to loud strangled barks from the vestibule and, with the baffled crowd parting before him, ambled out of the room. Trying not to laugh, Hanna followed him. Phil, who had expected at least a ten-minute speech, frantically consulted her running order. Aware that the TV camera was still running, she looked desperately at the minister who, whipping his notes from his pocket, leapt smoothly into the breach.

19

Outside on the library steps Fury was helping Charles Aukin into his overcoat. Hanna joined them and shook hands with Charles. "Are you sure you won't come back and have a drink?"

"No offense, Miss Casey, but I've had more than my share of drinks at crowded receptions. Fury and The Divil will give me a ride home and I'll be sitting in a tub with a crossword puzzle in no time."

Fury gave a contemptuous snort. "Well, if you're planning a bath you'll want to keep your coat on. I can't vouch for the heat of the water. There was a funny noise from that boiler of yours when we picked you up this evening."

"Yes, I had thought of asking you to take another look at it."

Exactly as Charles had known he would, Fury rose irascibly to the bait. "You had, of course, why wouldn't you? Amn't I the only eejit daft enough to try keeping it on the go? And I wouldn't have to if you weren't so bloody tightfisted that you won't get a new one installed."

Charles shot an amused glance at Hanna. "Now that, Miss Casey, is what the press calls insider knowledge. Let's hope the girl from the *Inquirer* never finds out."

Hanna watched his spry, elderly figure disappear into Broad Street, followed by Fury's lanky disheveled one and The Divil bringing up the rear.

Conor shook his head in amazement. "I tell you what it is, Miss Casey, I don't know how Fury puts up with him. That boiler at the castle's in rag order and your man won't hardly spend a cent on it. There isn't another builder in Finfarran that'd keep trying to patch it up."

And that was the thing about Fury, thought Hanna. He had a deep sense of obligation to the peninsula's landscape and buildings, and to the generations of tradesmen who had made and mended in the past. And it was a sense of obligation that extended to everyone who lived there. An eccentric, mildly malicious Wall Street banker wasn't someone he'd normally choose to spend time with, but Fury had worked out long ago that the owner of Castle Lancy was a lonely man. After years of globetrotting,

Charles Aukin's wife had died and was buried on a visit to Finfarran so, unwilling to leave her grave uncared for, he now lived in the castle alone. His refusal to update his boiler wasn't a sign of tightfistedness. It simply gave him an excuse to lift a phone. Hanna knew that each visit that Fury made to the castle ended with a drink or a cup of tea and a chat with Charles. What few people would ever know was that Fury, at the eleventh hour, had suggested the gift of the psalter, and that the old man's gratitude for his companionship was what had saved Lissbeg Library last year.

Looking back from the courtyard into the crowded exhibition space, Hanna found herself longing to get away. The heat and the wine and the speeches seemed to have nothing to do with the exquisite book glowing quietly in its glass case. Inevitably Jazz or Louisa would need her attention at some point, or Mary Casey would have to be dug out of Malcolm. And Phil had already asked her to pose and smile for the cameras later on. But right now the minister seemed good for at least another twenty minutes. Surely no one would notice if she took a break?

Conor came onto the library steps with a platter. "Didn't the girls do a great job with the food? Watch out for the salt caramel, though, The Divil's been there before you."

Hanna shook her head. "It's all lovely but I'm fine. What I fancy is a breath of fresh air."

"Right, so. Should I go back in and look interested?"

"Do. Say I'll be back myself in a minute."

Conor nodded obediently. "No problem. The Mayor's up after the minister, so I'd say you could take your time."

As Conor disappeared back into the vestibule, Hanna slipped into the nuns' garden through the side gate from the courtyard. By this time of the evening the garden belonged to the birds. As she walked under the trees that bordered the wide herb beds a goldcrest darted past her, making for the fountain. Evening sunlight fell on the row of stained-glass windows that had once lit the nuns' refectory. Beneath them, cast-iron railings enclosed rows of gray headstones. The sisters' graveyard was now cared for by the volunteers who worked in the garden. Recently, beehives had been restored to the corner where the nuns had gathered honey and collected beeswax to make candles and sweet-smelling polish. Stepping from the shade of an alder tree, Hanna walked down a gravel path between the herb beds, brushing her hand across a rosemary bush to release its spicy fragrance. Where four paths met, the statue of St. Francis with his arms extended stood on its plinth; the water gushing from the flowers at his feet made ripples in the granite basin.

Passing the fountain, Hanna went and sat on a wooden bench. It was made of silvery, time-bleached timber but a plaque on its back rail was newly inscribed to "Sister Michael, born Sarah Cassidy, a worker in this garden." With a pang of regret Hanna remembered the little lay sister whose energy had inspired her to unite the community and save Lissbeg Library. For more than seventy years Sister Michael had cared for the herbs in the garden and worked in the convent kitchen. She was buried now under lush grass in the quiet railed enclosure. Shading her eyes from the setting sun, Hanna squinted at the hills beyond the town. They were dark blue in the evening light against the huge westerly mountains.

There was the scrunch of footsteps on the gravel and, before she could turn, a familiar voice spoke behind her. "Great minds think alike. However . . ." Brian Morton sat down on the bench and held up two glasses and a bottle ". . . some of us have sense enough not to abscond without bringing the party with us."

It was six months since they saw each other alone, and now he was here she hardly knew what to say.

"How did you know I'd been drinking white?"

"Because I've been watching you all evening."

He filled a glass and held it out to her. They sat there for a moment saying nothing. Then she looked him in the face. "I meant to call you."

Taking the bottle by the neck he burrowed the base of it into the gravel so it wouldn't tip over. Then he sat back and sipped his wine.

"How do you like your exhibition space?"

"It's beautiful."

"You weren't very forthcoming at the planning meetings."

She remembered those agonized hours when they'd sat on the same committee trying to avoid each other's eyes.

"Well, *you* did a pretty good imitation of the Man in the Iron Mask."

Brian raised his eyebrows, accepting the point. "I didn't write that blurb about translucence, by the way."

"I didn't think you did."

There was a long pause and when he spoke again he still didn't look at her. "Me too. I mean, I intended to ring you. Lots of times. But then time went by and I thought that perhaps you wouldn't want me to."

"Why?"

"Oh, for God's sake, Hanna, I don't know. Because you didn't call me first. Besides, you've been avoiding me."

He held his drink at arm's length looking at the sunset through the glass. "And I've been acting like some kind of stalker, with half of Finfarran looking on."

The goldcrest swooped from the fountain to an herb bed and disappeared under a bush. Brian darted a glance at Hanna. "How's the house?"

"Good. Better than good, I love it. You must come over and see it sometime."

The invitation was followed by a pause in which she would gladly have bitten her tongue out. She knew he was remembering the last time they'd been alone together, when she might well have invited him not just to the house but also into her bed and her life. It was the night of Jazz's accident and, at the time, he and she had been inching toward a relationship. But, unlike Malcolm, whose every move was calculated, Brian hadn't a manipulative bone in his body. Given her emotional state that night, he could easily have swept her off her feet. Instead he'd driven her home from the hospital after she'd seen off Malcolm, and then stood mutely on her doorstep while she decided what to do next. He hadn't tried to influence her decision. And exhausted, and desperate for solitude, she'd chosen to send him away. She hadn't meant for him never to come back again. That was just what had happened, it was never what she had meant.

Now, looking at him sideways, she thought that he hadn't changed. His lean body seemed perfectly relaxed and he looked back at her quizzically. For a moment she panicked, unable to think what to say. Then, as he'd always done whenever she seemed at a loss, he just changed the subject.

"Good necklace. It goes with the psalter."

It was a modern silver piece, shaped like a torc and set with an oblong of amber. The polished stone was golden as honey and dark as burnt sugar and, as she'd put it on, she too had been reminded of the glowing psalter.

"Where did you get it?"

"Ages ago at an exhibition in London. It reminded me of home."

"It's a beautiful setting."

Brian looked at it intently as if surveying a house. Embarrassed by the scrutiny, Hanna stood up and said that she ought to go in.

"I'm supposed to be there being helpful, so I shouldn't really have bunked off without a word." Brian looked at her quizzically again and suddenly she found herself smiling. "Oh, dammit, look, it's really strange seeing you like this and I'm not sure how to handle it. And I don't know if you've noticed, but Malcolm's here tonight."

He stood up and looked down at her gravely. "I thought the distinguished-looking bloke in Armani might be him. Well, there you go. I've always had lousy timing."

"No, I didn't mean that. He's not here because of me. It's . . . family stuff. And, if I know Malcolm, he'll be out of here as soon as he finds an excuse."

Picking the wine bottle out of its gravel pit, Brian reached for her wine glass. His diffident presence was very different to Malcolm's suave charm.

"Thank you for the invitation. I'll come by and see the house."

"Do."

"Okay. But only if you want me to."

Hanna grinned. "Remember Sister Michael?"

"The dumpy little nun in the gray anorak? Sure. I always liked the look of her. I'd say she takes no prisoners."

"Not anymore anyway." Hanna nodded at the nuns' graveyard. "She's in there."

Before he could apologize, she laughed at him. "She was well over ninety, Brian, I daresay she's glad of the rest. No, the thing is that Sister Michael was great for contradictory pronouncements."

"About what?"

"Well, me in this instance. One minute she'd say I'm a divil for rushing into things. And next minute she'd say I'm the world's worst when it comes to making up my mind."

"So which is it?"

Hanna looked up at him wryly. "I don't know. I never have done. She was probably right and it's both."

They stood up and he raised his hand as, if to touch her face. Then the gravel crunched and she turned and saw Malcolm walking toward them.

"Well, here you are, I wondered where you'd slipped off to." He joined them and took her by the elbow. The gesture was casual and his tone was warm, but, through his hand, Hanna could feel aggression, and his eyes, when they met Brian's, were cold as flint. Brian didn't move.

Hanna had an absurd vision of herself as Cora in a standoff between Hawkeye and Magua in *The Last of the Mohicans.* Irritated, she was about to pull sharply away. Then, out of the corner of her eye, she saw a glint of amusement beneath Brian's bullishness. He might be nervous and unsure where she herself was concerned, but evidently he wasn't perturbed by this ridiculous show of possessiveness. And nor should she be. With the ghost of a wink at Brian, she freed her elbow and smiled blandly at Malcolm.

"Now isn't this nice! I don't know if the two of you have met?"

20

Mary Casey's texts were always written in capital letters with no punctuation. Texting, she claimed, was meant to be brisk and efficient; you were shooting off vital messages, not writing school compositions.

Sitting in the June sunshine at the Garden Café, she was tapping out a message to Hanna.

IVE ORDERED 8 BY 10 THOUGH THAT PUP SAYS ITS
2 SOMETHING 3 BY 2 FIVE 4

Hitting SEND, she sat back complacently and watched as Louisa approached the table with tea things on a tray. Then, struck by a niggling doubt, she grabbed the phone and tapped in another message.

PHOTOS

And as Louisa arrived she added another word.

INQUIRER

Then, with the second text sent, she looked approvingly at the tea tray. They did a proper size pot in the nuns' garden and a grand shortbread biscuit. Turning to the center spread of this week's *Inquirer*, she twitched it toward Louisa.

"Look at that now! Two full pages in the middle as well as the big story on the front. I told you we'd need to whip in fast to get a few copies. They'll have sold out by dinnertime with all the photos inside."

As Louisa poured tea for the two of them, Mary seized her phone again.

"God, I'd better tell Hanna we came in for the papers as well as to order the print." She swiped the screen to unlock the phone, clicking her tongue in annoyance. "Ah, Holy God Almighty, I'm killed with the grease on this glass!"

DONT GO GETTING THE PAPER WEVE SIX COPIES GOT

She pinged the message off into the ether, started another: ME AND LOUISA . . . then stopped and hit DELETE. When Louisa had phoned her this morning it was clear that she wanted to talk. So maybe it was best not to alert Hanna until she knew what was afoot.

Louisa hadn't said much when she came and picked her up in the rental car, other than that Malcolm was back at the guesthouse waiting for a phone call from work. Still, no doubt she'd speak now the tea was poured, and Mary was content to wait. Meanwhile, having polished the screen fiercely, she thrust her phone into her handbag and returned her attention to the paper.

The largest photo in the double-page spread was of the minister from Dublin flanked by herself and Hanna. Mary scrutinized it carefully.

"I'd say it'll print up lovely. I'm not having it framed inside in the *Inquirer*, though. I don't know who your man thinks he's fooling with his better-than-half-price offers. Sure, you'd get twice the value in Frames2Go in Carrick."

Scanning the pages, she expressed polite regret. There was a grand shot of Conor McCarthy and that girl in the gift shop t-shirt. But wasn't it a shame there wasn't one of Jazz or, indeed, of Louisa herself who'd looked so great? As Louisa demurred, Mary took a piece of shortbread. Privately she thought that the poor woman had looked dreadful; what kind of a person would turn up to a do like that in a dowdy beige frock and a little cardigan? Still, she was nice enough in herself and you'd have to be civil. And anyone with half an eye in her head could see that she doted on Jazz. Indeed, the two of them had been watching her the other night like a couple of hens with one chick.

The poor child had looked awful nervy and thin in her yellow dress and the bright, dangly earrings, all the time moving round the room trying to avoid her father. God knows what Louisa must have felt and she standing by, watching that. As far as Mary could see, Jazz wouldn't even sit in the same car as Malcolm. Maybe Hanna had been right to keep things from her earlier; if his cheating had hit her so hard and she past twenty, how would she have coped if she'd heard of it in her teens? All the same, it had been good to see Jazz with Gunther. He was a decent, steady employer and he'd be sure to bring her home safe.

❦

As Jazz came into the kitchen, Susan had the *Inquirer* spread on the table. Gunther was standing at the counter kneading bread.

"It says here there was a TV camera, how come it wasn't on the news?"

Jazz glanced over Susan's shoulder. "I don't think the camera was from RTÉ."

"And how well Gunther didn't get himself in a photo we could hang out there in Reception!"

Gunther's diffidence was an established family joke. He grinned at Susan. "Actually, I was doing something more useful. I chatted the TV guy up."

"I don't believe it!"

He had recognized a German production company's logo on the camera. "So I went and talked to him. The program they're making is going to be shown throughout Europe. It's about cultural tourism in Ireland—places to go, things to see . . . places to stay."

Putting the bowl in the proofing cabinet, he came to sit beside Susan. "But maybe I should have posed for a photo instead?"

"Oh, for God's sake, Gunther, stop teasing and just tell me!"

"I thought they might be doing more shooting in the area, so I gave him a card."

"And?"

"And when he heard that I was German and I told him we have a guesthouse in an old forge, he said they might come here."

"What, stay here?"

"Shoot here."

"Oh my God! But that was Saturday. This is Monday. How come you didn't say a word?"

"Because I knew that if it came to nothing you'd be upset."

Susan was about to argue when her eyes widened. "Does that mean it's come to something? Did he call?"

"No, the producer did. They want to shoot an interview about how I first came to Ireland and what we've done here."

"But this is massive! We couldn't buy this kind of publicity."

"I know. But it's also a good story for them." Gunther looked at Jazz. "Don't you think? This beautiful Irish place I fell in love with. The beautiful Irish girl who fell for me."

Susan laughed. "Oh that'll be the line, will it?" She winked at Jazz. "And, of course, I don't speak German. So he can come out with anything he likes and I won't have a clue."

Jazz felt almost like an intruder. She looked at Gunther's hands, slim, muscular, and dependable, his broad shoulders and fair, curling hair. They were so happy here in their sunny kitchen with the back door open and the sound of the hens clucking and scratching outside. The air was full of the warm smell of baking and six-year-old Holly was sitting on the kitchen step, cuddling the cat. It was such a vision of contentment that Jazz was stabbed by envy. Why did some people get all the breaks while others got all the crap? Still, she told herself, if anyone deserved happiness, Gunther and Susan did. They were the hardest working people she'd ever encountered and, right from the day she'd arrived here, she'd been treated like one of the family.

Susan pushed the paper across the table. "Do you want to have this? There's a lovely picture of your mum and your nan with the minister."

Jazz shook her head. "If I know Nan, she'll have a framed print of that in every room."

The picture was nice, though. Mum was smiling and relaxed in her chic dress and silver-and-amber necklace, and Jazz reckoned that The Carrick Couturier had actually done Nan proud. She smiled. It was just like Nan to get herself bang in front of the cameras and typical of Granny Lou to keep away from them, avoiding the potential embarrassment of a family pic. Which was just as well because the idea of posing with Dad had made Jazz want to spit. He'd swanned round the exhibition as if he owned it, giving an impression of profound interest which she knew was totally fake.

And now, to her annoyance, she heard his voice

and the sound of car doors slamming at the front of the house. Leaving Susan and Gunther looking at the paper, she stood up and went through to Reception.

The front door opened straight from a gravel sweep into the wide hall with its low beamed ceiling. Granny Lou and Dad had just come in. He gave a huge smile when he saw her and Jazz felt her own face freeze. She folded her hands and asked if they'd like tea or coffee.

"We serve it down here or you could sit in the garden or, if guests prefer, they can make their own in the bedrooms."

He was a guest here and that was how she proposed to continue to treat him, as just another client and all in a day's work. To her great satisfaction, she saw him flinch before he announced that he needed to take a phone call and would make his own coffee upstairs. As he made his way to the staircase, Susan came through from the kitchen. Jazz had a feeling that if Dad were here much longer she'd find herself taken to task; the Winterhalders wouldn't put up with a guest being made to feel unwelcome. But it wouldn't happen because he wouldn't stay a moment longer than he had to. Soon he'd be shoving Granny Lou down to Kent again, so he could get on with his own rotten life without needing to think of his family.

Susan smiled at Granny Lou and asked how she liked Finfarran.

"It really is delightful, there's so much to see and do. And it's so relaxing. Mary Casey and I had elevenses today in the café by the library. Such a charming place and quite a sun trap."

"Well, that's nice to hear. I'm glad you've enjoyed your few days here."

"Yes indeed." Granny Lou smiled broadly. "So much so that I've decided I'm going to stay on."

Susan looked disconcerted, then she spoke apologetically. "Oh, Mrs. Turner, I'm terribly sorry, but I'm afraid we're fully booked right through to September. Of course I'm very flattered and I'd love you to stay, but your room won't be available from tomorrow. I mean, neither of them will . . ." She glanced from Jazz to Granny Lou, looking troubled. "I'm sorry, I don't quite understand, were you and Mr. Turner both hoping to stay on?"

Granny Lou shook her head decisively. "Goodness me, no, Malcolm is far too busy. And it's I who ought to apologize, I haven't made myself clear. I won't be needing a room, Mrs. Winterhalder. I'm not sure exactly how long I'll be here in Finfarran. But I'll be staying with Mary Casey, so that's quite all right."

21

It was going to take a while for Conor to get used to the exhibition. It was weird seeing people milling around beyond the glass wall between the library and the exhibition space, lining up to look at the psalter and using the interactive screens. The guide on duty today was Oliver Bannister. Conor could see him counting out facts and figures on his fingers and answering questions from his group. It was a bit like having a TV on in the background with the sound down, though Miss Casey said that in no time at all they'd hardly notice it. And when you sat at the desk you had your back to the glass anyway, so Conor supposed she was right.

The rest of the library looked perfectly normal this morning. He and Miss Casey had been here with Phil all day Sunday, moving out the tables and returning things to their places. Bríd and Aideen had been in as well, clearing the catering stuff. The girls were bolstered by all the compliments they'd had about the food—according to Aideen, Phil had been delighted with the comments on the night and loads of people had retweeted photos afterward.

When Conor had given her a hand with the rubbish, she was dying to tell him some news. "One of the journalists came up and said he loved the goats' cheese. There was none of it in the goodie bags, so I got him a little box. I put it in one of the bags for him and he said he loved the concept. You know, medieval food to go with the psalter? And you know what he's going to do? He's pitching a piece to one of the Sunday supplements. A lifestyle thing based on my research!"

"How d'you mean, your research?"

"The leaflet Phil got me to write for the goodie bags."

The journalist had loved all the stuff she'd looked up about monks and medieval banquets. He'd said it was a really original angle on the exhibition story. "Because it's going to get covered by Arts pages but this would be kind of lighter."

"And do you get paid?"

Aideen's face fell and she said no she didn't. "He's the one who'll be writing it."

"Yeah, but it's your research."

"Ah Conor, all I did was dig round on Wikipedia."

"Sure, what would your man the journalist do but the same thing? And you can bet your life *he* gets paid."

For some reason that he didn't understand, Aideen had looked all hurt. So he'd hugged her and told her it was great. "It'll be like a big ad for HabberDashery." But that hadn't pleased her either and she'd shuffled and looked at her feet.

"I don't know if he'll mention the deli."

"He will of course, isn't the name there on the leaflet?"

Aideen looked sheepish. "I hadn't thought about that. I was just kind of amazed that he'd liked what I wrote."

Not knowing what else to do, Conor had hugged her again. As far as he could see, this fella had got himself a free story with his free goat cheese, and there was Aideen all lit up because he'd deigned to use her research.

A minute later she'd suddenly grabbed his hand. "God, Conor, what if I didn't get things right and he prints it and I get blamed?"

That was so daft that he'd almost said something impatient. But her eyes were huge and she really did look panic-stricken. So he put on a funny voice and said he'd go bail for her, and in the end he'd made her laugh.

Now, as he sat at Miss Casey's desk, he wondered how to help Aideen. She was pretty and clever and fun to be with, but none of that seemed to matter. The bottom line was that she'd no confidence and didn't realize how great she was.

The parking lot by the church in Knockmore was one of Hanna's regular mobile library halting places, and she often had her sandwich and a coffee there with the seniors at the day care center. But today, having made her halt, she drove on and found a place to eat her lunch in the sunshine. It was a low wall at the approach to a little bridge where the sound of rushing water was loud under the streaming reeds that fringed the riverbank. By contrast, the cattle in the fields on either side of her moved slowly through knee-deep pasture, tearing mouthfuls of grass and clover with soft drooping lips and powerful jaws. Biting into a sandwich, Hanna found herself mimicking the contented rhythm of their grazing. Her next stop before Ballyfin was at Owenacrossa, where Lizzie Keogh had lent Maggie Casey a suitcase. It was strange to think of the seventeen-year-old Maggie traveling these roads before her, passing under the same trees and hearing the sound of the river.

Pulling up her legs to rest her chin on her knees, Hanna remembered her own preparations when she'd left to go to England more than thirty years ago. After her initial training she'd worked for a year in a local library in Dublin before applying for a place on an art librarian's course over in London. She'd paid little attention either to her mother's massive disapproval or her gentle father's support. Instead, she was focused on her dream.

It was very different to Maggie's tentative, vulnerable experience sixty years earlier. Hanna had loved her first months in the big city, the pleasure of study and the companionship of the part-time jobs she'd taken to supplement her grant. When weekend work in a restaurant had proved uncongenial, she had just walked out. She couldn't exactly remember what had gone wrong—something about the head waiter being a creep or the bus route inconvenient. Whatever it was, she'd walked with no fear of the consequences. There were plenty of jobs to be had in London and plenty of employers happy to snap up a prepossessing, educated worker.

Back then she'd felt invincible. Her shabby flat-share high above a dusty Paddington street had seemed glamorous and, even if things had gone wrong, she'd had her safety net. For years her dad had continued to run the little shop and post office in Crossarra, just in case she might change her mind and come home to inherit the business. With that to fall back on, and a dream job in prospect, the cramped flat with its chipped bath, the makeshift meals, and the window through which you had to scramble to reach the tiny balcony, all seemed amusing. Like the flatmates she'd found through an ad in the *Evening Standard*, she'd known she was moving on to better things.

After the shabby rooms in Paddington there'd been Malcolm's far more sophisticated flat in a mansion block off Sloane Square, and then the late Georgian terraced house that she'd found and restored with such care. She was Mrs. Malcolm Turner QC by then, with new dreams invested in Malcolm's future and a shared life that had come to her out of the blue. And her own life had been jettisoned so lightly.

How did people find other people? You crossed the sea and came to a strange place and then one day, walking in a park or sitting in a restaurant, you met a man and decided to spend your life with him. How could you tell who he was? At home there'd have been no problem. Mary Casey would have known the seed, breed, and generation of him, and the neighbors would have had stories of his family reaching back to the Ark. If they'd met in Finfarran, could Malcolm have lived a double life for so long? During the bitter recriminations after Hanna had found him with Tessa, he'd sworn that he had acted for the best. He hadn't intended to fall in love, he said, it wasn't planned; Hanna had just had a miscarriage and to leave her then would have been cruel; then, as time went on, he couldn't bring himself to hurt her; and then she was pregnant again and there was Jazz.

A cow lowed in the meadow and Hanna wrapped her arms around her knees. Would she have coped if he'd left her after the miscarriage? Maybe so. But if he'd told the truth and divorced her then, she'd never have known the joy of loving their daughter. Anyway all this was stuff that she'd dealt with long ago. When she'd seen Malcolm the other day she'd had no sense of regret for having left him; all she'd felt was pity for the loss of his relationship with Jazz.

Pushing herself off the wall, she crumpled her sandwich paper angrily. She wasn't a fool and she knew quite well what was troubling her. It wasn't the past and Malcolm. It was the future and Brian Morton.

22

Having Jazz at The Old Forge was making a real difference. In previous years, with a full house, Susan had been torn in two. People who'd had a great time always wanted to linger and chat, and anyone with feedback, positive or otherwise, tended to demand attention. It was great to hear that guests loved the view from their room, and useful to know that they'd prefer more ginger biscuits and fewer macaroons on their tea trays, but it all took time and if she spent it that way the housekeeping didn't get done. But with Jazz on the team, the mornings were easier and Susan could even take a couple of hours off in the afternoons to run into Lissbeg or ferry Holly to a play date.

This afternoon Gunther wanted her to pick up some herbs from the nuns' garden when she went to the library for her book club—it was one of the volunteers' days in the garden, when trays of herbs were available for sale.

"No problem. I could take Holly with me, if you like, and get her out from under your feet." Susan found her book and then paused, looking uncertain. "Though, actually, I'm not sure I should."

She had thought of leaving Holly to play in the garden while she was in the library. Gunther often volunteered there and Holly loved weeding and raking the paths with a little rake and trowel. The other volunteers would keep an eye on her but, since today was a book club day, Darina Kelly's little daughter might be there as well.

"So what's the problem? Can't they play together?"

"Oh, honestly, Gunther, Darina's kids are a nightmare. The last time Holly played with Gobnit, she came home in floods of tears."

"What had happened?"

"I never found out, but I bet Gobnit started it."

"No, the poor child! Why would you say that?"

Susan looked at him affectionately. His kindness was the first thing she'd noticed when she'd met him ten years ago. She was earning the tuition fees for her next term in college by working in Carrick in a shop called Walking On Air. It was Gunther's first visit to Ireland and he'd already hiked across from Cork toward Kerry

and on to Finfarran. It wasn't a very romantic first en-
counter: his feet were giving him trouble, he explained,
and he needed a new pair of socks. She'd sat him in a
corner and gone to find what he wanted but, when she
came back to the bench, it was occupied by several small
children and Gunther was standing up. Meanwhile a
woman who could perfectly well have kept her children
with her was drifting vaguely round inspecting wind-
breakers.

Seeing Susan's face, Gunther had smiled shyly. "It's
no problem. Anyway, if I sit down I may fall asleep."

But actually it was just his nature; it would simply
never occur to him to sit while others stood.

He genuinely hadn't had much sleep the night before.
"I arrived late at the hostel. So I ended up in a top bunk
in a crowded room, which is not good for me because I
am long . . ." he stopped and frowned ". . . I mean tall.
So I don't sleep. And today I have thirty kilometers to
walk."

"You're never going to do thirty kilometers on blis-
tered feet!"

"I think you may be right. But I have a schedule.
And not a lot of time."

He had to fly home to Germany in a week, he said.
"But I cannot miss County Finfarran. People say it's so
beautiful."

"It is. I mean, Carrick's just a bog-standard town. But if you go west down the peninsula, it's amazing. There are great beaches and cliffs and gorgeous woodland."

"I come from a part of Germany called the Black Forest."

"As in the gâteau?"

"Schwarzwälder Kirschtorte, yes. But, you know, there is more to that area than this cake."

"God I'm so sorry! That must have sounded like someone going 'Ooh, leprechauns!' when somebody says they're Irish."

"Maybe a little bit."

His eyes were incredibly blue and they crinkled when he smiled. After she'd sold him the socks, Susan offered him a lift to Lissbeg. "It'll get you a little way down the peninsula anyway. I'll be leaving in half an hour."

They'd arranged to meet at a coffee shop but, when she got there, he was sitting outside on his rucksack.

"I know. I look like a miser. But I'm a student, I need to hoard my money."

When she laughed, he suddenly looked apologetic. "But you are kind enough to drive me, I . . . would you like a coffee? Shall we go in?"

She assured him she needed neither coffee nor gâteau,

and when they reached Lissbeg, she suggested a good place to stay. "You won't find it listed in the guidebooks. It's just a spare room in a farmhouse but they do B&B and it's really comfortable. And cheap."

She'd give them a call, she said, so they'd know he was coming. "It's about a ten-mile walk from here, on the edge of the forest. You shouldn't have any difficulty, even with the state of your feet."

That day, when she'd watched him walk off, limping slightly, she hadn't imagined she'd ever see him again. But a month later he'd sent her a postcard, addressed to the shop in Carrick, with a picture of a huge slice of Black Forest gâteau on the front of it and "Thank you" written on the back. And the following summer she'd looked up one morning to find him standing at the counter asking for socks.

The next year she visited his home in Freudenstadt, where his mum was a doctor and his dad was a civil servant. Gunther had left college by then.

What he'd always wanted, he told her, was to work in the hospitality industry. "And now I think that what I want most of all is to marry you and come and live in Ireland. We could have a B&B."

They were on a crowded bus that day and she'd had to lean in to hear him, so the proposal was no more romantic than their first meeting. But it was wonderful.

And by the time they'd jumped off the bus hand in hand and were walking through Freudenstadt's wide market-place they had made plans. Susan would go home and look for a suitable knackered-looking property. Gun-ther would pack up his life and fly over to join her. An inheritance from his godfather should be enough to give them a start in their business and, since their families had already met and liked each other, the prospect for the future was bright.

At the wedding reception Susan's mother had hugged the two of them. "I'm not going in for words of wisdom, it'll only make me feel ancient. I'll just say be kind to each other. If you do that you can't go wrong."

Now, seeing Gunther's instinctive sympathy for Da-rina Kelly's ghastly little daughter, Susan told herself her mother was right, and that she herself was a cow. It wasn't poor Gobnit's fault that she was underdisci-plined and overstimulated, or that she and her siblings couldn't get a word in whenever their mum was around. No wonder they were noisy and aggressive; and if other mothers kept their kids away from them, how would they learn to change? Pushing her library book into her bag, Susan leaned across the kitchen sink, where Gunther was peeling beetroot, and gave him a kiss.

"You're right, I'll take Holly. If Gobnit's there, it'll do them both good to work out how to get along."

In the nuns' garden, Susan and Holly found old Mrs. Reily sitting in the sun beside the fountain.

"Go on into your book club and don't be worrying about the little dote." Mrs. Reily smiled fondly at Holly. "We'll be grand altogether, won't we, pet? I'll mind you."

Holly looked at her severely. "I'm a brilliant gardener, Daddy said so. I don't need minding."

Then, before Susan could remonstrate, Holly leaned forward confidingly, placing a starfish hand on the old lady's knee. "But if you're waiting here for your daughter, I'll mind you if you like."

At the far side of the garden Gobnit Kelly was standing alone, hacking at the gravel with the heel of her pink Doc Martens. She was wearing a long, tie-dyed smock, obviously the result of one of Darina's evening classes, and her fair hair was beaded and plaited in unsuccessful cornrows. Susan smiled resolutely and waved her over to join them. For a moment the child did nothing. Then, with a banshee screech, she charged straight across the herb beds and came to a skidding halt beside the fountain. Deciding that this wasn't the moment for remonstration, Susan asked her cheerfully if she'd like to play with Holly.

Gobnit pursed her lips and waggled her tongue at

her. "No," she said, crossing her eyes hideously. Then she careered wildly away again, kicking earth onto the gravel.

Mrs. Reily winked at Susan. "*Briseann an dúchas trí shúile an chait,*" she murmured and turned her attention to Holly who was standing, arms akimbo, glaring at the state of the path.

Heredity breaks out through the eyes of the cat. It was an Irish proverb that Susan hadn't heard for ages. Old Mrs. Reily clearly belonged to the school that had more faith in nature than nurture. If the proverb was right, Susan told herself wryly, poor little Gobnit Kelly didn't stand much chance of redemption. As for her own family, she added with a grin, she'd better hope that Holly's offer to mind old Mrs. Reily showed that Gunther's inherent kindness had turned out to be a dominant gene.

23

Mary Casey's bungalow was built to her specific design. Not, she explained to Louisa, in terms of drains and materials. That class of thing was Tom's province. What she'd done was make certain it had double glazing; central heating; a proper, decent-sized kitchen with all modern appliances; and a bright light in the middle of every ceiling. Because she wasn't getting any younger and she couldn't be dealing with squinting at a book or trying to scrub an old range with a Brillo pad. She'd had enough of that all her life without having to cope with it in her retirement.

Flinging open a door, Mary stood back to let Louisa enter. Then she darted past her and adjusted the framed photo from the *Inquirer* which stood dead center on the windowsill. There was a second print in her own bedroom and a third on the TV in the lounge. You wouldn't be sure what the light might do to them, but they all faced different ways so with luck they'd be fine.

"This was Hanna's room when she and Jazz were here, and you have your own bathroom just across the hallway. I have the en suite in the master so there's no way we'll be tripping over each other in the mornings."

It was gratifying to see Louisa's appreciation of the bedroom. Mind you, she'd have nothing to complain about, even if Mary did say it herself. You couldn't beat it for the flowery wallpaper and the grand garden view. Tom had been a great one for flowers. Years ago, when they moved to the bungalow, he set pots of night-scented stocks and evening primroses on the patio. They were still there now and they made a lovely smell with the windows open in summer.

Louisa was a great gardener herself over in England. When Mary and Tom flew over for Hanna's wedding he and Louisa spent half the reception wandering round the grounds of the big house in Kent, talking away about flowers. Afterward, when they were home again, he'd sent her some seeds from the primroses. Not that there'd been any funny business, because you'd never get anything like that with Tom and, if Mary was any judge of character, Louisa wasn't that way either. She was a quiet, respectable woman and you could tell she'd leave a kitchen spotless.

Looking at her now, Mary was glad that she'd offered her the room. They weren't twenty minutes chatting the other day in the nuns' garden when she'd seen that Louisa was dying to spend time with Jazz. And why wouldn't she be? You couldn't see the poor child the way she was without wanting to get to the bottom of it. But she didn't want Jazz to feel that she was on top of her.

"No one wants their grandmother hanging about where they work. I do hate to disappear after a long weekend, though, having had no chance to talk to her. I mean, not properly." Louisa had looked troubled. "And, actually, I could do with a break myself. I'm rattling round that house in Kent on my own since George died, and I hesitate to go up to London these days because Malcolm is always so busy."

Mary's lips had tightened at the mention of Malcolm. But there'd been no point in raking over those old coals. Louisa was lonely and worried about her grandchild and God knew those were two things that Mary could understand. George had been a bit like Tom, in fact, in a posh, English way. Quiet-spoken and devoted to his wife. He'd died suddenly, too, just like Tom did, and the big house that Louisa was left with was miles from the nearest neighbor. It looked like a million dollars, of course, all chintz and *Country Gardens*, but no one could call it cozy. Mary hadn't been there since the wedding, but she'd never forgotten the spacious bedroom she and Tom had slept in, or the living room with the two big doors that opened onto a terrace. No wonder Louisa felt lost there with no one to keep her company. And the truth was that, for all its cozy comforts, Mary felt the same way in the bungalow. Looking at her spare room with the painting of the collie dog in its gilt frame on the dressing table, and the grand memory-foam rug beside the bed, she told herself it was nice to think that, for a while at least, someone would be sleeping here again.

What with the brilliant weather and the number of visitors to the psalter exhibition, the Garden Café had underestimated its requirements for the day and sent a text to the deli for more sandwiches. Having hurried over to deliver them, Aideen waved to little Holly Winterhalder who was crouched down by the camomile bed, raking the gravel path. Then she dodged through the traffic on Broad Street and returned to Habber-Dashery, where Bríd was clearing up behind the counter. The lunchtime rush was well over but these days there was always plenty to do. It was a far cry from the long afternoons back when they'd first opened, when they'd often stood round twiddling their thumbs, longing for someone to come in.

"How're they doing at the café?"

"Grand. They may have to up their midweek order, though. Between the crowd working in the garden and all those sunburned tourists going through the psalter exhibition, they were nearly out of sandwiches by two."

"We'll be taking on staff next." Bríd winked at her. "Or giving ourselves a raise."

"I think that's called losing the run of ourselves. We'd do better to up our repayments to the bank."

Bríd laughed. "I'll tell you what it is, girl, that Conor McCarthy has taken over your brain."

Aideen bridled. "What's that supposed to mean?"

Bríd looked at her in surprise. "Jesus, Aideen, it was just a joke. Lighten up, will you?"

Aideen clattered a pile of Tupperware containers into the sink. She could feel her face going scarlet, but she couldn't help it.

Bríd turned and eyed her shrewdly, fists planted on hips. "So what's going on with you and the man with the piggy bank?"

"I don't know what you're on about."

"Come on, Aideen. Spill."

She knew she was cornered. Wrapping her arms

round her chest, she hunched her shoulders. "I'm just . . . I don't want to talk about Conor."

"Right." Bríd reached for the coffeepot. "If you don't want to talk about Conor there's definitely something going on."

After half a cup of coffee and a lot of wriggling, Aideen finally admitted she was kind of freaked by a photo. "It was in the *Inquirer.* In the middle pages. You must have seen it."

"A photo of who?"

"Of Conor, you dork. With that girl from the gift shop."

"So what?"

"Well, look at them." Aideen produced a copy of the paper. Spreading it out on the counter, she shifted a bowl of mayonnaise and turned the pages round so Bríd could see them.

Bríd looked. "Okay, I'll say it again. So what?"

"He's got his arm round her."

"Presumably because that's the way he was told to stand."

"And she's looking over her shoulder, all sort of come-hither."

" 'Come-hither'? What have you been reading, Jane Austen? No, hang on, she was the classy one, I probably mean Mills & Boon. Ameena is looking over her shoulder because she was told to turn round. To show off the back of her t-shirt. With the exhibition logo on it. For God's sake, Aideen, it's called product placement. That's what we were all there for, remember?"

"Yes, but . . ."

"And she's not come-hithering Conor, is she? She's looking at the lens." Actually, she said, pulling the paper closer, Ameena Khan was making a great job of it. "She looks like a model or something, I bet Phil was pleased."

And that was the point, Aideen wailed, that's what everyone was saying. It was what two customers had said that morning and she hadn't known where to look.

"What, they came in and made an announcement?"

"No, they were just talking to each other. But they kept going on about how lovely she looked. And . . ."

"Yes?"

"And one of them said she and Conor made a great pair." As soon as she'd said it out loud, Aideen looked stricken. "I know. I know it sounds stupid. But they do. I mean, look at her, Bríd, she's all shiny and golden."

"She's a kid who's just finished her Leaving Cert. And this is Conor we're talking about."

Aideen hung her head. That, too, was the point, she said. Why would Conor want to settle for someone who'd scraped through her own exams on a wing and a prayer? "He's probably going to go off and be a librarian. And I'm just thick."

"You're making it awful hard right now for me to argue with that." Bríd stood up and shook the paper briskly. "Look, you know yourself that I'm right. It was all just posed. Phil was pushing people round like a sergeant major. Did you not see Miss Casey stood up with your man from Carrick?"

"Who?"

"Your man the County Librarian. Phil had the two of them beaming at each other for the photographers, and practically sitting hand in hand for the TV. And he was the guy that would have had Miss Casey on the scrapheap. I'd say she hates the bones of him, but she did what she was told."

"Really?"

"Really. Because what else could she do? Stamp her foot and say no? She was being professional and so were Conor and Ameena."

Aideen bit her lip and stared at her coffee cup. Then, in a small voice, she said thanks. "You're right. I'm an eejit."

"You are. And come here to me."

"What?"

"Promise you won't be a bigger eejit and go off and tell all this to Conor."

"Okay."

"Do you mean it?"

"Yes."

"Well, I hope you do, because if he hears it he really will think you're thick."

24

August 14th, 1920

I got a postcard today from Mrs. Donovan. She'd put it inside in an envelope and stuck down the flap. I suppose she thought it'd be read by the Keane crowd that run the post office if she sent me the open card. It was just to say that Mam had got my letter. I wish Mam would write to me herself, but Mrs. D says she don't be doing much. She goes down to the edge of the cliff sometimes and stands looking out at the ocean towards America. I sent her the address of this place, so she should know that I'm over in England, not there, but it sounds like she's very weak and low. There was a letter from

Lizzie Keogh today as well. She hasn't heard any-
thing from her brother so there's no news of Liam.
I worry all the time about how I'll send money to
Mam. I wish it was Lizzie beside her and not the
Donovans. Mrs. D wouldn't see Mam wronged but
I don't trust Paud. He got us a fair price for the cows
all right but at the same time, you wouldn't be sure
of him. I wish to God Liam was home.

There was a knock at the front door and Hanna, who
was lying on the bed reading, rolled over and pushed
Maggie's book under the pillow. She hadn't been ex-
pecting anyone. Going through to the other room, she
saw Brian Morton framed in the open top of the half
door like a painting on a wall.

"Hi."

"Hi. Come in."

He hesitated. "I don't want to disturb you."

"No, come in, I was only reading."

"I would have rung, but I happened to be passing
and it was easier just to come by."

There was a pause in which they both considered
the unlikeliness of anyone happening to be passing
down the narrow lane that led to Maggie's place. Then
Brian laughed. "Actually, I'm crap at phone calls, so I
decided to chance my arm and just come round."

"Well, you're welcome."

But he still hesitated on the step, as though afraid to trespass on dangerous territory. With a fleeting vision of them both being stuck there forever, Hanna turned away and made for the kettle.

"Would you like a cup of something? I've been dying for tea and too lazy to make it."

It was a bare-faced lie, but it got him over the threshold. As she filled the kettle and switched it on, he stood looking at the room. "Well, you and Fury O'Shea made a job of it between you."

Hanna found herself feeling absurdly pleased.

Brian leaned back against the doorframe. "Let me guess, the color scheme's not entirely your own."

She laughed. "You mean the dresser? It's an *homage* to the past."

"I haven't seen that shade of red in donkey's years." Brian crossed the room to inspect the dresser. "It's a super piece of furniture, though. Must have been built at the same time as the house."

"Fury remembers it from Maggie's time and he's about twenty years older than I am. And so do I, from my childhood. You know, even though the place was nearly a ruin when we started working on it, there were still some things of Maggie's standing in the dresser."

Brian lifted down a pottery bowl the size of a large cappuccino cup. "Was this hers?"

Actually, she told him, the bowl was one of four produced by Mary Casey when, grudgingly, she'd accepted that Hanna was moving out of the bungalow.

The worn glaze was cracked here and there, but a brave pattern of flowers still glowed beneath it. Like the shawl that Hanna now kept on the back of her fireside chair, they had once belonged to Mary's own mother.

She took the bowl from Brian and turned it in her hand. "The old people used them as teacups, like the coffee cups you see in rural France. Apparently they called them basins."

"Do you use them?"

"Yup. All four in strict rotation. I use one for my morning coffee each day, sitting above the ocean. On a bench, by the way, that Fury built and painted to match the dresser."

The kettle was boiling so she moved back to the worktop. "We could have coffee now if you'd prefer it."

He shook his head and went to examine the shawl. It was made of thick beige wool with a broad black-and-cream band around the edge and a fringe a handspan deep. Brian spread it out to admire it. "So many houses must have had stuff like this that just got thrown away."

"Or chucked out into sheds. And the trouble with the Irish climate is that anything organic like wool and timber just rots in the damp."

"There must have been a shed on this site at some point."

He replaced the shawl on the chair and went to the door and looked out, his shoulders blocking the light that had been pouring in from the garden. For a moment Hanna thought of telling him about how she'd found Maggie's book under fallen shed walls at the end of the house. Then she changed her mind; something of Maggie's own wariness possessed her, and the thought of sharing the half-read story seemed wrong. Instead she made tea and carried it to the table with some biscuits, serving it in mugs that she'd bought in a Carrick shop. Brian sat down by the window, his long body relaxed in the kitchen chair. As Hanna pulled a chair up to the table, her own shoulders tensed, anticipating the look or the words that would thrust them back to the awkwardness of the last time they'd met. But instead, he continued to ask her about the house.

Two rooms and a tiny extension, he said, must make for pretty cramped living. "Are you finding it works?"

"Perfectly. Why not? A whole family lived here when Maggie was growing up."

"How many of them?"

Hanna realized that she didn't know. "I don't think my mother was a great fan of my dad's family. She certainly wasn't crazy about poor Maggie. So I never heard much about them when I was a child."

Brian seemed incurious. Families could be odd, he said, and, getting up, went over to look at the fireplace. There, with his back against the chimneypiece, he considered the bedroom door. "People always assume that whole households squashed into one bedroom. Actually, most teenagers had left home for work by the time their siblings were toddlers. Anyway there were settle beds in kitchens and half lofts up in the roof." He moved purposefully away from the fireplace. "Nice to see an original interior door. Do you mind if I go through and look?"

Before Hanna could reply, he had crossed the room and disappeared into her bedroom. Hanna burst out laughing. As she struggled to regain her composure, he peered back around the door.

"What's up?"

"Nothing. It's just . . . Oh, I'm sorry . . . It's just, six months ago there was this big deal about whether you'd cross the threshold. And just now you were faffing about again, hanging around on the step. But get a bourbon cream and a sip of tea down you, and you're straight into the bedroom."

He grinned. "Professional interest. Though I have to say that's a pretty dashing kimono." Unhooking it from the inside of the bedroom door, he dangled it from one finger. "That's a serious weight of silk! Having said that, I'm not sure that silk's the best choice for the damp Irish climate."

"Well, you can put it back and mind your own damn business. You're worse than Fury O'Shea. He may have taken liberties with my paintwork, but at least he didn't comment on my kimono."

"Fair enough." Brian emerged cheerfully and rejoined her at the table. "I like the color scheme in there, by the way. Simultaneously vibrant and tranquil. It suits your style."

25

There was a tap on the door and Conor's mum asked if he was ever coming down for his breakfast.

He opened his eyes and groaned as he squinted at the time. Breakfast was out of the question; he and Joe had masses to do before the vet arrived in an hour. Swinging his legs out of bed, he decided to give the shower a miss. A morning grappling with calves and a few hours raking muck would put paid to the good of it. And with Aideen coming over later he'd want a proper stint in the bathroom to get himself up to scratch. Yesterday he'd nipped over to the pharmacy and got a new tin of hair gel. The last one had a cool citrus smell that turned out to be disastrous. It attracted midges. This one said "Unscented" in big letters and came in severe black packaging. Conor just hoped that its rugged masculinity wouldn't send a challenge to the horseflies.

Dragging on his clothes he glared at himself in the mirror, wondering if he should have had his hair cut. Then he told himself not to be stupid. He and Aideen had already gone leppin in and out of bed all across Italy. Mind you, they hadn't had much of a chance since then. It wasn't often they could go to her place and he couldn't bring her here. However, he told himself firmly, that was beside the point. The point was that today was no big deal. No need to make a fuss or start getting nervous. She was just coming over for tea with his family and why make a big deal of that?

Down in the kitchen his mum had given his rashers and eggs to Joe. As Conor came in she lifted a plate of toast off the range.

"I've no time, Mam. I'll drop back for something later."

"I know you, you'll get stuck into the work and you won't be back again till dinnertime. Take the toast, there's butter on it."

Conor picked up a fork and speared one of the rashers on Joe's plate. Shoving it between two bits of toast, he poured himself a mug of tea. Unmoved by the larceny, Joe kept eating. Their dad, who was sitting at the table, rustled his newspaper angrily. He was always irritable in the mornings and worse on the days the vet came; unable to do farmwork anymore because of his injury, he had never really reconciled himself to his sons being in charge. Orla, Conor's mum, glanced nervously at her husband.

"You'll be in this afternoon, Paddy, will you? Don't forget Conor has his girlfriend here for tea."

Hunching his shoulder, Paddy glared at his paper. "A late start and an early finish, is that it?"

Orla flinched. There wasn't a right thing to say when he got that way, and the more you annoyed him, the more you annoyed him, because he hated the way he reacted. It was like living in a hamster wheel.

Conor tried to sound cheerful. "Everything's in hand, Dad, don't worry. Isn't it, Joe?"

Joe dipped a bit of fried bread in the yolk of his second egg and said nothing. As far as he was concerned, the less said by anyone when Paddy was like this, the better. Conor sometimes wondered if he was right. Joe had called him a fool once, over a pint in Crossarra. He was as bothered about Paddy as Conor was, he told him, but there was no point in stirring up shit if you couldn't do something to clear it. According to the doctor, their dad's moods were caused by his medication and putting up with them was "the least worst option." The implication was that the occasional ratty moment beat suicidal depression, and that the heavy doses of analgesics kept Paddy from roaring like a mad bull. Which was probably true enough. Conor reckoned it wasn't just the tablets, though. You'd have to be a pure eejit not to realize that Paddy had a right to be fed up. How would the bloody doctor feel if they tied him hand and foot and let other people take over his job?

Aideen had decided that her outfit for tea at the farm was a no-brainer. Bríd would fall about laughing if she turned up at the deli with stuff to change into, so whatever she wore would have to be okay for work. In the end she did her nails the night before, used a deep-heat conditioner on her hair in the morning, and put on a clean pair of jeans and a newish top. Now, in case of a major, mayonnaise-related wardrobe malfunction, she buried another pair of jeans and a shirt at the bottom of her bag and, avoiding the creaky step on the stairs, slipped out of the house. By 8 A.M., they'd normally both be making sandwiches but today Bríd got a lie-in because she'd be coming via the cash and carry, which didn't open till nine. The trade-off was that Aideen would get off that afternoon at half four.

It was nice sharing a place with Bríd and nicer still that the house hadn't had to be sold. A few years ago, when Aunt Bridge died, no one had quite been sure what might happen. Aideen's dad had never been round at all and her mum had died in Carrick hospital having her, so Aunt Bridge and Gran had brought her up. Then, a few years after Gran died, Aunt Bridge, who was really Gran's cousin, had had a massive stroke. Aideen hadn't even known she was ill, but the rest of the family rallied round when she found herself alone in the middle of her Leaving Cert, and Bríd's mum, who was lovely, said she could stay with them.

She'd kind of sleepwalked through the next few months and then she'd found that Aunt Bridge had left her the house and a bit of money. So when Bríd came home from a course she was doing in Dublin, they'd opened the deli together and decided to share the house. It was only a little ex–council place on the edge of Lissbeg, but Aideen loved it. Aunt Bridge had been great for painting and decorating, so it hardly needed any work. She kept her old bedroom and Bríd had Gran's big one. Aunt Bridge's room was now a little office where they'd set up the computer and had meetings with the accountant.

She was still bothered about where she stood with Conor. It was all very well for Bríd to make pronouncements but, if she were the one who had so much to lose, she might shut up and think twice. Then again, if Bríd had been right about the *Inquirer* photo, perhaps she was right about the other thing as well? It ought to be possible just to turn round and ask Conor what they were saving for. Not in any awkward was-that-a-marriage-proposal way but casually, like it didn't matter. And maybe she would. But it was inevitably going to be awkward, now that she'd gone and left it so long. So maybe if she left it a little bit longer things might work out on their own. But, God, wasn't it awful the way being in love turned you into a desperate coward? The thing was she was so happy she couldn't believe it would last.

It was a busy day in the deli, with no mayonnaise-related or other disasters, and Conor turned up at four thirty on the dot. Aideen could easily have got out to the farm herself but they both loved the Vespa: in fact, though she hadn't told anyone, she was thinking of getting one herself. He looked awfully clean when he stuck his head round the door for her, and Bríd grinned.

"God, Conor, you could eat your dinner off you, what's going on?"

Before he could answer, she narrowed her eyes at Aideen. "Actually, here's another one all tidy and well scrubbed. You're not off to see the priest?"

Aideen wanted the floor to open up and swallow her, but Conor just laughed. And by the time they'd cleared town and were whizzing down the road, she just felt excited. The speed and the sun and the glittering light and rolling fields were gorgeous. She wasn't that used to spending time in the countryside because Gran and Aunt Bridge were townies born and bred. To them, city streets and country lanes were equally unattractive. Lissbeg was the only place that you'd want to be. When Aideen was growing up she'd felt the same; the little town was friendly and quiet and the orderly routines of her life had made her feel safe there. You could walk down from the housing estate to Broad Street along paths that were properly paved and brightly lit. Gran was years older than Aunt Bridge so things like that mattered to her; she liked having the post office round the corner and the doctor's office just a few steps from the door. And Aunt Bridge was totally immersed in Lissbeg's social life. She was a member of the French Circle and the Sewing Group and walked briskly each week to the library and the Film Club. The idea of living way out in the country appalled her. You'd be up to your ankles in mud half the time, she told Aideen, and life on a farm, for a woman, was no life at all.

So when Conor steered the Vespa into the farmyard, Aideen wasn't sure what to expect. The farmhouse wasn't pretty. It was a gray, two-story building with a lot of square-looking barns and outhouses round it, roofed in green corrugated iron. Aunt Bridge had always wrinkled her nose at the thought of smelly yards but, as Aideen took off her helmet, the place smelled much like Lissbeg without the exhaust fumes. It was really quiet, too, except for birds singing and a big dog who came up barking. For a moment she worried about her clean jeans but Conor clicked his fingers and the dog sat down at once.

"She's only curious. She won't hurt you."

"She's grand. You never said you had a dog."

"You couldn't get far rearing cattle or sheep without one. We have two, actually, and this one's just had a rake of pups."

It seemed rude to ask to see the pups before she met his family, but Aideen was dying to have a look; she'd always wanted a puppy herself but Gran had had allergies.

Conor winked at her. "I'll take you to see them later. Come inside and meet my mum."

She'd seen Mrs. McCarthy before, as a customer in the deli. She was slim and wiry like Conor, and shorter than her husband, Paddy, who was huge like Conor's brother, Joe. One night in Italy, Conor had told her his dad suffered from depression. He seemed smiley enough now though when he shook Aideen's hand. Mrs. McCarthy gave her a hug and said for God's sake to call her Orla.

"It's nice to see you here, you're very welcome."

Paddy urged Aideen to take a seat. She could tell by Conor's face that he was relieved. Maybe he'd thought they wouldn't take to her, but, more likely, he'd been worried that his dad would be in a bad mood. One of the easy chairs by the range had a massage cushion on it, so Aideen chose the one opposite. The kitchen was lovely—masses of worktops and an oven and things on one side and the range and the easy chairs on the other with a big table in the middle. There was a window looking out on a side garden with trees and a clothesline, and a hill beyond that with sheep in a stone-walled field. And there were other fields all around. Conor had shouted things about them over his shoulder as they'd whizzed along on the Vespa and, despite her helmet, Aideen had gathered they all belonged to the McCarthys. But mostly she'd just pressed her face against his back and loved the feel of him.

Orla must have been baking all morning because there were scones and a cake on the table and a grand warm smell in the room. When she saw Aideen looking, she laughed apologetically. "I didn't know what to give you since you make all those lovely party cakes yourselves."

"God, no. I mean, what you've done looks delicious. Anyway, Bríd's the baker, not me. And you know that retired guy who used to work at the Ballyfin Bakery? He does all the bespoke cakes and Bríd does the muffins and the rest."

A large cat jumped from a chair to the table and Orla scooped it under her arm. "I hope you don't mind cats?"

Aideen shook her head and advanced a hand to the cat, who sniffed disdainfully. There was a kind of awkward moment when no one seemed to know what to do next. Then somehow they were all sitting round the table and Paddy was telling her about a cat they'd had years ago who was mad for marmite on toast.

After tea Conor took her up to the cow shed where the border collie, whose name was Bid, was suckling the pups.

"You never know where she's going to decide to have them. I had straw down in a shed by the house but she took a notion to the cow shed." He bent down and touched the dog's head with his finger. "She's got a mind of her own, haven't you, Bid?"

"Can I pick one up?"

"Better not. She gets nervous if you touch them when they're this small."

Bid's eyes were black and her long, drippy tongue was deep pink. She had two russet-colored patches on her forehead like eyebrows and the long, silky hair on her body was black and white. Her feathery forelegs were russet too and the five wriggling puppies had the same blotchy coloring. One, whose tail twitched in ecstasy as he butted his mother's paps, had pure-white hindquarters. He was like a dog in a cartoon made of two halves stitched together. Aideen squatted down beside them, looking but not touching. Then, as Bid's eyes rolled anxiously at Conor, she moved back and stood up.

"Will we go for a walk?"

Conor looked at her. "Would you like to?"

She smiled back at him happily. "Yeah, I would. I'd like to know stuff about the farm."

26

Somewhere behind The Old Forge something moved. In the bracken at the edge of the forest a creature was hunting for food. Jazz tried to catch a glimpse of it, but the wash of moonlight on the landscape dimmed as clouds swept over the sky. There was an east wind blowing. Pushing open her window, Jazz leaned into the night.

She had fallen into bed after an exhausting day, certain that she would sleep, but a nightmare had jerked her back to consciousness. Lying on her back, with sweat cold between her breasts, she'd stared at a shadow on the ceiling. Then, fearful of falling asleep again, she'd huddled into her kimono and gone to open the window. It was a dormer with a built-in seat and, kneeling on a cushion, she leaned out as far as she could, swinging her shoulders and turning her head to the sky. The pewter clouds were backlit by the hidden moon. Straining her ears, Jazz could hear rustling in the bracken and in her mind a shrew or a mouse screamed, caught in the predator's jaws. Her sweat-soaked t-shirt felt chilly and her kimono held no warmth. She shut the window, and crouched on the window seat trying to control her heart.

Driving her car round the roads near the forge was absolutely fine. In fact, none of the country roads presented a problem, so long as she chose a time when she felt safe. Not early mornings, when she might meet tractors or delivery vans, or midafternoon, when kids were being brought home from school. Not milking-time, when cattle emerged from fields or farmyards. And not at night, when hares froze in the headlights with eyes glazed in terror, their pale fur spiky like barbed wire. But other times, when the roads were empty, and she could stop the car when she felt afraid. Driving to Lissbeg was a marathon, though, and the main road to Carrick was impossible. Even if she could manage to join the flow of traffic, she knew she would never get out again, and keeping that close to the car in front was enough to make her throw up. She had tried the main road only once since the day she was supposed to go back into Carrick to the nightclub. But it was no use. And what was she going to do now?

Her mum's car had been totaled in the accident but Mum had replaced it and, afterwards, Dad had bought Jazz a Fiesta of her own. In the weeks that followed, through trial and error, she'd worked out what she could deal with. And, as if she were secretly illiterate, she'd learned how to cheat and cope. Coming up with excuses had meant being endlessly inventive. But sooner or later, she'd assured herself, things would have to get better. She wouldn't be this way forever and, in the meantime, no one would know.

Now, with her forehead against the windowpane, she rationalized the nightmare that had jerked her out of sleep. This morning, she had woken to a sense of returning confidence. She'd been sleeping better lately and feeling good about work. Dad had taken his fake affection and sickening charm back to London. And Granny Lou was staying in the bungalow with Nan. Which was nice. Weird, of course, but all the same it was good to have her around.

So maybe things would be fine. A bit more practice on the country roads and the panic attacks would stop. She'd be bowling off to Carrick in no time. She'd even be able to drive to Cork to go shopping or to meet Carlos if he happened to have a stopover. He could still be a friend. It would be a strange dynamic to begin with, but that was life, you adjusted to things and moved on and, in time, you found you were happy. It was that or find yourself stuck with nowhere to go.

Today she'd had a few hours to herself before her evening shift. Lately, in her free time, she'd tended to drive somewhere close to the forge and park down a track or a lane. Then she'd sit in the car and wait till she was due back at work. But this afternoon she'd made up her mind to keep driving. The road was narrow but comparatively straight and there wasn't a vehicle in sight. Wriggling her toes to relax them, she'd eased her grip on the steering wheel. These were the things she was having to teach herself. There was no need to hang on to the wheel like a limpet, or to lean back as if her body weight could control the speed of the car. And it was important not to clench her jaw or to keep holding her breath.

And at first it had gone brilliantly. Driving became almost automatic again, and her mind had turned to a dotty guest who'd been outraged to find that the guesthouse had no gym. Susan was ultra-efficient in smoothing his ruffled feathers but back in the kitchen her comments would have stripped paint. If he wanted to keep fit, she'd said, he could try running up and down stairs all day dealing with thundering eejits like himself. Her scathing list of the performance-enhancing drugs he probably traveled with had them in fits over their coffee and, driving in the sunshine with her elbow out the window, Jazz had giggled again. Then a battered red van had emerged from a driveway up ahead. It was a good two hundred yards away and the driver was easing gently onto the road. But Jazz panicked. Stamping on the brake, she felt her mouth stretch in a scream as the car seemed to hurtle forward out of control before skidding to a stop. She sat rigid in terror as, a safe fifty yards farther down the road, a man got out of the van. Then, to her horror, a mottled ball of hair and teeth flung itself at the window behind him and blunt, curved nails shrieked on the glass. She screamed again, like a stricken hare, and burst into tears.

"Jesus, girl, you'd want to calm down, you scared the arse off The Divil."

Up to then Jazz had only been aware of him as a stork-like figure in a waxed jacket but, as the man leaned on her car roof, she saw it was Fury O'Shea. His eyes narrowed as he peered in at her. "You're the Casey girl?"

Jazz carefully moistened her lips with her tongue. "Yes."

"Are you all right?" He reached in through the window and opened her door. Then, once she was out of the car, he took her by the elbow. "What you need is some air."

The next thing she remembered wasn't fresh air, though, it was the smell of linseed oil and sawdust. His elderly Jack Russell terrier was banished to the back of the van and she was sitting in the cab sucking a sweet. Fury was older than she'd expected, having heard Mum's stories of him knocking up concrete and heaving timbers onto roofs. He put the packet of barley sugar into the glove compartment and turned in his seat.

"I can tell you what you're doing wrong, but you won't listen. And that's because you're a Casey, as pig-headed as they come."

To her own surprise, Jazz had found herself arguing. "Everyone says I'm the image of my dad."

"I'm not talking about what you look like, girl, sure that's only skin deep."

"And what do you mean, you know what I'm doing wrong?"

"Well, The Divil himself could see that you shouldn't be driving."

There was a shrill bark from the back of the van and Jazz jumped.

"Look at you, for God's sake, you're a bag of nerves." Fury regarded her complacently. "And what do you do about it? Grit your teeth like your mother would and never think of asking for help."

He unwrapped a sweet for himself. "Maggie Casey

was just as bad as the pair of you. And I knew her in her old age, mind, when she hadn't a tooth in her head." He paused to grin at his own joke and then poked Jazz's arm with a bony finger. "Tell me this, Miss, have you ever been up on a scaffold?"

"A scaffold?" Jazz looked at him blankly, imagining masked executioners and Henry VIII's wives.

"Twenty stages high, maybe, with huge gaps in the planks and your hands stuck to the ladder. Any builder with a grain of sense will tell you it happens to the best of us. And that trying to pretend that it doesn't is the worst thing a man could do."

Discovering that her hands weren't shaking anymore, Jazz had turned on him angrily. "I don't know why you think that has anything to do with me. Look, thanks for the sweet, but I'm fine now. I'm sorry to have been a bother."

For a moment he'd watched her thoughtfully as she wrestled with the door handle. Then he'd leaned across, thumped it with his fist, and pushed the door open himself. "And I'll tell you something else, Miss, about fearless eejits on scaffolds. They're not just a menace to themselves but to everyone round them."

Afterward, when she'd got back to the forge, she'd told herself he was a lunatic—"eccentric" was the word that Mum had used, but he must have gone downhill since. Susan had taken the evening off to drive Holly to a sleepover, and a party of unexpected hikers had meant that Gunther was rushed off his feet. Between waiting on tables and answering queries, she'd almost forgotten what had happened, and all she'd wanted at the end of her shift was to close her eyes and sleep. But somewhere at the back of her mind the whole thing must have festered. And tonight, in her nightmare, the cow's bones clattering onto the road had become The Divil's curved black toenails scrabbling madly at the window.

27

Miss Casey was coming out of the library as Aideen crossed the road. They met at the horse trough in the middle of Broad Street where the council's red geraniums were glowing in the sun.

"How are things going in HabberDashery?"

Aideen said they were grand. They'd had a lot of tourists in who'd come to Lissbeg for the exhibition. Wasn't it great altogether, she asked Miss Casey, the way people loved the psalter? They got so lit up and excited when they talked about it.

Miss Casey smiled and asked if she liked it herself.

"Oh my God, it's so beautiful. I keep going in to have another look each time you turn one of the pages. Did you see the one with the butterflies riding on snails as if they were horses? And the rainbow out over the sea?" Even the names of the colors were gorgeous, like ultramarine and yellow ocher and umber. And lapis lazuli. That was a blue stone that came all the way from Afghanistan. Along a trade route they called the Silk Road. On camels at first, pacing across the desert, and then over the sea to Ireland in wooden boats. She had looked it all up one day on the internet. It was magic. And did Miss Casey know that the base of the paints could be honey or oil or egg?

"Or even earwax!"

"No!!"

"Yes. There's a book about medieval paints in the library if you'd like to borrow it."

Aideen wondered if she shouldn't have mentioned the internet. That time when Conor had showed her the psalter, he'd said the same kind of thing—that she ought to go into a library if she wanted to look things up. But she always felt thick in a library because she never knew in advance what she was looking for. The internet led you on from one thing to another. And she hadn't settled for Wikipedia, either; some of the things she'd ended up reading were proper academic research.

Miss Casey smiled at her. "By the way, we're planning a Creative Writing Circle in the library. Not for a while yet, maybe in the winter when people are less busy. Conor said that he thought you might like to join."

That seemed weird to Aideen. Conor had never said a word about it. "You mean like a class?"

"Well, no. Just a group of people who'd come together and share their own writing. To develop their skills."

Suddenly Aideen felt cold. When she'd written the stuff for the exhibition opening, she'd thought it was pretty good. But Conor had seemed kind of iffy when she'd told him about that journalist. Maybe he'd thought she wrote so badly she'd made herself look like an eejit. Maybe he'd said it to Miss Casey, who'd said she should join a class.

She could feel herself blushing to the roots of her hair but at least her voice stayed steady. "That's nice of you to ask, Miss Casey, but I'm always awfully busy. And, look, I'm really sorry, but I ought to be getting on."

Then, seeing a gap in the traffic, she dived past a truck. Heaven alone knew what Miss Casey would think about her manners. All she herself could think of was to get away.

Later, when Bríd had taken a lunch break and nothing else needed doing, Aideen got some polish and a cloth. She always felt it was she who ought to keep the wall tiles shining because, back when they were designing the deli, it was she who had wanted them. Not everywhere, she'd explained to Bríd, because that would just be tacky. But two big panels of mirror tiles, one across from the other, would really work. They'd look modern and dynamic and they'd make the place feel bigger. Bríd had agreed, and when they went up they were perfect. The flowers on the counter and all the jars of peppers and olives and sundried tomatoes were multiplied in the mirrors, making the place look great. Aideen loved the flashes of color as she lifted a jar from a shelf or turned with a bowl in her hand. They reminded her of the reflections in the Houlihans' shop.

That was back when she was four, or maybe five, and HabberDashery was still an actual haberdashery, where two pint-sized sisters had worked together for years. Gran had had no use for needlework but Aunt Bridge was an expert. She was always working on something and practically every week, she and Aideen would walk to the Houlihan sisters' shop. It was old-fashioned even then, like a time capsule abandoned on Broad Street. Aideen adored it. There was a door with a brass handle and a bell that rang when you went in. Inside, where the till and the cool cabinets were now, there had been a long wooden counter and, behind it, sets of drawers and glass-fronted cabinets.

Houlihans' seemed to sell everything—threads and wools and laces, cards of needles and buttons, and round boxes of pins. Scissors hung in plastic sheathes on a revolving wire display stand, and dimpled steel thimbles could be tried on for size. At one end of the shop, cardboard spools of ribbon hung on parallel rods set in slots between two of the cabinets. The rods lifted down and the spools could be removed to measure the ribbon on the counter, but years of practice had made the sisters adept at measuring by eye. If Aunt Bridge asked for a yard of the two-inch green velvet or six of the pink silk grosgrain, the ribbon would be cut while the spool still hung on the rod. The length would then be meticulously measured against a brass rule that was screwed to the wooden counter. It was always spot-on. Then, when the small triumph had been silently acknowledged, the ribbon would be wrapped up in tissue paper and put in a brown paper bag.

And the reflections in the Houlihans' shop had been magical. High above her head there were two big mirrors, tipped forward like a tall person looking down. One was behind the counter between the cabinets and the other hung at the same level on the opposite wall. Each had an elaborately carved gilded frame, and worn Victorian silvering behind the glass. While Aunt Bridge matched yarn or selected broderie anglaise, Aideen would gaze at the image of one mirror in the other, enchanted by glimpses of familiar things from unfamiliar angles. In the worn glass everything looked warped, as if seen through moving water, and the brass ruler on the counter rippled like liquid gold.

It was she who'd come up with the name when they opened the deli. The original fittings were long gone when she and Bríd viewed the property, and the whole exterior frontage had been changed. But Aideen could remember a scroll saying HABERDASHERY etched on the Houlihans' window. She'd wanted to use it as a basis for the deli's logo, but she hadn't had the nerve to say. They'd ended up with a sharp, modern logo done by a guy up in Dublin and, actually, that was probably the better choice. They did have a bell that rang when the door opened, though, which reminded her of Houlihans'. And, by choosing the right moment, she'd got her tiles.

Now, as she polished them carefully, her phone rang. It was Conor sounding terribly chirpy and pleased. "Do you know what it is, you're a fierce hit with my mum!"

"How d'you mean?"

"I mean she thinks you're great. She says would you like to come over for tea again one weekend?"

"Of course. Yes. I'd love to."

"Great stuff. Listen, I'm ringing from work, I'll get back to you later."

Aideen was about to tell him that was grand, when she realized that it wasn't. Only this morning she'd been feeling really upset by him, so going all mushy at the sound of his voice wasn't on.

"No, wait, hang on a minute, there's something I want to ask you."

Her tone was sharper than she'd intended but, now that she'd started, she reckoned she ought to keep going. "Miss Casey came up and talked to me about her creative writing circle. I hear you told her you think I ought to sign up."

"Well, yeah. I do."

"And why would that be?"

"Well, because I think you're brilliant at writing."

Aideen leaned on the chiller cabinet, feeling completely confused. "I thought you thought I was crap at it."

"At what?"

"Writing."

"Why would you think I'd think that, for God's sake, when you wrote that great thing about the food?"

In the background, at his end, there was a loud scream and a clatter, and Conor suddenly said that he had to go. "It's that little monster Gobnit Kelly. Her mum dumped her here hours ago and now she's running amok."

"Look, don't worry . . ."

"No, but I *am* worried . . . are we okay?"

"We're grand. Really. I was just being an eejit."

"And you'll come to tea at the farm?"

He sounded so troubled that Aideen's eyes filled with tears. She opened her mouth to reassure him, but there was another crash in the background and he was gone.

Still leaning on the cabinet, Aideen stared at her phone. Nothing had been going on behind her back and he hadn't dissed her to Miss Casey. He thought she was brilliant at writing and his mum thought she was great. She'd have to get over her notion that people were always looking down at her. It was pure imagination and she ought to be ashamed.

28

Hanna's weekly route to Ballyfin took her through winding country roads to the point where the main route from Carrick veered south round the foothills of Knockinver, the mountain range that guarded the peninsula's western extremity. As usual, when she reached the main route she picked up speed. Then, reaching Ballyfin, she edged the mobile library van through the narrow streets. The little town had a string of hotels facing the golden beaches on either side of the old fishing port, and a central square of houses and shops built round a railed green with a pavement around its perimeter. The square and the streets radiating from it were late Victorian, the fishermen's cottages near the pier were far older, and the hotels with their health clubs and rooftop Jacuzzis were constantly being extended and updated.

At this time of year it was a fairly pointless stop on her schedule. In tourist season the local people hardly had a minute to themselves, and while tourists might well have been interested in walking round a proper library, they weren't going to borrow books from the van. When the crowds were gone, many of the hotel staff and shopkeepers were happy to put their feet up with a library book. But increasingly they tended to use the winter months to take their own vacations abroad. So, even in the off-season, Hanna sometimes spent the whole of her scheduled hour in the van in Ballyfin without seeing a single borrower.

Today, after forty-five minutes sitting in the cab, she was sorely tempted to leave early. At the far side of the square, directly opposite her parking space, was a small handsome building where a large sign saying INTERPRE-TIVE CENTRE almost, but not quite, obscured the word LIBRARY carved on the granite pediment over the door. The building had been built two hundred years ago by the de Lancy family, who'd stocked it with books and provided money for its upkeep. Subsequently, when the landed gentry were long gone, the council had taken over the building, removed the books to the County Library in Carrick and turned what had once been a focal point for the town into a "heritage experience" for tourists. Buoyed up by her success in saving her own library in Lissbeg, Hanna had once hoped that Ballyfin's might be reopened. But among the material removed from it was a local history collection donated by the de Lancys, and Tim Slattery was far too proud of how he'd displayed it in Carrick to allow it to be returned to Ballyfin. This was one of the downsides of coming home to a place still imbued with the tribalism of small rural communities—though his title was County Librarian, Tim, a Carrick man, would fight tooth and nail to retain what was in his own town. Hanna had accepted that pretty quickly. Anyway she'd had her fill of activism. This was to be a summer of pleasant days on the road and in the library, and long evenings in her garden or spending time with Jazz. Admittedly, the fact that her ex-mother-in-law had moved in with her mother was an unexpected complication. Then again, it might prove useful to have Mary's attention elsewhere if Brian Morton were to become a regular visitor to Maggie's place.

Hanna glanced at the clock on the dashboard. She'd arranged to pick up Louisa after work and take her to the house for supper. It hadn't seemed fair to expect her to find it in a rental car when she'd never been there before, so they'd fixed to meet in the nuns' garden in Lissbeg. If she left now she'd get there quicker by avoiding the rush hour in Carrick. But schedules were schedules, so she stuck it out to the end of the hour and wasn't even rewarded by a last-minute arrival.

By the time she reached Lissbeg she was hot and tired and regretting her invitation. Still, at least her mother wouldn't be there as well. When supper was suggested Mary's response had struck her as remarkably sensitive: she wouldn't like to be in the way, she said, Louisa and Hanna hadn't seen each other for ages and they'd want their own time to chat.

Later it had dawned on Hanna that Mary's favorite quiz show was on this evening, and that nothing on earth would have dragged her away from a million-euro rollover jackpot. Louisa, on the other hand, had seemed very eager to accept the invitation, so Hanna hoped that her staying with Mary hadn't proved to be a mistake.

When she got to Lissbeg she dropped into the library before going through to the garden. Conor was about to close for the day and a group of visitors to the psalter exhibition was exiting via the gift shop. She was talking to Conor by the desk when Ameena Khan looked in. She had locked the gift shop door and closed its window, she said, and the last of the group was gone.

"Right, so." Conor smiled at her. "I'll double check the lot when I'm closing up."

It struck Hanna that at Ameena's age Jazz would

certainly have scented mistrust and bridled, but Ameena just smiled back at Conor and said that was great. Perhaps, thought Hanna, she'd never had any of the normal teenage bolshiness. Or perhaps it was all behind her or yet to come. One way or the other, she was a pleasant, efficient presence in the building, and clearly she was loving her summer job.

Ameena explained that she was on her way to the café to meet her mum. "When we came to the exhibition she said she'd like to see the garden. She hadn't realized you could go there to buy herbs."

As they crossed the courtyard Ameena told Hanna that her mum was a great cook. "She learned from my nani in Pakistan who grew masses of herbs. Mum grew up in the country but we've only a tiny garden over here."

"Did you learn from your nani as well?"

"No, we lived in Karachi before we came here, so I didn't see all that much of her. Anyway, I was really small. I'm more of a pizza connoisseur myself, but I do love my mum's cooking."

When they got to the garden, Louisa was sitting at a table by the fountain chatting to Mrs. Khan. She pulled out a chair for Hanna. "Do you know Saira? We met at your exhibition the other evening."

Hanna shook hands with the shy-looking woman whose eyes were just like Ameena's. They had met again just now, said Louisa, and decided to take a seat together while they waited to be picked up.

Looking slightly surprised by the sight of the tea things on the table, Ameena offered to fetch another pot. "Would you like some tea, Miss Casey? It won't take a minute."

The cool fountain and the scent of sun-warmed herbs were too tempting. Conscious of an uncooked dinner at home, Hanna looked at the others. "Well, if Mrs. Khan has time for another cup . . ."

"Saira, please. And yes, I would love one. If you and Louisa are in no hurry to leave?"

Twenty minutes later the four of them were still sitting round the table and Saira's shyness had disappeared. She had walked round the garden several times before bumping into Louisa, and the layout and planting, she said, were extremely good. It really was a most impressive collection; she had counted several varieties and many species she hadn't seen before.

Catching Ameena's eye, Hanna winked at her. "I'm planting a herb bed at home in my own garden. Up to now I was really proud of my bog-standard parsley and mint."

Louisa laughed. "Well, if it's any consolation, I've always thought I was well up in herbs myself. But I'm nothing compared to Saira!"

"And I am nothing compared to my mother. She knew the herbs and all the spices and she could make medicines and cosmetics . . ."

"What, Nani could? Really? Like moisturizers and makeup?"

"And hair washes and scented oils. And far more practical things, like cures for ringworm."

"Yuck! Mum!"

Saira turned to Louisa. "This is the name for this infection? It's a fungus."

"That's it. But I didn't know that there was a herbal cure."

"My mother would say that there is a herb to cure everything. I don't know. I just cook and that keeps my family healthy! I do remember some cosmetic preparations, though. Many of them, actually. Rosemary made a hair conditioner and jasmine softened the skin."

"My daughter's name is Jasmine." Hanna smiled across the table at Louisa. "Do you remember sending me some from the garden in Kent before she was born?"

As soon as she'd spoken she wished that she hadn't. This was neither the time nor the place to remember that scented night in London when she'd told Malcolm their baby was a girl. He'd come home to the London flat with Louisa's bouquet of white jasmine, wrapped in damp paper to keep it fresh. They'd sat together staring at the scan that Hanna had been given in the clinic and, as she'd breathed in the scent of the flowers, she'd marveled at the thought of her baby. Jazz was to be their miracle child, born eleven years after the awful miscarriage that, according to her doctor, had left her unlikely ever to conceive again.

Now, for a moment, she found herself shaken by anger. That evening, in the London garden with Malcolm, she hadn't had a clue about his affair with Tessa, which had started almost as soon as they'd married and would last beyond their divorce. How could he bear to sit there that night and see her looking so happy? And how could she have been so easily fooled? Catching Louisa's eye, she smiled again, hastily. "Did we ever tell you that that was why we decided to call her Jasmine?"

It had been Malcolm's idea, but she had loved it, too. She remembered his excited phone call to his parents and the little pillowcase embroidered with jasmine sprigs that Louisa had sent her as a present when Jazz was born.

Saira beamed and said that in Persian "Jasmine" meant "fragrant flower." "You know, this, too, is a medicine. You use it to cure anxiety. And of course it promotes love."

Suddenly she glanced awkwardly at Ameena. "I mean . . . I don't know how you say this . . ."

Ameena grinned. "You mean it's an aphrodisiac."

Clearly, she was enough of a teenager to enjoy seeing her mum at a loss. Saira rallied and nodded briskly. "That's the word."

"But is there any scientific basis, Mum? Like pheromones or mood enhancers?"

Saira shook her head. "People have always believed such things, I don't know if they are true."

Louisa remarked diplomatically that she suspected the traditional romantic associations were just about the beauty of the flowers. "Fragrance certainly promotes wellbeing, but I doubt if it provokes love."

But Ameena, the A+ chemistry student, was doggedly pursuing her point. "Yes, but isn't the aphrodisiac effect about producing sexual desire? I mean that's measurable. Love isn't."

As their voices rose and fell round the table, Hanna sat back and said nothing. The memory that had stabbed her had left her strangely shaken. It was best, she thought, to give herself a minute before rejoining the chat. But lacing her fingers round her teacup, she told herself one thing was certain. She might never have loved Malcolm more than on the night when he'd given her those flowers, but now she felt nothing for him but a faint sense of distaste.

29

The menu Hanna had planned that morning involved a lamb casserole, but before she and Louisa left Lissbeg they picked up a couple of pizzas. They ate as soon as they got in, sharing the tasks of heating plates and tossing together a salad. Finishing the last of her eight-inch Fiorentina, Louisa sat back with a deep sigh of contentment.

"Oh dear, I'd no idea I was so hungry. And that was good!"

"Me too. Hanging round waiting for a casserole to cook wasn't really an option. Not after spending so long with Ameena and Saira."

Louisa reached out to gather the plates but Hanna stopped her. "Don't bother, I'll deal with them later. Would you like to see the garden now?"

"What I'd really like is a few minutes with my feet up. According to my doctor it's a good idea after I've had a meal."

"Of course." Hanna went and drew a couple of fireside chairs round to face the sunlight. "You haven't been ill?"

"No, no, I'm fine. It's just my age. And you get into routines, I think, when you live alone. After George died I had some kind of heart flutter and, though I'm perfectly well now, I find myself being careful. I suppose at the back of my mind I'm aware that if anything were to happen to me I'm a long way from help."

As they sat down, Hanna told herself that living alone must be really hard for Louisa. The manor house in Kent was a truly hospitable home. Malcolm's parents had always encouraged his school friends to visit and when he grew up it was a gathering place for his colleagues. There was a tennis court and a billiard room and plenty of space to lounge in, and a huge kitchen where Louisa was happy for guests to make themselves at home. George was equally sociable; he loved to share his carefully chosen wines almost as much as he loved to talk about them, which, as far as Malcolm's friends were concerned, made him the perfect host. But, looking back now, Hanna realized that in marrying Malcolm she'd taken over a sizable part of his parents' role in his life. The balance of power—or of responsibility—had shifted and, imperceptibly, Louisa's house parties for Malcolm's colleagues had become gatherings in the Norfolk cottage that he and Hanna had bought as a weekend home. As far as Hanna could remember, Louisa hadn't seemed bothered. But of course someone as dignified as Louisa was unlikely to have made a fuss. Hanna and Malcolm had continued to visit his parents and to encourage Jazz to go there with her friends. But Jazz spent far less time in Kent since moving to Ireland. So, it was little wonder that Louisa was feeling vulnerable as she grew old.

Reaching out, Hanna stirred the few sods of turf that were burning sweetly on the hearthstone. Even in summer, with the half door and windows open, she loved the glimmer of flame in the chimney place.

Louisa looked round appreciatively. "I like what you've done here. You always had good taste."

There was a pause in which Hanna replaced the poker by the fire and said nothing. Then Louisa caught her eye. "You might as well say it, dear, it's what we're both thinking."

"Say what?"

"That your good taste didn't extend to your choice of my son as a husband."

"No . . . well, perhaps, but . . . I mean . . ."

Suddenly Louisa looked extremely tired. "George was so proud of Malcolm, you know. An only child, so attractive and clever and charming. All George ever wanted was to give him the best chance in life. We both did. We wanted him to be happy. Well, you understand. I know how you feel about Jazz." She turned her head restlessly. "Sometimes I wonder how anyone dares to have children. How do we know how much damage they'll do? Or if it might be our fault?"

Hanna remembered her own notion that the way Louisa had raised Malcolm was the root of his ratfink behavior. It had never struck her that the same thought might have crossed Louisa's mind. She wasn't even sure how much Louisa knew about his cheating. Suddenly her mind spun off sideways. Tessa was one of the crowd from Malcolm's chambers who'd often driven down from London to visit his parents' house. On the weekends when Hanna hadn't been with him, had they slept in the same bed? After all, what could Louisa have done if he'd put her in that position—blow the whistle, destroy his marriage and break her granddaughter's heart?

Louisa leaned forward as if to touch her and appeared to think the better of it. After a few seconds she sat back in her chair. "I suppose I've been thinking about a lot of things since George died." She sighed and held out her hand to the fire's warmth. "I was very proud of George, you see, and of all that he'd achieved."

Still shaken by the thought of Louisa's possible collusion, Hanna tried to focus. Wherever this conversation was going, it didn't seem to make sense. George, as she remembered him, was an English squire as conceived by P. G. Wodehouse—genial, slightly bumbling, and certainly not the picture of a high-achiever.

Louisa had linked her hands in her lap and was turning her diamond ring. "George went to public school, of course, but rather a minor one. And he always said that if he hadn't won a scholarship, he'd never have got to Cambridge. There were several brothers and sisters, you see, so the money wasn't there. And when he came down his family insisted he go into his father's firm. It was a solicitors' office in a rather boring little country town. But, as it happened, he proved to be rather a genius at stocks and shares. So as soon as he could, he retired and we bought the manor."

Hanna was astonished. "I don't know why, but I'd always assumed that your family had lived there for ages."

"Well, that was the impression George liked to give." He wouldn't have lied, of course, Louisa assured her. It was simply that he was happy to have achieved a home that Malcolm could be proud of. "I mean somewhere pleasant and welcoming where he could bring his friends. Boys from school at first, you know. We sent him to Harrow, which was where my father had been. And George was so pleased afterward when Malcolm decided on Cambridge. He had George's rooms there, you know, in his first year. It was ridiculous how much that delighted his poor father." Louisa's voice wobbled. "Actually, I suspect Malcolm genuinely thought it ridiculous. But he'd never have let George know."

Hanna knew that was true. Malcolm might increasingly have taken the view that it was his wife's job to entertain his mother, but he was deeply attached to his parents and especially loving to his dad.

"I know how much you both cared for George. He was a very sweet man."

"Yes, he was. But I think I indulged him. And, of course, we both indulged Malcolm." Louisa looked at her sadly. "You see, I don't think George was very happy himself as a child. But the result was that Malcolm grew up with the idea that happiness mattered more than anything else. I think I saw it happening and I can't have thought it sensible, but I stood back and didn't intervene."

She looked so troubled that Hanna found herself echoing what Jazz had said on the beach. "Look, whatever you did, you did for the best and it's water under the bridge."

"Yes, but it's not, is it?"

This time Louisa did take her hand, which was unnerving because she wasn't normally the touchy-feely type.

"Malcolm turned up rather drunk one night just after you took Jazz to Ireland. No, listen, I want you to hear this. I'm not blaming you for taking her away. In fact, I understand. I gather from what he said that night that you'd found him in bed with Tessa. And that their affair had been going on for quite some time."

So it wasn't till after Hanna had left him that Louisa had learned of Malcolm's affair. Hanna's shoulders relaxed. In the last few years, she'd discovered far too many instances of friends who'd ranked their loyalty to Malcolm above what they owed to her. And each discovery had struck her like a blow. But now, even if the rest of her life were to be spent uncovering new cases of collusion, she knew that her ex-mother-in-law definitely wouldn't be one of them.

The knowledge pleased her almost more for Louisa's sake than her own. Bad as it was to find yourself cheated on by your husband, it must be worse to sit around knowing you'd raised a ratfink son. Wasn't that what every mother secretly worried might happen? Because the serial killers and fraudsters all had to be somebody's child. Deciding that this was a train of thought best not shared with Louisa, Hanna returned the pressure of her hand. It was okay, she said. Really. She and Jazz had weathered the divorce and everyone had moved on.

Louisa threw her a grateful glance. "I expect you're right. One of the downsides of living alone and un-needed is too much introspection. And don't assure me that I am needed, because it's patently clear that I'm not. George is gone, and Malcolm and I are light-years apart these days. I imagine I'll never stop doting on him, but I've nothing to offer that he needs."

"Oh, to hell with what Malcolm needs, Louisa! What you need right now is ice cream." Hanna crossed the room and opened the freezer. "Since we dined like kids at a slumber party, we may as well go the whole hog."

They carried their ice cream down to the bench that looked over the ocean and sat side by side with their feet propped on cushions of sea pinks. Then Louisa spoke with her eyes fixed on the horizon.

"Whatever about you and me moving on, it seems to me that Jazz hasn't. And if only Malcolm hadn't been so selfish, she wouldn't be so upset now."

"Yes, but you can't blame yourself for that."

"Can't I?"

"No, you can't. Mainly because there's absolutely no

point in it. Yes, if Malcolm had been spoiled a little less, perhaps he'd have been less selfish. And, by the same token, if I'd been a bit more suspicious, I might have been harder to fool. But you might as well say things would have been different if George's parents were kinder. And at that rate you could keep on going till you reached the dawn of time. Honestly, Louisa, everyone who's ever lived has been the sum of their ancestors' choices. That's the human condition. We just have to get on with things and play the hand we're dealt."

30

August 29th, 1920

I've moved out of the digs. The first week in Mrs. Spencer's I was out every day, looking for a job to suit me. What I really wanted was a place in a shop like Kate and Peg. I walked half the streets of Liverpool and didn't find one, so I was thinking I'd have to settle for what I could get. Factories do be terrible noisy. You go in to talk to the overseer and he'd be in a little room with a door to it and you'd still hear the noise from the factory floor outside. Some places have a rule about the girls not talking but, God knows, if they wanted to, I'd say they'd scream themselves hoarse. In a shop you could have a bit of a chat with your customers, and Kate and Peg's drapery has a room where the girls have their tea.

Anyway, one day it was pouring rain and I didn't feel up to going out. I was in bed in the room when the others had gone to work and the next thing in came Mrs. Spencer. She got red in the face when she found me in there and she flicked round with a duster and I told her she was snooping and had no business coming in at all. I was in the right of it too because it's a rule of her house that her lodgers do for themselves. She turned on me then and wanted to know why I wasn't out at work. She's a shrill woman with a pinched-up face and she was livid. The next thing her husband, the ex-sergeant, came in roaring. I wouldn't blame him either and he on night work and bad with his nerves. The Spencer one was spitting and she called me a liar. She told him she'd never have taken me in if she'd known that I didn't have work. I said I was no charity case and that I'd paid my rent on the nail. Then she shouted out of her and said I'd been walking the streets. Well, I had, of course, and I told her so, wasn't I only out to earn money? Then she dragged my suitcase off the top of the wardrobe and told me to get my clothes on and pack my things.

Peg nearly burst her heart laughing when she heard about it. She said I'd have fierce trouble keeping digs altogether if I was going to go round declaring I was a prostitute. When she stopped laughing she offered to tell Mrs. Spencer what I'd meant. But there was no point at that stage, and anyway I don't give a damn what that old cow thinks.

It was no joke that day, though, when they threw me out of the house. I was feeling bad and the rain was bad and I couldn't find lodgings. According to Peg, there's a power of women round here that had men who fought in the trenches and they won't take Irish lodgers because of our men fighting at home. I haven't said a word to Peg or Kate about Liam because you'd never know who you can trust or what would be safe. I wish I knew if Liam is safe but I've heard nothing from Lizzie.

I was knocking on doors for ages with my suitcase and it was getting dark when I saw a paper in a window saying a maid was wanted. It was a lodging house bigger than the Spencers' and the sign said the work was live-in. I knocked and the woman said her skivvy had left without working her notice. When you hear that you've a fair notion it might be a bad place. She took me in, though, and I've said that I'll stay till we see if we suit.

I've a room the size of a privy next to the kitchen and eight rooms to clean as well as the stairs. There's four flights going up the house and one going down to the basement, and there's the hall, the dining room, and the kitchen to clean as well. Mrs. Carr that owns the place cooks breakfast for the lodgers and she has a little girl who comes in to serve it up and wash the ware. Half of the lodgers is men and the little one does their boots for sixpence a pair each week. Mrs. Carr takes half of it.

The first day I was here Mrs. Carr had a laugh at me. I was down on my knees in the hall doing the bottom step. It was the first time I'd ever done stairs and I wasn't thinking. What I should have done was started on the landing and worked my way down from the top, and I'd have found that out soon enough when I came to kneel on the wet step I'd just scrubbed. But your one went past when I'd only begun and she stopped and called me a fool. What class of a place had I come out of, she said, that I didn't know how to do stairs? I was hard put not to tell her I'd come out of a house far cleaner than hers is. But I didn't want her throwing me out so I shut my beak and took the pail and went up to the first landing. There's ugly red and black oil-

cloth on the stairs and you scrub them with yellow soap.

I wasn't thinking that day because my mind was on the mountain. I was remembering how James drove over in the cart and offered to help with the turf. It was a long drive for him and Mam said he was very good. She was in no state to be working on the bog herself, so I'd been up and down on my own all that week with the jennet. It'd be easier driving in the cart, he said, and two of us cutting and footing would do the work quicker. James has great strength in his arms. His dad was able to spare him, he said, because we were neighbors in trouble. It's strange to think that was only a couple of months ago. Now the neighbors will have to draw home the turf that he and I cut for Mam.

We went up the first day with the sun on our backs and the high sky shining. We had a bottle of tea along with us, and a cake of bread that I'd made the night before. When we'd a few hours' work behind us we stopped for a drink of the tea, and James smoked a cigarette. There was a big stone above where we were working and I went up and lay there with the stone warm on my back. There was bog cotton moving in the wind all around me, and white butterflies dancing. If you look at them close you can see they've got pale green veins. We didn't talk much that day because I didn't know him. I'd only seen him a few times going to Mass. I don't know is there a church here near Mrs. Carr's house. I'd like it if there was because a church always smells nice.

I stopped writing just now to turn the light on. I've got this here on my knee and I sitting on the bed. If I was at home, there'd still be light on the mountain but over here it gets dark sooner and the houses are tall and crowded so it's hard to see the sky. There's great color and light here in all the shop windows, only I'm afraid to go walking the streets after what Peg told me. She says there's fellows always wanting you to go with them down the alleyways, and that's what that Mrs. Spencer thought I was at.

This Carr one makes a fierce fuss about wasting her electricity. The last time she found me with the light on she threatened to take out the bulb. You couldn't be sitting on the side of your bed in the dark with your mind on your troubles, though. And I want to write because if I close my eyes I'm always back on the mountain or under the trees in the place where we went in the forest.

31

Conor was scanning a book for Susan when Phil turned up with a magazine. The library had an order at the newsstand on Broad Street for newspapers and a few book-related magazines, but this was a glossy travel one. Phil was sounding really pleased.

"Talk about putting ourselves on the map!" She plonked it down on the desk and turned the pages. "Look at that! A piece about the psalter exhibition, masses of photos of the peninsula, and a half page about local food producers!"

Conor looked. It was a big feature about Finfarran, most of which, as far as he could see, had been lifted from the Edge of the World website—the bit about the exhibition was even called "The Book at the Edge of the World." But Phil was right, it was great.

Susan pointed at one of the photographs. "Bríd and Aideen will be pleased."

"I know!" Phil was beaming all over her face. She was about to go over to HabberDashery and show it to them, she said. They'd be delighted, and they'd every right to be. All the effort they'd put in to showcasing local produce at the exhibition opening had really paid off.

Susan edged round the desk to get a better look. "And there's their business card bang in shot. That's brilliant."

Conor was skim-reading the text. It was just as well, he thought, that HabberDashery's logo did appear somewhere on the page, since all the stuff about the food was taken from Aideen's leaflet. It was written by the journalist guy she'd told him about, and it was a straight steal of what she'd written herself. To be fair, though, it was great to see the business card propped up on a wooden platter of oatcakes with goat cheese and berries wreathed in green watercress.

A moment later the door opened and Ameena came in looking shy. She wasn't on the schedule for the gift shop today, so Conor was surprised. It turned out that Miss Casey had co-opted her to the book club.

"She said it'd be great to include some younger members. And Miss O'Rourke at school is always saying you want a broad range of experience for a résumé.

Like if your subject is chemistry you should have a hobby that's Arts-related. And I do love reading, so I thought it might be good."

Miss Casey had said she could choose the book they'd discuss at her first session. Her absolute all-time favorite was *The Periodic Table*, by a man called Primo Levi. "It's kind of about chemistry and sort of about the Holocaust. I don't know if you'd call it a memoir or a short story collection but it's really brilliant. I wasn't sure if it was right for the club, though, so I chose this instead."

She held up a copy of Arundhati Roy's *The God of Small Things*. "It was a big bestseller. I hope it's okay."

Susan said she thought it was great. She'd been dead tired the other night but she'd sat up in bed to finish it.

Miss Casey, who'd been setting out chairs in the Reading Room, came to join them at the desk. Phil, who was still immersed in the magazine, said Conor should do a tabloid-sized photocopy of the psalter piece and put it up on the noticeboard. She reckoned it was seriously good branding. Conor could see that Miss Casey was slightly sniffy about the idea. She'd had a bit of a rant a while back in the kitchen, saying that Phil was great at her job and all that, but the psalter was a cultural artifact and should be presented as such. Conor had told Aideen about it afterward and she'd said she reckoned it was just a matter of balance.

"You can't blame Phil for wanting to encourage the tourist trade and it's great that Lissbeg's getting a bit of a name. Miss Casey's got a point, though. We shouldn't get hung up on numbers." It was like sourcing stock for the deli, she said. "Say if we threw out a full Irish breakfast for half nothing with the cheapest ingredients you'd get from the cash and carry. We'd get streams of customers through the door okay, but in the long run we could lose our best customers."

She'd looked a bit flustered at that stage and tucked an escaping curl back under her headscarf.

"I'm not saying the psalter's like a plate of fried eggs and black pudding. I'm just saying that Bríd and I focus on quality. So I know where Miss Casey's coming from and I think she should stick to her guns."

Though the comparison was a bit iffy, Conor could see what she meant. Apparently she and Bríd had spent ages thinking about it. According to Aideen, it wasn't just a matter of getting people into the town and then getting their money off them.

"If we only think about numbers we could kill the goose that lays the golden eggs. People are dead choosy about holidays. Lissbeg could be flavour of the month one minute and the next thing you'd know we'd be deserted. Honestly, Conor, all it takes is a few reviews on TripAdvisor saying a place is overcrowded. And the whole point of increasing the tourist trade is to give people like Bríd and me a chance to make a living here where we were born."

She was right, of course. Still, she'd be sure to be pleased about the magazine photos and he supposed that the card in the shot counted as payback for copying what she'd written. It read awfully well, too. He'd been pretty impressed when he'd seen it on the leaflet but here in a glossy magazine, all laid out and surrounded by photos, it looked really class. Luckily they hadn't included the picture that Phil had pushed him into with Ameena. She'd looked great with the logo on the back of her t-shirt. But he looked like an eejit. Whatever way his hair had got ruffled when he'd been running round for Miss Casey it had all ended sticking up in spikes.

Susan, who'd arrived early for the book club, went through to the Reading Room with Hanna. Back at the desk Ameena and Phil were still examining the magazine while Conor was texting Aideen photos of the photos. Wasn't it great altogether, Susan said to Hanna, that Finfarran was getting the exposure? And had she heard about the television crowd that came out to the forge? "We had a German crew out for more than half a day, shooting a piece for a travel series."

"That's wonderful."

"It's perfect timing. Last year I was hard put to keep things maintained and do the paperwork. But these days, with Jazz on board, I don't have to play catch-up. So if the TV coverage pays off, we might even manage a holiday ourselves in the autumn. Can you imagine it? And the height of my ambition till now was the occasional afternoon off in town."

The possibility of a family vacation had only struck Susan lately, but, looking online, she had found herself enchanted by all the things they might do. She and Gunther might even go off on their own; they could spend a bit of time with his parents in Freudenstadt, leave Holly with her *oma* and *opa*, and take a few romantic nights on a Rhine cruise by themselves. And it was her diffident husband who'd made the TV thing happen. She could hardly believe that he'd had the nerve to go up and introduce himself. And more amazing still was the stuff he'd come out with in front of the camera.

"They didn't interview you, too?"

"God, no, I left them to it. I'm always saying I can't speak German, but actually I do have a bit. But what they wanted was the story about Gunther coming over to live here in Ireland. And he told it really well."

Gunther was a dote, she explained to Hanna, but he didn't go in for emotion. Nor did she, really, it wasn't her style. Maybe that was the reason the two of them were well suited. But when he was talking to the camera about the day they'd met, he'd said *sie war so schön*. Which meant "she was so beautiful." It had kind of blown her away. Afterward Holly had announced to Jazz that her daddy said her mammy was *so schön*. "And she is *schön* because she had beautiful eyebrows. Like Hairy Mollies."

It was the local kids' name for the black, furry caterpillars that Holly examined in forensic detail each time she found one in the garden.

Susan grinned. "I decided to take that as a compliment! And Jazz was very sweet and didn't laugh. She's terribly good with Holly."

"Well, that's nice to hear. She's not that used to kids, having been an only child."

"I'd say she got great training when she worked for the airline, though. She's very impressive at handling the guests." Susan hesitated. "I don't suppose that you're the one I should be asking, but do you think she's happy with us?"

As soon as she'd spoken, she could see that Hanna felt awkward. And of course she did because it was a dumb way to raise the subject—she ought to have put a straight question to Jazz. Feeling awkward, she apologized. "Look, I'm an eejit, I don't know what I was thinking of. I'll ask her myself at some point, don't bother your head."

The door slid open behind them and Darina Kelly bounced into the room. "Oh my God. Have you ladies seen *this*?!!"

She was brandishing a grubby-looking copy of the magazine Phil had come in with earlier. A moment later they were joined by Nell Reily, full of excitement because one of the photos featured a sample of her lace. Susan felt sorry for poor Ameena; something told her that, once again, the book club's discussion might not focus on their chosen title. Struggling to contain a giggle, she winked at Hanna and settled back in her chair to enjoy the chat.

But only a few minutes later her mind wandered. She'd asked Hanna that dumb question because beneath Jazz's air of efficiency something seemed to be wrong. So why was she feeling relieved that she hadn't had an answer? If she were a kind person, surely she'd care if Jazz was feeling unhappy? And if she were sensible, wouldn't she want to investigate before the problem affected the business? But perhaps she didn't want to open this particular can of worms. Because if Jazz was encouraged to articulate how she was feeling, might she not pack up her things and quit her job? And what would happen to the business then? If bookings increased as a result of the TV program, she knew she couldn't cope without Jazz there to help. They'd have to turn people and money away, which would ruin their own holiday. Feeling neither kind nor sensible, Susan assured herself that Jazz was a fully-grown adult and that, whatever her personal problems were, she could deal with them herself. You couldn't spend your entire life nannying your employees. Sometimes your own family had to come first. And that was the bottom line. Gunther had stood up in front of a TV camera and told the world she was beautiful, and nothing and no one was going to spoil her dream of romance on the Rhine.

32

From the top of Knockinver there was a three-hundred-and-sixty-degree view of the western end of the peninsula. Hanna lay on her back listening to the staccato sound of the shutter clicking as Brian took shot after shot of the Atlantic, shimmering like turquoise silk along the beaches far below. Her eyes closed and the sound of the camera became part of a subtler, wider soundscape in which the far-away cries of seagulls and the distant swell of waves against the cliffs merged with the song of a lark somewhere near her in the heather. Then she opened her eyes to find Brian had turned the camera on her. Laughing, she struggled to her knees, pushing back her hair.

"Hold it right there, that's lovely." There was another click and he lowered the camera and smiled at her. "That's the first time I've taken a shot of you when you haven't been looking grim."

"When do I ever look grim?!"

"Whenever you get all defensive. Which is constantly. Especially when you think you're being looked at."

She laughed again. "Well, in that case a decent person wouldn't stare at me through a lens."

"And miss two lovely shots like those? Sorry, Miss Casey, you're going to have to get used to it."

They had finished a picnic of cold chicken, rye bread, and fruit and were drinking wine that was rapidly growing tepid. Holding her glass away from her, Hanna tipped a few drops onto the springy heather as a libation to a droning honeybee. The fuzzy rear end, flecked with golden pollen, wriggled among the blossoms before the bee rose almost vertically and disappeared into the distance. Leaning back on her elbows she watched the clouds moving above her. Then she screwed up her face at the lingering taste of her last mouthful of wine.

"I told you we'd have been better with a nice bottle of cold tea."

Brian laughed. "Brewed over a turf fire with six spoons of sugar in the kettle? Nope. If that's the option, I'll settle for lukewarm Chablis."

"Did you ever go turf cutting?"

"Not with a jennet and cart like your great-aunt

Maggie. But there were people still saving turf in the Wicklow Mountains when I was a kid. One or two anyway. And there was an old guy who used to help my dad in the garden who retired to the shed now and then with a bottle of tea."

"You're sure it wasn't for a nip of something stronger?"

"Well, he could have had a naggin hidden behind the lawnmower. But I tasted his tea once and that was pure tannin and sugar."

The lark rose in one of the fields below them. Hanna lay back and closed her eyes again. On a leisurely stretch of their walk to the waterfall she'd told Brian about finding Maggie's book. His easy companionship always seemed to invite confidences, but, after she'd told him, she'd rather wished that she hadn't. Then, half as an apology for the awkward silence that had fallen between them, she'd hastily added that she hadn't yet mentioned the book to Jazz.

"My mother wouldn't be interested—she never liked Maggie—but Jazz would find it fascinating. I don't know why I haven't told her about it."

"If I were you, I'd want to finish it first."

"Would you? Why?"

"Because it must feel as if Maggie's talking to you. You want to hear what she had to say before you pass it on. I mean she started the diary when she was young, but she buried the box long afterward. You knew her in her old age and she left the house to you. It must feel like she's speaking to you from the grave."

Hanna had already realized that was exactly what it felt like. Sitting in her house or out in the garden with the handwritten book on her knee, she could sometimes have sworn that she'd heard Maggie's voice calling her to her dinner.

"What's the date of the final entry?"

"I don't know. I haven't looked."

They'd lost the thread of the conversation at that point because they'd come to a rocky place in the winding path. After a scramble they'd settled into a steady walking pace, pausing to look down a steep valley toward Ballyfin in the distance. The air was so clear that they could see movement on the deck of a fishing boat several miles below. With her mind still on the past, Hanna had tried to explain herself.

"Maggie was full of contradictions. I could see that when I was a kid and it never bothered me. In one way she was a free spirit who did exactly what she wanted. But in other ways she was rigid, so rigid you'd think she might snap."

Maggie had always scorned conformity. Why should she wear shoes if she liked to go barefoot? Who cared what the neighbors thought about how she lived? In

Hanna's childhood few people in Finfarran would turn away a visitor; there might be much rolling of eyeballs and subsequent cries of "wouldn't you *think*...??" but, even if someone arrived at midnight or mealtimes, the door would always be opened and the kettle put on for the tea. Maggie was different. If she didn't want to see you—and generally she didn't—she simply said so and slammed the door in your face. And she was the only woman Hanna had known who didn't go to Mass on Sundays. Once or twice she might turn up at the back of the church for a funeral, but otherwise she never darkened its door. To a twelve-year-old in the 1970s this had been heady example. Though, instinctively, Hanna had known that it mustn't be followed. Or even mentioned at home. She valued the freedom of Maggie's house too much.

Yet, for all her lack of conformity, Maggie had lived by certain unshakable rules. There was an exact moment at dusk when her curtains were drawn across the windows, and a specific order in which her dishes—which she always called "ware"—must be washed. And when Tom Casey suggested installing an oil-fired stove for her, she'd been outraged; there'd always been a fire on the hearth in her house and it wouldn't be she who'd change it. It had seemed to Hanna that, while Maggie appeared to scorn all conventions, her own rules appeared to carry a superstitious weight. And generally they centered on continuity. Her refusal to install the stove was all of a piece with her strictures about the curtains, the water bucket that must be replaced in its own particular corner, and her dinner of bacon and cabbage eaten on the dot of one o'clock.

The rule about reading held the same weight, but to say so to Brian seemed silly. How could she explain that her disinclination to turn to the last page to see how Maggie's book ended was a private expiation for breaking a childhood taboo?

Now, as the lark's song bubbled in the valley beneath them, she opened her eyes to find Brian looking down at her. The scrutiny was different now, no longer the impersonal gaze of an artist looking through a viewfinder. His face was narrower than Malcolm's, tanned and less conventionally handsome, and his dark hair was pushed back from his forehead. She knew that he had been married, but he wore no ring.

When he'd first spoken about his wife, Sandra, he'd said that she'd gone away. Hanna had assumed she'd left him but later he'd told her that she'd died. It was cancer, a blow so sudden and brutal that he hadn't been able to cope. Traumatized by her death, he'd gone to ground, locking his door and refusing to answer his phone. As a result, his fledgling firm had lost a valuable contract and, stricken by guilt, Brian had sold his house in Wicklow, made over the proceeds to his business partner and buried himself in a dead-end job with Finfarran County Council. It had been clear to Hanna when he told her his story that she was the first to hear it. And she'd appreciated the significance of what he had chosen to do: against his own inclination, he had let his emotional guard down in order to help her lower hers. That gesture of trust had been the start of their tentative relationship which now, after their mutual retreat, seemed to be starting again.

"I don't suppose that there's any point in my offering a penny for your thoughts?"

Feeling awkward, Hanna brushed lichen from her elbows. "Actually, I was thinking about Maggie."

"You were up until a minute ago. Then you started thinking about us. And, for God's sake, don't start fencing and ask me what I mean."

"Not even if I want to know?"

He groaned. "What do you think I mean? I mean we keep getting to the same point and then shying away from each other. Over and over again. And we've established that we both regret that, so what are we doing now? Honestly, Hanna, we're like a couple of kids behind the bike shed. Wouldn't you think that by this stage we're old enough to know better?"

Linking her arms round her knees, Hanna stared down the valley. Far below them a fishing boat was putting out from Ballyfin. It veered south at the head of the pier, its white deck flashing in the sunlight and its white wake trailing behind as it made for the open sea. When she and Brian had found this picnic spot, the first thought in her mind had been that the place had seemed ridiculously romantic. Now she turned and looked at him, facing the reason for that thought.

"Unless our respective ages are part of the problem."

Brian burst out laughing. "Ah, Hanna Casey, you're joking! What age do you think I am?"

"Younger than I am, anyway."

"I'm forty-eight."

"There you are, then, I'm nearly five years older than you."

"So?"

Hanna shrugged. "Nothing. It's just a fact. And maybe it's a factor."

"And maybe the tepid wine has gone to your head."

Hanna stood up angrily, shaking the jacket she'd spread on the ground to sit on. "Anyway, I'm getting cramped, let's move on."

For a moment Brian didn't move. Then he reached for his rucksack and began to pack up the remains of the picnic. It wasn't till they'd scrambled back down to the track that he turned and looked at her again. "You're right, you know, about one thing."

"What's that?"

"We're neither of us getting any younger. So if there is any kind of future for us, we'd want to stop wasting time."

33

Conor came down to the house from the top field dying for his dinner. He hosed his boots at the tap in the yard and went round to the back door where his mum was kicking off her gardening shoes by the step. Each year Conor or Joe dug a few ridges and set spuds and vegetables for her in the side garden. Paddy McCarthy was a great man for cabbage with his bacon, and they all ate as many carrots and turnips as they could get, but it was his mum who went for fancy stuff like the beans and the chard, planting some new vegetable every year and nursing her crop. This year she had yellow zucchini down near the apple trees and some class of a purple-skinned heritage spud in between her Queens and Home Guards. The basket she was carrying now was full of beetroot and baby kale leaves which she claimed were far nicer in salads than the lettuce you'd find in the shops.

In the kitchen the spuds were drained and drying and there was a great smell of onions from the casserole on the stove. Joe had driven Conor's dad into Lissbeg for an appointment at the medical center, so it was just his mum and himself at the table for dinner. He'd a power of work to get through before Aideen arrived for her tea later on, but Paddy and Joe would collect her. His dad had said it'd be easy enough, given how you had to sit round for hours at the medical center. He'd hardly be finished there, he said, before Aideen was ready to leave Lissbeg, so Joe could drive the two of them home together.

While his mum washed the salad leaves, Conor moved the spuds from the stove to the table and nudged the cat off a chair. Orla joined him with two plates of lamb stew and lifted the cover from a big dish of buttery carrots. There was nothing to beat her dinners after a morning's work.

"How's the tractor behaving?"

"Not a bother on her. She was coughing away the last day, though, so I might get Seán to take a look."

Each trip to the garage cost an awful lot of money, but the family was always aware that his dad's state was the direct result of taking stupid risks. Nine times out of ten Paddy would have jumped clear if a cow in labor had gone for him in a pen. But on the day of the accident he'd tried to head her off while Joe got over the rail. Joe had got out okay with no problem, but Paddy had rolled over the rail and landed on the top of his spine. Then the insurance lads were no good at all when he went to them with the medical bills; it turned out that the cover he'd taken wasn't nearly enough. Conor sometimes thought that half his dad's depression came from a sense of guilt. If he'd used better judgment, the accident wouldn't have happened, and if he'd taken out proper cover, then at least the bills would be paid. There was no point in dwelling on it, of course, and no way that you'd blame Dad. But if it wasn't for the accident, they might be living differently—or at least, Conor told himself, sadly, they would've had different choices. As things stood, they had no choice but to keep on keeping on.

The stew was great, but he drew the line at the salad. Orla laughed at him. "Are you sure? It'll put hairs on your chest."

"Have you not seen the ads on the TV? You're supposed to use a depilatory these days, to show off your fabulous pecs."

"Oh, yuck. Really?"

"A buffed body's your only man."

"Not in the films I saw when I was courting."

"Oh, please! You didn't call it courting?"

"Actually, no. We called it 'doing a line.' And hairy chests were the height of male fashion when I was doing one with your father. Mind you, so were bandanas and parachute pants, so maybe I should shut up."

She helped herself to salad and said she was planning to make a cake for Aideen. A proper one, based on a recipe, not thrown together the way she normally did them. And did Conor know if Aideen liked sundried tomatoes? Because she'd read a thing in a magazine about how savory canapés looked much better than sandwiches, unless you were doing a classic afternoon tea.

"Well, they sell them in the deli, but I dunno if she eats them herself. And you don't want to go making a fuss, Mum, she'll take us as she finds us."

"Oh right. So, you won't be up there in the bathroom later, scrubbing yourself with soap?"

Blushing, Conor told himself that was different.

Orla winked at him. "And why wouldn't you? I can tell you this much, a woman will always appreciate the trouble a man takes to please her. Some things never change." She got up from the table and went to refill his plate. "She's a lovely girl, Conor, I'm glad you've found her. And I know your dad feels the same."

Conor ducked his head and said nothing.

Coming back to the table, Orla looked at him shrewdly. "What's the matter, you haven't been falling out?"

"No, of course not, we're grand, it's just that . . ."

He stopped, wondering how on earth to go on. Whatever way he looked at things, he couldn't see the way forward. He was stuck on the farm as long as his family needed him. Not that he minded, because he loved it, but what about him and Aideen? Living with Paddy McCarthy was like walking on eggs. On a bad day his moods could make him vicious, and the things he'd say to his family often left poor Orla in tears. No one was sorrier than Paddy himself was afterward. But you couldn't expect Aideen to come and put up with it as well.

In the end it all came out in a rush and he looked at his mum apologetically. "I'm not blaming Paddy, I just don't know what to do."

Orla, who'd been standing with a tea towel in her hand, sat down and pleated it on the table. She took her time before she spoke. "Part of what your dad hates is the way we all look after him. No, hang on"—she shook her head at Conor who'd been about to speak—"it's not that he isn't grateful. He is. He's proud of you and Joe, the way you keep the farm going. And he loves me for trying to make things better—even when I make a bags of it and actually make them worse. But he hates the fact that the way he is dictates all our decisions. And, honestly, Conor, you mustn't let it affect you and Aideen as well." Whatever happened, she said, they'd find a way through it. And why did Conor think he and Aideen would have to live here on the farm? Didn't she have a place of her own and a business? Couldn't they find someplace together even if it meant having to make longer journeys to work? "Someplace between here and Lissbeg? I know Aideen can walk to her work at the moment and you're right here when you're wanted. But surely you could manage to work out some compromise?"

Conor looked at her blankly and her eyes opened in amazement.

"You're not telling me you haven't discussed it with her?"

"Well, no. I mean . . . no. I couldn't see where we were going, so I thought I'd wait till I could."

"But surely you talked about the future when you proposed?"

There was a long pause in which Conor felt his ears go bright pink. His mum stared at him for a moment and then sat back in her chair. "You haven't proposed to her, have you? Ah, for God's sake, Conor! And here's the poor girl coming to tea and me making chocolate cake with prunes!" Was he telling her, she demanded, that Aideen had no idea he wanted to get married? Then what in the name of God made him think that she wanted to marry him?

Conor stared at his plate of dinner, feeling his head explode. Maybe that time when he'd told Aideen they'd better start saving money, she hadn't understood what he actually meant. The truth was, he wasn't sure himself. But stuck with no way of taking things forward, there wasn't much else that he *could* say. God, though, it was fierce unromantic. It was the exact opposite of everything he felt. Aideen was gorgeous and beautiful with her shy smile, and her curling hair like a flock of birds, like it said in that poem about Absalom, and her way of putting her hand up behind his neck when they were in bed. He ought to have gone down on one knee to her beside some Italian fountain. He should have found a ring with a ruby in it as red as her red-gold hair.

Orla shook the tea towel at him and rapped smartly on the table. "You do want to marry her, don't you?"

"I do, of course."

"Well, in the name of God, Conor, would you ever get round to asking her!" Her expression softened and she put her hand on his arm. "All your life you've been a lad who's wanted to fix things for everyone. But the thing about getting married is that it's not all down to you. You can't expect Aideen to hang around while you go working out answers. She's got to be part of the decision-making. You need to work as a team."

She was absolutely right, thought Conor, stabbing his fork at his dinner. He'd gone at the whole thing arse-ways and he needed to change his tack. The thing to do was to sit down and talk it all over with Aideen. Some-how he'd never thought that she wouldn't come and live on the farm, but maybe his mum was right and they could find someplace for themselves. He didn't fancy moving into the house with Aideen and Bríd anyway, and Aideen wouldn't either. The few times he'd gone back to her room they'd always made sure Bríd was out. He didn't make enough money himself to go out and get a mortgage. But Aideen's house was her own and she could sell it. Or she could ask Bríd to move out. But would she want to? And how would he feel if he couldn't pay his way? Thinking about it, his mind went into overdrive. It shouldn't matter who paid if they were married: whatever they had then would belong to them both. Still, he wasn't sure that he'd like it. And he wasn't sure either how he'd cope not living at the farm. He'd be worried that Joe was getting things wrong without him. And how could he leave his mum to deal with his dad's depression alone?

"Conor!"

He looked up and found his mum smiling at him. "Talk about it to Aideen, you won't work it out on your own."

Absolutely. Definitely. She was right and that's what he'd do. Shoveling the last of his dinner into his mouth, he was struck by inspiration. He wouldn't say anything for a while yet till he'd do the proposal right. A proper setting with birds and a fountain and maybe music. Bubbling with excitement, he got up from the table and went to put on his boots. It'd take time and organization and he'd have to break into his savings. But, God, wouldn't it be fantastic when he saw the look on her face. He'd go to Carrick and find a ring that was really worthy of Aideen. And then he'd go down on one knee and tell her she was the love of his life.

34

Jazz felt the soft crunch of beechmast under her feet; even in summer the prickly cases of the fallen nuts lay thick on the forest floor. Seen from below against the bright sky, the dark branches and sharp-edged leaves looked like steel engravings. The paths were cool and shadowed, fringed with green ferns that curled from the earth like watch springs. When even the back roads near the forge became too much for her to cope with, the forest offered a place to walk unseen.

These days the growth was hardly managed and beech and sycamore jostled for space between older oaks and alders. She had parked the car in a shoulder off a track and followed a neglected path between mossy trunks and fallen branches. Here and there, jagged outcrops of rock were topped with rhododendrons,

shallow-rooted flowering invaders that gleamed between the dark trees. In the canopy of leaves above her,
birds whistled and sang. Now, with two hours before
her next shift at work, she could think about what she
should do.

Ever since meeting Fury O'Shea, she'd known that
she'd have to do something. Up to then she'd been convinced that, in time, she'd get her nerve back, but now
she knew that she ought to find help. It was dangerous to take a car on the road if you were too freaked to
control it—inevitably you'd end up crashing again and
this time someone else might well get hurt. Stamping
on a broken branch which produced a satisfying shower
of wood-chips, Jazz told herself crossly that Fury was
probably right—in many ways she was as pigheaded as
her mum was, each of them equally determined to do
things for herself. And apparently it ran in the family,
because Fury had said that Maggie Casey had been the
same. Bloody-minded, self-reliant women, the lot of
them. Which was why it felt so embarrassing to be acting like a wimp.

She had always admired Mum's confidence, the ef-
fortless way she'd run the London house and the Norfolk cottage, organized Dad's social life, and always
seemed in control. And she loved the story of how she'd
set off to chase her dream career. It must have been a big

thing, back in those days, to pack up and go to a foreign country to build yourself a new life. She'd asked Mum once if she'd minded giving up her career for marriage, and the answer she'd got had always stuck in her mind. The thing about dreams, Mum had said, was that sometimes they turned into prisons. You should never, ever deny yourself the freedom to move on and change. "I suppose I swapped one dream for another, and this one is just as fulfilling."

"Really?" Jazz could remember sitting in the London house wondering if that was true. It had seemed so unlikely that she'd asked again. But Mum was adamant. "Yes, really. I love the life that I have with you and Dad."

And even when the truth about Dad had emerged, Mum had just got on and coped with it. She'd walked away without a backward look and built herself another dream. And she'd done it alone while protecting Jazz in the process. It seemed there hadn't been a single moment when she'd cracked and needed help.

But now, pushing through a patch of whippy saplings, Jazz wondered if that was the whole truth. Maybe there'd been nights in Nan's back bedroom when Mum had had nightmares of her own. It must have been awful hearing the lies that Dad came out with when the divorce was over—and deciding on the right way to protect your kid couldn't have been easy alone. If Fury was right, Mum ought to have shared her problems. But who did she have to talk to but Nan, who'd probably have made things worse? And if all that was so, now that Mum had moved on and was happy, it wasn't fair to worry her again.

When Jazz was younger she and Mum had been best mates. Not in a lame, matching-outfits-and-days-out-at-the-beauty-parlor way. They'd both had lives that were far too full for that. But they'd loved each other's company and enjoyed each other's humor. Back when Jazz was still in kindergarten, Mum had taken her to a local library that was round the corner from the London house. It was a beautiful Victorian building and they'd always walked there, usually chatting so intently that it seemed to take no time. Then, on their way home with their arms full of books, they'd stop to feed birds in the park. At home there was a round shelf between the slender mahogany legs of a table in the conservatory, where Jazz had always insisted on keeping her library books. That was because Mum stacked her own books on the tabletop. It stood by a deep armchair next to the window, where they'd sit and read. Even when Jazz had graduated from the likes of *The Very Hungry Caterpillar* to *Alice in Wonderland* and *The Little House on The Prairie*, they'd sometimes squash into the chair together and read bits of books aloud. And each year, one or two of the books she'd liked most from the library would appear under the Christmas tree in beautifully illustrated editions found by Mum.

Jazz stopped to consider a shaft of sunlight, narrow as a pin-spot, falling directly through a gap in the leaves to the forest floor at her feet. The patch of moss that it illuminated glowed like a jewel on the path. She remembered the copy of Grimms' *Household Tales* that Mum gave her one Christmas.

It was a hardback edition, illustrated in the 1940s by Mervyn Peake, and it came with its dust jacket intact. Earlier that year Mum had read her some of Grimms' fairy tales from an anthology she'd chosen for herself in the library. But the pictures in that had been nothing at all like the ones created by Peake. From the moment Jazz had unwrapped the present, she'd known that she hated the book. The cover illustration showed a sinister, rearing bird with iron wings and a curved beak struggling to fly through a rain storm with two terrified children on its back. She didn't want to open it but Mum, who was delighted by her purchase, had urged her to show it to Dad. All the pictures had frightened Jazz, even the beautiful colored ones that appeared now and then among the disturbing drawings. There was one of three identical princesses wearing scarlet, whose long curling golden hair was twined with chaplets of pearls. Hovering in the center of the picture was a shining honeybee. It ought to have been enchanting, and it would have been if the other images hadn't lurked on either side of it, waiting between the pages to catch her by the throat.

Worst of all was the illustration to a story she'd loved when she'd read it in her library book. It was called "The Goose Girl" and was about a princess and her maid. They'd gone on a journey to another kingdom where the princess was going to be married, and her mother had given her a magic charm and the gift of a talking horse. But she lost the charm and, without its protection, she was forced to change places with her maid who'd taken the horse and her clothes. Somehow the next bit of the story had passed Jazz by on first reading. She'd failed to realize that, for fear of the horse revealing the secret, the maid had had it killed—after which, in the best traditions of fairy-tale horror, its head had been hung over an archway through which the princess, now slaving as a goosegirl, passed with her geese each day. And that was the part of the story that Peake had chosen to illustrate. Years later, when she'd found the book thrust to the back of a cupboard, she'd realized that it wasn't, in fact, one of his more powerful drawings. But the image of the horse's head nailed to the arch above the shrinking goosegirl had stayed with her for the rest of her life.

She'd never told Mum, who would have been horrified. And, looking back, she suspected that the version of the story she'd read in the anthology from the library had been watered down to make it acceptable for kids. Maybe it had or maybe it was just a question of selective memory. At eight or nine, all she'd taken in was the fact that the talking horse, whose name was Falada, had continued to comfort the goosegirl in her plight. Each day as she passed under the archway, the horse had called out to her, sympathizing with her sorrow: "Alas, alas, if your mother knew, her loving heart would break in two." And Jazz, who, to Mum's huge embarrassment, had been a fanatical My Little Pony fan, had chanted the rhyme under her breath as she'd combed her pink plastic unicorn's purple mane.

Ahead of her the path she was following branched in two directions, leaving her wondering which way she ought to go. She kept to the left, where the shafts of sunlight falling through the forest's canopy seemed brighter. Or perhaps there were just more of them, slanting through slender conifers as well as the spreading oaks. According to Mum, all this woodland had been managed for ages by Fury O'Shea's family. Then his brother had sold it off to some guy in Australia when Fury was over in England working on the sites. All the old fellows in Finfarran seemed to have the same story, they'd left school at fifteen or sixteen and gone to work on building sites in London or in the States. When Fury came home the forest had been sold and, by the sound of it, his elder brother had drunk himself to death on the proceeds. All that was left to Fury was a site on the edge of the forest by the road, where he'd built himself a house. That was the gateway he'd been turning out of when Jazz had encountered him the other week in her car. Mum once said Fury still went round as if he owned the whole forest. Then she'd laughed. "Actually, I should have said the whole peninsula. Fury keeps an eye on the lot of us, whether we like it or not."

Jazz didn't like the idea of him keeping an eye on them at all. She hated the thought of that annoying old man with his snappy little dog and his pronouncements on other people's business. Especially as, in her case, he might have been right. Now, walking from shadow into sunlight and back again, she hoped she wasn't going to meet him on the path. But she could hear nothing but birdsong and no tall figure appeared through the trees. Close to the earth, where bracken and ferns were green against bark and lichen, little creatures occasion- ally scuffled and stirred. But no human voice sounded in the distance and no hand parted the scarlet flowers that grew on the gray rocks.

Looking at her watch, she realized she'd been walking for half an hour. She'd need to leave herself time to return to the car and get back for her next shift. Before setting out she'd had a coffee in the kitchen where Susan was taking a batch of brown bread from the oven because Gunther was out in the van. The bread had cooled as Jazz had sat at the kitchen table and before she'd gone out Susan had urged her to make herself a sandwich.

"You hardly had time for a bite of lunch with all that ironing. Take something with you if you're going out and you can have yourself a picnic and a rest."

For the last while it had seemed to Jazz that Susan was eyeing her covertly, as if she was worried about her. Yet she wasn't as eager as she used to be to sit and have a chat. Still, business was building as the season progressed, so perhaps she was feeling pressured by the weight of work to be done. From Jazz's point of view, chats were best avoided anyway, because you had to keep warding off inquiries about how you'd slept and how you were. So she'd accepted Susan's suggestion with a smile and made herself a sandwich, enjoying the fresh-baked smell of Gunther's bread. Now, she reckoned, she needed to find a place to sit and enjoy it.

For a while she kept walking, disinclined to sit down

for fear of ticks and other insects in the bracken. Then she rounded a corner and found herself in a clearing, where the sound of the birdsong chimed with the sound of water falling on stone. It was a small, cleared space ringed with oak trees. In its center was a curved outcrop of red sandstone where a spring well bubbled up through a cleft at the base of the rock. Looking across the sunlit clearing, Jazz had the strangest feeling that she'd seen this sight before. She'd certainly never been this deep in the forest, though. So what was that about?

She stepped out from among the trees and moved toward the sound of the water. Then, as her sightline changed slightly, she saw why the rock seemed familiar. On the night of the exhibition opening Mum had demonstrated how digitized images from the psalter could be accessed on computer screens around the exhibition space. One was an illustration of a red deer running through a forest. Its feet and antlers were picked out in gold, and green leaves had been swept from the trees by the speed of its passage. Farther down the page, in another illustration, the same deer was standing by a curved outcrop of rock from which water was bubbling. Mum had told her that this was the first page of the psalter that she'd seen. "It was back when Fury took me to Castle Lancy and Charles showed me the manuscript." It had belonged to the de Lancy family, she said, since the time of the Reformation. "I'd no idea then that he'd end up giving it to the library. At the time I was just bowled over when he produced it from a drawer."

That was when Mum had realized that the psalter's illustrations included features of Finfarran's actual landscape. Fury had leaned over her shoulder and identified the rock as a landmark in the forest. He called it "Lackatubber," a name that came from the Irish and meant "the slab of the well."

"As the hart panteth after the water brooks, so panteth my soul after thee."

The psalter was written in Latin, but you could click the screen for a translation into half a dozen languages. Jazz had read out the text. According to a pop-up, it was Psalm 42.

Mum had smiled. "Kind of breathtaking, isn't it? We should go and find the rock sometime."

But they hadn't, and now Jazz had discovered it on her own. She knelt down by the well and put her hand in the water. It was warm to the touch. Behind her a twig snapped in the forest and she swung round in alarm. For a moment every muscle in her body tightened. Then she relaxed with a sigh of relief as Gunther stepped into the clearing.

35

Mary Casey polished her glasses, reassumed them, and glared at the computer screen. Then she right- and left-clicked aggressively with no idea what she was doing, and swung round triumphantly on Conor.

"It's broken!"

Conor patted her shoulder. "Don't worry, Mrs. Casey, I'm sure you haven't broken it."

"I never said I'd broken it, I told you the thing was banjaxed!"

At the far end of the library Hanna tried to focus on her own computer. Meanwhile the rest of the seniors in Conor's class happily abandoned what they were doing and turned to look at Mary. Last week she'd announced that the library desks were a health hazard; her chair was too low, its back wasn't straight, and the screen was at the wrong angle. Today, having been moved to another desk by Conor, she'd managed to erase her entire morning's work.

"Don't look at me that way, Conor McCarthy, I did nothing you didn't tell me to!"

With infinite patience Conor reiterated the importance of taking things gently. "You don't want to go bashing the keyboard, Mrs. Casey, you'd never know what might happen. And I'd hold back on the mouse too till I'd see where the cursor points."

Mary said that was all well and good, but what had happened to her letter? "I had three good pages inside in that computer setting out my case for compensation. The way those council lads treat trash bins is notorious!" She turned confidingly to her audience. "I have a grand plastic sleeve that goes all round mine, with big colored flowers on it. And it's perfect. You can put your bin out in the garden and you'd hardly know it was there. And what did those lads do when they emptied it out last Friday? Got half the muck of the seven parishes plastered all over me sleeve! Sure, if I put it out by the roses now you'd think I was after mulching them. Five euro that sleeve cost me inside in Carrick, and I a senior!"

By this stage the others were sitting back drinking it in; Mary Casey in full spate was far more entertaining than a session on using templates. At the other end of the library Hanna hunched her shoulders. She needed to get this e-newsletter drafted and sent before lunchtime. Trying to ignore her mother's voice, she tapped briskly at her keyboard. Then, realizing that she'd typed the words "DO JOIN OUR BOOK CLUB" three times in succession, she gave up and saved the unfinished document. It was good that Mary—who'd grown increasingly dependent—was getting out and being active. But it was infuriating that her chosen activity took place here in the library. On the plus side, of course, it was lucky that, so far, she hadn't joined the book club. Stifling a grin, Hanna decided to go for an early lunch. It was twenty to one on a slow morning and Conor would be fine without her.

Once outside, she crossed the courtyard and made for the nuns' garden. At a table near the fountain Saira Khan was sitting with a large cappuccino. As Hanna approached, she looked up and smiled, obviously pleased to see her. She was waiting for Ameena, she explained, whose shift would finish shortly. "I walked down to meet her because the weather was so lovely. Have you come to have lunch?"

Hanna said she had but it was a working one. "There's something I need to read so I'm going to tuck myself in a corner."

She smiled back at Saira and moved on, feeling

slightly guilty. She'd promised herself that morning that she'd spend her lunchtime reading the next entry in Maggie's book, but by no stretch of the imagination did that count as work; she could easily have stopped for a chat while Saira was waiting for Ameena. Briefly she hesitated, wondering if she might go back. But the moment had passed and, anyway, the pull of Maggie's story was too strong. Picking up a sandwich and a coffee in the café, she found herself a seat in a far corner of the garden and took the book out of her bag.

September 7th, 1920

The de Lancys are gone out of the castle now, back since the time of The Land War. That's more than twenty years the place has been left with none of the family living there. Dad took me to see it one time and Jim the caretaker showed us round. He said what the family didn't know about couldn't bother them. It's not really a castle, just a big house, but Dad said the walls around it are Norman and that the first de Lancys lived in a castle on the site. I'd say they had plenty of money always and where did they get it but out of the mouths of the people? It was no different here in England. I met a girl in a tea shop the other day whose granny worked in a cotton mill when she was only seven, and the mill owner lived in a big house and rented out slums to his workers. I don't know what the de Lancys will own if the lads free Ireland. They got out fast enough anyway at the first sign of danger, but I suppose you couldn't expect them to stay and be burned out or worse. That's the thing about the rich, they can always run away and find a welcome. The de Lancys went off to the States where they'd money invested, and there's Mam and the rest of Finfarran still paying out rents to them. I remember Dad saying that was all changing and Liam stamping round the house saying it wasn't changing fast enough.

There was a big room in the castle with books in it, covered with sheets, and Jim's wife took us up to it and pulled off some of the covers. She was a cousin of Dad's on his mother's side or I'd say we'd not have got in there. There were shelves of books reaching round the room and right up to the ceiling. They had wine-colored leather backs to them, and thick paper and brown leather covers. And each one had a gold stamp on the front that Dad said was the family arms. Mrs. Jim said she had to keep the light off the books and put a big fire in the grate each week so the room wouldn't get damp. I *asked her if she ever read them and she said that she didn't want to. She'd never seen the family reading them either. They'd hardly go up and set foot in the room the times that they used to stay there. I told her that if I had it, I'd be up there reading always.*

When the de Lancys were in the castle they employed a power of servants. Dad's father worked in the gardens and his mam minded the gatehouse. When he was small he worked in the house himself cleaning boots. Then the de Lancys leased him the farm of land when he and Mam got married. He always had great respect for the family because they'd given him that. Liam says they were damn lucky to get such an honest tenant. At least that's what he used to say to Dad's face. Behind his back I've heard him call him a lackey.

I don't know why I'm sitting here on the bed writing down all this rubbish. I suppose it takes me home again to be writing about Finfarran. I do think of it all times. I do dream of the forest. The other night I dreamt I was climbing Knockinver and Dad was with me, and Liam, and the dog was behind us. It was a grand day with the clouds flying and the sun shining on the mountain. When I woke up I thought I was home with Mam in the bed beyond me. Then I lay awake the rest of the night wondering was she all right. I do worry about her all the time when she's only the dog for company. Mrs. Donovan sent me a card the other day but she hardly put six words on it. Lizzie wrote by the same post and said that she'd heard from her brother. She made no mention of Liam at all and she didn't call her brother by name. I'd say that means that they're still on the run in the mountains. I know the fight is still going on, for you'd see it here in the papers. Lizzie said she went dancing one night and now she's walking out.

This isn't a bad place. Mrs. Carr has a sharp tongue in her head but she pays up what she owes you. I got my first wages this morning and it's great I've no rent to go out of it. My room's no bigger than a prison cell but it's warm because it's right beside the kitchen. I get the same food that the lodgers get and they pay through the nose for it. You'd have sausages and rashers and eggs for your breakfast, though they call the rashers "bacon." The tea's weak enough and the milk is skim, but she cuts the bread thickly. The work's not the worst either, though your back would be bad with the stairs. The trouble is that there's nobody here to talk to. There's a rule that I'm not to go standing around with the lodgers and no doubt Mrs. Carr wouldn't demean herself by having a chat with a skivvy. The little one that comes in by day to serve the meals doesn't say a word, and I hardly see Kate and Peg at all since I upped and left Mrs. Spencer's. I'll stick it out, though, for the time being for fear I'd find nothing better.

I had a bit of luck today, anyway. One of the lodgers left this morning and I found a book in his room when I was cleaning it. It's a lot of stories about an English detective. I don't know if I'll like it but it's all I've got so I'm going to take it easy. It's called The Memoirs of Sherlock Holmes *and it has a blue cover with a picture that says The Strand Library on it, and gold letters stamped into the cloth. I suppose I ought to give it to Mrs. Carr in case your man comes back looking for it. But he was a divil for smoking cigarettes out his window and throwing the ends in the chamber pot. And I said never a word to Mrs. Carr about that, so you could say he owes me a read.*

So Maggie had once stood in the room where Hanna had first seen the psalter and had dreamed of the mountain where Hanna and Brian had picnicked above the ocean. Closing the book, Hanna sat back in the sunlight. In her mind's eye, the psalter lay unseen in its drawer in Castle Lancy's book room, while the teenage Maggie climbed to the top of Knockinver on sandstone steps as worn as the castle's stairs.

Ameena gave her mum a one-arm hug and pulled a chair out from the table.

"I'm really sorry I'm a bit late, I was stuck with a brain-dead customer." Most of the people who came to the gift shop were lovely, she said, but now and then you'd get someone who shouldn't be let out alone. "She looked perfectly sane but, basically, she was raving. All she wanted was three of those framed lace initials, one for each of her kids. So it should have been straightforward. Wouldn't you think? But then it turned out that one kid was called Jacob and the *J* looked a bit boring so maybe the *S* would be better. Because sometimes they called him Sonny. And I'm thinking God knows why Sonny—who's apparently fourteen—is going to want a lace initial to hang on his bedroom wall. Honestly, Mum, by the time we'd worked our way through Melissa, also known as Baby-Girl, and Frances, or BooBoo, and Mr. Snuffles, the dachshund, I was seriously starting to lose the will to live." Ameena sank onto the chair and pulled a rueful face. "I'm really sorry you've been sitting here doing nothing but waiting for me."

"But I haven't. I've been drinking a cup of coffee here in the sun. And I've been thinking."

"What about?"

"Gardens. And Nani."

Ameena looked at her anxiously. "I know you miss her a lot."

"Of course. She was my mother. And I do get a bit weepy sometimes. But you shouldn't worry, Ameena. It's natural, just as it's natural for a mother to die before her daughter. *Insha'Allah* that is what will happen to you and me. And remember what Nani told us, we'll see her again in Paradise."

The Paradise thing was a bit too much for Ameena. You couldn't know what happened to people when they died, so why say you did? This wasn't something she wanted to pursue with her mum, though, especially since she hadn't quite made up her own mind. Some days it made sense to her. Other times Paradise just seemed bizarre.

The Garden Café provided little homemade biscotti with every cappuccino. Mum's was still uneaten on her saucer, so Ameena picked it up.

"Nice." With her mouth full, she gestured toward the café. "Will I go and get us some lunch?"

"Don't you want to know what I was thinking of?"

"Well, you said. Nani."

"And gardens. I walked around this one again. It really is beautiful. Very peaceful. Well cared-for. Well stocked. It reminds me of Nani's garden when I was a child. The light is different and so is the layout, but the smell of some of the herbs here takes me home." She pointed across the garden. "Have you read that sign on the noticeboard?"

Ameena shook her head. She hadn't even seen the noticeboard, which was over in the far corner.

"They're looking for more volunteers to look after the herb beds." Mum picked up biscotti crumbs with her finger. "I met a lady over by the polytunnel. I told her I'd like to sign up."

"Really?"

"Really. It's a walk from the house. This is a beautiful place. It's something I'd like to do. They're looking for people who would have some free time maybe twice, three times a week."

Ameena could feel herself smiling like the Cheshire cat. This was totally unexpected and it would never have happened if Miss O'Rourke hadn't told her about the job in the library.

Licking the crumbs off her finger, Mum smiled back at her. "And here's something I bet you don't know." She nodded at the herb beds enclosed between high brick walls and the side of the old convent building. There were insects humming in the foliage and the sound of water falling from carved flowers into the fountain. "The word 'Paradise'? It's an Indo-European word from a language that people once spoke in Pakistan. If you translate it literally, it means 'an enclosed garden.'"

36

Hanna's own herb garden was coming on nicely. As she'd piled up the stones to make her rock garden, she'd sunk pots and tubs of varying sizes between them and planted mint, marjoram, comfrey and lemon balm. Fennel had refused to take at first. Then it had appeared in the gravel near the end of the house, somehow having transferred itself to a place that it preferred. The feathery green shoots had taken root so firmly that she'd shrugged and let it be. Now, weeks later, it was several feet high, its stalks striped grass-green and pale yellow and its fronds casting shadows on her wall.

She was sitting on the doorstep in the evening sunlight when a volley of shrill barks announced that The Divil was scratching at her gate. Moments later, Fury

O'Shea appeared round the end of the house with the little dog fussing at his heels.

"Don't go getting up, I'll come and sit beside you."

Ignoring the space she made for him on the door-step, he sat on the ground, folding his gangling frame against the wall.

"You can't be comfortable sitting on gravel!"

"I'll sit where I like, Miss, without your say-so." He winked at her cheerfully. "So, tell me, how's the view from your own front step?"

"Heavenly."

Hanna looked down the sloping field, now tamed and beginning to look like a garden. She smiled. "I remember sitting here with a mug of buttermilk when I was small. It was an enamel mug with a chipped lip that my mother would have called a Health and Safety Hazard."

"Ay, well, Maggie Casey would pay no attention to a couple of chips on a mug. She was a great hoarder, that one. Nothing ever got thrown out."

"I looked for it when I was clearing the rubbish before you did the restoration. I suppose it was long gone by then."

Yet, strangely, she had found the tumbler that Maggie had used as a measuring cup when making bread. The green glass was thick with cobwebs but, unlike the more robust enamel mug, it had survived for decades in the empty house.

"I found it exactly where it had always been on the dresser, with a blue Milk of Magnesia bottle and a broken string of beads."

Fury raised an eyebrow at her. "Not rosary beads, I take it?"

"Artificial pearls. I can't imagine Maggie wearing them. Any more than I can see her carrying round a rosary. She was about the only woman I knew back then who didn't have one somewhere in her bag."

"She had no time for the Church, I'll tell you that much. The necklace might have been her mam's, she talked about her a lot. I'd say she was fierce fond of her."

With a pang of regret Hanna remembered that she'd scooped up the scattered beads in her hand and thrown them into the hedge.

Fury shrugged. "Or she could just have found them somewhere out walking. You'd never know."

That was the trouble, thought Hanna. You never did know. In so many families, old hatreds or alliances conspired to conceal the past. So, while objects remained when their owners were dead and buried, the resonance they carried was lost because their stories were buried, too. It crossed her mind to tell Fury about the book in the garden. But once again she found herself holding her tongue. Instead she stood up and suggested they walk down the field to the bench that looked over the ocean.

"You'll want to inspect your paint job. It's looking grand."

He met her eye with a malicious glint and said that he wouldn't doubt her. "You've been down there in the winter nights, covering it up from the cold."

Hanna had taught herself long ago not to rise to his gibes. In fact, she had come to enjoy them almost as much as he did. And now his sardonic intelligence chimed with the new aspect of Maggie she was finding in the book: they cast the same appraising eye on the world and found it wanting, though Fury had never withdrawn from it in the way Maggie Casey had.

As they walked down the field together, she glanced at her boundary walls. When she'd first encountered Fury, he'd told her he'd worked for Maggie when he was young. With both his parents dead and his brother about to inherit, he'd decided the time had come to get away. But he'd needed to earn the price of his passage to England and Maggie had been willing to pay him a fair wage. The O'Sheas were a well-respected family, and the people around had had sympathy for an orphaned seventeen-year-old, but the early 1970s were a hard time on the peninsula, when the weak were often cheated by the strong, yet Maggie Casey had paid on the nail and never tried to cheat him. And in the few weeks that she'd been his employer, they'd found that they got on.

"You built these walls for her, didn't you?"

He nodded, striding, stork-like, down the field. "I lifted every stone of them with my bare hands. She got her money's worth. We had great craic all the same, though. She was a mighty woman. She came home from England in the 1940s and lived here alone till she died."

He'd been long gone to England himself by the time Hanna had been sent round to Maggie's. The woman she'd known in her childhood had either been silent or fiercely petulant and, except for their indulgent feasts of poreens, they'd never had what you'd call craic.

Fury ginned. "People round here always said she was paranoid. She wouldn't talk to the half of them and she'd hardly let a soul in the house."

That sounded familiar to Hanna. It had been the cause of many rows in her childhood when Mary Casey couldn't see why Maggie depended so much on Tom.

When they reached the stile, she climbed over it and sat down on the bench. Fury scooped The Divil up under his arm and came to sit alongside her. The ledge between the wall and the edge of the cliff was fringed with grass. Tiny, white, star-shaped flowers grew between clumps of sea pinks. Out on the horizon, the last of the sunset reddened the darkening waves.

They sat in companionable silence watching the dusk creep down. Then Hanna asked Fury what he and Maggie had talked about.

He shrugged. "The iniquity of the neighbors. She was hot on that. And the way her dad would set about building a wall. It wasn't my way, I can tell you, and she swore that his way was better. I told her he was just a farmer and I was a craftsman born." Fury grinned reminiscently. "She nearly ate the head off me."

A line from the diary flashed through Hanna's mind. *Paud Donovan sold the cows for us anyway . . . He's taken the grazing too at a fair rent.*

She looked at Fury. "Do you know what happened to the farm? How much land was there?"

"I don't know. No more than a few fields anyway. It must have got sold off."

The clifftop fields on either side were thick with yellow furze. To Hanna's eye they looked as if they could never have yielded a living.

. . . the de Lancys leased him the farm of land when he and Mam got married. He always had great respect for the family because they'd given him that.

Bending to scratch The Divil, she remembered what came next.

Liam says they were damn lucky to get such an honest tenant. At least that's what he used to say to Dad's face. Behind his back I've heard him call him a lackey.

"Did she ever talk about her brother? Liam?"

"Liam? That was your dad's dad. She said he'd no interest in farming. I suppose that was why he took the post office and she was left living here."

Hanna was stunned. How idiotic not to have made the connection! How foolish not to see that the Liam of the diary had been her own grandfather. Liam, the brother about whom Maggie had worried. The freedom-fighter hiding out in the hills.

She looked up at Fury. "Did you know he fought in the War of Independence?"

"Did he? Half the men round here were involved. Women too. It wasn't something they talked about in my young days. Too many memories. Too much bad blood."

She knew he was right. Families had been torn apart by that war and the civil war that followed it.

"And Maggie said nothing?"

Fury shook his head. "Not to me."

So here was another story buried in old hatreds and alliances—yet because of Maggie's book it hadn't been lost beyond recall.

The Divil nudged Hanna's hand with his nose, looking for more attention. But her mind was elsewhere.

She found herself thinking about the choices made by the book club. The fact was that the more one relates to whatever it is that one's reading, the more one feels that it's an important book. The cookbook that had been handed on to Nell Reily by her mother. Oliver's theories about cover design and Darina's eagerness to link *Go Set a Watchman* to her heartthrob Gregory Peck. Ten minutes ago she herself had seen Maggie's book from a greater distance. Now that she'd realized Liam was her grandfather, things had subtly changed.

As Fury bent down and lifted The Divil to his knee, the little dog stiffened and glared at the ocean, presumably suspecting the gulls of being flying rats.

Hanna glanced at him. "Did Maggie ever tell you that her dad worked for the de Lancys?"

"She did not. If you'd believe half of what she said of him, he was ten foot tall and could run like some class of a cheetah. He'd win prizes at fairs."

"I think his parents had the gatehouse at Castle Lancy."

"Could be. Maggie never said."

"Charles wouldn't know?"

"God, I wouldn't say so, sure he only married in." Fury looked at her slantways. "Isn't there a power of de Lancy family photos inside in Carrick Library?"

For a moment, Hanna didn't understand him. Then she remembered old books of photographs taken in stately homes. They didn't just show the gentry. There were all those rows of servants lined up on lawns or on steps, some of them holding the brushes or spoons or tools that defined their work. Maggie's father had once been a boot-boy at Castle Lancy. And Fury was right. Among the local history collection that Tim Slattery had moved to the County Library were several albums of de Lancy family photos.

Suddenly, Hanna found herself tingling with excitement. Somewhere among the de Lancy photos she might find the face of the little boot-boy who had grown up to be her great-grandfather.

Fury caught her eye and winked at her. "No better woman than yourself, I'd say, for getting in for a look at them."

Hanna laughed. Tim's display of the memorabilia combined flashiness with inaccessibility in a measure likely to daunt even the most determined researcher. Which was the point. He was one of that breed of librarians who saw readers as anathema—a stereotype that, at one stage, she'd been close to becoming herself.

"I'd say you're right. Though to be fair, the collection's fragile and Tim does have a duty of care."

"Ah go on outta that and don't be making an eejit of yourself. Don't you know as well as I do that the man's a pompous ass."

Hanna grinned at him. "You might say so, I can't possibly comment. What about a beer instead?"

"Now you're talking." Fury stood up, neatly tipping The Divil onto the sea pinks. "You can put a bowl down, too, for the poor Divil. He's never been known to refuse a drop of beer."

37

CBASS 4T CAN U GT CAPERS LBEG WHN UR IN
THERE TRY HDASHERRY IFNOT NOPROB

Mary Casey stabbed at her phone and shot her text off to Louisa. Didn't the rental car give that woman great freedom altogether? And it was one of the many bonuses of having her staying at the bungalow, because she was always happy to pick things up in Lissbeg.

Mary was well used to getting her neighbors to run errands for her. Wasn't there many a thing poor Tom did for the neighbors when he was alive? In and out of half the houses in the parish, putting up shelves and cutting hedges, when there were plenty of others, and even relations, that should have been there before him. There was many a favor owing, she reckoned, and weren't we all here to help each other? Still, it wasn't easy to ask. You couldn't go putting too much pressure on Hanna or poor Jazz either, and they working. But Louisa was graciousness itself. So, with any luck, they'd have a grand tartar sauce tonight with their sea bass. Johnny Hennessy had dropped the bass off with her. And there was no need to feel beholden to him, Mary told herself complacently. This time of year people caught more fish than they'd ever want to be eating, and the same Johnny had no time for freezers. He'd sooner give it away and see it eaten fresh.

Louisa was great company round the house, too, and she wasn't the least bit demanding. The two of them had got things worked out fine. Breakfast was a thing that Mary hadn't been sure about at the beginning. What would a woman with a manor in England know about frying rashers? But then it turned out that Louisa knew a lot about rearing pigs. She had a neighbor at home who went in for Gloucestershire Old Spots and, apparently, the meat you'd get from them would be classed as top-notch. Mary had asked Ger Fitzgerald, the Lissbeg butcher, and Ger, who was very sound on rashers, had told her the Old Spot pigs were "only mighty." He'd never reared them himself, he said, or sold them in the shop either, but he'd tasted the meat all right. According to him, a woman who appreciated them lads could be trusted with anyone's breakfast. And he was right. Louisa had a great way with the frying pan and she'd baste you a lovely egg. Mind you, she hadn't a clue at the start when it came to black pudding. But she picked things up in no time, and she was happy enough to be told.

To begin with they'd eaten at the kitchen table, but one sunny morning Mary had come down to find breakfast set out on the patio. It wasn't what she'd been used to. In fact, it was the class of thing Hanna had wanted before she'd moved out into Maggie's. But Louisa had put out cushions on the chairs and laid the table properly and, with the sun shining, it all looked very nice. Mary hadn't been sure about eating in her dressing gown either but, from the first day, Louisa had turned up in hers. And, to be fair to the woman, she didn't look a bit sloppy. She was showered and decent, with her hair up on her head, like Audrey Hepburn in the movies, and a floor-length rose-patterned dressing gown with a white toweling belt. Mary couldn't abide a skimpy wraparound. But there was a great swing to Louisa's, which was lined with the white toweling, and she wore it with pink slippers with leather soles.

The next week, when they both went shopping, Mary had seen a blue one in Carrick that was pretty much the same. Not a copy, of course, but kind of similar. It had deep revers that were actually nicer than Louisa's, and cuffs that turned back and were piped in white. It wasn't cheap but, as she'd told Louisa, there was more than one season's wear in it. So she'd paid for it on her credit card and never regretted it since.

It was a lovely relaxed thing to wear over breakfast and, with Louisa around, the meal could go on for an hour. They'd be popping in to make more tea and toast, and even reading the papers. Mary hadn't looked at a paper for ages, and why would she with no one there to discuss the bit of news with? If you opened your beak to Jazz or Hanna, they'd say that you didn't know the half of it, but Louisa was civil and interested or, if she wasn't, she never let on. And, of course, they'd both be properly dressed in time to wave to the postman. So that was grand.

Leaving her phone on the kitchen table, Mary crossed the room to attend to the sea bass. It was wrapped in several sheets of the *Inquirer*, and already gutted by Johnny, who'd left on the head. A few times in the past she'd put similar presents out for the neighbor's cat. But not any more. Having Louisa around made all the difference: she had far less call to go texting Jazz or Hanna, with invitations she suspected they didn't want.

Running the fish under the cold tap, she watched the blood swirl down the plughole. In fairness now to Louisa, she'd always leave a spotless sink. And it was Louisa who'd told her about that new way of texting. You didn't put all the letters down, you just went for the gist. Malcolm had shown it to Louisa over in England, and she'd offered to teach it to Mary one night. But the last thing Mary wanted was secondhand lessons from Malcolm. She'd worked it out herself instead with no problem at all. Anyone could see it was just a matter of squashing the words up together; and if someone couldn't grasp what you meant, sure they'd call you and you could explain. Mind you, she'd had a fair few calls after that from Louisa, looking for explanations. But that was just to begin with. They were perfectly fine now.

So it was a fierce shame that Louisa was due to leave in a few weeks' time. Mary patted the fish with a piece of crumpled kitchen paper. There was a little vase of daisies on the windowsill that she hadn't noticed that morning. Unexpected things like that were the kind of things you'd miss.

Last night she'd gone outside to the trash bin. It was late enough and Tom's night-scented stocks were shining in the dusk. When she'd shut the bin, she'd seen a stream of light from between Louisa's curtains. It had fallen across the grass and made her smile as she'd turned to go in. She'd locked the back door as usual, sliding the bolts at the top and bottom and carefully putting the chain on. Then, as she'd crossed the hall to her own bedroom, she'd noticed the line of light on the carpet under Louisa's door. When she'd got into bed, she'd plumped up her pillows and turned off her own light easily. It was way easier to sleep well when you knew that you weren't alone.

38

It was a wet day and the NO VACANCIES sign was swinging in the wind outside the guesthouse. Susan was in the laundry room trying to do the ironing, and a houseful of guests kept wanting her attention. It was weird the way weather affected tourists. The feeling that they couldn't go out made everyone twitchy. One stalwart couple on a walking tour had leapt up from the breakfast table and plunged into the rain, but the other guests were mooching about, finding fault with their rooms and wanting extra milk for their coffee.

Holly pattered into the laundry room and announced that the fat ladies in Room 4 didn't know how to work the hairdryer.

Susan looked at her angrily. "We don't call people

fat, Holly, you know that. And you're not supposed to be hanging round the bedrooms."

With great dignity, Holly replied that she hadn't been hanging round anywhere. She'd been up on the top landing talking to Ginger when a lady came out of Room 4 with her head in a towel. "She said the hairdryer didn't work, but I know it does because Jazz always checks them. But *you* say I shouldn't argue, so I smiled and said I'd tell you. I was very polite and I didn't call her fat either. I only said it now so you'd know who I meant."

"Well, you shouldn't say it at all. And you shouldn't have Ginger up on the top landing. You know he lives in the woodshed because some guests are allergic to cats."

Holly's face fell and Susan felt guilty. "I'm sorry, pet, it's just that I'm really busy." She looked round and saw no sign of the kitten. "Where's Ginger now?"

"I *told* you, he's upstairs and I *know* he's not meant to be there. That's what I was *telling* him when the lady came out of her room."

Jazz, who was folding tea towels, offered to fetch him. "Come on up with me, Holly, and you can hold on to Ginger. I'll go in and see if I can help with the dryer and then we'll both bring him down." She held her hand out to Holly, throwing a glance at Susan. "The chances are that they just haven't switched it on at the wall."

Susan smiled at her. This sort of unstressed intervention seemed to be Jazz's expertise. Maybe it was part of the training she'd had at the airline but, whatever it was, it worked magic on days like these. Her own tension had relaxed as soon as Jazz had spoken and Holly's face had brightened as she'd taken the outstretched hand. Susan watched them go to the door together, fingers linked and arms swinging.

As they left the room, she called out to Jazz. "When you bring Ginger down, will you take him up to the woodshed? And tell Gunther we need more logs for the fire?"

Normally she wouldn't have a fire in the lounge this early, but this morning, seeing the weather, she had lit one before breakfast, and the next thing she'd know some guest would be saying the log basket wanted filling. That, or they'd be turning up in the laundry room offering to do it themselves.

Up on the landing Jazz found the kitten mewing forlornly in a corner. She scooped him up and gave him to Holly before knocking on the bedroom door. The problem with the hairdryer was indeed solved by turning on the socket and, before she left, the ample ladies were wreathed in grateful smiles.

On the way down the stairs, Holly lowered her voice to a confidential whisper. Didn't Jazz think the two ladies were very, very fat? Not in an ugly way, she explained, just big and shiny, like sea lions?

It was such a perfect description that Jazz laughed. "I suppose they are."

Holly nodded defensively. "I knew they were, but Mummy said I shouldn't say so."

The correct thing would have been to endorse Susan's verdict but, looking at Holly's earnest expression, Jazz smiled. After all, Susan herself had looked guilty when she snapped at Holly, and the poor kid had only been trying to help. Taking the kitten, which was struggling to escape, she squeezed Holly's hand. "Let's go up and see Daddy, shall we, till Mummy's a bit less angry?"

The woodshed was full of shadows and smelled of sawdust. As soon as they got there, Holly ran to her father, who swept her up in the air and swung her round. The little girl screamed in terror and delight, her arms and legs flying, and the kitten leapt from Jazz's grasp and scuttled away to its bed. Gunther set Holly down in a pile of wood shavings swept in the corner.

"There. Be quiet and make yourself a nest."

Holly giggled and obediently began to burrow amongst the shavings. Gunther sat on the sawhorse and looked at Jazz.

"Am I wanted indoors?"

Jazz shook her head. "No, Susan just wants logs for the fire. I'd say there's no rush."

He pushed his fair hair back from his forehead and smiled. "It's quieter here."

She nodded again. That's what he'd said when they'd met that day in the forest. He'd stepped into the clearing as she'd stood beside Lackatubber and smiled and told her he liked to go there because it was cool and quiet. She hadn't been surprised. He was a quiet person, strong and gentle, and probably in the wrong job. She'd wondered lately how on earth he'd come to marry Susan. They didn't seem to fit. Susan was all bustle and drive, determined to succeed in business. Gunther was reticent and shy and wrapped up in his daughter. She looked at him now, his blue eyes alight with fun as he laughed at Holly, who was solemnly dribbling sawdust onto her hair. If Susan saw her doing that, the chances were she'd be trying to stop her. Gunther's instinct was always to understand.

"Why does a bird need sawdust in its feathers?"

Holly made a face at him. "It's not sawdust, it's rain. I've gone and built my nest in the wrong place."

"Oh no! A bad decision. Now you will have to live with the choice you've made."

Holly's eyes were round as a baby owl's. "Why?"

"Because that is what birds and people must learn to do."

Jazz shook her head and smiled at him. "My mum says that dreams can sometimes turn into prisons. We should never deny ourselves the freedom to walk away."

In the forest they had sat on the stone by the fountain and, for no reason she could understand, she had found herself confiding in him. Gunther had listened thoughtfully, his head bent in the sun. She'd explained about the car and how the accident had unnerved her. And how she felt like a fool and was afraid to tell anyone else.

"But I know I have to. I mean it's either that or stop driving altogether, and how could I work if I did that? Here, I mean. How could I stay in Finfarran?"

"Do you want to?"

"Yes. I think so. The only reason I lived in France was because of my job with the airline. And that's gone now. And there's no reason for me to live over in London. That's gone, too."

As soon as she'd said it aloud, she was stabbed by its starkness. There was nothing for her in London now that she'd found out the truth about Dad. Everything she'd had over there had been built on his lies. People fell out of love, she knew, and that was just what happened—half the people she'd been at school with had parents who'd been divorced. But there'd never been a time in her whole life when Dad hadn't been cheating on Mum. Every Christmas, every birthday, every family outing now seemed hollow. Even the night when she'd been conceived, he'd been thinking of somebody else.

Pushing the thought away, she had turned to Gunther. "Would you help me?"

"Me? How?"

"The thing is that I panic when I'm driving alone. Not always. Sometimes. But if someone was with me, I know I could get over it. Someone who'd just come along."

That was all she'd wanted. Someone she could trust.

He hadn't been sure at first, especially when she'd said that it had to be secret. She'd tried to explain. "I don't want any fuss. Don't you see? I just want to get over this and get on with living my life."

He'd looked doubtful and, to her horror, her eyes had filled with tears. She hadn't wanted to cry and she'd only just managed to stop herself. Then he'd put his arm round her shoulder and she'd known that she'd be all right.

39

Conor was on his way to buy an engagement ring for Aideen. It would be red gold, he'd decided, as red as her hair. He'd looked up rubies on the internet and the cost of them would frighten you, so the big, shining stone he'd imagined would have to remain a dream. But, when he thought about it, he'd told himself that she might think a big stone was flashy. Something understated might be better. Actually, the first time he'd showed her the psalter, she'd been far more interested in the little pictures in the margins than in the big ones. And even with the full-page picture of the gold women going up the mountain, she'd been drawn in by little things like the nests of colored birds.

Conor steered the Vespa neatly between a tourist coach and a truck. There was a shop in Carrick with a website that showed a couple of rings he might manage. According to the blurb, they were designed and made in-house, though, which might be iffy. But they were real gold, with real stones that weren't as expensive as rubies. Diamonds, he had discovered, could cost ten times the price of a bull calf.

On the second day that Aideen had come to tea, he'd arrived in from the field and found her inside in the kitchen. Apparently, when Paddy and Joe had turned up at the deli, she'd said she could take off at once. He'd planned to shower and change before she got there but instead, when he came in all mucky and sweaty, she was sitting there talking recipes with his mum. Joe was at the table with a mug of tea, and their dad was sitting in the easy chair looking almost cheerful; the old dog, who'd been allowed indoors since Paddy had had his accident, was leaning up against him with his muzzle on his knee. Aideen looked great. Her cheeks and her nose got freckled in summer but, for some reason, she never went pink like a prawn. Instead her skin was a lovely gold where it wasn't freckled and her eyes went a deeper blue. She was wearing jeans and a cheesecloth top and a lot of silver bracelets. But she had little gold hoop earrings on, so it wasn't like silver was her thing. Actually, she liked all different kinds of jewelry. In her bedroom at home she had a big bowl of rings and bracelets on her dressing table, and chains and necklaces hung at the side of the mirror.

His mum had smiled when he came in and Aideen had jumped up and hugged him. It was the first time she'd done that in front of the family and he didn't know where to look. Out of the corner of his eye he could see Joe making a face at him; but even though Joe could be an eejit you could tell that he liked her, too. She looked totally at home in the kitchen. She wouldn't let him go up and change either, when he said that he'd have to go out again later for the cows.

The chocolate cake was magic, you wouldn't notice the prunes at all. Mostly when Paddy came home from the doctor, he'd be bad for the rest of the evening: he'd go up to his bedroom and watch TV up there. But that day he'd stayed down in the kitchen talking and making a game of Orla's canapés.

"Isn't it far from sundried tomatoes we were reared?"

Orla had laughed back at him. "You speak for yourself, Paddy McCarthy! Anyway weren't you the boy buying me jugs of retsina when all belonging to you were still drinking pints?"

They'd gone to Greece on a vacation back in the 1990s, she said, and Paddy had come home with notions. He'd even gone in for baseball caps and flip-up sunglasses which, let's face it, looked pretty weird on the farm. She'd put manners on him as soon as they were married, she told Aideen, winking, and look at him now, in a knit sweater from Penney's and a pair of Lidl's cords.

They'd sat round laughing and talking till it was time to go up for the cows. Conor had been going to leave Aideen in the kitchen, but she'd announced that she'd brought her wellies. So the two of them went out together and idled up on the Vespa; the cows were up in the hill field, so it was easier to take the bike. Bid came out of the shed barking when he whistled to her. She was fed up with her puppies by then and happy to be back to work.

It was a smashing evening. A grand bit of sun and plenty of wind to keep down the midges. Aideen sat on the back of the bike with her arms round his waist and her chin on his shoulder. Halfway up he'd stopped and showed her the field where he'd lost the sheep. He'd only been small then, maybe ten or eleven, and Paddy had sent him up to move some ewes. But when he got up there he hadn't shut the field gate right and, by the time they were moved, hadn't three of the buggers gone missing? He'd nearly died.

Aideen was wide-eyed. "What happened?"

"I was round the roads on my push bike for hours afterwards. And in the heel of the hunt they came home on their own. I never left a gate unchecked after that day anyway. And fair play to my dad, he never rubbed the lesson in." That was the way with Paddy, he'd told her. "He was hard enough, but you couldn't call him a bully. And when he saw the state of me that day, he knew he'd no need to say more. I'd say my pride was hurt more than anything. The ewes wouldn't have gone far, anyway, and there's not much traffic round here."

Aideen had said that was why she liked the farm. It was quiet and you'd love to be surrounded by green fields.

When they'd got to the hill field the cows were waiting. Bid brought them round and Aideen got off the Vespa to shut the gate. She hopped back on in her muddy wellies as Conor turned in the road and began to follow the cows. Bid wove to and fro behind the lot of them, twitching at their heels and urging them home, as if she was the one in charge. Conor had steered past the plodding beasts as they came down to the farmyard. Usually, he'd dump the bike by the ditch and go to let them in; he couldn't leave the yard gate open lately because Dom Byrne was forever shifting sheep up and down the road. But, before he could park the bike, didn't Aideen jump off it a second time and go over to do the gate. You'd think she might be afraid of the cows when she wasn't used to being close to them and one that had brushed by her was all covered in muck round the back. But not a bother on her. She'd even spread her arms and turned a divil that was making for the ditch. Then she'd held back till Conor had got them through to the shed for the milking, before she'd closed the gate and gone up to the house.

The inside of the jeweler's in Carrick was a bit hushed and gloomy, but the guy in the suit at the counter was nice enough. Conor came out and told him straight what he wanted. He'd have bought Aideen the moon and the stars if he had the option, but the money wasn't there and that was that. Anyway, his mum was right, they ought to be thinking of finding a place together, so the more they saved the better, from that point of view. He asked about the rings that he'd seen online and the guy sort of raised an eyebrow. They were made by the owner's father, he said, and they wouldn't be what you'd call classic. But Conor stuck to his guns, so your man went off to get them. By the looks of things they were kept in some cupboard out the back while the classic stuff—which meant diamonds in platinum settings—was all laid out on velvet in the front.

As soon as the guy in the suit disappeared, Conor took out the tea light. He'd worried for days about how he'd size the engagement ring, when the idea of using a tea light had hit him like a bolt from the blue. Aideen was a great one for creating an atmosphere when they went back to her bedroom. Not that either of them needed much encouragement when they got there, but he loved the way she'd have candles up on the bookshelf and tea lights on the dressing table reflected in the mirror. The bowl she kept in front of the mirror was made of cut glass and silver and the little lights flickered off that as well; she'd told him her gran just used it as an ornament, but she had it full of bracelets and rings.

In the beginning he'd thought he'd sneak a ring from the bowl and take it with him to Carrick: but he wasn't sure how long it would be before they'd be back in the bedroom and if she found a ring had gone missing it might spoil the surprise. So he'd planned the whole thing out as if he was 007, and left the wine down in the fridge when they'd gone upstairs with the glasses. Then he'd whipped off his clothes and stuck them on a chair and got into bed before her, so she'd been the one who'd have to go back downstairs. As soon as she was out of the room, he'd shot over and grabbed a tea light, but the thing was roasting hot and burned his hand. Then, when he tried to get it out of the little tin yoke it came in, the liquid wax splashed up and hit him on the tit. It hurt like hell and even James Bond would probably have let a roar out of him. But he'd kept his cool and managed to get the tea light out of the tin yoke. Then he'd turned it over and taken an impression of a ring. The wax had cooled real quick so it didn't get smudged or anything, so he chucked the ring back in the bowl and stuck the tea light under his clothes on the chair. He was about to make a leap for the bed when he saw the tin yoke still there on the dressing table. So he'd doubled back and had it crushed in his hand when Aideen came in with the wine. She looked a bit surprised to see him standing stark naked in front of her mirror, but he'd grabbed her quickly and kissed her, and carried it off with an air.

Now he held out the tea light to the guy who'd come back with the rings. Your man looked a bit sniffy but he got the idea. He took the dimension of the impression with a ruler and said it was a standard size. Then he put a tray of rings on the counter and swung a lamp round so Conor could see them. All the rings were made in the same red gold. The guy said the stones were gemstones, and he kind of curled his lip. Amethysts, he said, and garnets, and citrines that Conor first thought were amber—though, looking through them, he found one as pale as a lemon. Some of the stones were faceted like Aideen's cut-glass bowl. Others were just polished. The garnets were red, like rubies, and the amethysts were violet, and there was one, called agate, that looked like an emerald. Conor reached out to pick it up, thinking of how Aideen had said she liked green fields. And then, at the back of the tray, he saw another ring. He lifted it and felt the weight in his hand. The deep-blue stone was set in a round, gold rim that held it like the tin yoke had held the tea light. It was polished smooth, but when you moved it you could see gold flecks running through it.

It was lapis lazuli. And it was perfect.

40

Hanna ran up the steps to the County Library, carrying the keys to the van. It had been another sunny day and even the back roads were dotted with rental cars and walkers. The crops in the fields were beginning to ripen and, with the tourist season in full swing, the lines for the mobile library were getting shorter every week. Knowing the rhythm of her neighbors' year, a lot of the books she carried now came from the children's collection; they were a boon to mothers whose kids were becoming bored by the long summer holiday.

Having left the keys at the reception desk, she dug in her bag for the swipe card that gave access to the Staff Only corridor. Beyond the security door, and below in the basement, was a warren of storerooms for material that wasn't on public display. As always when she came to the County Library, she found herself feeling guilty. Had the campaign to save her own library not been successful, this could have been a state-of-the-art building instead of a slightly shabby one with an inconvenient layout and a lack of space. Yet few, if any, of her colleagues seemed to blame her. In the end, even people whose working conditions would have been improved by the centralization of the county's library services had recognized that the alternative proposal made a lot more sense. Not only had Lissbeg Library and the county's mobile library service been saved, but wider investment in the whole peninsula had proved better for everyone. In fact, when the dust had settled and the banners had been put away, more than one of Hanna's colleagues had sidled up to her and said that they'd supported her campaign. None of them had said it openly, but that was hardly surprising; unlike her, they still had to work in close proximity to Tim.

She herself now saw as little of Tim as she could. Of course there were meetings and social occasions when they couldn't avoid each other. But, despite his continued animosity, he was no longer a threat. Even though it was housed in Lissbeg, the psalter had brought him kudos; and, judging by his behavior at the exhibition opening, he'd settled for basking in that. All the same, Hanna was glad that, by this time of the evening, he was unlikely to be at work. He was a great man for end-of-day, off-site meetings that allowed him to combine library business with drinks in his favorite bar.

As she approached the staff-only door, it was opened from inside and she found herself face to face with Brian Morton. She stopped awkwardly on the threshold, intensely aware that her colleague at the reception desk could see them. She and Brian hadn't been in touch since the day on the mountain that had ended in painful silence. They had walked back to the car carrying the debris of their picnic, and nodded goodbye without even a peck on the cheek.

Now he seemed unfazed, even pleased to see her. Standing in the doorway, he explained that he'd been going through the county records. "I'm supposed to be advising a planning committee and I wanted to check something out."

"Can't you get all that digitally these days?"

"Should do, but half of it isn't available. You know yourself what digitization costs."

She did. The library's local history collection had recently been augmented by material from the 1920s and 1930s, but most of it was still down in the basement in boxes, and none of it was likely to be digitized for some time. That was what she'd come here to look at; along with the de Lancy photographs, it might yield information about Maggie's dad and Liam.

As Brian stepped back to let her pass, she hesitated. "You don't want a cup of tea, do you? We could go down to the canteen."

It wasn't a canteen really, though that's what it said on the door; it was just a room with tables and a coffee machine where the library staff went on their breaks. There was a water cooler, and a kettle on a table in the corner, and a fridge where people put salad pots or sandwiches they'd brought in to have for their lunch.

Hanna led the way down the corridor. When she'd left Brian in the parking lot at the foot of Knockinver, she'd worried that perhaps their brief rapprochement was over. Maybe he'd disappear again as he'd done before. And if he did, she couldn't blame him. Ever since the night of Jazz's accident she'd felt she'd been behaving like a character in a Georgette Heyer novel, leading him on and then smacking his wrist with her fan. It wasn't what she'd wanted, but nor had she wanted to fall into bed with him just on the rebound from Malcolm. Besides, she felt her emotional energy ought to be saved for Jazz; how could she forgive herself if, by chasing her own happiness, she made matters worse for her daughter? What right did she have to move on from her divorce while the child whose life it had turned upside down was still struggling with the fallout?

The room was stuffy and a bit dingy but Brian slumped cheerfully onto an orange plastic chair.

"So tell me what you're here looking for. Something to do with work?"

Over tea she told him about her conversation with Fury. "I don't know why I hadn't realized that Maggie's brother was my dad's father."

"What, you never knew your grandad?"

"God no, he died when my dad was only a toddler. And his wife wasn't long after him. Dad was raised by a cousin who came in to run the post office."

She could remember Tom telling Jazz about it years ago, on a summer visit to Finfarran; there'd been an envelope of old photographs he'd produced one day on the beach. A shabby, crumpled envelope that might once have held a birthday card.

"I'd never seen it myself when I was small. There may have been a photo of Liam in there but I don't remember. Well, there must have been. A wedding shot or something."

A line from the diary flashed through Hanna's mind. *John Joe Quinn, the editor of the* Inquirer, *got the word last year to destroy all photos of the lads out on the hills.*

She sipped her tea thoughtfully. She had forgotten

that until now. Maybe she wouldn't find anything down in the boxes in the basement. It was a long shot at best.

"What happened to your dad's envelope?"

"Probably stuck in some drawer in my mother's bungalow." She hadn't even considered asking Mary, not wanting to open that particular can of worms. Now she shrugged. "It's a perfect metaphor. There are masses of photos of her people and practically none of his. They must have been self-effacing. Like himself."

But in Liam's case, of course, there could have been another reason. If he'd gone on, as so many did, to fight in the Civil War, his instinct afterward might have been to keep a low profile. He had died in the 1940s when those emotional and political wounds were still raw. Hanna remembered what she'd told herself when she'd sat on the bench with Fury, that old hatreds and alliances conspire to conceal the past.

Brian put his mug down, stood up and held out his hand. "Let's go and explore together, you've got me interested now."

But there was nothing. The material in the boxes, which ranged from the turn of the twentieth century to the 1930s, had been roughly sorted by year. In the run-up to the centenary of Ireland's Easter Rising, Tim had put out several calls on local radio for anything relating to 1916 or to the founding of the State. There were newspaper cuttings and letters, obituaries and applications for military pensions. The library staff had organized a series of oral memory sessions at which older people made recordings that kids from the local schools had later transcribed. It was all there in the boxes, and all fascinating, but none of it mentioned Liam.

Working their way through the decades, Hanna and Brian noticed there was very little about the Civil War years in which old comrades had fought and died over the terms of the treaty agreed with Britain at the end of the War of Independence. As Fury had pointed out to her, some memories were tainted with too much bad blood.

Eventually, Hanna sat back hopelessly. Seeing her disappointment, Brian reached out and gave her a hug. For a moment she stiffened but then she leaned against him, smelling the cotton fabric of his shirt. Seconds later she pulled away, reminding herself that she wanted to see the de Lancy collection upstairs.

Up in the public area, having summoned the necessary step stool and keys to the locked bookcases, she carried the Victorian albums to a desk. They, too, yielded nothing she had hoped for. There were pictures of servants all right, solemn and respectful and lined up in rows, just as she had expected. Several groups included little boys, aproned or holding garden tools. But few of the photos were dated and none came with lists of names. Even those of the gentry were anonymous. Like any other family, the de Lancys seemed to have failed to anticipate a time when the beauty in the bustle or the tall man with the shotgun would no longer be instantly recognizable as Aunt Flo or Cousin Jim.

Brian, who'd helped to carry the albums, looked at them over her shoulder. Eventually Hanna turned and urged him to go. "This is completely pointless and I've interrupted your work."

"You haven't. I hadn't intended to go back to the office. I was planning to walk round to The Royal Vic."

"God, you're as bad as Tim Slattery!"

"No, I'm not. I didn't fancy cooking tonight, so I thought I'd get supper there."

He looked down at her troubled expression. "What was the big deal about finding a photograph?"

"Oh, I don't know. I think I just got diverted by the thought of seeing his face."

"Liam's? Or the Victorian boot-boy's?"

"Either. Both. Someone linked directly to my father. Maybe I thought they'd bring me closer to him."

"But what about Maggie?"

It was a fair question and, now that he'd asked it, she feared that she had the answer. Like Mary Casey, she'd been thrusting Maggie aside to get at Tom. Perhaps there was more of her mother in her than she'd ever cared to admit.

Brian lifted a couple of albums and moved toward the bookcase. Did she want to come with him to the hotel, he asked, and grab a steak in the Grill?

Hanna shook her head. "I'd love to. Really. But I told Jazz I'd be home tonight and she might drop in."

He walked over, stepped on the stool, and replaced the albums on the shelf. Then, turning round, he looked down at her quizzically. "I don't need to say it, do I?"

"I don't know what you mean."

"Yes, you do. I was going to inquire if you ever took time for yourself."

"You mean time for you."

"I mean time for us."

And there they were, back again, exactly where they'd been last time. It was idiotic to get angry, so Hanna laughed.

There was a pause in which they both said nothing. Then Brian reached out and touched her face with his hand. "You're right, you know—I do mean time for me. Which is a bugger because I swore to myself that I wouldn't be one of your projects."

This time Hanna really didn't know what he meant.

He came back and picked up the last of the albums. "What was it the nun in the anorak said? Sister Michael?"

"That I'm useless at making up my mind."

"Yes. I remember. But that's not how I see you. I see someone so wedded to guilt that she doesn't know how to let go."

She opened her mouth but, before she could speak, he interrupted her. "And, seriously, Hanna, I don't want to be yet another case you feel bad about. Spare me the indignity of that."

41

Ameena met Conor in the vestibule when she arrived for her afternoon shift. As soon as he saw
her, he told her she had a rare spring in her step.

"Have I? It's a gorgeous sunny day."

In the shop she climbed on a chair and opened a
window. When she'd done that, she went back to the till
and looked around happily. Just as she'd thought from
the beginning, this was a great place to work. The design of the shop was stylish and the things on sale were
cool. It was great, too, that her mum had got used to
her working, and that she loved working in the nuns'
garden herself. Like Ameena in the shop, she'd begun
with just a few sessions but now she was volunteering
in the garden four days a week. Smiling at a customer
who was approaching the till, Ameena told herself life

was utterly brilliant. No wonder Conor had said she'd a spring in her step. Though, actually, it wasn't just the shop that was making her feel fizzy and light-headed, it was the fact that tonight she'd be going on a real date with Lar.

He was the last person on earth that she'd thought she'd fancy. When they'd fixed to go out with the rest of the class on the night their exams were over, they'd both just seen it as convenient—he had just broken up with his girlfriend and she wanted a date that didn't drink. She'd gone to meet him in town wearing Nani's green-and-silver sari and, though all the other guys were just casual, Lar had arrived in what looked like his grandad's tux. At first she'd thought he'd imagined they were going to a debs dance, but then she realized he was wearing it for a laugh. And for a while that night she'd been pretty annoyed because it seemed like the joke was on her. But actually it was just his sense of humor; he was witty and sharp and charming and really intelligent. And soon his crooked mouth and his dodgy tux hadn't mattered at all.

She'd already started to fall for him by the time the evening was over, and he hadn't even kissed her goodnight. The next day she'd told herself that he was an awful eejit and for several weeks she'd managed to believe her own lie. And then, out of nowhere, he'd turned up in the gift shop and asked if she fancied lunch. Even that day there'd been nothing you'd call romantic; they'd eaten quiche on the bench by the flowery horse trough and afterward he'd just wandered off with a wave. But last night he'd phoned her when she'd been sitting at home watching TV, and announced that he'd been working himself up to asking her out on a date.

"So, for God's sake, don't go getting all coy or say that I've missed my chance. Honestly, Ameena, I feel like a total plank. Are you up for it? I'll come round at eight."

He hadn't been charming, or even witty, yet she'd been an absolute walkover. She'd never been more excited in all her life.

Conor was back from his lunch break in time for Hanna to get ready for the book club. There had been a message from Ameena saying she'd love to keep on with the club but she couldn't fit it in around her work. Hanna had smiled when she saw it; something had told her after the last session that Ameena wouldn't be back. And the truth was that the club had its own dynamic; trying to change it by injecting new blood had never been likely to work.

It was Oliver's turn to choose a book and, to Hanna's relief, he'd come up with something sane, though he'd used his usual method of selection. It was Seamus Heaney's second poetry collection, *Door into the Dark*.

"I'm telling you, Miss Casey, I spotted it from the far side of the road. I knew it'd be a great book altogether, and I was right."

With a flourish, he'd thrust a Faber paperback under Hanna's nose. The cover was sparsely designed in red, black, and white, with a line drawing of an anvil immediately under the title.

"Look at that there now for a real book, Miss Casey. That's a man there now with a great eye. Just that one image of an anvil, with the red line going round. You'd feel the very weight of it in the drawing. And the poems he wrote inside are just as good."

It had seemed easiest not to challenge his assumption that Heaney designed his own book covers, so Hanna had just nodded and noted his choice. Later on, when she'd ordered up copies of *Door into the Dark* through the inter-library loan system, she'd realized in dismay that none of them was the edition admired by Oliver. And now, to make things worse, Susan arrived armed with her own copy, a prized Faber first edition with no image on the cover at all.

Oliver's brow furrowed at the sight of it. The colors,

he said, might well be the same but begob you'd miss the anvil. The anvil was the point. The thing that mattered. He opened his copy at the poem called "The Forge." As everyone else followed suit, Hanna told herself that at least they'd got on to the text. Oliver whacked the poem with the back of his knuckles. This, he said, was what the whole book was about. A young lad looking into a forge. And the sound of the hammer on the anvil. The anvil, mark you. That was the vital image. Heaney compared it to a unicorn, of all things. And it was a fair enough description, though Oliver didn't much like it himself. He liked the next bit better, where it's called "square" and "immovable." Because that's what you'd find an actual anvil was. Square, bar the pointy bit, which might or might not cause you to think of a unicorn. And definitely immovable. You'd have a hard time trying to lift one anyway. "Immovable" was what poets called a right word.

Susan said there were over thirty other poems in the collection. So you couldn't just announce that the book was all about an anvil.

Oliver crowed in derision. Then why, he demanded triumphantly, had yer man put an anvil on his cover? And why had he called the collection *Door into the Dark*? He could have called it *My Second Poetry Collection*. But he didn't. Not at all, of course he didn't. He was tipping you the wink. And he'd want to give you a steer somehow. Because he had to stick all the others in to justify the price.

As Susan, the owner of a first edition, waded into battle, Hanna abandoned hope and let her own mind slip away.

September 23rd, 1920

Dad never brought me to the forge when the horse wanted shoeing. It was a man's place always. Mam said they used to idle time away, standing with their backs to the door. I asked James about that when we were saving the turf. He laughed at me. Dad laughed at Mam as well. He said there was business done at the forge door and many a bargain made.

A forge is always built at a crossroads near to wood and water. Wood for the fire and water to quench the heat. James said there was healing in the water where the smith cooled his irons. He said an apprentice wouldn't be let shoe a horse until he could lift the anvil. I asked if he could lift one himself and he laughed again. He said men had less strength in their arms these days than they used to have, and less strength in their souls to confront temptation. It was pitch black inside a forge, he

said, but the fire would sear your eyeballs. He said
the sound of the hammer on the anvil was like the
sound of a church bell.

The entry had ended there. By the next, written weeks later, Maggie had left Mrs. Carr's. It was a catalogue of complaint about the meanness of her employer, who had found her hoarding food and thrown her out. There was no return to the story of the smith who had come to save turf for her mother, and no mention of Liam except to say that she'd heard he was safe. She was working in a factory and she didn't like the noise there. She wanted to go home but she couldn't; and there was no explanation why.

When the book club left the library, the battle was still raging. Oliver and Susan were giving each other no quarter, though Hanna noticed that, much like herself, Darina and Nell had tuned out. As she tidied up the Reading Room, she reflected that at least the row had been sparked by the book they were meant to be discussing. And that was a vast improvement on previous weeks.

Conor was the last to leave the library. Miss Casey had hurried off soon after the book club was over, which was fine by him because he was hoping to see Aideen after work. He'd lock the place up when everyone was gone and saunter over casually, and if he caught her he'd take her somewhere and produce the ring. This morning he'd told himself firmly that it was high time he got on with it. He'd been carrying it round for more than a week, waiting for the perfect occasion, but at this rate they'd both be drawing their pensions before they ever got engaged.

On the stroke of five thirty Ameena stuck her head in. She'd locked up in the gift shop, she said, and she wasn't working tomorrow. So she'd see him next time she was in. As soon as she'd gone, Conor went through the exhibition space to have a quick look at the shop. If anything at all wasn't properly shut the alarm went mad when you set it, so he always checked the doors and windows before closing the place up. Ameena had always been totally reliable, but it never hurt to make sure.

Seconds later, having grabbed Jimbo in the courtyard and told him to watch the library, he was charging down Broad Street after her. She'd been going at a great pace, and when he caught her by the arm he made her jump.

"What is it? Did I forget something?"

Conor said that yes, actually, she did. "It's no big deal at all because I shut it, but one of the windows was open in the shop."

Her hand flew to her mouth. "No! I am *so* sorry! Was it a top one? It was really hot in there and I opened it when I came in."

"Listen, it doesn't matter a damn, it's fine, I always check the whole place anyway. I just thought that you might remember this evening and get in a flap."

Next thing he knew, she'd flung her arms around him and, caught off balance, he lurched sideways and grabbed her round the waist. When they righted themselves, they were both giggling like eejits and, before she turned away, she pecked him on the cheek. Sure as fate, she said, if he hadn't bothered to find her, she'd have remembered the window halfway through her date.

Conor turned away, rubbing his cheek where she'd kissed him. Through the moving traffic he could see Aideen standing on the pavement outside the deli. Beaming happily at the sight of her, he bounded across the road.

42

Brian chose the sepia option and the sunlight on Hanna's face turned to amber and umber. Then he clicked CANCEL and watched her hair and eyes come to life again, and the heather behind her turn to amethyst and gold. For a moment he stared at the screen doing nothing. Then, with the slightest pressure of his hand, the image changed to black and white.

Pushing his chair away from the desk he went to the fridge and got himself a beer before taking a sketch pad and a box of charcoal and going out onto the balcony. His flat faced west and the setting sun was still warm on the bench by the rail. Settling himself in a corner with his back against the wall, he opened the beer, turned a page and selected a stick of charcoal. The first sweep of charcoal on paper captured the turn of her head.

Not picking up the phone and calling Hanna was turning out to be the hardest thing he'd ever done. But he knew that he mustn't. What he'd told her in the nuns' garden was true—for six months after he'd driven her home from the hospital, he'd kept his distance simply because he hadn't known how to approach her. The parting had been too complicated. Had he crossed the threshold that night, he knew they'd have ended up in bed; and at the time she had been so shocked and exhausted he'd feared she'd regret it later. But though he had walked away then, he'd never intended not to come back. Now it was different. A new realization had come to him when he'd taken her photo on the mountain, and it had crystallized on the day that they'd met again in the library in Carrick. For both their sakes, Hanna was going to have to make a decision. The next move was hers, and hers alone.

Her face was emerging now on the paper before him, the wide-set eyes, the broad forehead and the strands of dark hair blown by the wind. He had seen her appear to age ten years overnight when Jazz had her accident, and watched her face soften over the last months as newfound pleasures in her job, her house, and her place in the community had combined to make her relax. Summer sun had tanned her face and the hours she'd spent working in her garden had seemed to loosen her limbs.

Smudging the little wrinkles round her eyes with his thumb, he sketched in her straight, uncompromising eyebrows, and unconsciously added the crease that appeared between them whenever she was troubled. Reaching for a swig of beer, he sat back and considered the face in his drawing. It wasn't the open, laughing expression he'd caught in the photo on the mountain: it was the grave, thoughtful Hanna that he'd first learned to love.

With the beer can in his hand, he rested his eyes on the horizon. Every evening as he sat here, he was conscious of her distant presence. Only a few miles away she was probably working in her garden or sitting on her bench above the ocean drinking a glass of wine. Sometimes he wondered if she thought about him at all. And ever since that night at the exhibition opening, he'd flinched at the thought of how much she might think about Malcolm. It wasn't the ex-husband's Armani suits or that carefully cultivated ambassadorial air that bothered him. Well, not much. It was the fact that Hanna and Malcolm shared a past that no outsider could ever access, and the certainty that Hanna's focus on Jazz would always keep Malcolm on her mind.

Restlessly, Brian turned again to his drawing, sketching the outline of a necklace around her neck. It was the silver torc set with the oblong of amber that she'd worn on the night that they'd talked in the nuns' garden. For a moment the charcoal faltered and, with a grin, he realized that another image had formed between his brain and his hand. It was the dumpy little nun in the gray anorak who'd said that Hanna was the world's worst when it came to making up her mind. The chances were, he told himself, that he wasn't alone when it came to feeling frustrated; Hanna was probably suffering as well. But that didn't make his own state of mind any easier, or lessen the sense of humiliation he felt when people like Conor McCarthy shot him a knowing glance. The truth was that he, too, hated the thought of being looked at. He had come to Finfarran after his wife's death to escape from sympathetic eyes.

Charcoal on paper couldn't achieve the sheen of amber and silver. He returned to Hanna's face, which was nothing like Sandra's. Her grave expression had nothing of Sandra's brilliance and the silver threads in her dark hair made his wife's memory seem unnaturally young. But then she *had* been young—ten years younger than he was—and fragile as a fledgling bird by the time she died. And now here was Hanna, very different and nearly five years his senior, with her solid grace and her square hands on which she wore no rings.

Her hands with their unvarnished nails had been the first thing that attracted him, along with the resolute set of her shoulders and the crease between her eyebrows that he'd wanted to smooth away.

The sketch had reached that dangerous stage at which adding anything more would surely spoil it. It was good. Somewhere behind the wary eyes he had now caught the sense of freedom and laughter he'd seen when he'd taken her photo. Carrying his sketch pad, Brian walked back to his desk. The black-and-white image of Hanna on the screen looked up at him, frozen in time with a hand raised to her hair. Reaching for the touchpad, he clicked back to the first of the two shots he'd taken that day on the mountain. He had turned away from the ocean and captured a moment of total stillness, her face composed and attentive and her eyes closed. The click of the camera's shutter had jerked them open. Somewhere above them a lark had been singing and far below on the beaches there were waves like turquoise silk.

Aware that his own eyes were pricking with tears, Brian slammed the laptop. Then, tearing his sketch from the pad, he went to the fridge for another drink. Later, having eaten and made himself coffee, he found a knife and cut a mount for the drawing, using a piece of gray card that matched the color of the paint on Hanna's windows. Later still, having sprayed it with fixative, he placed it between two layers of corrugated cardboard, taped them together, wrapped them in brown paper and tied the parcel with string. He had almost written her name and address when he realized that he mustn't. For the sake of them both, the next move had to be hers.

43

Jazz drove as far as the point from which she could see the turnoff to the main road and then drew in to the entrance to a country road. The grass in the narrow lane that snaked away between the fields was knee high and the hedges that bounded it were shaggy with summer growth. Clearly no animals or farm vehicle had taken it for weeks so, knowing her car wouldn't be in anyone's way, she parked it tight against the hedge and set out to walk the last mile to the bungalow.

Being a pedestrian on the main road in high season wasn't pleasant or relaxing but, although her confidence had improved, she still couldn't face the drive. Life really was better, though. Much better. And it was all due to Gunther. At first he'd been iffy about the whole idea of secrecy and, in retrospect, she'd wished that she'd never used that word. Secrecy sounded dodgy. What she'd meant was something else. Privacy. Space to work things out. No one could be expected to build up confidence in front of an anxious audience. She knew perfectly well that Mum and the grannies were worried. They could tell that something was wrong, though they didn't know what. But she didn't want them fussing around, trying to help her with her driving, and the thought of trying to articulate her nightmares to anyone struck her dumb. Even Gunther knew nothing about the nightmares. That wasn't because she didn't trust him. On the contrary, she literally trusted him with her life.

He was calm and endlessly patient but he told it like it was; she was shaken, he said, but she mustn't let that define her, all that she needed to do was regain her nerve. Driving the car with him at her side, there were times when it seemed to Jazz that she was like Holly that day in the woodshed, frightened but utterly confident in his strength. It was funny that she liked that. She hated the idea of Susan coming over all mumsy, which she certainly would if she knew what was going on. Susan's brisk effectiveness would make you feel twice as inadequate. Gunther would never lie to you or make you feel stupid and lost.

They'd chosen the less scenic roads because they were less traveled. Then, as her confidence mounted, she'd agreed to try the tourist routes, closer to the beaches and cliffs. Gunther had grinned and told her that sharing a road with rental-car drivers was the best kind of challenge. "Most of them will probably be more nervous than you."

In one way that was terrifying but in another she found it reassuring. And anyway, she knew he would never let her come to harm. Once, she was behind a tourist who clearly hadn't a clue how wide his car was, and had probably never driven on the left. After crawling along at a snail's pace, clinging to the ditches, the driver had suddenly accelerated and swerved across in front of her for no apparent reason. Her instinct had been to scream and cover her eyes but, with Gunther beside her, she'd managed to take appropriate, sensible action; and a few minutes later, when she found a place to pull in, she was relatively calm. It was a psychological turning point. Since then she'd had fewer nightmares and whole hours in the car might pass with no sensation of panic. Gunther had said yesterday that soon she'd be driving the main road. Now, walking steadily toward Nan's bungalow, Jazz felt that he was right.

Louisa closed the book she was reading. The scent of the flowers in the pots outside the open window was beautiful and the comfortable chair she and Mary had

carried in from the living room had turned her bedroom into a pleasant retreat. Mary, she knew, felt the
same about her own bedroom. And, indeed, about her
kitchen, which was an eccentric mix of 1980s state-
of-the-art fitments, a huge fridge flanked by a plastic
altar to Padre Pio, and an oversized pine dresser that
displayed her collection of crockery. The kitchen had
rather taken Louisa's breath away at first, but it was
functional and surprisingly pleasant to work in. And, in
typical Mary style, the lines had been drawn at the out-
set. She had declared that she and Louisa were well past
the age of behaving like kids in a flat-share. "You're a
welcome guest and I'm glad to have you, but this house
is mine and not yours."

But, despite her manner, Mary was not unimagina-
tive and, though she frequently chose to ignore them,
she was shrewdly aware of other people's needs. In fact
Louisa had come to admire her: they respected each
other's private space and took pleasure in each other's
company and, over the past few weeks, had fallen into a
pleasant habit of sharing the tasks of cooking and cleaning the house. It hadn't taken long for Louisa to see that,
under the aggression and apparent eccentricity, Mary
was enduring widowhood with remarkable levels of re-
silience. Or that, like everyone her age who lived alone,
she was facing a daunting future.

Now, laying her book on the windowsill, Louisa got up and moved to look out at the garden. She had been sitting down for an hour and her hip was stiff. In purely practical terms, she thought, the elderly have good reasons to be selfish; our strength needs to be hoarded not only to deal with grief, disappointment, and apprehension but with the minor physical aches and pains that are part of growing old.

When Louisa joined her in the kitchen Mary was icing a cake. Neither of them had talked much about their concern for their granddaughter, but each had tried on different occasions to sit down and chat with Jazz. Both had failed. It was obvious that she was avoiding being alone with either of them, and that, Mary announced now, boded no good at all. "I tell you, the trouble with that child is she's far too like her mother!"

She piped parallel lines of chocolate over vanilla icing, expertly using a fork to feather the result. It was Jazz's favorite sponge cake, layered with jam made from garden blackcurrants. Tom had planted them years ago and they still produced a great crop under the old net curtains he'd always spread over the fruiting bushes to keep off the birds.

With an approving nod Mary watched Louisa begin the washing up—they were wholly in agreement on the foolishness of using the dishwasher for the bowl and the few bits of cutlery it took to make a cake. The cake tins were already there in the sink. They were the easiest thing in the world to wash if you soaked them first. Wasn't it an awful shame that Louisa's son hadn't taken after his mother? It was hard to believe that a woman like her had raised a pup like Malcolm, though, in fairness, there was plenty about Hanna-Mariah she wouldn't want blamed on herself.

As she moved the cake from the wire rack to a platter she told herself there was a fair bit of Malcolm in poor Jazz, too. Secretive like her father and headstrong like her mother, though God knew she had a loving heart. It was a bad mix if you were young and troubled. And here was the poor child coming over today because she was too good at the bottom of it all to keep refusing her grannies, and too sly not to grab the chance of avoiding a tête-à-tête. That was what Louisa had said anyway when Jazz had sent the text to her.

"She's banking on our not ganging up on her. And I think she's right, I think it would be too much."

Much as it went against the grain, Mary had to agree. They'd just give Jazz tea and get her to sit in the garden; you couldn't force her confidence and a rest would do her good. Mary scattered a few blackcurrants round the cake for decoration. If it had been down to her, she'd probably have tackled Jazz head-on now she had a chance. But Louisa was right and, to be fair to her, she hadn't hammered home her point. She'd often make a statement and leave it so, and allow you to come round to it; and somehow she never made you feel she was treating you like a fool.

At least it'd be good to see Jazz again and get a decent meal inside her. Earlier on, Louisa had made a grand plate of different sandwiches—the paté and smoked salmon that Jazz liked these days, and the egg and tomato with salad cream ones that she'd loved when she was a child. Mary had done sausage rolls as well, the kind Tom and Jazz had had when they used to come home from swimming; the secret was to put mustard into the mix. The table was laid with the tea set she kept for state occasions. She'd worried that that might be going too far, so she hadn't put down a tablecloth. And she'd used the ordinary jug for the milk, which toned things down a bit.

Now she glanced at Louisa, who was hanging up the tea towel. Mentally, she knew, they both had their fingers crossed.

But in the end they'd hardly sat down to the table when Jazz announced that she only had an hour.

"Susan's nipping out to get a haircut, so I said I'd be back to help Gunther put Holly to bed."

Mary bristled immediately, not liking the sound of that. She could see Louisa trying to signal caution, but the thought of Jazz being treated like a skivvy was too much. Wasn't she at the forge to work in the guesthouse, not to be used as a babysitter? "Do you know what it is, girl, you'd want to be careful and watch your back! God knows what they'll have you doing next if you put up with that class of nonsense. Sit down there and don't move at all till the proper time for your shift!"

The moment she'd spoken, she knew that she'd made a mistake. Jazz didn't argue, but the rest of the meal was stilted and before the hour was half over she'd pushed her plate away and checked her watch. Louisa tried to keep things going by chatting about the garden, but Mary could have told her it wouldn't work. This was Hanna all over again, ready to bolt whenever she felt cornered.

After another awkward ten minutes Jazz stood up decisively and kissed them both on the cheek. "It's been lovely. Really. I've really loved seeing you."

And then off with her so fast that you'd think the hounds of hell were behind her. And her two grannies left on the doorstep, waving like a couple of fools.

Back in the kitchen Mary looked at the table. The dish of sausage rolls was untouched and the grand cake uneaten. With her hands shaking, she gathered the plates and looked in distress at Louisa. What was going on there at the forge anyway? And why couldn't a grown man put his child to bed on his own?

44

The irritated woman from the pharmacy must have spoken several times before Conor heard her. He only realized she was there when she rapped sharply on the desk and asked if he was deaf. She had a pointy nose and a ghastly orange blouse on her that made her look like a pumpkin, and she was one of those eejits who came in looking for a "nice book." God alone knew what they thought a nice book was or why they couldn't go find one themselves on the shelves. And this woman belonged to a particular subsection of eejitry because what she wanted was a nice book for her husband who, if he was daft enough to marry the likes of her, must be pretty stupid, too.

Pulling himself together, Conor asked politely what kind of books her husband liked.

"Oh God, I don't know. He never seems to read anything I get for him. Coming in here on his behalf is a sheer waste of time."

Controlling himself with an effort, Conor asked what his hobbies were.

The woman looked at him disdainfully. "He doesn't have hobbies. He's a dentist."

Wearily Conor got up from the desk and led her toward the LATEST READING trolley. Perhaps, he suggested, she might find something here. Then, before she could open her beak again, he thrust a book into her hand and retreated down the room into the kitchen. Miss Casey didn't like him to leave the desk unattended but if he had to cope with any more from the pumpkin he might just explode. What in the name of God had happened with Aideen? Miserably, he took out his phone and looked at her last text.

stop calling n coming round stop bothering bríd n me stop it

Slumping against the work surface, Conor absently ate a custard cream. Nothing made sense to him anymore and everything had gone wrong.

It had begun the evening he'd crossed the road planning to make his proposal. Now, for the hundredth time, he tried to remember what had happened. He'd left Ameena on the pavement after telling her he'd shut the window. He'd seen Aideen standing outside the deli. She was looking great in a pink skirt and a little yellow t-shirt. He'd dodged across the road as far as the horse trough. Then a truck loaded with silage bales had cut her from his view. But she was still there when it passed and he'd run over to join her. He hadn't noticed at the time but, thinking back, he supposed she looked kind of pale.

He hadn't had a proper night's sleep since and, lying awake in the small hours, he'd remembered, too, that she was sort of tense and weird when he'd kissed her. Unyielding, that was the word. Anyway, whatever way she was, she'd been strange for the rest of the evening. He'd planned to take her up on the cliffs and maybe propose to her there. Now, eating another custard cream, he fumbled sadly in his pocket for the engagement ring; the box was lined with pleated satin like a coffin and the blue stone in its red-gold setting was exactly the color of her eyes.

With the way she'd been for the rest of the evening, he'd given up on finding the right moment. Half the time it had seemed to him that she wasn't with him at all. He'd be talking away and suddenly see that her eyes had gone blank. At one point she'd said she wasn't well and he'd asked if she'd got her period. The look she gave him then was something he'd never seen before.

So the whole evening had been really odd and she'd gone home early. And then, somewhere round midnight, he'd got the first text.

Sorry. We r not going2 work. Lets 4get it

It had made no sense at all, so he called her at once. But her phone was off.

Since then, she never seemed to have it on. He'd called and sent texts all night and gone round to her place next morning, but it was no good. He'd tried catching her in the deli, where he could see her through the window, but as soon as he'd reach the door, she'd always be gone. Bríd would be there behind the counter saying she wasn't available, though Conor knew perfectly well she was just inside in the room where they hung the coats. One time he'd gone and stood outside, waiting to catch her when she was going home. It was Bríd who came out.

"Look, would you stop stalking her, Conor, she doesn't want to see you."

Conor knew that he'd looked at her with his jaw hanging down like an idiot. Bríd was a bit pink in the face, but she stood her ground while he gaped at her. Then she said she had nothing else to say and told him to move along.

He'd kept trying ever since, of course, but that had been more than a week ago. At one point he'd sent Aideen a letter asking her to tell him what he'd done. The next day a reply had come in a notelet that had little flowers on it. His heart had leapt when he'd seen it but then, when he opened it up, he couldn't believe his eyes.

If you don't know, there's no point in my telling you.

He'd been standing in the cowshed and he'd roared out like she could hear him. "Holy God Almighty, Aideen, what are you doing to us?!" There she was, going on like someone in a soap opera, and here was he, literally feeling his heart had exploded in his chest.

Now the same feeling swelled up in his throat and he choked on the dry biscuit. As he stood there coughing, the pharmacist tapped on the kitchen door. "I can't quite make up my mind between these as a nice book for a dentist."

She was holding a couple of books in her hand and both of her choices were crazy—*Doctor Zhivago* and Zadie Smith's *White Teeth*.

Conor clenched his hands, saw his knuckles whiten, and wondered if he might kill her. Then he spat biscuit crumbs into the sink and steered her back to the desk.

45

The fennel that had transplanted itself to the end of the house was now almost as high as Hanna's shoulder and the wild foxgloves that clustered at her gate had begun to scatter their purple flowers onto the path. As she came home from work, she broke off a few fennel fronds and carried them indoors. One of the seniors in Knockmore had presented her with a couple of mackerel, which went well with a fennel-flavored stuffing, and tonight she planned to eat one sitting outside. Summer had really set in now and recently she had lugged her garden table, made from the stand of Maggie's sewing machine, as close to her burgeoning rock garden as she could. To her gratification, the herbs did a great job keeping flies at bay. So for the last few weeks she had dined there in happy seclusion, surrounded by pungent lemongrass, mint and basil, and the oilier scents of rosemary and lemon thyme.

Leaving the fennel by the sink and the mackerel in the fridge, she went through to shower and change before starting to cook. Louisa had brought her a present of a bar of soap from London, scented with essential oil, flecked with deep-purple lavender flowers, and beautifully shaped to fit snugly in the hand. The tiny bathroom built by Fury was lit by a sloping window in the roof, through which she could see the sky as she stood in the shower. It was a far cry, she thought, from the tin bathtub used by Maggie, which used to hang on a nail on the back of the old shed door. As a child she'd once asked Maggie where she got hot water to fill it and was jeered at for not knowing it was heated on the fire. Maggie's towels had been threadbare and rough, but all the same they were lovely; she had thrown them out on a bush to dry, where they'd captured the scent of the furze.

As Hanna tied the belt of her kimono after her shower, she told herself that the texture and smell of laundry dried in the sunshine was one of the joys of living here in the house. Mary Casey delighted in her huge washer-dryer that rumbled away each evening in the utility room off her kitchen. But, whenever she could, Hanna followed Maggie's system of drying sheets and clothing on a clothesline and throwing towels over a bush. Now, for old time's sake, she took her towel out to the nearest clump of furze and spread it over the prickly branches and coconut-scented flowers. Even at this time of the evening, the sun and the warm breeze would dry it in no time.

As she turned to go back inside, she saw that her windows wanted cleaning; once again the wind from the ocean had crusted the glass with salt. Looking at the panes, which were shadowed but still translucent, she thought of the frontier cabins with their windows made from marriage certificates greased to let in the light. This time she remembered where she'd read about them. It was in Conrad Richter's trilogy of novels *The Trees, The Fields,* and *The Town.* She'd first found it in London when Jazz was a toddler, and had been gripped by the saga of three generations of the Luckett family who'd emigrated from Pennsylvania to Ohio in the wake of America's Revolutionary War. At the time she'd thought she'd just been entranced by Richter's use of language, and the epic endeavor of this tight-knit family "who followed the woods as some families follow the sea." Now it occurred to her that his heroine, Sayward, was not unlike Maggie Casey. Each was a resolute, observant woman, raised to poverty and hard work, and given to mulish reticence. And both had lived through extraordinary periods of change. Perhaps, on some level, that was why Hanna had been gripped by Richter's novels and read all three back to back. At the close of the third book, she remembered, Sayward, who has lived to a great age, lies on her deathbed with her youngest son sitting beside her. They've never been close, and for years have hardly communicated. Looking at her face, dark and implacable, as if carved out of oak wood, he realizes he's been carrying around so many questions to ask her. But she's already deep in a coma and it's too late.

As Hanna chopped fennel and grated lemon and breadcrumbs to stuff her mackerel, she remembered the secondhand bookshop on the Charing Cross Road where she'd picked up *The Trees*. It was strange that she'd bothered because, in an Oliver way, she'd been underwhelmed by its dust jacket. Though, having read the book, she'd felt it would have taken a Dürer or a Peake to produce the right illustration; the spare evocation of light and space, the intense awareness of the protagonist, and the barefoot family in single file walking through the deep forest. She had no idea where that copy was now; all she could remember was that she'd discarded the dust jacket on her walk home, and that the abstract design on the book's burlap boards had delighted her for years. It was suggestive of a handmade quilt or a linen sampler—the sorts of things that, as Brian had said, rot away with the passage of time.

She hadn't seen or heard from Brian since that day in the County Library and whenever she thought of him, she found herself feeling bereft. And a bit dismayed. Had she really become so used to his forbearance that she assumed he'd just turn up again? Appear in some doorway and smile at her and act like things hadn't gone wrong? If so, she'd been mistaken. The next move was evidently down to her.

With her dinner cooked and eaten and a glass of white wine at her elbow, she moved her chair round to face the sunset and returned to Maggie's book. After the entry dated September 23rd, there were more pages of arbitrary material: shopping lists, records of savings, and carefully transcribed verses from popular songs. Flipping past Gershwin and Irving Berlin, she found pages with strips and corners torn off, as if Maggie had turned to the book if ever she needed an odd scrap of paper. Further on, an advertisement cut from the *Liverpool Daily Post* offered "Lastix Bust Bodices at Highly Competitive Prices." It was attached to the yellowed copybook with a pin that had left rust spots on the page.

The next diary entry had no specific date, just the month and the year.

December 1920

*They're after burning out the center of Cork.
The newspapers here say the lads in the hills have
started mounting reprisals. Lizzie wrote and told
me her brother Seán is dead. She said nothing at
all about Liam and I think that if she'd have heard
something bad she'd have told me. I'm sending bits
of money all the time to Mrs. Donovan but there's
still no word from Mam. I must have sent half a
dozen postcards now and I wonder if they're up
on the mantelpiece. Mrs. D says Mam don't have
the heart to write, but she's glad to be getting the
money. I don't know is that true. I wish to God I
felt I could trust Paud. I wish to God I knew who to
trust of the lot of them. You couldn't be sure.*

Hanna stared across the boundary wall beside her
house. According to Fury, that neighboring field had
belonged to the Donovans, and the house they had
lived in had stood there as well. Both the house and its
owners were gone by the time she herself had been car-
ing for Maggie, though she thought she remembered
ruined buildings there when she was small. Probably
the fallen walls were still to be found beneath the furze.
The Donovans, Fury had told her, had left Finfarran

for America during the Civil War. Maggie had never spoken a word about them and, as a child, Hanna had never thought to ask.

Turning the pages, she realized there was only one more diary entry. The remaining pages contained lists of addresses that looked like potential employers, notes of the times of trains from Liverpool to London, and a hand-drawn sketch of a gravestone with the words "Seán Keogh. RIP."

So Lizzie's brother had died in the war while Liam had survived. Obedient to her self-imposed discipline of reading one entry at a time, Hanna closed the book and focused her eyes on the horizon. Right up until the day she'd died Maggie Casey had clung to her independence while her relatives itched to see her safe in an old people's home. It wasn't just a case of Mary wanting to dispose of an irritant. Hanna knew that Tom, too, had been troubled by his stubborn aunt. In the end it was he who had found her one morning when he'd dropped in to bring her a paper—she'd fallen or had a stroke going down to the well.

Hanna could vaguely remember the whispers going round at the funeral, neighbors agreeing it was the grace of God she'd been found by Tom, not "the child." It was only later that she'd realized they'd been talking about herself. Now, for the first time, she wondered how things might have been if she had found the corpse. Not just for her, but for her parents. Had they never foreseen that possibility when they'd effectively made her Maggie's caregiver? She knew that her father would have blamed himself for giving in to her mother. Would Mary have been able to accept her own share of the blame?

Knocking back the last of her wine, Hanna stood up and shook herself. There was no point in looking back and second-guessing the past. Maggie herself had had an expression for it. "If ifs and ands were pots and pans, there'd be no work for tinkers." And there was no point in apportioning blame either. From one generation to the next the whole world over, most families just got on with things and did the best job they could.

46

The dreams were getting less frequent now and driving was far less frightening. Tonight Jazz was wakeful only because the moonlight was so bright. She had woken from a deep sleep to find it falling straight on her pillow and, getting up, she had gone to look out at the night. Every tree in the forest seemed to be etched with silver. The land below her attic window sloped gently upward to where a deep belt of bracken marked the boundary between the edge of the forest and the field behind the forge. Gunther and Susan had planted apple trees in the field when they'd first bought the property and now, leaning out of the window, Jazz could see little clusters of fruit gleaming on the branches. There was no wind at all.

Recently Holly had taken to demanding a bedtime story. She wanted Jazz to read to her, she said, because Mummy didn't have time.

Susan had pointed out that Jazz was there to help with the guests. "She's not here to go running round after you, so stop pestering her."

Jazz said she didn't mind. She could read something short for Holly while Susan caught up with the emails from Gunther's suppliers. "Would that help? Then one of you could look in and just say goodnight."

Generally it was Gunther who put his head around Holly's door at bedtime. It had been much the same when she herself was small; Mum had read her bedtime stories and Dad had come in and kissed her goodnight. Then they'd gone out of the room together, leaving her feeling safe.

Looking through Holly's bookshelf she'd found a collection of fairy tales. Holly had announced that they were her favorites and, wriggling confidingly into the crook of Jazz's arm, she'd declared in a throaty whisper that the best stories to read were ones about princesses. Turning the pages, Jazz had found "The Queen Bee."

"Will we have this one? Do you know it?"

She recognized it herself. In her childhood book of Grimms' *Household Tales* it had been illustrated by the color plate of three princesses in scarlet, whose long hair was twined with chaplets of pearls. Back then, frightened by the dark images that surrounded it, she had failed to see why the focus of the picture was a shining honeybee.

It was a classic fairy tale about how greed inevitably leads to bad luck. Three brothers set out on a journey and the youngest stops the others harming creatures they meet along the way. Then they come to an enchanted castle where everyone has been turned into stone. A little gray man meets the brothers in the doorway.

Holly's eyelids were drooping. "What did he say?"

Tucking her in, Jazz had read on about how the man had set the brothers tasks to break the enchantment. The first was to collect a thousand pearls, scattered in a deep forest. The second was to find the key to the princesses' bedchamber. The third was to pick out the youngest princess, though all three were alike.

"What happened then?"

Seeing that the little girl was half asleep, she'd summarized the rest of the story. "The older brothers were mean and cruel, so no one wanted to help them. So they failed to fulfil the tasks. But the youngest brother asked for help from the creatures he'd protected. So ants found the pearls for him. Ducks brought the missing key from the bottom of a dark lake. And a queen bee found him the youngest princess."

"How?"

"All the princesses had tasted something sweet before falling asleep. The oldest had sugar, the second had syrup, and the youngest had tasted some honey. The queen bee picked her out and everything wrong was right again."

"Did they marry and live happily ever after?" Holly's voice was as drowsy as the droning of a honeybee.

The door had opened and Gunther was smiling at them. Jazz closed the book and said that of course they did, they'd married and lived in the castle forever and their little girl was called Holly.

She'd smiled back at Gunther, who'd gone to bend and kiss Holly. Jazz had kissed her, too, before they'd turned to leave the room. Then, just as Gunther switched the light out, Holly had sat up in bed again, belligerent and sounding wide awake.

"But the princess wasn't asleep at all, you know she wasn't. *You* said that she'd been turned to stone."

Susan reckoned that late evening was the best time to do admin. Between the guesthouse, the goats, and the family there were several different files and accounts to keep updated and, with everyone else in the house in bed, she could tackle them without being interrupted.

This week most of the guests were on walking holidays, so they tended to go to bed early and rise at the crack of dawn. Gunther was due to do tomorrow's early breakfasts and Jazz already knew which rooms needed a change of linen. In the morning she herself would need to juggle the orders of goat cheese she'd be sending out to customers and the weekly supplies for the guesthouse kitchen that she'd be ordering in.

Holly had been difficult and hard to settle earlier, crying for no apparent reason and wanting her light left on. But now she was sleeping soundly. So, with most of the ground floor in darkness and the lights going off in the guestrooms upstairs, Susan had urged Gunther to go on up to bed.

"I'll just do an hour at the screen and be up after you. You know yourself I sleep twice as well if the work's out of the way."

He'd kissed her and said that if she sat up too late, he'd be downstairs looking for her. And he would, too, bless him. But he was as knackered as she was, and it was he who had the early start.

The takings were looking impressive. As she'd hoped, the TV coverage had made a noticeable difference, bringing guests from Germany and from Austria, where the program had aired as well. And the steady stream of returning guests had continued to build also; people who'd found The Old Forge in the early years of the business seemed to feel proprietorial about its growing success. It was lovely to see old faces again, and to feel your guests were rooting for you. And it was brilliant to know that her plans for a family holiday were still on track.

Looking at the figures, she realized she could go online now and book the Rhine Cruise. It would be a lovely surprise for Gunther, to whom she hadn't yet said a word. On the other hand, it wouldn't really make sense. If the plan involved leaving Holly for a while with the grandparents in Freudenstadt, it wasn't fair to go choosing dates without contacting them first. She had the website bookmarked on her computer, though, and now, when she should be working, she allowed herself a sneaky peek. The boats were gorgeous, all sleek and white and luxurious, and the staterooms looked like something out of a film. Susan was well aware of the effect of a fisheye lens on a photo, and the glamour extended to the shots of the cruise line's passengers, who all appeared to have tans and designer clothes. They were models, of course, and she knew that the rooms had been carefully lit for the photographs, but all she could see was herself and

Gunther lounging round drinking champagne. Besides, with her professional head on, she'd checked out the cruise line carefully and anyone could see that it offered a wonderful trip. Almost all the feedback came with four- or five-star endorsements, and lots of professional travel writers had written it up as well. The champagne would probably amount to a single glass on embarkation, and most of the actual passengers were likely to turn up in t-shirts and shorts, but they wouldn't be doddering retirees and the whole thing wouldn't be a rip-off. It was the perfect choice for a romantic break with an occasional touch of luxury, and heaven knew that she and Gunther had worked hard to deserve it.

Meanwhile she needed to get on with the blasted accounts. Banishing the website, she clicked on a folder called GOAT STUFF and reached for the mug of coffee by her side. An hour later her phone rang and it was Gunther calling from the bedroom.

Susan smiled. "Are you not asleep yet?"

"No, I was reading. Are you not coming to bed?"

"Ten minutes."

"Make it five."

"You'll be asleep by then."

"I don't think so."

Laughing softly under her breath, she logged out and went upstairs.

47

On her way to the Garden Café Louisa made a detour to the gift shop. She was due to go back to Kent soon, and a card from the library to say thank you to Mary seemed like an appropriate choice. It was going to be hard to leave, she thought, and not just because they'd enjoyed each other's company. The fact was that both of them were still worried about Jazz.

Ameena Khan, who was behind the counter, showed her a display of cards on a carousel. Louisa examined a series of reproductions of floral details from the psalter, and chose a group of buds and blousy roses in deep pinks against a startling blue background. They were a good compromise between the vivid beauty of the manuscript and the exuberance of Mary's personal style. As she paid for the cards, she smiled at the thought of the bungalow's back bedroom wallpaper. Though she'd kept her countenance when she'd first seen it, her initial reaction had been horror; and that night the sight of her own rose-sprigged dressing gown lying on the lurid duvet had made her wince. Even now she felt more comfortable with her eyes on Tom's pleasant garden and her back to Mary's riotous quilt and rosy walls; but no one could deny their energy and warmth, any more than you could deny the warmth of strangers in Finfarran greeting you when you passed them by in the street. It had taken a while to get used to that, too, and to the nods and waves from unknown drivers on the roads. But now, she thought ruefully, it was going to be strange to return to her life in Kent.

As she approached the fountain carrying a glass of iced mint tea, she saw Saira Khan working on one of the herb beds near a worn timber bench. Skirting the granite basin where the water gushed from the flowers round St. Francis's feet, Louisa approached the bench and greeted her.

Saira looked up in surprise. "Louisa! How are you?"

"I'm very well. And it's good to see you. May I sit down?"

Saira brushed earth from her hands and gestured toward the bench hospitably. "Of course. Come and talk to me."

Louisa held up her glass of mint tea. "Would you care for one of these?"

Saira shook her head. She'd keep working, she said, because she was due to finish soon. But it was nice to have someone to chat to while she weeded the last of the dill.

Louisa set her glass on the bench and sat down a little stiffly on the end nearest the herb bed. Saira, who'd been kneeling on a waterproof cushion, got up and held it out.

Louisa shook her head. "That's very kind but, really, no, I don't need it. The bench is perfectly comfortable, this is just old age."

In fact the feel of the sun-warmed wood at her back was delightful. She turned to look at the plaque that was screwed to the rail behind her. It was newer than the wood to which it was attached and an inscription had been picked out in red paint against the polished brass: SISTER MICHAEL, BORN SARAH CASSIDY, A WORKER IN THIS GARDEN.

Saira knelt down again and explained, as she weeded, that Sister Michael was one of the last of the nuns who'd lived in the old convent.

"I never knew her, but the volunteers say she was a very holy lady." Her brow wrinkled and she sat back on her heels. "One of them called her cute as a fox, but I'm not sure what she meant."

"I think that in Ireland 'cute' can mean resourceful. Wasn't Sister Michael involved in the campaign to save the library?"

Saira nodded. "Maybe. Everyone here knows each other so well, sometimes I don't like to ask. I know they have great respect for her memory." She looked toward the railing that enclosed the nuns' graveyard. "And I like that they planted marigolds on her grave."

"I believe that's a Muslim tradition?" Realizing she wasn't sure, Louisa faltered. It felt idiotic and somehow offensive not to know something so fundamental, though, on the other hand, she knew just as little about Roman Catholic rites.

Saira brushed earth from her hands again and glanced toward the graveyard. "They are part of the Hindu tradition, but not of ours. And, like those nuns, we Muslims don't have large gravestones. My mother was fond of marigolds, though. I think of her when I see them. She said that, like jasmine flowers, they promoted love." She smiled at Louisa. "In many cultures they are seen as holy. And they have numerous medicinal properties. Cosmetic ones, too."

"Face creams and shampoos again?"

"And massage oil. Where I grew up everyone's granny made that."

She came to sit on the bench beside Louisa. "I ought to

go and wash my hands and get ready to pick up Ameena. We said we'd walk home together when she finished work."

"I saw her just now in the gift shop. She's such a polite, helpful girl."

"Her teachers always say she's very clever. I'll miss her when she goes away. I don't think she'll come back."

Stretching her legs out, Saira leaned back, drawing her orange scarf forward over her dark hair. It was strange, she said, to have imagined Ameena would want to settle down in Lissbeg. "Though I didn't imagine it, really. I just hoped."

"What makes you think she won't want to?"

"I don't know. Perhaps it's not what I think, it's just what I'm afraid of. But I know there's no point in trying to hold her back." She glanced at Louisa, suddenly looking mischievous. "And perhaps I'm completely wrong. These days there's a boyfriend."

Louisa laughed. "That can be a game changer."

"And who knows whether for bad or good? My mother would have told me to leave it in the hands of God." Saira linked her own hands in her lap. "Anyway, I'm glad to have found this work in the garden. I don't think I've ever felt I've put down roots in Ireland. Maybe this is where I'll begin."

Roots. That was the nub of the matter. As Saira got

up and left to meet Ameena, Louisa sipped the last of her mint tea. No one could blame Hanna for uprooting Jazz from London and, once the child had settled in Finfarran, she'd seemed to be doing well. It was a place she knew and loved since childhood, and she'd gone off to train for the airline job with a group of friends from Lissbeg. Then, later, the French flat-share had provided a taste of independence. Yet all this was in the context of a sense that London was where she belonged. It was her home, the place she'd been born and where she grew up. And now that sense of security was gone. Malcolm's selfish lies had made her an exile from London, while the surgeon's embargo on a career in travel had uprooted her from France.

And no one, Louisa repeated to herself, could possibly blame Hanna. Where another woman might have been crushed by Malcolm's betrayal, Hanna had bravely returned to her own roots and started her life again. The trouble was that Maggie's house, which anyone could see had been her salvation, literally had no room in it for Jazz.

In practical terms this was no real problem. It was a given that Jazz would always have a place to stay at the bungalow and Malcolm would gladly have bought her a property anywhere she liked. But living with Mary Casey wasn't the answer. And knowing the truth about

Malcolm, Jazz would never accept his help. What was needed was something that would allow her to put down her own roots here in Finfarran. Something that would make her feel that this was her home.

At the far side of the nuns' garden the volunteers who had finished work were laughing and chatting over coffee. As Louisa watched, they were joined by a group who'd emerged from The Old Convent Centre. Among them she recognized the framer who worked with Nell and old Mrs. Reily; Trish, the girl who made chocolates; and Phil, the woman who was in charge of the center's space to rent. According to Hanna, the decision to turn the old convent into a hub for business development had changed these people's lives. Young and old, and coming from widely differing backgrounds, they had all harnessed inherent talents to open up creative possibilities.

A bird fluttered up from the flowers round the fountain and swooped across the garden to perch on the back of the bench. Sister Michael, who'd been cute as a fox, lay beneath gray stone and marigolds. Fearlessly, the bird turned his head and fixed his eye on Louisa. Crushing a leaf of mint in her fingers, Louisa considered a plan.

48

The last entry in Maggie's book was written in blue biro and headed "Finfarran 1963." Hanna blinked as she read the date: it was the year she herself had been born. The handwriting, which was recognizably Maggie's, was no longer reminiscent of a schoolgirl's. Peering closely at the pages, Hanna could see that, once again, several had been removed with a sharp blade by a steady hand. The missing pages were just before this final entry. The entry itself began with three brief sentences.

Tom came round. Black hair, tall as a rake and not a spare pick of fat on him. He's the image of Liam when he was the same age.

They were followed by a gap of several lines.

Hanna sat back and marveled. She hadn't needed a photo after all, because Maggie had given her the answer that she'd been seeking in Carrick Library. Liam, the grandfather she'd never met, had been the image of her father, Tom. The rush of warmth that came with the knowledge surprised her. Laying the book on her knee, she wondered if Tom himself had ever known; with a father who'd died when he was a toddler, he might have been dependent on Maggie's memories to give him a sense of self. But Maggie had been so close-mouthed that perhaps she hadn't said.

Looking down at the book on her knee, Hanna continued reading.

One thing I remember is how I missed the cows when they were gone. Paud Donovan took them to the market in Lissbeg for me three days after Dad was shot. The neighbors couldn't go minding them forever and I couldn't leave Mam long enough to milk them or take them to the field. I couldn't tell what would happen to us and Mam wouldn't stop crying.

The neighbors buried Dad and Hannie. I wanted to go to the funeral but Mam got worse when the coffins were carried from the house. One of the Donovans would have sat in with her but she screamed till I took off my coat. I was afraid Liam would go to the burial ground, but he didn't. Paud said the word was that he was back in the mountains. I prayed he'd stay there.

The night Dad was shot the Tans left their truck way up the road and came down to the house on foot. If some of them hadn't had drink taken we'd never have heard them coming. But one of them fell as they came round the gable before they kicked in the door. Liam was inside in the room with his rifle catching a wink of sleep. The rest of us were round the fire in the kitchen when we heard the noise outside.

When Dad looked up and saw them passing the window he knocked the lamp off the table, then as the door smashed in he was out between them like a bull at a gate and away over the ditch. The officer and a couple of the Tans ran out to fire at him and I think the one that was left in the house with us didn't know what to do. Anyway, he stood there doing nothing for a minute. Then he must have realized that Dad escaping out was a diversion, because he went for the door of the room. Mam and I tried to stop him, though I'd say Liam had got out the back and gone as soon as he heard the row. I was listening out and I heard shots fired up on the road.

Hannie heard the Tans firing at Dad and she ran after him out the front door. I don't think the one who hit her knew she was only a child. She came up behind him in the dark and he swung round and got her on the side of the head with the butt end of his gun. I was on the threshold by then but I couldn't get to her in time.

It was black as the hob of hell outside so I thought Dad might have got away. The Tans didn't go over the fields anyway, to see if they'd hit him. When the officer saw what they'd done to Hannie, and the men he'd left up on the road came down without Liam, he swore and ordered the lot of them back to the truck. The neighbors found Dad in the morning. He'd got most of the way across Donovan's field when a bullet got him in the neck. Hannie lasted till the next day but the doctor said her skull was fractured and she died.

There was another gap of a few lines and the entry continued in a different ink.

I think Mam had accepted that Liam might be killed. Two lads who had joined the Volunteers with him died in an ambush that April and another was pulled behind a truck by the Tans and shot. Liam was her only son but if the news had come that he was dead I think Mam could have taken it. He was ready to die for Ireland and she'd have said it was God's will. What she never expected was that Hannie and Dad would go first. And what she had on her mind afterward was that Liam would never have come home that night if he hadn't heard she was sick. It was only an old cough that was troubling her but someone had told Liam that she wasn't great. They'd been up in the hills beyond in Cork for ages so he couldn't have come then even if he'd wanted to, but in April the lads had been ordered back to Finfarran and that had brought him closer to home.

They'd only been back a day when he turned up. There'd been a price on his head for ages, getting bigger with every ambush, so he should have known better than to come. He was dead tired when he came in the door, and we'd only chatted a small while when he went down to the room to sleep. Mam had made tea and boiled eggs. He hadn't a pick of fat on him. Liam hadn't seen Hannie for more than a year and he couldn't get over how big she'd got. He had barley sugar in his pocket for her *twelfth birthday he was after missing, and she said he'd missed Christmas and my seventeenth, too, so where were the presents for them? Mam said that just seeing him was a tonic, like Christmas had come again.*

He was in good spirits that night and he said he had a good commandant so he reckoned they could hold out for months if they had enough bullets. He said the English were running scared and they'd soon have to treat. He was right, too, but when the end came it was too late for Dad and Hannie.

Hanna closed the book and sat back in her chair, her eyes on the window through which Maggie's father had seen the men approach. The family must have sat up late that April night if it was dark when the door was kicked in. But of course Liam would only have moved under cover of darkness. Perhaps his arrival had woken them and his mother had raked the ashes from the fire and built it up to make his tea.

Hanna threw turf on her own fire and shivered. Liam must have loved his family deeply to have risked that visit home to his ailing mother. What had it been like to live with the knowledge that his father and his little sister had died because of that visit, while he himself had survived?

49

A few minutes before closing time Charles Aukin strolled into the library followed closely by The Divil. Given the old man's status as the library's bene-factor, Hanna didn't complain, but when Fury arrived a few minutes later she told him in a steely undertone that dogs were still not allowed.

He responded by tipping The Divil out the doorway, using the toe of his boot. "What are you so afraid of, Miss Casey—that he'll go round eating your books?"

Ignoring him, Hanna turned her attention to Charles, who had taken to dropping in to the library each time she was due to turn a new page of the psalter. According to Fury, who gave him a lift to Lissbeg, he was missing its presence at the castle.

"Mind you, I'd say he hardly noticed it when he had

it. But 'twas there if he fancied a quick flick through it of an evening."

The idea had made Hanna wince. She herself never touched the psalter without an intense awareness of its age and it shocked her to think of generations of de Lancys flicking through it whenever the humor possessed them.

With Charles at her elbow, and Fury and Conor behind her, she went through to the exhibition, opened the glass display case, and reverently turned a page to reveal a new spread. The text on the left-hand page was Psalm 147 and the illustration that faced it glowed richly, like a case of jewels. Conor reset the screensaver on the interactive screens around the walls. Hanna was about to comment to Charles on the success of the technology when she remembered Conor joking about how Aideen found it boring. These days any reference to Aideen, however remote or tangential, seemed to wound him, so, leaving her thought unspoken, she looked at what she'd revealed.

Dominating the page, which depicted a rural landscape in various seasons, were the muscular rumps of three huge horses. Two stood with their heads down, contemplating clumps of daisies. The third was looking over its shoulder at the figure of a small smith with a large horseshoe held in a pair of pincers. The surrounding fields made a backdrop of green pastures, yellow corn and snow on the backs of woolly sheep. But the central focus was the horse that was staring at the smith. It was rendered in pale blue against a pink crossroads and had a rather attractive squint in its left eye.

Fury, who was peering over Hanna's shoulder, gave an appreciative chuckle. "So what exactly would we be looking at here?"

Conor clicked on a screen and found the translation of the psalm.

"Um . . . 'He telleth the number of the stars' . . . hang on . . . 'prepareth rain for the earth . . . giveth the beast his food' . . . nope, here we go, it must be this." Having glanced ahead to see if anything further on might be more relevant, he read out the tenth verse. " 'He delighteth not in the strength of the horse: he taketh not pleasure in the legs of a man.' "

Charles winked at Fury. "You can't beat a picture of a cockeyed horse."

Seeing Conor's slightly shocked expression, Hanna hastily explained to him that a lack of interest in men's legs and the strength of horses was the psalmist's way of presenting a God of peace. "Warriors rode horses in battle, you see, and armies able to march long distances would have been highly trained."

"But why would the verse about horses be important?

I mean why did your man decide to paint that one and not one of the others?"

Pleased to see him interested, Hanna said that, for her, that was part of the psalter's attraction. No one knew why the illustrator had made that particular choice. Maybe he just liked the sound of the verse. Perhaps part of his duties had involved working in the monastery's fields. The horses he'd created looked more like the farm animals that had once congregated round the horse trough in Broad Street than the thoroughbred chargers of antiquity.

Leaning over to look at the psalter, Conor agreed with her. They could be Percherons or Shire horses, he said, showing more animation than she'd seen in him for weeks. But only a few moments later he wandered back into the library looking glum.

As Hanna secured the display case, she found Fury beside her. "Woman trouble there, I'd say."

Hanna grimaced. "Something's gone badly wrong, I think, but I don't like to ask him. It's so sad. Aideen was always dropping in for another look at the psalter. I imagine that's what Conor was thinking about just now."

"It's a strange thing the way that yoke means something different to everyone."

The same thought had crossed Hanna's mind. "Do

you think Charles comes to visit it because it reminds him of his wife?"

Fury snorted derisively. "I do not. Sure, isn't she still up there at the castle? If he wants reminding he only has to visit her grave. No, I'd say he's genuinely missing the odd look at a blue horse. It was a wrench, you know, handing it over. That's the way the rich are, they're bred to hang on to their plunder."

Hanna shook her head at him. "The de Lancys acquired the psalter perfectly legally. They bought it at the time of the Reformation. They even kept the receipt."

"And where do you think they acquired the money to buy it?"

She grinned, remembering a line from Maggie's diary: "I'd say they had plenty of money always and where did they get it but out of the mouths of the people?" She quoted it to Fury, who chortled. "Sure even a cockeyed horse could see she was right."

As they turned to go, he looked back and winked at her. "And didn't Charles do right to give it back to the people? Maybe he's kept his wife and himself out of hell." Watching her startled reaction, he threw back his head in delight. "Begod, you're the best woman in the world, Hanna Casey, for rising to an easy bait!"

She conceded the hit by making a face at him. "So you don't believe in divine retribution?"

"Not for something as complex as colonization. I'd say even the Almighty would break his shins on that. And didn't we drive the poor buggers out in the end anyway? And leave all the beautiful houses we'd built for them crumbling away into bits."

Conor came through and joined them, having checked the doors and windows. He looked so down that Hanna felt like giving him a hug. Instead she watched him trail miserably toward the kitchen to collect his helmet and gloves.

Fury glanced at her sideways. "God, the young think their troubles will last forever! And the desperate thing is that it's when they're low that they tend to make stupid decisions."

Hanna looked at him anxiously. "You don't think that Conor's likely to go and do something silly?"

"I wouldn't say so, no. Hasn't he a farm and a family to consider?"

Then, as they left the library, Fury mentioned in passing that he'd seen Jazz a fair few times driving the back roads with Gunther. "I gave them a wave and The Divil barked, but they never noticed me at all."

50

Mid-gray wasn't a color that Hanna would have chosen for her own toenails, but on Jazz's tanned feet it looked really good.

"In my day we stuck to scarlet."

"What do you mean, 'in your day'? There's life in the old girl yet."

"That's a foul expression. And in my case it's debatable."

"Well, people gasp at your outré choices. I remember you being the first of your friends to go in for gray paint."

"On windowsills, yes. Not my feet."

Jazz grinned and jumped from one rock to the next, her espadrilles swinging from her hand. Hanna followed a little more carefully, feeling the seaweed scrunch and slither under her bare heels. They reached the sheltered inlet they'd been making for and trudged up the beach to where the base of the cliff met the fine, silver sand. Jazz spread out a sweatshirt and sat down, pushing up her sunglasses and blinking at the cloudless sky.

Settling herself with her back to a rock, Hanna nudged her. "The whole point of wearing sunglasses is to protect your eyes from the sun."

"Do mothers ever stop prodding their daughters and making pronouncements like that?"

"Well, you've met your grandmother."

Jazz chuckled and put her glasses back on. "Just so long as you recognize the similarity."

Hanna reached into her bag and produced the plastic folder, which Jazz received with a smile.

"Is this it? Maggie's book?"

Hanna nodded. She had phoned last night and arranged this outing in order to hand the book over. Lately, Jazz had been so evasive and distant that Hanna had half-expected a text saying she couldn't turn up. But now, as she removed the book from the folder, Jazz was looking relaxed.

"I thought you said it was a diary?"

"I said there were diary entries. But not in any logical sort of order. There's other stuff as well. And some pages have been cut out."

Jazz investigated the binding. "Why?"

"Who knows? Maybe just for the paper."

"And she'd buried it in a box? Why? Because the bit about the Black and Tans was so sad?"

Watching her flick casually through the pages, Hanna felt obscurely protective of them. To her, both Maggie's book and the house were links to a fragmented past. Fury's insistence on retaining the color of the dresser and Brian's awareness of the underlying integrity of the structure both depended on an awareness of what had been there before. So did her own new sense of Maggie's personality, found in the handwritten pages that so easily might have been lost. But for Jazz, that awareness was missing. So although she might find the book interesting, the links just wouldn't be there.

"Don't get it covered in sand!"

She had spoken louder than she'd intended and Jazz looked slightly surprised. But she replaced the book in its wallet. Hanna smiled apologetically. "I don't know why she buried it. Yes, probably because of that. Families didn't talk much back then. I mean about the Tans. Or the Civil War."

Or about Mary's jealousy and how Tom had put up with it.

"So did Liam fight in the Civil War as well?"

"I don't know." Hanna could hear herself beginning to sound like a parrot. "It sounds daft but, really, I don't. That's the point, I think. What's there is there and that's all she left to us. The gaps might just be arbitrary, but they may be there by choice."

" 'When there's holy war going on in the background, people want to protect their kids.' "

It was evidently a quote but Hanna didn't recognize it.

Jazz flashed her eyebrows at her ironically. "That's what you said to me about your divorce."

There was a pause while Jazz put the folder in her bag and they lay side by side in the late-evening sunshine. The heat seeped into Hanna's bones, and the knowledge that she and her daughter were here and happy together filled her with pleasure.

"You know, you could say that the book stretches across five generations. Maggie's dad was your great-great grandfather."

Jazz's hand moved in the sand beside her, working it out on her fingers. "That's cool. What was his name?"

"John. She just calls him Dad."

When she'd finished reading the book, Hanna had

searched the 1901 and 1911 Census records and found the names. Hannie had appeared in 1911 as well, aged three. She had been fifteen years younger than Liam, who was ten years older than Maggie. It was a small family by Irish standards, so the chances were that there were other siblings who'd died. But those were the only names that Hanna had found. There were other records she could have trawled through. Birth certificates, registers of deaths and marriages.

"But I didn't."

"Why not?"

"I tell you what, you can be the one to take it further. It'll keep you off the streets."

"No, but seriously, Mum, why not? Aren't you interested?"

"Kind of. Yes and no."

How to explain her lack of interest in scrolling through online information as opposed to the intense pull of the handwritten book? It was like Aideen's reaction to the psalter: she hadn't been interested in the digital screens that gave access to so much detail. What had drawn her in was the thought of the moving pen. Remembering how Conor had told her that, Hanna sighed. He was still withdrawn and she couldn't bear to see him in such low spirits.

Jazz looked round sharply and narrowed her eyes. "What's up? You've got that mumsy look again."

"No I haven't."

"You have so!"

"Well, okay, I was thinking of Conor. He and Aideen broke up."

"Oh, Mum, for heaven's sake!"

Hanna looked at her in genuine incomprehension.

Jazz shook her head. "It's like you *need* someone to stress over. If it's not Dad, it's Granny Lou, and if it's not her, it's me. And now it's poor bloody Conor. What you should do is get yourself a life."

She reached out just as Hanna had done and nudged her in the ribs. Then she grinned as Hanna pulled away.

"Honestly, Mum, you should. You're enjoying your job, you've got your own place, why don't you just chill out a bit? Ask that nice Brian Morton round and open a bottle of wine."

"You wouldn't mind?"

"Why on earth should I?"

"Well, you're still upset about Dad."

"Ah, look!" Suddenly Jazz's English accent disappeared and she sounded pure Lissbeg. "Will you have a bit of sense? I'm not six years old, Mum, and you're not getting any younger. You don't have to put your life on permanent hold."

Ignoring the echo of what Brian had said, Hanna sat up and put her arms round her knees. "You are still upset, though, aren't you?"

"If I am that's between me and Dad. You can't hover over me forever, Mum. I've just got to get on and chase my own dreams."

Hanna looked at her thoughtfully, chewing her lower lip. Under the relaxed surface Jazz was still brittle and nervous. Maybe even more than she'd been before.

"You're not feeling isolated away from your own friends?"

"I'm fine."

"And you're getting on well with Susan? And with Gunther?"

For the briefest of moments she felt Jazz stiffen beside her. Suddenly Fury's voice echoed in her mind. He'd seen Jazz a fair few times driving the back roads with Gunther. And, now that she came to think of it, she had once seen them herself. It had been a misty day and she'd glimpsed the car only for a moment, but Gunther's broad shoulders and blond hair had been unmistakable. At the time she'd thought nothing of it, but now she recognized the blank look Jazz used always to assume when caught out as a child. Before Hanna could speak, the childish look became adult aggression.

"What are you saying?"

"Nothing at all. It's just . . . I know I shouldn't worry, love, but I want you to be happy. And to be careful. Just, you know, to take care."

She wasn't even sure what she meant herself, or whether Fury's comment had simply been an observation. But now, suddenly, Jazz was on her feet, swinging her bag onto her shoulder, brushing sand off her skirt. "Someone's been gossiping, haven't they? Running to you with lies."

"What? No. No one."

"God, Mum, it's despicable!"

Hanna struggled to her own feet, feeling dreadful. "I'm not saying you've done anything wrong . . ."

"Well, thanks a million for that!"

"It's just . . . look, no one's been spreading gossip. I saw you with Gunther myself."

"And?"

It seemed to Hanna that a pit had opened at her feet. Then an expression she knew all too well smoothed the feeling from her daughter's angry face. It might have been Malcolm standing there confronting her, his mind inaccessible behind the familiar armor she had seen him assume in court. Jazz bent to thrust her feet into her espadrilles; the gray polish on her toes was stippled with shining grains of sand.

Still trying to grasp the implications of what was happening, Hanna held out her hand. "Look, don't just walk away. We need to talk."

It was a waste of time and she knew it. As Jazz turned to walk away, she'd already gone far beyond recall.

51

Whenever Aideen arrived to open up the deli, she checked her phone or pretended to look for something in her handbag; she couldn't bear to raise her head for fear Conor might be over the way. Even though HabberDashery and the library were separated by Broad Street with its traffic and its central island with the flowery horse trough, they were far too close together. And the ghastly thing was that everyone who knew her knew what was going on. Bríd had more or less given up asking what had happened, but motherly customers kept smiling in a knowing way and wanting to know how she was doing. The worst were the ones who flicked their eyes across the street. How was Conor? Had she been in to the library lately to have a look at the psalter? One woman even leaned on the counter and talked for hours about the book club. It sounded gas, she said, and her own daughter was planning to join in September. Why wouldn't Aideen think about going along? It had been impossible to know whether she was shoving her oar in or didn't know what she was saying. And whichever it was didn't matter. Any mention of Conor or the library, innocent or intentional, left Aideen on the verge of tears.

Howling into her apron at the deli wasn't an option, though. And at night she had to stick her head under the pillow, otherwise Bríd would come in and give her another lecture. So the only time she could really cry was on long walks in the evenings, and then she'd have to run upstairs when she came home, to hide the state of her eyes.

Without saying anything, she'd fixed her shifts to avoid arriving or leaving work at the same time as Conor, but, even on the days when he worked on the farm, she felt tense. He was always having to come in to Lissbeg for something. Her stomach lurched at the sight of him and once, when he'd turned a corner and seen her, he'd nearly crashed the Vespa into a van. The idea that she could have killed him left her feeling sick for hours and she'd ended up making a whole batch of pesto with sugar instead of salt. It was the same when she had to deliver stuff to the café, the thought of the library across the courtyard was more than she felt she could bear.

Now the door opened with a ring and a violent rattle and Miss Casey's noisy mother swept into the deli. Controlling her gut reaction, Aideen smiled and asked if she could help her. Mary Casey nodded at a tabloid-sized sheet that was framed on the wall behind the counter. It was an enlargement of the magazine article about the opening of the psalter exhibition. Recently Aideen had wanted to remove it, but Bríd had gone mad.

"That article is the best ad we've ever had for our services and I'm damned if we're going to take it down to satisfy your neurosis!"

Recognizing that she was serious, Aideen had given in. Because she worked with her back to it, she didn't have to see it anyway, except on unguarded occasions when she'd catch its reflection in a mirror. Like everything else, she'd told herself sadly, the joy of the mirrored walls around her had turned to a source of pain.

Now Mary Casey waved her hand at the article and announced that she was looking for the makings of the yokes they'd had that night in the library.

"The canapés?"

"If that's what you want to call them. I'd say they were morsels of bread and bits of fish. Anyway, Mrs. Turner, who's staying with me, was very taken by the taste of them, so I said I'd come in and see how you made them up."

Aideen explained that the bread had been a special order from the Ballyfin Bakery. "But we stock some of their artisan breads here now. That was the rye."

"Artisan, is it? You mean overpriced! Still, Mrs. Turner liked it, so I suppose I'll take a loaf."

Aideen smiled. "We served them with organic smoked salmon and watercress. And we used either a mustard or a horseradish cream dressing under the fish. I could make you a couple of pots to take out if you like."

"Go on, so. And I suppose I'll have to take the organic stuff if you haven't got anything normal."

As Aideen began on the dressings, Mary leaned heavily on the chiller cabinet. "You must have been spitting feathers when you saw how that pup from Dublin stole your work." She nodded again at the article hanging on the wall. "Wasn't half the stuff he said in there cribbed out of your leaflet? According to my daughter Hanna, he'd want to be ashamed." Not, she added hastily, that her daughter had said such a thing in so many words. "No, I noticed it myself as soon as I read the paper. And when I pointed it out to Hanna, I could see she was very shocked. Well, not shocked, exactly. But I said it to her and I could see that she took my point. Well, she's a librarian. Plagiarism's an open book to her."

Leaning into the cabinet, she peered at a bowl of artichoke hearts. "I couldn't be doing with these things, they're slimy and that's a fact."

Aideen heard herself saying inanely that artichokes were fierce healthy. Anything to keep Mrs. Casey from banging on about the library.

"Mark you," said Mary, "I wasn't the only one very impressed by your leaflet. Plenty of the ladies at my computer class thought it was great as well. Did you research it on the interweb?"

Keeping her head down, Aideen said that she did.

Mary reached over and prodded her. "Do you know what it is, girl, you're a fool to yourself! And don't tell me I don't know what I'm talking about. I do! Any lad who can teach a crowd of seniors how to compute is worth having. Mark you, there's a few of us still having trouble with Windows 10. But that's no fault of poor Conor McCarthy's. What did you think you were at when you let him go?" Squaring her shoulders, she looked at Aideen, whose lower lip was trembling. "Ah, name of God, child, don't start fussing, I'm only telling the truth."

For a moment Aideen was sure she could control herself. Then, to her horror, her nose streamed and she opened her mouth and bawled.

After that it all got confusing. Bríd appeared through

the door with a box from the cash and carry. Aideen found herself in the back room, sobbing into the coats. Out in the shop she could hear Bríd talking to Mrs. Casey.

"Not at all, don't be daft, she's grand really. She's had a touch of the flu and it's left her a bit depressed."

The dressings were only half made, the bread wasn't packed, and Mrs. Casey was announcing loudly that girls today were far and away too touchy. But somehow Bríd got her smiling and out of the shop. Aideen could hear their cheerful goodbyes on the doorstep. Then the shop bell rang as Bríd closed the door and came marching through to the back.

"Right, that's it, get yourself a coffee, we're going to talk."

She had turned the sign on the door over and pulled down the blind.

"But what about the customers?"

"Damn the customer we're going to have soon if you keep on like this."

Bríd pulled a stool from behind the counter and ordered Aideen to sit on it. She herself paced round the floor like a lion lashing its tail. "This has got to stop, Aideen, and you know it. What in the name of God happened just now?"

Aideen blew her nose and took a scalding gulp of coffee. "She was talking about the exhibition over at the library . . ."

"And?"

"And I was grand, I was mixing a couple of dressings . . ."

"And?"

Aideen's voice rose to a wail. "And she gave me a prod and starting saying I shouldn't have left Conor."

Bríd came very close to her and glared into her eyes. "And you know bloody well that she was absolutely right."

She jerked another stool round and sat down facing her. "Okay, I'm done being the nice guy. I've covered your back and sent him away and watched the two of you droop like a couple of eejits. And I still don't know what the hell it was he did wrong. Well, you can fill me in now, girl, and I won't take no for an answer."

Aideen looked away and bit her lip.

"I mean it, Aideen, this place is my livelihood. I've a right to know what's going on if it's going to affect your work."

In the end, it all came out in another flood of tears.

Bríd sat back and stared. In God's name, she wanted to know, was Aideen out of her mind?

Aideen groped for another tissue. "I'm telling you, I saw them outside the library. They were kissing."

"No. What you told me was that you saw her kissing him. On the cheek."

"He had his arm round her."

"And?"

"And he came over the road to me like nothing at all had happened."

"That would be the clue, Aideen. Because obviously nothing did."

"But . . ."

"This isn't to do with Conor or Ameena. This is all about you."

Aideen stopped sniffing and gaped at her. "I haven't done anything!"

"Yeah, you have. You've decided you're not good enough for Conor. But you haven't worked out what that's all about. Instead you've gone blaming him."

"That is so not true. I never said he was to blame."

"Who is, then? Ameena? The big, bad foreigner coming here Taking Our Men?"

"Of course not!"

"Of course not. So who, then? Who is it about if it's not about either of them?"

Aideen stared at her, looking stricken. Bríd got up,

went to the counter and cut two pieces of cake. She dumped one on a plate and shoved it under Aideen's nose. "Here, get that into you. They say sugar is good for shock."

Taking a forkful of the other slice, she leaned against the counter. "In case you haven't noticed, Ameena Khan is going out with Lar Walsh. Oh, what am I saying? You won't have noticed because *you've* been going round with your head stuck up your own arse."

Aideen's jaw sagged.

"And don't go making matters worse by saying that proves she's a slag."

"I wouldn't . . . !"

"Good. At least you're not that stupid." Bríd put her plate down and scowled. "Actually, if anyone's to blame it's probably me."

"Why on earth?"

"Because if I'd had an ounce of common sense, I'd have forced you to say what was wrong. Instead I was being all sensitive, thinking Conor had done something dreadful. God knows why, because, let's face it, he's not exactly the type."

Her tone was so dismissive that Aideen bridled. "What do you mean by that?"

"Well, he's no Lothario, is he?"

"That's a rotten thing to say!"

Bríd looked at her for a moment and burst out laughing. "Oh, for God's sake, will you get over the road and get groveling."

There was a long pause and then Aideen stood up and blew her nose. As she opened the door of the deli, Bríd shouted after her. "And while you're at it, why don't you find out if the two of you are engaged?"

52

All the rooms at the forge had been booked by a bachelorette party. The bride-to-be was a Dublin girl who worked in Stuttgart and had seen Gunther's interview on German television. Her mates were old school friends and colleagues from work, all a few years older than Jazz and behaving like giggling teenagers. Jazz was well used to dealing with the type; she had served drinks to the likes of them many a time on crowded planes to Torremolinos and Malaga. There was no harm in them and the best way to cope was to laugh along and join in the banter.

The trouble was that she didn't feel like laughing. Her row with Mum two days ago had left her feeling rattled, and the bachelorette party's rowdy jokes had begun to annoy her. This morning they'd all turned up to breakfast wearing red devil horns and angel wings, falling about laughing about what Gunther had said about Susan. The chief bridesmaid, who had organized the trip, jumped on a chair and made a speech. "Settle down, settle down, ladies!! This is our last day in *Fun*farran and tonight we're going to hit the town of Carrick. And I want to remind you that it's clearly the place to find the perfect husband! Clodagh's found hers already"—she paused for the cheers and then went on, raising her voice even louder—"so the rest of us better get a move on! And don't forget that our lovely hostess found a man in Carrick who was willing to get up on TV and tell the whole world that she's gorgeous! Now *that* is what I call sexy!!"

The room went wild and Jazz, who'd overslept after a broken night, thought her head was going to split.

Waving her napkin round her head, the girl finished up triumphantly. "And they met in Carrick where *we* are going to be dancing till dawn tonight! So, get a good breakfast down you, girls, you'd better be on your marks!"

When breakfast was over and the tables cleared, Jazz had a croissant and a coffee in the kitchen and then went through to reception.

Susan was upstairs, doing the guests' bedrooms. Jazz was tempted to pop up to her own room where Maggie's book, which she'd read till the early hours of the morning, lay on the unmade bed. But there were umpteen bar bills to be printed out and emails to be dealt with, so tidying her own room would have to wait.

As she sat working at the computer, the bachelorette party came crowding into the hall, laughing and chatting. She smiled and said goodbye, thinking that it was a hundred years since she herself had gone off with a crowd of mates for a day's pampering. And the trouble was that she couldn't see where or when it might happen again.

Then the phone on the desk rang and she picked it up automatically. "The Old Forge Guesthouse, Jazz speaking, good morning, how may I help you?"

Her voice was professionally charming, but her mind was still on the bar bills. Then she heard the voice on the line and it was Dad.

"Look, sweetheart, don't put the phone down, I really want to talk to you."

Jazz was outraged. She'd rejected about twenty calls to her mobile since he'd gone back to London, but it had never struck her that he'd have the neck to call her here at the desk. For God's sake, it could have been Susan who'd answered!

"What the hell do you think you're doing, this is my *work* phone!"

"I know, but we need to talk."

"I don't need to talk to you. Not now, not ever."

"Well, I need to talk to you, darling, so please just hear me out. I know that you're angry and you've got a right to be. And I know you want to punish me, and I do understand. But if punishing me means hurting yourself, I can't just look on and say nothing."

She opened her mouth and he must have heard her angry intake of breath.

"No, listen. Please. Once I've said my say I promise I won't call again. Look, I wasn't supportive when you decided to work for the airline. And I'd be lying if I said that, after the accident, I hadn't hoped you'd come home and take a degree. But I do understand that it's your life. I just can't bear to see you waste it. At least there was some sort of career path available at the airline. What kind of future do you think you'll have working at the forge?"

It was as if he had chucked a glass of water in her face. Blinking, Jazz struggled to find the words to answer him but, before she could summon her wits, he kept going. He was used to this, she thought bitterly, with his years of striking poses and speaking in courtrooms. His voice now was urgent but it was level and controlled.

"So, here's the thing, I want you to remember that I earmarked money for your education. If you don't want to go to university, you can use it for something else. It's always seemed to me that you've got entrepreneurial flair. Think about it, darling. Ask yourself where you plan to be in the future. You might do a course in marketing or, I don't know, something else. Something that would give you choices and let you move on."

Jazz found her voice, though when she spoke she seemed to be choking. "No, Dad, *here's* the thing, and I can't say it any plainer. Get out of my life and stay out of it and don't call me again!"

She slammed down the phone and shrank back from it, as if it were going to bite her. Then, to her shame, she felt her eyes filling with tears.

At that moment Gunther came through from the kitchen. Groping for a Kleenex she knew she didn't have, Jazz turned her face away. But she couldn't stop her shoulders shaking.

"Jazz? What has happened? What's the matter?" His kind face was troubled. "Are you all right?"

"Yes. Of course. I'm sorry . . ."

"Tell me what has happened."

Instead she buried her face in her hands and heard herself start to sob. In a way, the sound was pleasing, because it drowned the voice at the back of her mind telling her Dad was right. What *was* she doing here and where did she think she was going?

Feeling Gunther grasp her elbows, she lowered her hands. His blue eyes were full of worried concern. Then, as they looked at each other, he suddenly wrapped her in a bear hug. She squeezed her eyes closed so tightly that sparks flashed in front of them, and she felt her tears seep into the fabric of his shirt.

Then she pulled away blindly and grabbed her bag from the shelf beneath the desk. The bar bills hadn't been finished and there was a mound of other work to do, but nothing mattered now but her impulse to run.

53

A ideen had spent the whole night, with her head under the pillow, trying to avoid the thought of what she'd done. Bríd was right. She needed to go and find Conor and grovel. He wouldn't take her back now, of course, but she had to apologize. How could she think that someone like him would go around the place cheating? It was like Bríd said, if she loved him at all she should have shown him more respect. And what would he think if he knew what she'd been thinking about Ameena? She had seen Ameena with Lar Walsh and she *had* dismissed her as a slag. But if she couldn't even admit that to Bríd, how could she say it to Conor? And was wanting to tell him everything just more self-indulgent crap?

Because that's what she did want. She wanted to rush out the door in her nightdress with her rat's-nest hair and run down Broad Street, straight into Conor's arms. She wanted to tell him what she'd done and say she was sorry. And after that she thought she'd quite like to die.

When she left the deli yesterday she'd thought she'd go over the road at once, but then she hadn't. Instead she'd come home to her room and cried for hours. At one point, when it seemed she had no tears left, she'd gone to look in the mirror, feeling curious. This was how a person looked, she'd thought, when her life was over and done. It was kind of interesting as well as tragic and she'd leaned in close to examine her eyes. Then she'd remembered seeing Conor standing in front of her dressing table, looking a bit odd with nothing on. Well, not odd, really, because he looked gorgeous. He had lovely muscles in his shoulders and his skin was golden brown. Not freckly like hers, but properly tanned. And he had gold hairs on his arms that were soft if you rubbed your cheek against them, and narrow hips and straight legs like those statues you'd see in Rome. Just thinking about him, her eyes had filled and her face in the mirror had gone all blurred and fuzzy. She remembered the way he'd turned that night and swept her into his arms. She'd had the bottle of wine in her hand, but it was ages before they'd drunk it. And that was the last time he'd been in this room.

Now she slumped on the end of the bed and told herself to get on with it. She couldn't stay locked in her room forever with a face like a saggy balloon. Last night Bríd had come home and gone to bed without talking to her. Aideen had heard the front door, and the sound of Bríd in the kitchen and the loo, and her bedroom door closing. This morning she'd heard the shower running and the door slamming as Bríd went out to work. She ought to be there too but she'd known that she couldn't face Bríd until she had talked to Conor. So now she'd better take a shower herself.

Half an hour later, with her hair washed, she walked down Broad Street. Everything looked normal. People were going in and out of shops and businesses; tourists were looking at maps; and beside the deli the old clock with SEED MERCHANTS written on it still had its hands stuck at a quarter to three. Over in the parking lot she could see Conor's Vespa. Outside the library a line of people were waiting to be ushered through to the exhibition. Unable to cope with the thought of pushing past them, Aideen crossed to the center of the road and sat down by the flowering horse trough. There were fallen geranium petals like little rubies scattered all over the bench.

Ten minutes later she couldn't delay any longer. The line had cleared and, behind her, she was aware of Bríd glaring beadily at her through the deli's glass door. Aideen stood up wearily, wishing that she'd worn a different t-shirt. The one she'd pulled on after her shower was way too faded and stretched.

When she went up the steps she could see through to the exhibition space. Oliver Bannister was waving his hands and giving a talk to the crowd. There were a couple of guys with backpacks, a bunch of schoolkids with what looked like somebody's mother, and a whole lot of smiling Americans clutching guidebooks. Standing in the vestibule, Aideen gritted her teeth. Through the door on her right she could see that there were browsers in the library. An old guy reading a newspaper, a group of young mums in Children's Corner, and a few people looking at books on the shelves. With his back to the glass wall between the library and the exhibition space, Conor was sitting at the desk.

It struck Aideen that she couldn't possibly walk in and disturb him. He was working. The place was crowded. She couldn't just push the door open and announce that she needed to talk. Everything seemed to slide into slow motion and, for an awful moment, she thought she was going to faint. The next thing she knew, he had looked up and she found herself falling through the door.

Then Conor's arms had grabbed her and the two of them kept interrupting each other.

"I'm sorry . . ."

"No, I am . . ."

"I ought to have explained . . ."

She wanted to tell him everything but she couldn't because he was kissing her. He was really squashing her ribcage but she didn't want him to stop.

Then somehow he was standing on the desk, scrabbling in the pocket of his hoodie. And then he was down on one knee up there, holding out a little box.

It was the perfect ring and he put it on her finger and it fitted perfectly. It had traveled all the way from Afghanistan on the Silk Road with boxes of spice.

She stood there in silence and the silence turned to clapping. And all around her people whistling like a football crowd. The young mums and the old guy with the newspaper, and, weirdly, Miss O'Rourke who used to teach her science at school. And Gobnit Kelly was swinging from the shelves in Children's Corner. And behind the desk where Conor was standing like Cú Chulainn, all the tourists at the psalter exhibition were cheering and waving beyond the glass wall.

There was going to be masses of time for talking later. Right now she held her hand out to Conor. He pulled her up beside him and the cheering got even louder. Then he pushed her hair back from her face and bent his head to reach her and she was aware of nothing but his kiss.

54

It was a small pub that Jazz hadn't been to before. Others of the same design up and down the peninsula had knocked down their internal walls to accommodate tourist parties; but here the interior was still divided into two small rooms, with the muddy-brown varnished bar in the center and a "snug room" to one side. The tiny windows, framed by yellowing lace curtains, hardly let in any light and the large TV screen over the bar dominated the space.

Peering through the gloom, Jazz saw that the place was almost empty. The tables inside the door were unoccupied and the room beyond contained no one but a group of three or four lads. She couldn't tell if they were locals or tourists, and she didn't care. What she wanted was a drink—preferably a large one—and a seat by a fire. But the fireplace here just contained a pile of ash.

When she'd rushed blindly from the forge she hadn't had a clue where she was going—she'd told herself that she just wanted to go somewhere and think. Then, driving away, she'd seen Gunther standing on the doorstep staring after her. That was when she'd realized that she didn't want to think at all. Instead, driving, which had been such a bugbear, had become a source of solace. Concentrating on nothing but the road, she had felt insulated from the world outside. She'd spent hours driving fiercely and aimlessly round and round the back roads until a point came when her mind was no longer prepared to remain blank. That was when the thought of a drink and a fire had begun to possess her, and she'd pulled into the roadside, having seen the little pub.

It was a place that would probably be cheerful when it was crowded but now, with no fire, and rain rattling the windowpanes, it was bleak. Jazz went to the bar and ordered a brandy. Then she slumped onto a banquette covered in torn red plastic, and glared at the rings on the table where the bartender put her drink. On the TV screen, a weather woman mouthed her way through the forecast; Jazz wondered sourly why she'd chosen underwear that sucked her in and pushed her up in such unflattering places.

Swallowing half her brandy in a gulp, she shuddered as it burned her throat and settled warmly in her stomach. Then, taking another sip, she clenched her teeth. The truth was, she told herself, that Dad was just part of the problem. She'd actually been secretly angry with Mum for months. And with Nan. They'd known what Dad was like and they'd lied about him. Or prevaricated. Or whatever. The bottom line was that she'd gone round like an idiot believing in Superdaddy while everyone all around her played along. Nan might have thought it was wrong, but she hadn't done a thing about it. And even if Mum had felt tortured, she ought to have had more sense.

Finishing her drink, she went and tapped on the bar for another. In the back room the group of lads were sitting round drinking pints. One of them tried to catch her eye and she looked back at him coldly. She was sick to death of cocksure males turning on the charm.

It was chilly on her side of the bar where the wind blew under the door and stirred the ashes in the grate. As she finished her second drink, she realized how long it was since she'd eaten. In most pubs of this kind you could buy chocolate or a packet of crisps or peanuts, but when she asked the bartender he shrugged and said he had none.

Through a door behind him she could see a glimpse of a family kitchen with a kettle on a stove, and for a moment she thought of asking if he'd make her a sandwich: judging by his morose appearance, though, she reckoned it was unlikely.

As she hesitated, unsure of what to do, one of the guys from the back room came round the bar carrying a packet of biscuits. "If your man's got nothing to eat, do you want one of these?"

They were staying at a hostel down the way, he said, and they'd dropped in for a pint after going shopping for stuff for their dinner. Feeling a bit muzzy, Jazz accepted a chocolate chip cookie. Then, seeing him order a round of drinks, she rummaged for her purse.

"Look . . . let me pay for those."

He laughed and said that the price of a round was a hell of a price for a biscuit.

"Well, actually, you're saving my life, because I'm starving."

With another laugh, he put the packet in her hand and, the next thing she knew, the rest of the lads were all round her. The first guy, who said his name was Dean, carried the drinks to her table. Jazz and the others followed him and, still trying to find her purse, she took her place at the end of the banquette. To her surprise, there was a brandy among the pints.

As she dithered about paying for the drinks, Dean slipped in beside her. He was wearing a large down jacket and, squashed into the corner, she began to feel less chilly. There were four guys, about the same age as she was, with Dublin accents and the air of having already downed plenty of pints. One of them took the packet from her hand and shook all the biscuits onto the table. There was a kind of laughing scrum in which they all grabbed them, and Jazz ended up with only one. She ate it in two bites washed down with a fiery slug of brandy. Sometime later another glass appeared on the table, but by then she was not just muzzy, she was feeling sick.

The conversation was almost entirely about football and there must have been a moment when she nodded off because, suddenly, her head jerked and she felt Dean's hand gripping the back of her neck.

"Wakey, wakey." He was moving her head back and forth like a puppet's and she didn't like it.

Struggling to sit up straighter, she realized she was pinned into the corner, between his body and the end of the banquette. Dean was the only one on her side of the table. The others, laughing and shiny-faced, were crowded together opposite her with their pints in their fists.

"Tell you what . . ." One of them leaned toward her. "Why don't you come back to the hostel with us and we'll all have a bit of dinner?"

"Jaysus, yeah, why don't you?" Another guy, with a stud through his nose, breathed Guinness into her face.

The first guy slammed his glass onto the table, aiming for a beer mat and missing. As the mat shot sideways onto the floor, Jazz tried to stand up.

Dean held her round the shoulders. "Ah, Jazz, c'mon now, don't be a killjoy."

When had she told them her name? She struggled to free herself, but he took her by the hair and pushed the glass of brandy to her lips.

"C'mon, love, finish your drink and we'll all go home for dinner."

His grip on her hair was hurting her and the other guys sniggered when the brandy ran down her chin. Terrified, she lurched forward, upsetting the table and sending the glasses to the floor. Then there was a clatter of curved nails on bare floorboards and a Jack Russell terrier hurled itself out of the snug.

As Dean made a grab for Jazz, and the other guys scattered, The Divil planted himself four square in front of them, his hackles rising and his teeth bared.

"Jaysus God Almighty!" The guy with the stud, who had aimed a kick at him, screamed as the terrier's teeth sank into his ankle. Then Fury O'Shea spoke from the door of the snug.

"Right, so, that's enough of behaving like four-year-olds. Come on, Miss, you're going home."

He jerked his head at Jazz and clicked his fingers at The Divil, who fell back and subsided at his feet. Two of the guys were mopping their groaning mate's bleeding ankle.

Ignoring them, Dean clamped his arm around Jazz's shoulders. "It's a free country, isn't it? She can come or go as she pleases without some oul fella rappin' out orders."

There was a long pause in which Fury just looked at him. Jazz felt the grip on her shoulder slacken and—conscious of behaving exactly like The Divil—she staggered obediently over to Fury, who gripped her by the arm.

Then there was a rush of wet air that took her breath away as he marched her out the doorway, and the smell of sawdust and linseed oil as he hooshed her into the passenger seat of his van.

As they rattled down the road with The Divil in the back, Jazz concentrated hard on not throwing up. The effects of two chocolate chip cookies and several glasses of brandy hadn't been good.

Beside her in the cab, Fury was whistling through his teeth. Ten minutes passed before he glanced across at her. "Is there any chance at all, d'you think, that you're ever going to grow up?"

Jazz wriggled round indignantly to face him. His bony shoulders were hunched under his waxed jacket and he wore a disreputable woolly hat over straggling, gray hair.

She raised her voice over the sound of the van bouncing through potholes. "Look, I'm sorry, I know I should be grateful for what you did back there."

Fury gave a loud, ironic snort. "Damn right, you should."

"But it's really none of your business how I choose to live my life."

He didn't reply. Instead he kept whistling tunelessly and she slumped back in her seat.

It seemed ages before he spoke again, glancing across at her mildly. "I told you once that cocksure people were a danger to everyone around them. The same goes for people who cringe and cling and can't let go."

Jazz felt too muzzy to respond to him, so she kept her eyes on the windshield where the wipers were turned on full against the driving rain. Focusing again on the world outside, she realized that the pub must have been Fury's local; she had driven in ever-decreasing circles till she'd ended up back on the forest road.

They were driving between the forest and the cliffs with the forge not a mile up ahead. Dimly, she told herself that she wouldn't have far to go back and pick up her own car. But the hypnotic swing of the windshield wipers was making her feel so sick and so dizzy that all she wanted was to fall on her bed and sleep.

Fury dropped her off just before they came to the gate of the forge and she stumbled round to the back door alone. The lights were on in the kitchen. Through the window she could see Gunther and Susan at the table. Holly was sitting between them in her nightdress, clutching Ginger the kitten and drinking a glass of milk. Jazz wondered if she'd had a nightmare and was being comforted before being carried back up to bed.

She slipped past the window unnoticed and entered the house through the darkened laundry room. Then, unable to face the family in the kitchen, she groped her way upstairs to her room and fell on the bed.

The last thing she was aware of was the sight of Maggie's book lying beside her, and the sound of it slipping from the bed and hitting the floor.

55

The writing was in pencil and the entry was headed "August 15th, 1940. Finfarran." Released from their homemade binding, the other pages lay scattered on the duvet. The brown paper cover, separated from its cardboard backing, had drifted onto the floor. Jazz stared at the page in her hand. She had opened her eyes to find her head pounding and her mouth like sandpaper and realized that she'd fallen asleep sprawled on her unmade bed. Then, as she'd wriggled upright, she'd seen the book on the floor beside her. Its spine had been split by its fall from the bed and, picking it up, she'd realized that between the brown paper and the cardboard there was some kind of soft padding. Mum would probably have got all precious about preserving the integrity of the cover. Screwing up her eyes against the painful morning sunlight, Jazz had gone for a Stanley knife.

As her interest grew she began to forget her hangover. The pages she found within the binding matched the number and size of those cut from the book. The use of the sewing machine and the handwritten name on the cover suggested that Mum had been right to think it was Maggie herself who had made the binding. So the evidence indicated that it was she who had concealed the pages hidden within it. They were written in the same schoolgirl hand as the bound pages written in the 1920s.

Liam has gone away out of this house and I've told him he's no longer welcome. He's been itching to marry Mariah Keane from the post office back in Crossarra these last fifteen years. He can go there and be done with it now that Mam's dead and buried.

I got back from England in time for the funeral and when I saw the way the house was I was furious. The place was like a shed by him. There was no comfort in it. I said nothing at all when I came in the door, nor at the church nor in the burial ground. I stood while the priest squeezed out his prayers and the neighbors shifted and snuffled.

And then when Liam came home after dark I knew he'd been drinking with his cronies. I'd seen the lot of them at the back of the church with their black suits and their swagger. They were all out like himself in the past, fighting the British to begin with. Then Liam and a couple of others were in the crowd that held out against the Treaty to the last. Some of the men at the funeral today spent months in prison with him, and I'd say one or two are touched in the head after what they went through.

There's nothing wrong with Liam, though. I wouldn't grudge him a drink, but the way he talked when he came back home had me raging. Mam never said a word against me, I know that much. She never had a bad word for him either, but when she wrote and told me she'd left me the house, she thanked me for sending the money. She'd had nothing from the bold Liam in all those years he'd been away. And now I can see that when he came back he was good for nothing either. Not a lick of paint on the house by him, nor a clean sheet to a bed. And Mam's ware that was always clean thrown up in a heap on the dresser.

And then to stand up with his back to the fire and say I'd deserted my duty. He was half-drunk with his bloodshot eyes and his big belly swinging, and he roaring out that when he'd come home poor Mam was here like a shadow. I wouldn't doubt him. Why wouldn't she be with her husband dead and her heart grieving for her daughters? I told him it wasn't me that brought trouble into this house in the first place. I said that I'd never have gone away if I'd had any choice in the matter.

In my own mind I was screaming though I kept my voice quiet. I didn't say it was because of him that my own trouble followed. Why would I give him the satisfaction of knowing why I had to go?

I just told him to go to Mariah Keane because the house and the field are mine now. The rest of the land is long gone and he and Mam have been living on what I sent them. I won't go back to England. He can seek his bit of a pension if Dublin will let him have it. He can write up and send them a list of his medals. One way or the other, it's true to say that he gave his life for Ireland. He took ours while he was doing it, though Mam seems never to have blamed him. I do, though. I'll blame him till the day I die. Not for doing what he saw as his duty, in spite of all that followed. But for coming here on the night of her funeral and saying I deserted mine.

So Liam *had* gone on to fight in the Civil War. Jazz laid the page on the bed and picked up another. Wriggling back against her pillow, she drew up her knees and settled the pages against them. When she finished, she closed her eyes and felt tears slipping under her eyelids.

The row with Mum hadn't just been about her drives on the back roads with Gunther; she hadn't wanted to admit that lately they'd been going for walks in the forest. Ever since she'd stalked away from the beach, she'd been telling herself that she'd nothing to be ashamed of. It had simply happened by accident. After they'd stopped driving together she'd met him there by chance. It was just like the first time. She'd walked the winding path to Lackatubber and he'd stepped out into the clearing. It was coincidence and their friendship was nobody's business but their own. Now, with the sunlight flooding her bed, she knew that that wasn't true.

And even with her eyes closed, she could still see Maggie's handwriting.

The priest came up when me and James were in the forest. I'd say he'd been peeping and prying round us for weeks. We'd gone to a place where James and his wife used to go before they were married. I knew well myself what I was doing. James said she hadn't

*been out much lately because of her having a baby.
And I said to myself when I heard that, what matter? What she didn't know couldn't hurt her. And
James said it would kill him if he couldn't see me.
That's what a man will always say so I didn't take
that much notice. I knew it would kill me, though,
to be sitting all day in the house seeing Mam.*

"What she doesn't know can't hurt her." That was
presumably what Tessa and Dad had told each other
about Mum.

Maggie's priest seemed to have been frothing at the
mouth like Moses in a B-movie. The first thing he'd
done was order James to go home. It must have been
awful. According to Maggie, he "went away like a
whipped dog with his tail between his legs." Jazz imagined the young woman sitting at home holding her baby.
Had she ever asked herself where her husband went
when he went out?

*The priest turned on me when James was gone and
I didn't know what he'd say to me. My mind kind
of went off sideways. I was wondering if James
came offering help when we buried Dad and Hannie because he'd had his eye on me always and was
just waiting for his chance. Then it struck me that,*

*whatever else went wrong, I had the turf cut for
Mam anyway. And then the priest told me he'd give
me a choice. I could get on a boat and go away off to
England. Or he'd preach against me from the pul-
pit and shame me before the world. He stood there
with the birds singing all around him and asked me
how could I let that happen to Mam? She'd lost all
she had and Liam might never come back to her. So
how could I rob her now of her good name?*

Jazz read on: It appeared that James, too, had been
ordered to leave the parish. Had his wife demanded
to know why her husband had decided to uproot the
household? Or did she know better than to ask, for
fear of the answer? And what of the child to whom the
move could never be properly explained? Had it grown
up out of touch with its extended family? Did it find
out later and have to deal with the thought of what its
father had done?

And what of seventeen-year-old Maggie, faced with
that stark choice? It wasn't something she could have
talked through with anyone around her, least of all her
mam. And there was all that stuff about feeling sick on
the boat. Might she even have been pregnant? Whatever the case, she must have believed that the priest
would carry out his threat. Judging by the fact that he'd

made it, she was probably right as well: he sounded bonkers. Even so, Jazz wondered, had he actually saved a marriage? And was it worth saving if it was built on lies? Pulling a face, she remembered Mum trying to tell her that these things were complex. Maybe they were, but one thing was clear enough. In seeking some kind of comfort Maggie had ended up causing chaos. And, with far less justification, Jazz herself had risked the same end.

She remembered Susan laughing one day in the kitchen. Gunther was the kindest man you could meet, she'd said, so kind that he'd let the worst in the world take advantage of him. All these weeks had it really been a case of the blind leading the blind? Or had one or both of them simply chosen to close their eyes to the truth? She didn't know. Nor, remembering his arms around her, did she know how she'd manage without him. But she did know she was going to hand in her notice here at the forge.

56

By the time Hanna had coaxed flames from a handful of sticks on the hearth, the kettle on the worktop was boiling. Taking the thick shawl from the back of the chair, she threw it round her shoulders and went to make coffee. As she lifted a bowl from the dresser, Fury appeared at the door.

"I wouldn't say Maggie Casey ever drank coffee."

"All I can remember is very stewed tea with the sugar boiled down to syrup." Hanna held up the cafetière. "Will you have some of this?"

"So long as it comes in a proper mug with a handle. None of your arty-farty blasts from the past."

He went to the hearth and encouraged the flames with a couple of sods of turf. Hanna poured him a mug of coffee and filled herself a bowlful. As they sat down opposite each other, The Divil put his nose round the door. Fury jerked his head at him and the little dog pattered over and lay with its chin on the hearth.

"I heard that Jazz will be moving on from the forge."

Of course he had. There was no piece of news in Finfarran that Fury didn't have before the rest. Hanna had sometimes wondered if he did it by osmosis. She nodded and said she was glad.

"You are, of course, doesn't it give you a whole new series of things to worry about? What'll happen to her now? What might go wrong? How does she feel?"

"Well, that's where you're wrong, because I think she'll be okay."

Last night as she'd sat up late by the hearth, she'd heard the sound of a car outside on the road. When she opened the door, the envelope she found on her doorstep contained Maggie's book and a scribbled note.

Sorry I took it apart. You know yourself we can have it rebound if you want to. I've given in my notice at the forge. Don't fuss. I'll find something else. J.

Now she got up and fetched the padded envelope from the bedroom. "I don't usually entertain wearing my kimono. Have a look at that while I get decent."

When she came back, Fury had built up the fire and the pages were scattered around him. Over more coffee she explained how she'd found the book. Then she brought him the tin box and the greaseproof bread wrapper. It was just like Maggie, he said, to squirrel things away.

Hanna picked up a page. "I suppose she stuck with domestic service when she was over in England."

"She told me she was a housekeeper. Maybe she worked her way up."

"All those years spent over there when she could have been here with her mother."

Fury shrugged. "It's not like she had a choice."

"And I suppose that as soon as her mam was dead, the priest's threat meant nothing. If she didn't give a toss about what the neighbors thought, she could settle back here and be damned to them."

"The chances were that the priest knew that as well. I doubt he said a word in the heel of the hunt, with Liam a local hero and Maggie's story nearly twenty years old."

"But when I was a kid, hardly anyone would speak to her."

"She was always a sour-faced old besom, so I'd say it worked both ways."

Hanna frowned. "She worried about sending money home via the Donovans. They lived next door. She says a couple of times that she didn't trust Paud, the husband, though she liked the wife." She searched through the pages. "But you're right. She seems to have had a down on everyone. Right from when she went away. '*I wish to God I knew who to trust of the lot of them. You couldn't be sure.*'"

Selecting a page from the floor, Fury read a line from it softly. "'*The Tans left their truck way up the road and came down to the house on foot. If some of them hadn't had drink taken we'd never have heard them coming.*'"

His face was expressionless as he looked at Hanna, whose eyes widened. "Oh my God. It wasn't a random raid. They knew what they were there for . . ."

Fury nodded. "Someone must have informed on Liam, and Maggie thought it was Paud."

"But was it?" Hanna looked up suddenly. "What happened to the Donovans?"

"I don't know. Like I said, all I know is they left Finfarran during the Civil War."

Because they'd been the informers? Or because people thought so and they were hounded out? She frowned again, trying to make sense of it.

"But if they were the guilty ones, and they were gone, why would Maggie be so mistrustful of everyone else?"

Then, with tears in her eyes, she looked over at Fury. "She never knew. She could never be sure. It could have been any of the neighbors. She couldn't even be certain that there'd been an informer at all."

The Divil twitched in his sleep and Fury laid a hand on him. "Bad times. No wonder people didn't want to talk about them." He stood up. "You're right. She couldn't know. She just lived with all that poison festering inside her. And she didn't have anyone to talk to, so she wrote it down in a book."

When they'd finished their coffee and he moved to go, Fury stopped on the threshold and looked at her. "Did anyone ever tell you what happened in Castle Lancy at the end of the Civil War?"

"No. What?"

"The de Lancys were long gone out of the place by that stage. I suppose they didn't feel safe as soon as the War of Independence started."

Maggie's lines echoed in Hanna's head. *They got out fast enough anyway at the first sign of danger, but I suppose you couldn't expect them to stay and be burned out or worse.*

Fury had set his back against the doorframe. His face was in shadow and she could only hear his voice. "The castle was empty with only a caretaker in it. The war was almost over and the diehards were more or less fighting with their backs to the wall. It was clear enough that the treaty made with the English was going to stand. But a crowd of them raided a train and got hold of a helluva lot of munitions. Guns and bombs and ammunition. And they took it up to the castle and told the caretaker to get lost."

There was a plan to liaise with some other crowd, he said, to get the stuff spread out to other pockets of anti-treaty lads still up in the hills. But then the castle was surrounded and they knew they hadn't a hope.

"So what did they do?"

"Gave themselves up in the end, but not before they'd decided to blow up the castle. They didn't want the treaty lot to get the munitions back."

"But how come the castle's still standing?"

"Apparently they ended up scrapping amongst themselves. Somebody reckoned there'd been enough destruction. And they got taken prisoner while the scrap was still going on."

Winking at Hanna, Fury turned and clicked his tongue at The Divil. Hanna gasped, her tired mind grasping what she'd just heard. According to Charles Aukin, the psalter had always been kept in the castle's book room.

Fury flashed his eyebrows at her. "So if the whole place had gone up, the Carrick Psalter would have gone with it. They say it was just one man who managed to hold the others off."

"Maggie says Liam was one of the men who held out to the end."

Seeing her expression, Fury laughed and shook his head. "You want Liam to be the man who saved the psalter, don't you? So do I. But the truth is, nobody knows."

57

WE R ON R WAY ETA 5 OR SO LOL NAN

Jazz looked at her phone and grinned. According to Mary Casey, if LOL didn't mean "lots of love," it ought to. That's what she meant by it anyway. And if people thought it meant something different, they must think she was somebody else. Those were the kinds of Nan conversations that drove Mum nearly frantic. Jazz herself didn't mind them, at least not on a sunny day like this.

She parked the car and walked through to the café in the nuns' garden. All summer long she had dreamed of hanging out here, but couldn't, and now she'd managed the drive with no problem at all. The garden was beautiful, a paradise tucked away from the busy traffic on Broad Street. The herb beds smelled lovely and the statue of St. Francis was surrounded by swooping birds. Jazz got herself a drink from the café and sat at a table by the fountain. Then she opened her phone again and scrolled down to the message she'd had from Carlos.

You could tell that he hadn't been sure of her reaction; the tone veered between serious and half-jokey, and the selfie he'd sent showed him pulling a mournful face. He'd moved out of the flat in France, he said, and the thing he'd had with Sarah was definitely over. How about a drink or a meal next time he had a stopover somewhere like Cork?

Jazz held up the phone and took a selfie with the fountain shining behind her. Then she shot it back with a message saying "Maybe." Though she wasn't going to make it easy for him, it would be nice to see Carlos again.

As Louisa and Mary cut through the courtyard to the café, Conor and Aideen emerged from the library holding hands.

Mary stopped in her tracks with her arms akimbo. "Now so! You've had sense at last!"

Conor looked sideways at Aideen, who blushed bright scarlet.

Mary poked her in the ribs, "Well, come on! Give us

a look at the ring." She reached out, grabbed Aideen's hand and raised a disparaging eyebrow. "Well, I wouldn't exactly call it the Koh-i-Noor."

Louisa murmured deprecatingly, but Conor threw his head back and laughed. It was better than that, he told Mary. Way, way better. It was lapis lazuli all the way from Afghanistan. And it was the exact color of Aideen's gorgeous eyes.

Crossing the garden, Louisa shook her head at Mary, who stopped and turned on her. "What?"

"You might have been a little more tactful."

"Ah, for God's sake, Louisa Turner, do you not know me by now?"

"I suppose I should know that tact is too much to ask for."

"Well, don't worry. I'll leave this next bit to you."

They joined Jazz in the sunshine by the fountain with a tray of tea. Louisa pulled over a chair from another table.

Jazz looked at her in surprise. "Is someone joining us?"

"In a few minutes. I wanted to have a quiet word with you first."

Louisa folded her hands and declared that she'd come to a decision. And not one that she'd rushed into either, so Jazz was to listen and not argue.

"I've decided to sell the house in Kent." It was far too big for her now, she said, and much too isolated, and it made no sense to stay there since she'd be forced to leave in the end. "So I'm selling up and using the money to invest in a start-up business."

Mary reached for the teapot. Louisa extended her cup with a nod and looked calmly at Jazz. "Don't gape, dear, I've thought it through and I'm really rather excited. I'm going to invest the proceeds of the sale in a venture here in Finfarran. Organic herbal cosmetics. I've done the research and it's evident that there's an Irish market to be tapped into."

"But, Gran, you've got no experience in business."

"Well, of course I shan't be running it myself."

"Who will, then?"

"I'll need a manager. And a partner. Someone I can trust who'll work with me on a proper business plan."

"But what about product?"

"Well, that's the idea. We'll need to develop our own. With grant aid, perhaps, at the R&D stage of the process. And maybe a certain amount of investment later on when we're bigger." Louisa smiled and opened a sachet of sugar. "Fortunately, we won't require a start-up loan."

"Whoa, stop, hang on a minute. You can't sell up and risk all you've got on some daft notion like this!"

"Actually, dear, I can do whatever I like. Your grandfather left the manor to me, along with considerable savings. I can dispose of them in any way that I choose. Of course, I've always intended to leave what I have to you. But I do hope to be around for some time yet."

"Well, of course . . . I didn't mean . . . I mean your money is yours to do whatever you like with. But . . . but what about Dad? The manor's his home."

"Nonsense, Jazz, that's just pure sentiment! Your father left home more than thirty years ago. He can't expect me to keep his teddy bear waiting in his room."

A goldcrest landed on the ground beside them and started pecking at crumbs.

Jazz frowned. "But where are you going to get all these people? Investors? A business partner?"

"Oh, I don't think that finding investors will be a problem when we come to it. There are plenty of big guns in the City to whom George and I played host. People Malcolm brought to the house, you know, when he was building up his own contacts. I've no doubt at all that they'll pick up the phone if I call."

Jazz leaned her elbows on the table and stared at her. "And this business partner, who's that going to be?"

"Actually, dear, I was hoping that would be you."

Before Jazz could react, Louisa selected a shortbread biscuit. "You and I in partnership, a unit here at first, in

The Old Convent Centre. We'd find ourselves a manager locally. You'd be the creative marketing director. And Saira Khan will help with the R&D."

"You've asked her already?"

"Of course, dear, she'll be here to join us in a minute."

"And what'll you do if I'm not up for the job?"

"Find someone else, of course, though I wouldn't like it. Why? Do you have something else that you'd rather do?" Louisa looked at her blandly and sipped her tea.

Jazz wasn't sure whether to feel furious or excited. Already ideas were beginning to bloom in her mind. They could source their herbs from the nuns' garden, at least while they got started. Later on they could buy some land or, better still, find different producers up and down the peninsula. Nan's neighbor Johnny Hennessy had a garden full of herbs. Sourcing from different places could mean a range of distinctive brands. Crossarra Cleansing Cream, say, or Lissbeg Lip Salve. Ballyfin Bath Oil. Something from Owenacrossa, maybe, but that would need more thought. Hearing her own mind whirring, she found herself laughing. Then her brow knitted and she looked at Louisa again.

"But, just a minute, if you sell the manor, where are you going to live?"

"Well, I shouldn't like to lose my foothold in England altogether. So I might take a pied-à-terre in London, or point out to your father that his house is too large for his needs. All I'll want over there is a bed and a bath."

"You mean that you're planning to base yourself over here?"

At the other side of the table Mary Casey tossed her head. "She will of course, and why shouldn't she? She's going to live with me."

Jazz stared at Louisa, who smiled sweetly. "We have it all planned and costed, haven't we, Mary? It's the perfect practical solution for us both."

"We've been to an architect and he's going to turn my bungalow into two flats." Mary slapped her hand decisively on the table. "Half for Louisa, half for me, and a shared kitchen-diner in the middle. And we'll each decorate our own flat whatever way we like."

Jazz grinned. "So who'll decorate the middle?"

"We'll come to a compromise."

Louisa nodded serenely. "After which we'll do it Mary's way. It's all going to be fine."

Mary's lip trembled a little and she jabbed her finger at Jazz. "And don't go pointing out to me that your grandad built that bungalow. If I fancied a change, he'd tell me to go ahead."

Louisa nodded. "So, here we are, pulling up old roots and putting down new ones. I know it's a bit surprising, and I don't need an instant answer. But I hope you'll decide that you'd like to do the same." Raising her teacup, she smiled at Jazz. "Your grandfather George was remarkably good at business. What's bred in the bone will out in the blood, as the saying goes."

Mary Casey bristled. "And there's plenty of get up and go on the other side of the family. Your grandfather Tom was the first postmaster in Crossarra to install an electric bacon slicer."

Jazz looked from one smiling face to the other, feeling the future bubbling inside her. It was nothing like what she'd feared or expected and she knew it was going to be great.

58

Finfarran. September 1975

It's right that the child should be called after Tom's mother but I'm glad he named her for Mam and Hannie too. She's twelve years old and her hair and eyes are just like Hannie's. I know well that her mam sends her round because Tom has been here too much. In a way I'm glad that he doesn't be here like he used to. He was always asking questions about his father, and how could I tell him that Liam and I never spoke after Mam died. How could I tell a word of it to anyone? Hate came into this house on the night that Dad and Hannie were killed.

Hanna hardly opens her mouth and I say little enough. She's a great worker. I went to Lissbeg the

*other day and got an appointment with the solicitor.
I want her to have this house and the field when I'm
gone. Maybe one day she'll need a place where she
can feel safe and be happy. If she does and she has
this place, I think Mam would be glad.*

Had it not been for Jazz, Hanna told herself, she
would never have seen this. And now, having read it,
there seemed no need to preserve it. It was meant for
her and not for anyone else. The writing was crammed
onto a sheet of paper smaller than the pages of the copybook. Hanna recognized it as blue Basildon Bond. Tom
Casey had sold it, along with Staedtler pencils and Biro
ballpoints, from a shelf in Crossarra post office when she
was a child. She remembered him bringing a pad of it to
the house as a jotter when Maggie had complained that
she couldn't remember half of the things she needed to
buy in Lissbeg. Mary Casey had tossed her head and
pointed out that, by that stage, Tom himself did most
of the old lady's shopping. But Tom just shook his head.
When you're old, he'd told her, "you still want to feel
that you've some control over your life."

Now Hanna folded the page and held it over the fire.
The rest of the book, in its waxed bread-wrapper, lay
in its biscuit tin on the dresser. One day she might have
it rebound. One day she would give it to Mary Casey to

read. One day, almost certainly, Jazz would go online and construct a proper family history, with dates and names gleaned from official sources. She herself was happy with Maggie's half-told, half-remembered story, with all its gaps and uncertainties and all that it left unsaid.

A flame leapt up from the fire and she loosened her hold on the paper. As she watched it turn to ashes on the hearth, a breeze blew in from the half door, touched by the rich scents of early autumn. Then Brian spoke behind her and she looked round at him, smiling. He was standing in the bedroom doorway in jeans and a t-shirt and his feet were bare.

"Good morning." He stretched luxuriously, his arms reaching above the height of the low lintel. Then he looked at her appraisingly. "It really is a good kimono. You should always wear silk in the mornings, despite the Irish climate."

She laughed. "I always do."

"So much I have to learn about you." He crossed to the half door and looked out at the garden. Outside the sun was shining and gulls wheeled above the ocean. He moved back toward her and took her elbows in his hands. "And so weird to wake up here, in your beautiful bed."

Hanna's heart lurched as he smiled down at her.

Last night she had lain awake while he slept beside her and the sound of his even breathing had lulled her to sleep. As soon as she'd read what Maggie had written, she'd known that she had to call him. And Jazz, who was an adult now, not a child, had clearly known it, too. Attached to the sheet of blue notepaper there'd been a yellow sticky note with a single line in red biro.

Put that bottle of wine in the fridge and call that nice guy now!!!! ☺

It was the next step, the logical thing, the right way to thank her lucky stars for the gift of a place where she could feel safe and be happy. She owed it to Maggie, to Jazz, and to herself to accept the gift and move on.

Brian dropped a kiss on the top of her head and glanced back at the bedroom.

"I've been lying in there looking at the light through the window. We could do an extension at the end wall and double the size of the room."

Hanna looked at him blankly. "An extension? Why?"

"Well, I know this once was a family home but, honestly Hanna, it's a bit small for the two of us."

The two of them? Hanna's mind went into overdrive. Did he think she was going to ask him to move in? No, hang on, did he think he could just move in without even asking? How in the name of God would she deal with this?

Before she could speak she realized he was looking down at her, laughing. "Fury O'Shea is right, you know, it's child's play to wind you up."

"You mean . . .?"

"I'm joking. Of course I am. This is your house, I'm not about to invade it. Let's just start with the fact that we've finally spent a night together. God alone knows where we're going to go from here."

Still shocked, and slightly angry, she drew away from him, frowning, but he pulled her back and traced her eyebrows with his thumbs. Her shoulders relaxed and she found herself laughing back up at him. After all those months she had made him wait, she supposed he had served her right.

Seeing her thought, Brian bent down and kissed her. "There were two of us in it, you know, my love. And each one as bad as the other."

Hanna wasn't sure if that was quite true but this was no moment to argue. Something told her they had plenty of time for that.

"Tell you what, let's start by sharing the workload. You wash up last night's glasses and I'll make a start on breakfast."

She gave him a push toward the sink and went to switch on the kettle. While it boiled, she went to the dresser and took down a couple of bowls. With the coffee made, she found cream and sugar and assembled them on a tray with the bowls beside them. The worn glaze was cracked here and there but the brave pattern of flowers still glowed beneath it.

Brian smiled as he crossed the room to join her, making no offer to lift the tray, since this was her house and her kingdom. Then they walked together into Maggie's garden with the gulls wheeling above them and the last of the summer sun warming the earth.

Acknowledgments

My thanks to my brilliant editor Hannah Robinson, and to everyone at Harper Perennial, New York, who has worked so meticulously on this US edition of *Summer at the Garden Café*, and to Markus Hoffman at Regal Hoffmann & Associates.

I also remain very grateful to all at Hachette Books Ireland, and, as ever, to my agent, Gaia Banks, at Sheil Land Associates, UK.

About the Author

Felicity Hayes-McCoy was born in Dublin, Ireland, and graduated in English and Irish from UCD in the 1970s. She then built a successful UK-based career as an actress and writer, working in theater, music theater, radio, TV, and digital media. As well as the successful Finfarran series of novels, she is the author of two memoirs, *The House on an Irish Hillside* (UK: Hodder & Stoughton, 2012) and *A Woven Silence: Memory, History & Remembrance*, and of *Enough Is Plenty: The Year on the Dingle Peninsula*, a lifestyle book illustrated with her own photographs (Ireland: The Collins Press, 2015). She and her husband, Wilf Judd, divide their time between London and Ireland. With him she wrote *Dingle And Its Hinterland: People, Places and Heritage* (Ireland: The Collins Press, 2017).

HARPER LUXE

THE NEW LUXURY IN READING

We hope you enjoyed reading
our new, comfortable print size and found it
an experience you would like to repeat.

Well – you're in luck!

HarperLuxe offers the finest in fiction and
nonfiction books in this same larger print size and
paperback format. Light and easy to read, HarperLuxe
paperbacks are for book lovers who want to see
what they are reading without the strain.

For a full listing of titles and
new releases to come, please visit our website:

www.HarperLuxe.com

HARPER LUXE

SEEING IS BELIEVING!